CONNIE BROCKWAY

"Romance with strength, wit, and intelligence. Connie Brockway delivers!"

—Tami Hoag, *New York Times* bestselling author

"Brockway's lush, lyrical writing style is a perfect match for her vivid characters, beautiful atmospheric setting, and sensuous love scenes."

—*Library Journal*

"If you're looking for passion, tenderness, wit, and warmth, you need look no further. Connie Brockway is simply the best."

—Teresa Medeiros, bestselling author of
The Bride and the Beast

PATTI BERG

"Patti Berg is an exceptional voice in the field of romantic fiction today."

—*Romantic Times*

"One of the best spinners of tales the genre has to offer."

—*Affaire de Coeur*

"Keep on writing, Ms. Berg. You've got the gift!"

—*Rendezvous*

more ...

My Scottish Summer

Connie Brockway
Patti Berg   Debra Dier
Kathleen Givens

WARNER BOOKS

A Time Warner Company

WARNER BOOKS EDITION

Copyright © 2001 by Connie Brockway
Copyright © 2001 by Patti Berg
Copyright © 2001 by Debra Dier
Copyright © 2001 by Kathleen Givens
Compilation copyright © 2001 by Warner Books, Inc.

Cover design by Diane Luger
Cover art by Franco Accornero

Warner Books, Inc.
1271 Avenue of the Americas
New York, NY 10020

Visit our Web site at
www.twbookmark.com

For information on Time Warner trade Publishing's online publishing program, visit www.ipublish.com

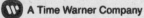 A Time Warner Company

Printed in the United States of America

First Printing: July 2001

10 9 8 7 6 5 4 3 2 1

Contents

Contents

Lassie, Go Home

CONNIE BROCKWAY

Acknowledgments

Dog people are simply some of the most generous, enthusiastic, and lovely people around. I had the pleasure of learning about Border collies, sheepherding trials, and the United States Border Collie Handlers' Association from Becky Beckman of Rising Sun farms, Chuck O'Reilly, at whose farm I saw my first national trial, and Bill Johnson, whose Border collies joyfully haze geese here in my home state of Minnesota.

And thanks, Jenny Simonson, for telling me about Wally Szczberiak!

1

"Yo, Braveheart! Whoop! Whoo—"

Devlin Montgomery's head popped through the neck of his cambric shirt just in time for him to glimpse a pair of long legs flailing above a hedge. Then he heard a thunk and a groan.

Damn American tourist, he thought, striding over to make sure the Yank hadn't killed herself. And yes, it had to be an American—such an enthusiastic holler could only come from an American.

It wasn't human kindness alone that hastened his steps. Lawsuits and Americans went hand in hand, and the Strathcuddy Faire, a new entrant in the lucrative business of annual Highland games fairs, couldn't afford any litigious actions. Besides being bad publicity, it would cut severely into the purses awarded to the winners of the various contests, and Devlin Montgomery, who had every intention of winning several of those purses, badly needed the cash.

Dev looked over the top of the fence capping the yew hedge. A woman lay sprawled in the clover. Platinum blond hair tumbled about her shoulders, half covering her face. She was twisted at the waist, her long jeans-clad legs bent to one side and her arms thrown wide. The position drew attention to her bosom.

Dev sucked in a low whistle. It was a bosom well worth drawing attention to, and right now it was stretching the printing on a snug fitting, and garishly plaid, T-shirt that read "Sassy Lassie."

He suppressed a groan. God deliver him from tourists.

As he watched she spat a hank of silvery hair out of her mouth. He vaulted lightly over the rail, landing beside her.

"Are you all right?" he asked.

A pair of eyes flashed and disappeared behind the curtain of hair. She moaned but made no attempt to straighten herself. His concern redoubled. "Miss?"

"Perfec-lee fine," she slurred out.

Oh, yeah. Definitely American. Not an East Coast or southern native, though. California blonde?

Dev knelt beside her, carefully brushing some of the hair from her face. What he uncovered would have made a Viking papa proud. Wide cheekbones flared above a firm, clean jawline. Her nose was short, her lips were full and plush. True, the brows and lashes were darker than that which usually went with such a blond mane, but then there was no saying she was a real blonde. Especially that shade of blonde. She *still* would have made a Viking papa proud. Especially if the length of those legs translated into the height he suspected she owned.

"Can you move anything?" he asked.

"Courth . . . course I can, silly. I can move everything," she said, eyes still shut.

It didn't sound as if she were in pain, but maybe she just couldn't *feel* any pain. Maybe she'd broken her back.

"How do you know?" he asked worriedly. "Do you think you're moving things? Because if you do, you're wrong. Nothing's moving."

"I'm not *that* tanked," she said with a touch of asperity. Abruptly one hand rose and the fingers wiggled. "There," she said. "See?"

One eye opened a slit, and she peered up at him. Blue eyes. A blue-eyed maybe blonde. His breath hitched. Okay. So he'd once been a touch susceptible to that particular combination. He was older now, not so easy to impress. Ha.

"Braveheart! You're still here," she said in the happy tones of the pleasantly sotted.

"Yeah," he said. She'd dimpled as she said it, and he caught back a low whistle. She was as cute as a newborn giraffe. "Ah, can I do anything for you, miss?"

"Oh, yeah," she breathed, still gazing raptly up at him. "Speak Sean Connery for me."

"Huh?"

"Ya know—'Ye seem to hae fallen on yer nut, haven't ye, ye great heeland coo?'"

Caught off guard by the atrocious and disarmingly canny impersonation, Dev broke into laughter. She couldn't be too badly hurt.

"There's a sport." She grinned foolishly, her eyes unfocused and sappy with expectation.

"Sorry. I don't do Sean Connery."

"Wish I could," she mumbled morosely, rolling her head to the side. Abruptly her dazed gaze sharpened. She darted a glance at him out of the corner of her eye, squirmed a little closer to his knee, and . . .

His eyes narrowed. "Are you trying to look up my kilt?"

Her head snapped back to its original position. Her blue eyes went round as she donned an abrupt and completely unconvincingly innocent expression.

"Well?" he prodded sternly.

"Maybe," she allowed and sniffed. "What's the big deal, anyway?"

Americans and their kilt fetishes. He brought his face closer to hers. "If you found out the Secret of the Kilt," he whispered dramatically, "you could never leave the country."

She snorted, but he noted that a wave of color had unrolled up her throat. He rose to his feet and held out his hand.

"Here. Let me help you up. Braveheart would never leave a damsel in distress." She hesitated, so he added, "Especially an American damsel. They sue if you don't meet their expectations."

"Hey. Scots aren't supposed to be sarcastic." She didn't move, just lay on her back.

"I'm half French," he explained pleasantly.

"You don't look French," she said suspiciously.

"I know. I look like Braveheart. Of course, there is a slight matter of my having eight inches on Mr. Gibson."

"Oh? Where?" As soon as the words were out she clamped a hand over her mouth. Her fair skin flooded with an intense blood-orange color.

"Five," she mumbled into her palm.

"What?" Dev asked, confounded and bemused; the color of her eyes was exactly the color of the pansies growing untended beside his back door, and just as velvety—

"I had five Scotches at the Scottish tasting booth." Her gaze looked abashed above the gag of her hand. "I mean *Scotch* tasting booth!" She started giggling.

Five? Good Lord. No wonder the girl couldn't get up. Or even sit up, for that matter. He moved around to her head and squatted down, wrapping his arms under her arms and lifting. She hung like a sack of wet wool.

"Why did you have so many?" he grunted, heaving her to her feet.

Toni Olson squinted thoughtfully up at the blue, cloud-clotted sky, vaguely aware that the gorgeous Scot she'd spied earlier that day hurling a telephone pole around was propping her up. *Why* had she tasted so many whiskies? Because they were there, that was why. There and cheap, and she was on the last few days of a dream vacation–cum–business trip before returning to Minnesota.

She couldn't ever remember feeling so . . . so free. And delighted. It must be the clean air sweeping in off the sea, or being up in a real, live Scottish valley, or seeing her first guy in a kilt who wasn't either eighty years old or blowing into a bagpipe or both.

But when she'd seen this man, who was the culmination of every one of her lustful, Braveheart-induced fantasies, stride around the corner of the tent in nothing but a kilt, she'd reacted the same way her niece did every time Wally Szczberiak walked on the court for the Timberwolves. She'd whooped. For the same reason she'd drunk all the Scotch: he was there.

He really was gorgeous, she thought, twisting around and grinning at her hero. More-than-Mel might have ridden from the pages of a history book, leading a horde of painted savages on some sort of heroic assault. He had a hard, square jaw, a cleft chin, and a firm, wide mouth. He had red hair, too, but not carroty red. It was dark auburn that fell in loopy curls on the back of his neck and went particularly well with his dark, coffee-brown eyes.

Added to all this masculine beauty was a body that shouted, "National underwear ad campaign." Tall, lean, lithe—if she hadn't had so much to drink she could have come up with more and better adjectives. She still could have if he hadn't put his shirt on. Too bad. Right now all she could remember was that his stomach was as corrugated as a mile of country road and muscles had bunched all over his shoulders, chest, and arms as he'd put on his shirt.

"Miss, are you *sure* you're all right?" he asked. He had her upright now and kept one hand on her shoulder while cautiously relinquishing his grip on her with the other.

"Ah-huh. Why?"

"You look sort of goofy."

Some of the glow around More-than-Mel faded. Braveheart wouldn't have used a word like *goofy.*

"What say we get a spot of something in you to soak up the spirits, eh?"

Dinner and a date with Braveheart? Hot damn. "Hoo-kay," she said, turning around—oops. Mistake. The world caught up to her feet and kept moving right on by. She swayed, tilted, and began to pitch forward—

—and a strong hand curled around her waist. Without even a grunt this time, the gorgeous Scot picked her up and resettled her on her feet, facing him. She found herself staring at the tip of his nose.

It had been a long time since Toni Olson, onetime all-state center for the Edina girls' basketball team, had looked up to meet a man's eyes. She did so now and all she could think was that it was obscene that those lashes should have been wasted on a man.

"Begads, luv." The gaze traveling down her body was as slow as molasses, sending tingles along her skin. "I'm surprised you don't have a chronic nosebleed all the way up here."

The tingles stopped. Another comedian. "*You* seem to have adapted."

"Aye. But I'm a braw manly man, and you're just a—"

"Don't say it." If she had a penny for every would-be comic who thought it hilarious to call her a wisp of a girl—

"—pale American who can't hold her liquor." His black-brown eyes sparkled.

"Oh." Points to him for ducking the obvious. Points to him for still being here. Most men would have left her flat on her back burping Scotch and moaning. Not that she needed any help. She was perfectly capable of taking care of herself. She was a practical, sensible Minnesotan.

She started to sway again. He grabbed her arm, steadying her.

"Can you walk, or should I carry you?" he asked.

Toni shot him a darkly suspicious glare. His expression was perfectly sober. He meant it. If she said the word, this poor man would risk condemning himself to a life of chiropractic care in order to carry her somewhere. She could just imagine what *that* would look like, all six feet one and one-half inches of her sticking out at odd angles as he staggered toward the fairgrounds gasping, "Help!"

"Nah-uh. But thanks. I jes . . . I just need to walk a lil bit."

"Sure," he said offering his arm, and a nicely muscled arm it was, too.

"You have very nice manners for a Scot," she said graciously.

"We Scots are known for our good manners."

"No, you're not," she replied matter-of-factly.

"No?" He definitely sounded amused. What had she said that was so funny? "What are we known for then?"

"Kilts," she replied, pleased with her insight. "And Scotch. And thistles. Mel Gibson—"

"Mel Gibson isn't Scottish!" he said, sounding indignant.

"Don't be such a stickler," she answered. "He looks good in a kilt. Almost as good as you."

She tripped, but he caught her against his hip. He had big, strong hands. Her heart started pitter-patting with teenage lust. And she wasn't a teenager. Far from it. She was twenty-five. She pulled her thoughts back to the matter at hand and caught sight of his strongly muscled calves.

"You got nice legs," she said sincerely.

"Back atcha." He really sounded amused now. She grinned, inordinately pleased with the offhand compliment.

They'd made their way to one of the tented booths crowding the side of the gaming field. A middle-aged man with huge, red muttonchop sideburns snored in a chair behind a counter. More-than-Mel picked up a scone from a plate balanced on the edge of the counter and handed it to her before filling a paper cup from the pitcher of lemonade beside it. He put it in her free hand.

"Eat. Drink. I'd add 'Be merry,' but I think you're already there."

She complied, chomping off a third of the biscuit. It was hard and salty with way too much baking soda, nothing as good a Patisserie Margot's. But she was a guest. "Yum."

"Birdie makes the best scones in Scotland."

Toni mumbled noncommittally around the dry crumbs. Poor More-than-Mel if he thought this was what a scone was supposed to taste like. Her hero dropped a couple coins into a tumbler with an "Honor System" placard taped to it. Not surprisingly, it wasn't exactly overflowing.

"Where's Birdie?" Toni asked.

"Birdie wouldn't be caught dead at a Highland fair. She disapproves of them on principle."

Birdie probably wouldn't be caught dead admitting to making those scones. Toni sure wouldn't. She took a sip of lemonade. It was watery. "She doesn't have anything against making a buck off the tourists though."

"Of course not. She's principled but practical."

Toni nodded with grudging understanding. In spite of

having spent every last dime on T-shirts, treacle pudding, and tartan throws on her way to picking up her prize pooch before heading back to Grim Reality—aka Hopkins, Minnesota—she considered herself acutely practical.

A voice distorted by a bullhorn and distance called out for the next set of contestants to take the field for the hammer toss.

"Hey," Toni said, peering up at the gorgeous Scot. "Am I keeping you from something important like dancing under a flaming sword or something?"

He bit his lip. "Nah," he said seriously. "I heard they scratched the limbo from the program."

"Oh." She smiled.

"Look," he said. "You can't get behind the wheel in your present state. Let me drive you to your inn."

She shook her head fervently. "No. I couldn't ask. You'll miss the hammer heave or whatever it's called."

"Hammer toss, and I've already competed in my weight class."

"Ah!" she said, liking the picture her imagination conjured up of this man bronzed and gleaming with non-smelly sweat, flinging a manly-sized hammer yards beyond his puny competitor's range. "Did you win?"

"Didn't even place."

"Well, there's probably some other sport you need to be here for."

"Rugby. But not for a couple hours. Where are you staying?"

"Strathcuddy Inn."

"I know it well. It's only five miles or so up the road. I'll drive you there and trot on back here in plenty of time for the kickoff."

She frowned peevishly. Somehow she'd gotten the idea that if she made all the appropriate noises about not imposing on him and he made all the appropriate noises about it being no trouble, they'd eventually end up back at the inn eating haggis in the moonlight and gazing soulfully into each other's eyes. Or engaged in other, equally interesting, pastimes.

Apparently he hadn't shared her vision. He was just being polite.

"So where's the auto?"

She jerked her thumb in the direction of the car lot. "There."

She wasn't sure she wanted to go back to the inn just yet. She'd been having a grand time. Scotland was everything she'd dreamed it would be—except for the food.

High, barren moors and pine-shrouded mountains, purple heather and leathery burgundy gorse, the west of Scotland embodied the romance of a hundred Hollywood movies. She'd lunched on terraces overlooking shaggy Highland cows placidly grazing the banks of lochs— *lochs,* by heavens!—followed the paths purportedly traveled by cattle-thieving clansmen and border lords, quaffed tepid beer and gnawed on castle rock, toured the haunted ruins of a dozen abbeys, and today, on her way to Oronsay Kennels, stumbled on a real, live Highland fair.

No. She didn't want to go back to her inn. But she supposed if she insisted on staying now, she'd only look like a pathetic American, hanging around hoping to spend more time with Laird Luscious. Which was true, of course, but a girl had her pride.

"Come along then," he encouraged her. Heaving a resigned sigh, she allowed him to lead her to the parking lot, where she pointed out the tinny little Volkswagen van she'd rented.

He helped her into the passenger seat before going round and sliding in behind the wheel. He turned the ignition, and the beast grumbled to life. "Ach, love, I see you went all-out renting the sporty model."

She studied him suspiciously. The full effects of the scotch had begun to fade a bit. "Was that 'ach' for my benefit?"

He gave her a charming, heart-tipping grin. "Busted. Now, sit back, relax, and enjoy the scenery."

Somehow she avoided making the obvious comment.

She would have been heartened if she'd known that Dev was biting his own tongue to keep from making a similarly cheesy remark.

He looked over at the tall, willowy Nordic princess, and he didn't want to play rugby. He wanted to stay with her and see what odd, funny, and disconcerting bits would next escape her lips. As long back as he could remember, he'd never ditched out on a rugby game. But if he didn't have a dozen of his mates counting on him to return, he sure as hell would now.

One thing was for certain; if the ride to the inn was half as interesting as the last half-hour had been, he'd be heading back to Strathcuddy Inn first light tomorrow. He pulled out of the parking lot. "So, darlin'," he said, trying to sound offhand, "might your driver ask your name?"

"Toni," she said. "Antoinette Olson."

"Part French?" he asked sardonically.

She shook her head. "Nope. In America you don't have to have an ethnic background to have an ethnic name. We're very democratic."

"So I've been told."

She hiccuped and blushed. When was the last time he'd seen a girl blush? She was lovely.

"My middle name is Chosposi," she continued. "It's Hopi for 'Bluebird Eye,' and before you ask, I'm not Hopi, either."

"Good God," he blurted out.

"Mother went to Berkeley," she said primly.

"It's a charming name. So . . . unexpected."

She nodded, sending the curtain of blond hair rippling. "Thanks. Tit for tat. What's your name?"

"Devlin Montgomery. Dev for short."

She gave a short guffaw that she immediately covered with her hand.

"What was so funny about 'Devlin Montgomery'?" he demanded.

"Nothing," she said, keeping her face turned forward. But her lips kept twitching with irrepressible humor.

"What?"

"Well . . . come on! *Devlin Montgomery?* I couldn't have named you better myself."

"I must be missing something."

"Well, look at you!" she declared, giggling. "You look like you should be on a billboard advertising Loch Liquor or something. You know. The kind with a dark, craggy mountain looming in the background and you in the foreground, a bottle of whisky in one hand and a sword in the other."

"Sounds a mite hackneyed."

"Yeah. Well, that's my point."

All right, perhaps it had occasionally occurred to him that his name had a certain romantic quality to it. But what most interested him was her previous words. "And what do you mean, 'look at me'?"

She blushed again. He bet she wasn't nearly so forth-coming when she was sober. She blushed too easily and too readily to be in the habit of saying whatever came to her mind. And what an interesting mind it was. Malt whisky billboard, indeed.

"You must know you are gorgeous."

"Must I?" Sure, in the last five or six years he'd grown accustomed to a certain amount of female attention. But he still found it unsettling, as if any day he might wake up and discover his mum was paying the girls to do a bit of fawning.

He glanced at Toni. He bet this tall, stately creature wouldn't have spared him a passing glance ten years ago. Then he'd been nothing but a scarecrow with braces. He hadn't even gone to the local deb ball, and that in spite of the invitations that came with being the school's rugby captain.

She still hadn't answered. Probably thought he was fishing for a compliment, which he was. He wouldn't mind being fawned over by Toni Olson. He wouldn't mind doing quite a bit with Toni Olson, he thought.

"Are you ogling me?" she asked. But he had her mark now, and nothing that popped from between her lips was likely to catch him off guard.

"As it happens, I was."

"Oh." She opened her mouth, shut it, turned, and stared straight ahead again. He grinned.

"What? You can blurt out candid comments, but I can't?"

She swung around to face him. "That's not it," she said. "I was *trying* to decide if you were pulling my leg."

"Not without an invite." He leered at her. "My mum raised me to be a gentleman."

Out of the corner of her eye he saw her swallow. A tad bit of an innocent, then, in spite of that eight-inch comment.

"I was rather hoping you might burst out with a hearty 'damn' at that particular juncture," he said.

"I *like* gentlemen," she replied. "I'd hate it if you turned out to be just another guy with notches on his bedpost."

He chuckled at the idea. "No worries there, luv. My bedpost is sadly unmarked."

"So you say."

"We can take the next turnoff, and I can show you," he suggested.

"No. I mean, no, thank you," she said, suddenly prim. But she kept stealing glances at him when she thought he wasn't looking, and the color in her cheeks stayed high.

"Another day, then." They passed through the village, and in a few minutes they were rolling into the Strathcuddy Inn's yard. A chicken squawked at their arrival, and a white cat scooted out from under a wooden bench beside the front door.

The sun was just kissing the tops of the mountains to the north. He got out of the car and went round to Toni's side, opening the door and holding out his hand. She clasped it gratefully, and he pulled her up and out. It was a unique pleasure to be able to speak to a woman without getting a crick in his neck. She was just the right height. Just the right height to . . .

He leaned in and kissed her.

His lips touched hers, and her world tilted right back

out of orbit. He settled his mouth more firmly, putting his arms around her to draw her closer, steadying her, holding her upright. His kiss was firm and heated and hungry.

His muscular length tensed, his arms tightened, and the kiss deepened even more. Her thoughts spun, whirled, senses clamoring for attention. He drew back a little, their lips clinging sweetly, so gently, his polishing, coaxing . . . Her mouth opened.

His tongue slipped into her mouth and found hers. Little sparks shattered against the back of her eyelids. She sighed a surrender to pleasure as her hands slipped around his waist, bringing their hips into contact. With a deep urgent sound, he tipped her back, his strong arms supporting her, and bent over her, kissing her even more deeply, his fingers tunneling through her hair . . .

A lamb bleated nearby, penetrating her fast-fleeing thoughts. Lamb? Her eyes flew open. Lamb. Scotland. Scotch.

This wasn't Minnesota. Sure, she could take him up to her room and make love until the sun rose above the western edge of the Grampian Mountains. But he wouldn't be calling the next day. Or any day after, for that matter. He'd be a souvenir.

Or she would.

He felt her hands on his chest and then, suddenly, she pushed herself away, breaking off their ardent kiss. She braced her arms straight, her palms flat on his heaving chest. Her own chest was doing a fair amount of heaving itself, and her eyes were dilated, bright with trepidation and arousal. Abruptly he realized he was still holding her, pulling against her push. He released her.

Her lips looked full, bruised. Had he done that?

"What was that?" she asked breathlessly.

Chemistry, he thought blankly. He'd heard about but never experienced it, instant electrifying sexual attraction set to blaze by any contact. Even a simple good-night kiss. Good-night, not good-bye. It couldn't be good-bye.

"I don't know." He tried to make his tone light. "But I want to find out. How about you?"

He waited for her answer, willing her to say yes.

"I don't know," she said, her gaze searching his face. "I'm leaving Scotland in a few days, and I have some business I have to take care of before I go."

He mustn't scare her, which is just what he was doing. He could see the uneasiness in her eyes.

"Let me write down my number," he said. "If you have time after you're done, please call me."

"Really?"

Dear Lord, did she think he was kidding? "Yes. Really. I'd love to . . . I want to . . . Geez. Why do you have to leave in a few days?"

"Plane ticket. Nonrefundable."

"Damn it."

"I thought you were a gentleman." There was a little note of amusement in the breathless admonition.

"I am. Sorry. When? Two days? Three?"

"Four."

"Damn it." He raked his hair back, casting about for some way to keep her in Scotland longer.

"Look, it's been a while since we left the fair," she said. "Your friends'll be expecting you."

Was she trying to get rid of him? "Da— Sorry." If she wanted him gone, he'd best go. He strode over to the van, rummaged around in the glove compartment, found a piece of paper, and scribbled his number down on it.

"You're right, of course. I'd best be off." He couldn't give her some hackneyed phrase. "It was fascinating meeting you, Toni Olson. I hope you call. Please do."

And then he did something that in the coming years he would look back on and be impressed by. He started down the road, and he did not look back. At least not until he was fairly certain the darkness concealed him. Then he did turn. But she'd disappeared.

2

"**O**uch."

The road beneath the van had more ripples in it than Dev Montgomery's stomach, and that was saying a lot. Each time the van hit a rut, it jumped like a jackhammer, driving pain straight into Toni's temples. She deserved it, both for drinking too much and for making a complete ass out of herself.

She touched her hip pocket where she'd stashed the scrap of paper with his telephone number. She'd never use it. How could she?

"I've an extra eight inches on Mel."

"Where?"

She winced. And then she'd said, "You must know you're gorgeous."

And had she really said she wished she could "do" Sean Connery? And she couldn't have tried to—please God, let this memory be wrong!—peek under his kilt!

And then to cap it off, there'd been that kiss.

She could still feel the rising pitch point of desire, the heat of lips, the fierce pull of attraction . . . She was lucky she hadn't woken up in the same bed with him.

Or maybe that was unlucky. She wasn't sure.

That was the problem. Everything she'd done since she'd fallen off that damn fence made her look like an easy American girl on the prowl. But in truth, she'd never been promiscuous, not anything even remotely like it. Dev Montgomery, however, had made her want to toss a lifetime of caution aside and leap feetfirst into his bed. It was unnerving, and that alone, she decided as she rolled up the van window against the chill air, was an excellent reason for not calling him this morning.

Along with her aforementioned shamelessness.

No, she wouldn't be calling him, now or ever. Just the thought of facing him again drove the blood boiling to her face.

She was so immersed in her thoughts she nearly missed the battered sign on the side of the road that said Oronsay Kennel was about ten miles east. She stopped the van, reached into her purse, and pulled out a bottle of Tylenol, dumping three capsules into her palm before popping them into her mouth. With a sense of getting her due, she chomped down on the bitter pills.

No more mooning over Dev Montgomery. Her life was about to change; she was on the cusp of taking possession of the finest dog in the world, a dog she'd longed for since seeing his image on an Internet video loop last year: Grand International Champion Nolly's Black.

Nolly's Black would be the basis not only for her own business, but for a program of introducing European bloodlines into her dogs' pedigrees. If things went as well as she had every reason to believe they would, she would live the life she'd always dreamed about—May through November in two of the world's most gorgeous "summer" cities, Minneapolis and Saint Paul, and the rest of the year traveling in warmer climes.

Several companies had already offered her lucrative contracts for her and her dogs' talents. Nolly's Black would increase the snob appeal immensely among the higher-end suburban companies.

She stepped on the gas, lurching onto the pitted road, her headache fading with her anticipation, thoughts of Devlin Montgomery usurped by the image of a glossy, black-and-white blue-eyed Border collie. By the time she pulled to a stop in front of a neat stone building bearing the Oronsay name, the throbbing in her head had subsided to a dull ache. She got out of the car, looking around with interest.

It was small. She'd expected a large facility with shining kennels set in rows behind modern buildings. Instead the famous Oronsay kennels looked like someone's converted garage. No more than a dozen runs extended from the side of the building, and only half of these contained dogs—two bitches with litters, a couple of young dogs, and an old campaigner snoozing on a rug. At the far end of the building an old Volvo station wagon stood with its hood wide open, a light rain anointing its automotive innards.

She walked around the side of the building. Behind it,

hidden from the road and a short distance up a narrow lane, she saw a small—a really small—castle. Half of it was tumbled in picturesque ruin; the other half was pock-marked with new brickwork and large modern windows. On the renovated side a drift of smoke rose from a thoroughly modern smokestack. She grinned, the romantic part of her nature elbowing aside her practical—and most often louder—side.

It really was a castle, no matter how diminutive, and people really did live in it. Amazing. She'd toured roughly a hundred castles since arriving, castles being something of an obsession with her, but she hadn't been inside one where the heirs of the original occupants still lived. They were probably associated with the kennels. Probably the owners.

She wondered if there was any chance of her getting inside. Maybe if she played her cards right and hinted to Mr. McGill, the kennel manager with whom she'd corresponded, that she'd like to meet the laird or lairdess—was there such a thing?—she'd be invited up to the castle for an introduction. And a scone. Maybe they even knew Devlin Montgomery.

But first things first. She found a door marked Office and entered. Inside was a large room filled from floor to ceiling with shelves displaying well-dusted trophies, cups, and ribbons. Pictures of dogs—oil paintings, watercolors, and photographs—papered the walls, leaving hardly any space bare. A carved and battered desk that Toni was certain belonged on the *Antiques Roadshow* stood squarely in the center of the room, and behind this, stooped over a ledger book, sat the quintessential Scottish laird.

His elderly face was lean and ruddy and fierce. A spider's web of tiny veins mapped his beaky nose, and bristling white brows stood out like shelves above his little piercing blue eyes. Thinning white hair lay smoothly across a freckled, domed head. He silently mouthed numbers from the ledger he pored over.

With a start, Toni realized he hadn't noticed her entrance. She cleared her throat noisily. He glanced up and then, seeing her, popped to his feet.

He wasn't very tall. The sports coat he wore—tweed, of course—had leather patches at the elbows, and his trousers bagged at the knees as though he spent a good deal of time kneeling in them.

"Aye?"

He actually said "aye" as an inquisitive! Toni nearly sighed with pleasure. She held out her hand, extending it over the desk. "Hello. I'm Toni Olson, and you must be Donald McGill. It's so nice to meet you." Her hand hung unaccepted in the air. The fierce blue eyes were staring at her blankly.

"Mr. McGill?"

"*You're* Tony Olson?"

"Yes. Oh." She suspected the reason for his pole-axed expression. "Toni. Short for Antoinette. You were probably expecting a man?"

"Bloody well right I was," the old man exploded, taking Toni aback. "I thought you were a man, and I was having a hard enough time with it as it was, but now that you're a woman . . ." He trailed off, shaking his head.

"Now that I'm a woman, what?" Toni asked, a deep fear beginning to take root.

"Well, a deal's a deal no matter what, I suppose," the

old man muttered, ignoring her remark. She didn't press the matter. For a second there she thought the old man was going to renege on their deal.

That couldn't happen. She'd already made a down payment of half the price of the dog, and her check had already been cashed. That, along with the cashier's check made out to Oronsay Kennels that she carried in her purse, had effectively wiped out her bank account. Even her credit card was maxed out, run up to the hilt with the presents and things she'd purchased over the last two weeks.

"Thank you," she said. "Now, if I might see him."

"Aye," McGill groused sullenly. "Soon enough fer that. You need to know some things about the beastie before you go carryin' him off to yer Minna-Soda."

"Of course." She must play this cautiously—not give him any excuse to back out of their deal. She sat down on the only other chair in the office. "What can you tell me about Blackie?"

"Well, first off, he's no kennel dog. He's been treated like a prince by some that ought to know better since the day he was whelped. No concrete runs for him, ye ken. Ye'd break his heart if you put him in solitary, and that's all it is, tha damned kennels with their chain links and not a dog to keep company with. Such cruelty is solitary confinement, as sure as you're standin' here. A dog's a pack animal. He craves companionship as much as you or I."

Toni, who'd worked with dogs all her life, was in complete agreement, but she couldn't help the prickle of resentment that crept up her spine at his belligerent tone, or the fact that he was lecturing to her even after they'd had a fair amount of correspondence on this very subject.

Unless he thought she'd just been acting agreeable in order to purchase the dog.

"As I told you," she said, "I have no intention of putting him in a kennel. He'll be living in my house. Probably sleeping on my bed."

"Yer naught thinkin' of tryin' to make him a lady's pet, are you?" McGill asked suspiciously. " 'Cause he's no pet. He's a working dog," he cautioned sternly.

"He'll work, all right. Five or six times a day at least."

That impressed McGill. He peered at her as though suspecting she was lying. "That's a fair day's work. Unless you mean by work a few exercises."

"No," Toni replied. "I mean work. As in 'work for his kibble.'"

"I dinna know Minnesota had so many sheep."

Toni laughed. "Oh, it doesn't. At least not that I know of. But geese it has in spades."

"Geese?"

"Yup. Big Canadians. They're everywhere, a plague on Minnesota's landscape. Every golf course and every park, every stretch of grass by any bit of water, is ankle deep in—"

"You're gonna use Grand International Champion Nolly's Black to chase geese off golf courses?"

McGill erupted from his seat. Toni stared at him. His face and throat were violently red. His jowls quivered. His hands clenched and unclenched into white-knuckled fists at his side.

"Yeah . . ." she said slowly, worried the old duffer was going to keel over.

"Over my dead body!"

Exactly what she'd been thinking.

The fire engine red had morphed into a sort of magenta color, and his neck was swelling up alarmingly, like a bullfrog's.

"Take it easy," she said, standing. "You might pop something if you go on like this. Listen. Is there someone I can call—"

"I'll be fine just as soon as you leave here, miss! So please do so. *At once.*"

She studied him narrowly. As soon as she realized he wasn't going to explode, she considered his words. She didn't like them. Not one bit.

"I'm not leaving without my dog."

"He isn't yours, yet, lassie."

"I have a signed contract. You've deposited my money in your bank, and I have a cashier's check here with your name on it. In my book, that makes him mine."

"Well"—he slapped his hands palm down on the desk, leaning over it and thrusting his red, angry face into hers—"we're in Scotland now, Missie, and what is or isn't in your book don't matter here."

"Oh?" she asked quietly.

Toni was normally very easygoing, but the same tenacity that had allowed her ancestors to endure near Arctic winters now surged forth. She had bought this dog. She had scraped and saved and sacrificed in order to buy this dog. She wanted this dog. And by God, she was going to *have* this dog.

She had contracts to honor. Plans she'd spent a year devising. Two lovely young border collies waiting to be made mothers by a Scottish stud.

She laid her hands on the desk and shifted her weight forward until her eyes were on a level with McGill's, inches from his face. They both understood the rules in this game: Don't blink.

"I wouldn't be so quick to discount my book if I were you, Mr. McGill. Your government sure won't, and it might prove a costly mistake if you do. In fact, I guarantee it. Now, if you don't hand over my dog, I'll sue your Scottish ass as quick as you can say Bonnie Prince Charlie."

He sucked in a breath through his teeth. "Such foul language! I never hoped to hear a lass—"

"Can it, McGill," Toni said curtly. "Let me make myself even clearer. I have a plane ticket with reservations for one dog to be transported from this country to mine, and that ticket is nontransferable and nonrefundable and confirmed for three days hence. Come hell or high water, Mr. McGill I intend to be on that plane. *With my dog.*"

His brilliant blue eyes narrowed on her. "You don't understand. This dog, Miss . . . Miss Olson, he's not just any dog. There's been a Nolly's Blackie with the clan for near two hundred years, and every generation carefully accounted for and recorded in that very book." He pointed at a heavy, battered-looking leather tome sitting in a place of honor in the middle of the bookshelves.

"Why, there are heads of state sitting on thrones today who don't have a pedigree as fine and unblemished as his. And you want to use him, a Grand International Sheepherding Champion, the distilled essence of the perfect sheepdog, valiant, bold, Nolly's Black to"—he sputtered, the red flooding his cheeks once more—"to . . . *chase geese?*"

Toni'd heard the arguments before. While she too believed that a working dog not only should but *must* work in order to be happy, she was just as sure that to a herding dog, what it herded didn't make a damn bit of difference. She'd seen Border collies herd ducks, sheep, geese, and if those weren't available, children, and always with the same intensity and desire.

Unfortunately, their human handlers were far more prejudiced.

"Believe me, he'll adore chasing geese, and they present some pretty unique situations, you know. They swim, and we have lots of lakes, so that he'll have to—"

"He won't 'have to' anything!" McGill's attempt at reasonableness had apparently ended. "He's not going with you. I'll write you out a repayment check right now, and you'll be off. I'm sure you'll be able to find some poor daft herder who'll sell you his dog for a tenth of what you were going to spend on Blackie."

"*Am* going to spend on Blackie. You don't seem to understand. I don't wany any dog. I want Nolly's Black. He's going to be the basis for—"

"For what?" sneered McGill. "For a Grand International *Goose*herding Champion?"

There was no sense talking to him. It wasn't that he couldn't understand. He wouldn't.

"Please go get my dog, or I will be forced to call the local authorities."

That chased the sneer from his thin lips. "Now you don't want to do that, miss. I'm sure we can come to some sort of an understanding. I have a fine young—"

"My dog, Mr. McGill," she said loudly. "Now, please."

"If you'll just listen to reason—"

"Look. I'm giving you until the count of five to leave

this office and go get me my dog. If you don't, I'm going to dial 999."

He pressed his lips tightly together and marched around the side of the desk. He was small but nasty, and the fact that he had to crane his neck to glare up at her didn't decrease his ferocity. She quickly back-stepped as he stomped past, stopping halfway through the door to turn and glare at her.

"Ye'll not take exception to me havin' . . ." He stopped. Whether his lips were trembling with rage or some other deep emotion, she couldn't say. He hitched his chin up proudly, and continued. "Ye'll not mind me havin' a bit of a farewell with me lad, would ye?"

Her anger abruptly dissolved. How in God's name could she refuse? She wasn't heartless. The reminder that she was taking this man's dog from him hit her with almost physical force. She could only guess what it would mean to her if some stranger were to come and take her dog away.

"Of course," she gasped, suddenly abashed. "Of course! You say good-bye to him. Take as long as you like."

"It'll be a spell. Blackie . . . he's up to the castle." The old man wiped the back of his knuckles across his eyes. "The . . . the only home the dear little fellow has . . . has ever known!"

And with a sound like a sob he swung around, slamming the door behind him, leaving Toni to watch him trot, head bowed with the strength of his emotions, past the window. She gulped, feeling like a villain, and wandered over to the wall to read some of the framed newspaper clippings.

It took her a good half-hour to finish reading them, and another to leaf through the photo album and studbook. By the time she'd finished, she was feeling less like a villain and more like a victim. McGill was certainly taking his own sweet time with his good-bye. A person could be halfway to Fort George in the time it was taking him to . . .

Suspicion hit her like a sledgehammer.

No. He wouldn't. He couldn't. She hurried outside. The rain had stopped, but a bracing wind had replaced it, pushing the clouds overhead.

"McGill!" she hollered. "McGill!"

The dogs in the kennel, up for a bit of afternoon sport, barked encouragingly.

"Mc! Gill!" She ran around the side of the building. The van stood where she'd left it, and farther along the Volvo still immodestly exposed its engine. Thank God for that. She hurried back the way she'd come and headed up the path she'd seen McGill take. Maybe the old guy was really still up there, sobbing into Blackie's ruff.

Close up, the castle lost a lot of its charm. Someone was obviously working on a major renovation, and she could see why. Rubble might look quaint from a distance, but it smelled bad up close. The damp stone scattered about the unrepaired section smelled unpleasantly organic and stale. On the other hand, the newer section looked too new. Why, no one had even bothered to take the windows' e-rating stickers off.

She banged on the newly hung door. Nothing. She banged harder. A voice shouted for her to come in.

She eased open the door and stepped inside. It was a disaster. A painter, a carpenter, and a fast food delivery-man had obviously had a gigantic brawl in this room, because the evidence of all three professions was scattered across what she judged just might some day become a kitchen floor. She pulled her fascinated musings back to the matter at hand.

"McGill!" she shouted. "McGill, where are you? I want my dog! Now!"

She heard the sound of booted feet approaching from the other side of a closed door across the room. She lifted her chin. No more screwing around.

The door opened. He stood backlit against the bright light, tall and lean and broad-shouldered and gorgeous. He was wearing jeans this time, and damn if he didn't look just as good in Levi's as he had in a kilt.

Her eyes grew round. Her jaw grew slack. Her heart started racing as she remembered with exacting detail the shape and texture of his mouth.

His brows dipped in a scowl. So much for their happy reunion.

"McGill left about an hour ago," Devlin Montgomery said. "Now, what's this about a dog?"

*I*t didn't take an advanced degree in engineering—
which, by the way, Devlin had—to figure out what
had happened. The van's fuel tank cap lay alongside a
half-empty bag of sugar by the back tire. That coupled
with the fact that McGill, Blackie, and an ancient Land
Rover—according to Dev, the only other vehicle the kennel owned—had vanished told the story; Blackie had
been dognapped.

"Your manager has stolen my dog!"

Dev frowned, unwilling to trust his eyes. He'd spent
the previous evening on the rugby field muffing every
other play he'd been involved in until finally his team-
mates had permanently sidelined him. He hadn't cared.

He'd spent the hour thinking about her: her round

American accent, the naughty-nice quality of her grin, the way her blush tinted her skin, the Caribbean sea color of her eyes . . . but mostly her response to their kiss; the way her breasts had flattened against him, the tip of her tongue meeting his.

He'd gone to sleep fantasizing about her, awaking aroused and uncomfortable, cursing himself for an idiot but nonetheless spending the day hanging about waiting for a call that hadn't come. He'd thought about driving in to Strathcuddy, but was afraid that if he did, she'd call while he was en route, and he'd miss her altogether. But now she was here, demanding he hand over his dog.

"Listen," he said, having a hard time getting fantasy and reality to jive. "McGill wouldn't steal Blackie. Any more than he'd sell him. Blackie isn't even his to sell. He's mine."

"Yours?" She'd shed the atrocious "Sassy Lassie" T-shirt and was wearing something soft and pink that accented the highlights in her hair. The color in her cheeks was a delicate woodland bramble rose, and—

"Well?"

"What? Oh. Yes. Mine. I hand-raised him. I trained him. I even ran . . ." Dev trailed off as he met Toni's eye.

"Who the hell are you?"

"I thought you didn't like bad language?"

"Some situations warrant it," she said crossly.

What had happened to the sloshed hero-worshiping, or rather Braveheart-worshiping, lass of yesterday? Oh, yeah. She'd sobered up. And looked to be paying a penalty for yesterday's frivolities, too, if the dark circles beneath her blue eyes were any testament.

"Now who are you?"

"Devon Angus—"

"Who *are* you?"

"I, ah, I own the castle."

Her amazing eyes widened. "You're the laird?"

He hated to kill the soft light of grudging adoration dawning on her face, but he couldn't pose as something he wasn't. "Down, Lorne Doone. There is no laird, at least not officially. Hasn't been for generations. It's more a tourist come-on nowadays, and I don't have anything to tour." He waved his hand around.

"But if there was a laird, would you be it? Or your father?"

He snorted. She was tiptoeing around a case of Highland worship. He'd seen the signs before, mostly down at the local pub when the tourist bus came through. But while his mates weren't averse to using Robert Burns's more lurid prose to their advantage when they encountered an attractive tourist, Dev never had. However, looking at Toni Olson, he was willing to make an exception. "My dad, I suppose."

"And McGill is . . . what? A trusted family retainer," she breathed. Then, as though caught with her pants down, she scowled fiercely.

"I guess so." McGill *had* run the kennels for his family for the past forty years, as had his father before him. And McGill was certainly trusted and excellent with the dogs. It was the making money part that McGill had trouble with, which was why Dev was here, fixing up one of his family's decrepit castles and hoping to make a go of the kennels.

The Montgomerys were bright and charming, but earlier generations had also been notoriously impractical.

Consequently the family had as many failing businesses as they had varied ones. His generation couldn't afford such dilettantism.

He could see in Toni's face her struggle to sublimate her rising rapture—Scandinavian practicality versus American romanticism.

"Well," she said sternly, "your retainer just made off with my dog."

Scandinavian pragmatism one, American mawkishness zero. Damn.

"I have the contract that proves the sale right here." She snapped open a sheaf of papers.

"Listen," he said, holding up his hands in a pacifying gesture, "I believe you. You have a bill of sale for my dog, signed by McGill. But first things first. I've got to find McGill and Blackie, and then we'll get this sorted out."

"Fine. Where'd they go?"

"Specifically? I haven't any idea."

"That's just great." A little note of fear had entered her voice, and all sorts of manly protective instincts Dev hadn't even known he'd possessed came roaring to the front. He stepped closer to her and touched her arm. She was too miserable to even note the familiarity.

"What's the matter?"

"I told you yesterday. I have nonrefundable, nontransferable tickets. I've made reservations for Blackie to be on the same flight with me three days from now, out of London. If I miss that flight—I can't miss that flight."

An unpleasant suspicion took hold of Dev. "Does McGill know about this?"

She thought a minute. "Yeah? So?"

"He's gone to ground," he told her flatly. "As far as

McGill is concerned, he only has to stay out of your way until your plane leaves, and he figures he's home free."

"The . . . the . . ."

"Blackguard?" Dev suggested.

"I was thinking of something a bit more colloquial," she said.

Dev smiled in spite of her grim expression. She might be a much cooler and more remote woman than the tipsy lovely he'd kissed yesterday, but the humor was still there.

"And let me tell you, Mr. Montgomery," *Ouch.* "Your manager has figured wrong. I may be forced to leave here without my dog, but I won't give him up. I'll get a lawyer. A really nasty Scottish lawyer."

"Hold on," Dev said. He couldn't afford a lawsuit. Not that he wouldn't spend his last penny protecting what was his if he thought his principles were being tested—he would. But he wasn't certain right now who was right and who was wronged. Clearly, Toni didn't have any such moral dilemma.

"McGill hates cities. Doesn't trust the motorways, and he's driving an ancient Land Rover."

"Yeah?"

"I think I know where he's headed."

"Where?" she asked.

"The Great Hebrides Sanctioned Trial on Mull starts tomorrow. McGill was planning on attending. I know he entered a dog. I thought that's where he'd gone when he came in and fetched Blackie. If you wanted to stay lost for a few days and you had a Border collie, what better place to hide?"

He started past her, but she caught at his arm. The

touch was electrifying, stopping him as effectively as a brick wall. "Where are you going?"

"To Mull." He couldn't think very clearly with her holding his arm like that. The scent of her herbal shampoo filled the air between them, along with a heated wave of awareness. The memory of their kiss ambushed him in a stampede of desire.

"How?" she asked. "He ruined my car, and he took yours."

"I got me bike," he answered in thick Scottish brogue, trying for a brashness that would disguise her effect on him.

"Motorcycle?"

"Yeah."

"Good. I'm going, too."

He frowned. "No. The roads are too rough, and the bike's suspension is old. You'd shake some teeth loose, and I don't want to be responsible for your orthodonture on top of everything else."

"Aha!" she crowed. "then you *do* concede that the dog is mine!"

"I don't concede anything. Except that this is a mess, and we need to get it straightened out. And I'll be able to do that a good deal faster without you coming along for the ride."

"Listen," she said, stepping nearer and tapping him in the sternum with one finger, "I have a vested interest in this. How do I know you won't just putter off to Oban for the afternoon and leave me here with no way out?"

He felt himself stiffen. "Because you have my word."

"Yeah. Well, I had McGill's word, too, and his signature, for whatever good it did me."

"Ow. That was cold."

His words drew a quickly suppressed grin from her. "I'm a businesswoman, whatever you might think. My actions yesterday were entirely out of character—"

"Lord, I hope not," he said with a lopsided grin.

She blushed prettily and scowled. "Don't try and side-track me, Montgomery."

Okay, he thought, *marginally better than Mr. Montgomery.*

"Now, I don't want to call the cops on your trusted family retainer, but I will unless you take me with you."

He eyed her speculatively. She was standing with her hands on her hips, but there was a shadow in her eyes that belied her aggressive stance, a touch of pleading. She didn't want to call the cops but clearly felt her back was to the wall.

His thoughts took an improbable and devious turn. If he took her with him, there would be other compensations. He'd have a chance to be with her, to see if attraction this potent had at its base something more than pure animal lust. Not that he was deriding animal lust. Not at all.

"Okay. Get your money and whatever things you might need for a night on the town, providing the town is population one-fifty. Meet me down at the garage. And put on a jacket," he advised, looking out at the gathering clouds. "Rain jacket."

She darted out, leaving him to make a quick call to his mother's house in Aberdeen so that his youngest brother could come out and watch over the dogs. As he'd hoped, his brother was happy to assist. Anything to get out of one of their mother's dinner parties. Then Dev stuffed a change of socks, underwear, and another shirt into a pack and went down to meet Toni at the kennels.

She was waiting for him. She'd put on a Burberry and donned a pair of red cowboy boots in place of her Adidases. They brought all sorts of wicked thoughts boiling to the surface of Dev's imagination, of her long legs still in those red boots, wrapped around his . . . *Steady, boy.*

He opened the garage door, went inside, pulled the drop cloth off his bike, and rolled her outside. Toni sucked in an appreciative whistle, thereby rising in his already high opinion of her. Not only did she have looks, wit, and a love of dogs, but she could appreciate a work of art when she saw it, too. What more could a man ask?

He donned his helmet, straddled the shining black Harley, and stomped on the gas pedal as he turned the throttle. The rebuilt 1958 engine purred to life. He held out his hand, the spare helmet dangling from his fingertips. She put it on quickly, shoved a black backpack under the bungee cords he'd strapped across the back rack, and scrambled aboard, hesitating a second before positioning her hands gingerly on his flanks.

He grinned and gunned the motor. The bike jumped. Toni gasped, plastering herself against his back, her arms flying around his waist as she held on for dear life. She felt good clinging to him. There was strength in her arms, and her long legs bracketed him with fascinating pressure. Her face burrowed comfortably against the back of his neck. Her warm breath brushed his ear.

His grin broadened. With a little finesse he could make the trip to Mull last hours.

4

*M*ull was one of the most picturesque of the Scottish Isles. The terrain ranged from softly rising mountains cloaked in fragrant pines to wind-savaged stretches of coast framed by the winding single-track roads that skirted the island. Toni was certain she had a bruise for each rut in the road that bisected the small fishing village of Tobermory.

The island, usually a mecca of solitude, was inundated with visitors. The little hamlets teamed with campers and day trekkers who'd come not only for the field trial but because of Mull's deep burns and shaded glens, pretty greenness and hushed beauty. In short, Mull made as spectacular a setting as a sheepherding competition could want. Indeed, the local inhabitants had raised a fair around the official trial proceedings.

There were handlers, trainers, owners, spectators, and families, all enjoying the festival atmosphere. As such, every small inn and bed-and-breakfast on the island had been booked.

It was pure chance that Dev and Toni walked into a farmhouse B&B just as the proprietress was taking a phone cancellation. The rate she quoted them was outrageous. Toni could see by the set of Dev's jaw that he didn't like being taken advantage of, but he looked at her wind-burned face, and the combativeness drained from his expression.

"Fine, we'll take it," he said. She looked at him gratefully, and his expression softened further.

The stout, grim Scotswoman led them up a steep flight of stairs, her back stiff with disapproval as she flung open the small door and stood aside. The room inside was charming, decorated in pale blue-sprigged wallpaper and starched white cotton eyelet curtains. A delft-blue slipper chair stood at the foot of a single white bed . . . *single*.

Toni's gaze flew to Dev's face. He was regarding the narrow white counterpane with bland disinterest. An image of all six-foot-whatever of him and all six-foot-one-and-one-half-inch of her together on that bed flooded her imagination. They wouldn't be able to draw breath without smashing into one another.

But there was really no where else either of them could sleep. The slipper chair was too dainty, and the floor, well, only a braided rag rug covered the rough boards. If Dev felt as battered as she did, he wouldn't be thrilled at the prospect of camping out. She steeled herself against weakening. Too bad. Just because she'd acted like . . . like some sort of nympho yesterday didn't mean she was easy. Not that he'd given any indication he— She frowned. What was wrong with him anyway?

"Do you have anything else?" she asked the proprietress. "Anything with a bigger bed?"

"This ain't Cupid's gymnasium, missie," the Scotswoman clipped out. Toni's lips twitched, her humor restored.

"Believe me, lady," she answered, "Cupid could shoot his entire quiver into my hind end, and I wouldn't so much as twitch. We just want to sleep." She turned to Dev. "Right?"

"Right." He nodded. He needn't be so agreeable.

"Well, you'll have to make do," their hostess said, not in the least mollified. "This is all that's available, and yer lucky to have it. How many days did you say ye'll be staying?"

Dev grimaced. "Best make it two." He held up his hand, stopping Toni's protest before it began. "Look. You've seen the place. It's overrun. If we don't find McGill tomorrow, we'll need to look until we do. If time gets too tight, you can hire a car to get you to Glasgow."

"Oh, yeah?" she said, trying unsuccessfully to keep the panic out of her voice. "And who's going to pay for this car? I'm maxed out on my credit card!"

The proprietress nailed her with a glower that proclaimed her every dark suspicion justified. "If you're staying two days, I'll be needing the next day's rent. In advance. In cash."

"Smooth move, Minnesota," Dev said, pulling out his

wallet. He peeled off three-quarters of his remaining bills and plopped them in the woman's outstretched hand. "And I'll pay for your car, if it comes to that. It's the least I can do for all the trouble McGill has caused."

The woman sniffed once, to make sure she left no doubt about her opinion on her two new tenants' morals, and left, closing the door behind her.

"Okay," Dev said moving toward the bed and flopping down on his back in the middle, "I've got thirty pounds ten in my wallet. If we don't eat too much, that should last us the next few days." He eyed her up and down. "I suspect you eat a lot."

And here she'd just been thinking how charming he'd been. "No more than any other Amazon," she said flatly, winning a laugh from him.

She swung her backpack up onto the slipper chair. The day's drive had flung mud all over her jeans, and her once pink sweater looked more "ashes of roses" if one was being kind, "dingy Kool Aid stain" if one wasn't.

"Not to worry," Dev said from behind her. "We'll eat on the cheap, but we'll eat well. It's something of a point of pride with me."

He really was being awfully nice. And he hadn't once brought up her outrageous behavior of the previous day. She owed him an apology and, by gum, she'd give him one. There was a reason the media had coined the term "Minnesota Nice." Most of them thought *nice* was synonymous with *placid*.

Toni knew differently. She suspected the Minnesotan temperament was the result of a gene seeded eons ago during the interminably long Scandinavian winters, when frigid weather kept people huddled inside together for weeks on end. If you didn't learn to keep your thoughts to yourself and remain obstinately polite in the face of any provocation, you likely ended up arguing with, say, Uncle Sven—who didn't tolerate cabin fever very well but *had* had the foresight to bring his ax with him into Der Winterhut. Those who made it through the "long night" in one piece were generally those predisposed to reticence. Yup, everything she'd done after that fourth Scotch had been totally out of character and she needed to own up to her sins.

She drew a deep breath and turned to face Dev. "I'm sorry for whooping at you like that yesterday, and, ah . . . for trying to look up your kilt, and for, er, any untoward comments I might have made. Did make."

He'd folded his hands behind his head and was regarding her oddly. "Did you just say 'untoward'? I didn't think people really spoke like that except in old Merchant-Ivory films."

She would *not* be sidetracked. She needed to do this. "We use those words in Minnesota. Sometimes. If warranted."

"Warranted?"

"Stop it. I was rude. Please accept my apology."

He grinned, an absolutely delicious, wicked, and incorrigible grin. "Don't think twice about it."

Women probably whooped at him all the time.

"Thank you," Toni said. "I mean it. You've been really decent about all this. I mean, here I've come to take your dog away, a dog you didn't even know was sold, and you go out of your way to see that he's returned to—"

"Hold on, Snow Princess. I'm reuniting you and McGill. I'm not conceding anything about Blackie yet, all right?"

"But he's mine!"

"Nah-uh." He shook his finger. "Not gonna discuss it until I hear McGill's side of the story. Then, calmly and collectedly, we'll all decide what we're going to do about the situation."

"I've told you. I don't have the time or the money to sit around Scotland and let *you* decide *anything*. As far as I can see, you're not even involved."

"I own the dog."

"Your manager, who I assume was invested by you with the authority to make these sorts of decisions, sold the dog to me."

Aha! She had him. She could see it by the slight flicker in his eyes.

"Let's just find McGill first, agreed?"

What else could she do? She needed him, and he knew it. Not only did he have the financial resources to continue this search, he knew the land and the people. He knew who to ask, and what. She nodded unhappily, and he suddenly sat up, reached out, and chucked her lightly under the chin.

"Ach! Don't be lookin' like a lost lambikins, lassie. Things'll come oot right as rain, ye'll see." She couldn't help but laugh at the thick accent.

The smile died from his mouth, but the warmth stayed in his eyes as he held out his hand. "Truce?"

She held out her hand. Slowly his long fingers wrapped around hers, their heat sinking into hers, just as the heat from his big body had warmed her all day, his breadth protecting her from the wind.

He was big, strong, quick-witted, and trustworthy. Oh, yeah. And drop-dead gorgeous.

He moved closer, his gaze becoming sharper, more intent. The air seemed to have fled her lungs, leaving her a little light-headed, a touch breathless. She could see the rise and fall of his chest beneath the soft, worn chambray shirt. He was breathing harder, too. His hand still held hers, tightening, drawing her nearer, and she was going, melting toward him like candle wax beneath a flame.

Warning bells went off just in time. What the devil was she doing? In three days she'd be gone and never see him again. She'd be chasing geese around golf courses in Minneapolis, and he'd be here, bricking up his castle walls, melting other women with his dimples and smoldering gaze. No matter what he said, no matter that she'd really believed him when he'd said there weren't any notches in his bedpost, she wasn't going to be the first because . . . Because why? Because that's not the type of woman she was.

She pulled back, smiling nervously. A flicker of irritation? distress? passed over his features, and then he let her go, turning aside, and the moment was gone. She felt empty and uncertain, as though she'd misunderstood something important. But a woman like her, a woman alone, with no one but herself to look after her, couldn't afford to take chances with her heart.

Heart? What was the matter with her? Next she'd be convincing herself she was involved in the love affair of the century.

He walked past her, heading for the en suite bath. "I need a shower," she said. She opened her mouth to reply and slammed it shut.

He didn't mean . . . Nah. They'd been on the road all

afternoon. She needed a shower, too. But after he came out and it was her turn to clean up and she'd shed her dusty clothes and stepped into the tub and grasped the handle to turn on the water, she couldn't help noticing the chrome was ice cold.

*S*omehow he was going to get through this night. He wasn't precisely sure how yet, but if he kept her up long enough, he was certain he'd think of something. So far the best diversion he'd managed was to stumble around Fionnport's three streets, eating pub grub and chatting up some of the local boys in hopes of finding McGill.

Happily, the old reprobate wasn't to be found; the truth was that Dev was far more interested in being with Toni Olson than finding Donald McGill. And Dev had the oddest feeling Toni felt the same. Time and again they'd be laughing or discussing something, and Toni would suddenly get a frosty expression and withdraw from the conversation, as though she had to remind herself, and sternly too, that she was here on business and that theirs was simply an expedient and temporary relationship. She was right, of course. How could it be anything else? And it was for the best. It really was, because he had a feeling Toni Olson would take a lot of getting over if a man was so inclined. And he wasn't . . .

But damn, he was having a hard time keeping his hands off her.

Especially now, when they were back in this warm, cozy room while the wind lashed the windows and the rain beat on the roof and she looked like something a man conjured from erotic dreams, sitting cross-legged on the bed, her hair spilling down her back, her eyes dark in the soft glow of the single lamp.

They'd also decided early on that the only sensible thing to do was share the bed, he on one side on top of the blankets, and her on the other, beneath. But since then, no one had mentioned it. Beds. Sleeping. Or anything vaguely related to either.

He glanced at the clock. It was twelve forty-five, and Toni was punch-drunk with fatigue. But she didn't seem any more anxious to crawl into bed than he did. She squirmed on the bed, wincing a little.

"Something wrong?" he asked.

"Cramp in my calf. I've never ridden a bike that long before."

He ducked his head guiltily. She'd spent more than an extra hour on that bike, clinging to him simply because he liked the feel of her there. He should make amends. He rose from the slipper chair and sat down at the foot of the bed, reaching out and encircling her ankle. She straightened, startled.

"Relax," he said, drawing her leg out and over his thighs. Gently, he began massaging her calf, but the red cowboy boot impeded him in his self-assigned task. He grasped the heel of the boot and stripped it off her leg before working his fingers under her jeans and up her calf. He kneaded the svelte muscle deeply.

Had he thought of this as a task? He meant "penance." She drew in a little hiss of pleasure, letting her head fall back, her throat arched for a lover's kiss. She groaned. He tensed.

"That," she said, "is incredible."

This suddenly didn't seem like such a great idea anymore. Sure, she might be feeling no pain, but the same could most definitely not be said for him. He had one hell of an erection, and he didn't think he could stand another thirty minutes of frigid water.

"We better get to sleep," he said suddenly, dumping her foot off his lap and avoiding her look of surprise. "We've got a long day ahead of us."

She looked hurt. Hurt and bewildered, and his reaction, in his current state, was to become irritable. Couldn't she understand he was trying his damnedest to be noble here? What was wrong with American women that they couldn't appreciate a bloke's gallantry?

He stood up. "You want the bathroom first?"

Her eyes shot sparks. She rose in one fluid, mouth-drying move and, without glancing at him, snagged her backpack from the floor, went into the bathroom, and closed the door.

Dev closed his eyes and prayed for a little self-understanding, a little bit of enlightenment as to what was going on here. He couldn't remember ever having been so powerfully attracted to a woman. Not only on the physical level, on other levels as well. It didn't make sense. He'd known all sorts of wise, smart, pretty women. Okay, not too many had been built like Valkyries and had eyes that you'd never forget no matter how long you lived, or lips that smiled that easily, that piquantly.

It was probably just that she was American and therefore a little exotic. . . . The door swung open, and Toni came out, blushing as red as a beet, but her expression defiant.

She was wearing a plaid negligee. An honest-to-God Black Watch plaid baby doll with little neon purple thistles forming spaghetti straps. But most startling, in place of panties she appeared to be wearing a piece of shag carpet, or a muppet, or a . . . With a start, Dev realized it was supposed to be a sporan. A fake fur sporan.

It should have been ridiculous. He should have been laughing himself sick. He wasn't. His mouth was bonedry, and he could feel his pulse hammering away in certain parts of his anatomy.

The deep vee of the neckline revealed twin mounds of pale honey-colored flesh and the fascinating valley between them. The silk fabric flirted with the tops of thighs so smooth and silky the light seemed to gild them. She put her hands on her hips, and the movement set her breasts jouncing. His throat closed.

What the hell did she think she was doing?

"What the hell do you think you're doing?" he demanded, his voice rough.

"I grabbed the wrong backpack out of the van."

"Huh?"

"I took the wrong backpack. I had two. One with my things in it, and one with souvenirs I'd brought for my friends. This was supposed to be a gift for my college roommate!"

"That?"

"A gag gift," she said, her fiery complexion burning even brighter.

"Well, you can't wear that to bed."

She stared at him, her mouth slackening before snapping shut and her eyes flashing. "What do you mean, I can't wear it to bed?" she asked grimly.

"Nah-uh." He shook his head back and forth vigorously. He wouldn't get an instant of sleep lying next to her knowing she was wearing nothing but *that*. "You're not wearing that. Not if I'm going to share the bed with you."

"Why?" she demanded. "Because this little number just jettisons me into the ranks of Ultimate Seductress? Right." She cocked a brow, challenging him to agree.

What could he say? "No."

She heaved a gusty sigh. "Oh, can it, Montgomery. I'll be under the blankets."

She thought he was mocking her. He felt the blood climb in his own throat this time, feeling more than a little ridiculous that the sight of her in that thing could affect him so.

She started to brush past him. He stepped in front of her, blocking her way. Anger, frustration, and the humiliating realization that she didn't see him as a threat drove him. "You'll be under *me*, if you wear that thing into that bed."

She gasped, and the color drained from her cheeks, leaving her eyes looking even bluer than before. Blue like the heart of a flame. Blue as in blue words. Blue as in furious.

"Look," he said, gritting his teeth. "You just go back in that bathroom and put back on that pink sweater thing and your jeans."

Her eyes flashed more blue fire, and she didn't say a word. She merely spun on her heels and marched back into the bathroom. Thank God. He relaxed. If he'd had to—

Splat!

A soggy, heavy wad of denim hit him squarely in the chest and fell to his feet. It was Toni's jeans, sopping wet.

He looked up. She was still wearing that plaid baby doll, her arms crossed squarely over her breasts.

"I washed my jeans, but since you're so hot and bothered, *you* can wear them!"

He stared at her, the wet splotch on his shirt spreading. She didn't understand. Not at all.

"I'm tired," she said grimly. "I'm going to bed. I suggest you do the same. Somewhere you can feel relatively certain you'll be able to resist my irresistible allure."

She paced past him and snatched the cover back from the bed, sat down, and snapped the blankets back over her. She glared at him once, scooted to the far side, and flipped over, presenting him with her back. "Men!"

The light blanket molded to her shoulders and followed the flowing line of her torso to the sharp dip at her waist before climbing the sweet, round curve of her hip. He stared at her.

Jeans or baby-doll plaid. Fully clad or half undressed. It didn't matter at all. With a soft curse he strode over to the tiny slipper chair and flopped down in it. He made his hands relax over the ends of the arms and stared purposefully out the window into the black island night.

*S*he must have drifted off to sleep, because when she opened her eyes, the room was steeped in darkness, only the light from the car park outside offering any illumination. She pushed herself to her elbows and looked around. She was alone in the bed. Dev was sprawled over the slipper chair, on the ottoman, and on a little table he must have dragged over to prop up one stocking-clad foot.

It was that drat stocking—argyle, of course—that

tugged at her heart. Everything about Devlin Montgomery testified to his being self-possessed, confident,
and supremely competent. But that sock, worn at the heel,
bleached by too many washes, reminded her that he was
only human, sometimes uncertain, even vulnerable. Even
a little stupid in the way men were so often stupid: about
women.

Like she really believed he found her irresistible in
this stupid plaid nightie with its absurd polyester fur un-
derpants. Worse, she'd suspected that he was making fun
of her womanliness. She hadn't been amused.

But that sock made her forget her anger and want him.
Right now. She wanted to nip his strong, dark throat, to
run her fingers through his crisp, tousled hair, to feel the
rasp of his beard on her palms as she held his face and
nibbled at his lower lip.

If only there were more time. But they didn't have
time, and how could she trust emotions and desires that
had bloomed full-blown in one short day?

5

"What a beauty!" Toni whispered reverently, pointing at the Border collie shedding out a recalcitrant ewe. "Look at him. Power, presence. He'll be spectacular when he gets a bit of seasoning."

Devlin watched Toni with growing respect. They'd woken early and eaten breakfast under the baleful eye of their hostess, an eye made even more baleful after she'd seen Toni's T-shirt, bright blue and two sizes too small, which said, "I Just Washed My Kilt and I Can't Do a Fling with It!" Toni wore it with as much dignity as she could muster, only laughing after their hostess had left the room.

Dev was glad. She obviously didn't hold last night against him. In retrospect he supposed he had overreacted a bit. But then again, that was easy enough to say when she was fully dressed and it was daylight and they were heading out on a motorcycle. Night might tell a different tale.

Afterward they'd driven north on the island to where the first test was being held. The chances were overwhelming that McGill wouldn't be able to stay away. Added to which Dev knew some of the professional handlers in attendance. They might help him locate his missing manager and, more important, his missing dog.

But as soon as they'd discovered that the third test was under way, Toni had been trapped, her attention riveted by the competition. Though he'd realized early on that Toni's enthusiasm wasn't simply the result of having watched *Babe* one time too many, he soon recognized her expertise. She knew dogs, and she *really* knew Border collies. She loved the breed. As he did. Which only made his attraction to her deeper—and more impossible to act on.

He didn't want a simple tumble in the sack—well, actually, he did, but he didn't think "simple" was an option anymore. If it had ever been. Instead, he wanted to learn everything he could about her. She was too good to be real, but in fact, she was real. And wonderful.

"You don't run sheep, do you?" he suddenly asked, drawing her intent gaze away from where the red-and-white dog had successfully separated the ewe from the rest of the flock and was circling the pen.

She looked at him. "Why do you think that?"

"You've mentioned being too many places. People who have livestock can't leave them."

She nodded. "Busted. I don't own any sheep." Something in the way she said it, a little gruff, a little defensive, made him suspicious.

"You're not one of these people who want to turn the breed into the perfect little urchins' pet—the family wagger, all boundy with joy when Daddy comes home from work and 'Look! He's brought me slippers!' are you?"

"No," she answered. "I've been around working dogs all my life. When I was a kid, my family fostered service dogs from puppyhood until they were ready for formal training. Later I got a job training them. My dad was a cop in the K-9 division too, so we always had a working dog at home with us."

She suddenly grinned. "Sorry. Bit more information than you asked for. It's just that I want you to know that I respect what's going on here. I've had pets, and I've had pets who had jobs. In my mind that's the best situation of all. There is nothing more beautiful, or more joyful, than a dog that's doing what it was bred to do, whether that's pointing a pheasant, finding cocaine at a baggage claim, guiding someone across a city street, or herding a flock of—whatever."

"Whatever?"

"Look," she faced him, squaring her shoulders, "I chase geese for a living. That's what I bought Blackie to do. That and act as the base for a breeding program I've been developing."

"Geese?"

"Geese. Minnesota is the land of ten thousand lakes. Most of those lakes have golf courses attached to them. The ones that don't, the ones in the Twin Cities, have industries and corporate headquarters adjacent to them. Geese come flapping down the northern flyway from

Canada, take one look at all that suburban green and all those little lakes, and see a goosey counterpart to La Costa Spa."

"Yeah?" he said slowly, sure he was missing the point.

She gazed at him in exasperation. "Let me put it this way: The suburban green is a good deal greener after the geese arrive. In fact, the sidewalks, the parking lots, the driving ranges, the putting greens, the soccer field, and the sandlots are all green. Or rather greenish. If you know what I mean."

"I see. And the dogs chase them off?"

"Yup. We haze geese. Initially it takes anywhere from twice a week to four times a day, but within a few weeks we're going out purely on maintenance calls. And the dogs"—her gaze fastened levelly on his—"love it."

His thoughts whirled. "You wanted to buy a Grand International Champion so that he can chase geese?"

"Live in my house, drive around with me, be my constant companion, make sure planes can safely take off and land at private airports, keep playgrounds and parks and golf courses clean, and yes, chase geese," she said flatly. "Believe me, geese are much more formidable and five times nastier than sheep. Chase a sheep, and you've mastered a Schwartz toy. Haze a goose, and you've vanquished Attila the Hun."

"*That* formidable?"

She eyed him narrowly. "Ever been attacked by a goose? It's not fun. Not only do you look stupid, but it hurts. Why, an enraged goose nearly drowned a dog in Lake Champlain last year."

"I had no idea," he said, trying desperately to keep from laughing.

"Look, Sheep Boy. When was the last time you got attacked by a ewe?"

He *did* burst out laughing. "Got me. Never."

She smiled smugly. "Okay. Maybe geese aren't exactly Bengal tigers, but they're pains in the butts."

"So what do you do about them?"

"Haze them."

"How's that work?"

"Well, to start out, I scope out the business that contracted me to rid them of geese. See where the geese are hanging about and what time they arrive and leave.

"Then I bring a couple of my dogs out. Usually I'll send each dog in the opposite direction to circle in and drive the geese into the air. Of course on golf courses the geese are as likely to flap off into the water hazards and jeer at the dogs from the safety of the water. But my dogs can herd even in the water."

"Really?" he asked, impressed. Getting a Border collie into the water usually took a bit of doing; to have them actually take direction once there was impressive.

"Yup," she said proudly. "And I've taught them a bark command."

"Huh?"

"They bark on command even in the water. Scares the bejeezus out of the geese. I can haze most areas in twenty minutes or less."

"And it sticks? The hazing?"

"Oh, yes." She nodded. "Much better than any other methods they've tried and with much less of an environmental impact. I know of a business that used to set off pyrotechnics and sound cannons. The neighbors complained."

He laughed. "I should imagine."

"But with dogs, usually the geese have learned not to come back to an area within a few weeks. After that it's just a biweekly romp on the grounds for my dogs—just in case some goose scout is watching to see if we're being vigilant." She smiled dreamily.

"Goose scouts."

"Oh, yeah." She nodded sententiously. "They have scouts, moles, spies. A whole goosey intelligence network. I told you, they're a very worthy opponent."

He burst out laughing.

"Besides which," she continued, an impish light in her eye, "there's something satisfying about watching a bunch of geese light out in front of a really intense Border collie."

"And you can make a living at this?" he asked curiously.

"Oh, yeah," she said in such a way that his interest was piqued even more.

"How much?"

Her smile became complacent. "Enough to get me out of Minnesota anytime from November through April. Geese," she lectured knowingly, "are a seasonal problem. So I make a tidy little sum during the season and get to go other places during the winter."

"Like Scotland." He suddenly saw a lot of virtue in her profession. "You might be able to come back to Scotland this winter. If you wanted to." He tried to sound nonchalant.

"Yes. I suppose." She blushed and looked away. "Maybe we'd better keep looking for McGill and my dog."

He agreed, watching the unconscious sway of her hips as she strode over the grassy field. He felt the pull of attraction and resolved not to do a bloody thing about it. He would convince her to come back to Scotland this winter and spend some time with him. He would use as recommendation the fact that he hadn't pushed her for a physical relationship. He wouldn't give her any opportunity to think he saw her as a one-night stand or a casual relationship. Because whatever the hell his feelings for her, they were most definitely not casual.

They had so much in common, it was—dear God, he couldn't believe he was saying these things—as if they were meant to be together.

"So being a Scottish laird isn't one long, happy stroll through the glen?" she asked, twirling her straw in the coke bottle.

"I told you, I'm not a laird. A laird is a chieftain, a martial leader. I couldn't even raise a pony parade, not even if I bribed the local tots with toffee pudding."

She laughed. He was so exasperated with her romanticism that even when it had faded, she kept up the mooneyed pretense, just because she liked teasing him. Though he gave as good as he got—she'd heard more barbed editorials on American politics than in a Dennis Miller routine.

"What I don't understand," she said, glancing at him sidelong, "is why you're going through all the trouble of fixing up your castle if you don't really like being a laird."

"I like having a roof over my head." He smiled. The dimples in his cheeks were fascinatingly boyish. "My family owns all sorts of things. The odd castle here, a decrepit warehouse there. A fishing boat that's been in dry dock since the war, and a newspaper that hasn't printed anything beside notices of Kirk rummage sales in twenty years. And a kennel."

"But the Oronsay Kennels are world-famous."

"I know. But you don't make money on a kennel that has fifteen dogs. The kennel is just a very celebrated hobby, is all. I was hoping to turn it into a going concern."

"Why?"

He chuckled. "I told you. I like having a roof over my head. The castle was there for the asking, the kennels had a good rep to build on. It seemed better than moving to Aberdeen and working for a living. We Montgomerys find the notion of working for a living most distressing."

She smiled. He could claim to be a slacker, but she'd seen the work he'd been doing on that castle and heard the detailed and thoughtful planning that had gone into his proposed renovations. Once the rest of the renovations were complete, it would once more become a cohesive whole, a place with both modern and historic elements.

"So, just how are you going to go about making the kennel a going concern?" she asked.

He stopped, cocking his head and studying her intently. The sun glimmered on his dark red hair, warmed the toffee-brown depths of his eyes. "Do you really want to know?"

She did. She wanted to know everything about Devlin Montgomery. "Oh, yes," she said.

He smiled and proceeded to tell her.

$\mathcal{T}$he salt-kissed air whistled past Toni's ears as Dev expertly guided the vintage bike toward the headlands at the

western edge of the island. Overhead, blue rivers chan-
neled their way through towering white canyons of
clouds. Toni pressed her head between Dev's shoulder
blades, using his broad back as a windbreak, soaking up
the heat from his body.

She was miserable and elated and despondent. They
had everything in common. They were both oldest unwed
children. They both enjoyed traveling—in comfort. They
both loved dogs, scuba diving, Douglass Adams, and the
Iron Chef. They had the same sense of humor and the
same ideas about the proper work-versus-play ratio. And
they both wanted each other so badly she was afraid to
buy the balloon a kid offered her for fear the damn thing
would stick to her hair, the air between them was that
charged with electricity.

And she was going away tomorrow, even if she
didn't find McGill and Blackie. She could not imagine
leaving with things so unfinished between them, but she
was a realist, a practical, imperturbable Minnesotan.
This wasn't a movie; she wasn't going to arrive at
Heathrow two days from now and discover Dev had purchased the seat next to hers on the plane. Anything that
was going to happen would have to happen here. Today.
Tonight.

She wasn't very experienced. She'd never been carried away by her emotions—and were these even emotions? What if they were just pheromones or hormones
or some other sort of moans? But darn . . . they seemed
like emotions. They seemed honest and certain and
strong, strong enough to sweep her off her feet and carry
her beyond the stars with only one thing to cling to—
Dev.

Was it a mistake to make some bittersweet memories, even if that's all she'd take with her when she left? She closed her eyes. No. Absolutely not. Now she just had to convince Dev, and if last night was any evidence, that shouldn't be too hard.

6

"Drat. Your ten beats my seven," Dev said, trying to keep the relief out of his voice. "Your call. What do you want me to take off next?"

Somehow what had started out as a gin game had morphed into a "friendly" game of strip poker. Honorable intentions aside, Dev hadn't had quite the willpower necessary to say no when she'd suggested it. He should have. He should have realized straight off that there wasn't any such thing as a friendly game of strip poker when Toni Olson was the only other player.

When the realization *had* struck him, he should have called quits. Unfortunately, once again, he didn't have quite that much manly fortitude. So instead he played on, flirting with masochism, deciding he didn't much care for it, and finally tried desperately to lose every hand. Because he didn't think he could handle watching Toni Olson doff one more article of clothing.

She sat cross-legged on the end of the bed, well within arm's reach, her T-shirt's hem grazing the lace-trimmed leg opening of her panties as those vampish red cowboy boots flirted with him from beneath the satiny smooth skin of each well-toned thigh. If he won another hand, what would he ask her to shed—shirt or fantasy-inducing boot?

He shook his head and glanced up quickly enough to note the slow, knowing curve of her lips. What the hell had happened to her much-vaunted luck? No matter how abysmal his hand, hers was equally lousy. If it weren't so screwy, he'd think she was trying to lose, too, as eager to push him to the limits as he was to keep from going there.

He didn't want a tumble, he wanted more. He wanted a relationship. There. He'd admitted it. He wanted Toni Olson in his life for a long time to come.

"Shirt."

"Huh?"

"Take off your shirt."

Shirt, jeans, boxers. Three things left. Surely she wouldn't ask him to take off the boxers? But then again, what difference would it make? As soon as he stripped off his jeans, she'd realize the state she'd put him in. If she didn't already.

He unbuttoned his shirt and wrenched it off, excruciatingly aware of her gaze on his chest, the heat in her regard, and the interest. She liked what she saw. Dev offered up a word of thanks to his mom for making him build her that stone fence around her garden this summer. Toni caught her bottom lip under her edge of her front teeth. Too sexy. He looked away, tossing the shirt onto the slipper chair. "Deal."

"Hm?" She gazed at him with vague eyes.

"Deal the cards."

"Okie-dokie," she said happily, expertly shuffling the cards. She dealt the cards rapidly and scooped hers into her hand, fanning them, quickly selecting two, and dumping the rest on the bed.

He picked up his cards. Two pairs. Queens and threes. If he got rid of the queens and one of the threes, that should pretty much assure that he'd lose this hand.

"Three." He held out his hand. She counted out the cards. He fanned them and smiled. A three, a two, a five an eight and a ten.

"Gee," he said laying his hand faceup on the bed. "I can't believe I'm having such bad luck. So . . ." He unsnapped the brass rivet at the top of his jeans and had partially unzipped his fly when her hand covered his. He inhaled on a sharp hiss.

Her hand dropped. She drew back. "Not so fast, Dev. I'm afraid my luck's deserted me." She spread her cards. Five single numbers, seven high. "What'll it be?"

"Boot!" he grated out.

She stretched her leg out, putting her red boot in his lap. "A little help, please?"

She sounded a little nervous, and her gaze was a trifle wary. Wary, hell, she should be running for the door!

He grabbed her boot heel, frantic to get this done with, and pulled so hard he yanked her from a sitting position flat onto her back. She landed with an "oof!" At once he rose to his knees and hunched over her, bracing his hands on either side of her shoulders.

Mistake. Her hair spread across the bed like a silk shawl. Her breathing came rapidly between her lips, the agitation causing her breasts to move tumultuously beneath their tight cotton cover. She gazed up at him, a question in her lovely blue eyes, a question he couldn't fathom and thus had no answer for. All he knew was that she was on her back beneath him.

He swallowed. "You all right?"

"Yeah. Just surprised."

"Sorry." He forced himself to sit back, this time taking her foot in one hand while clasping her calf with the other. It was just as satiny smooth and warm as last night. With a grim set to his mouth he pulled the red boot off and dropped it to the floor. He should have dropped her leg, too, but this whole debacle had been a treatise on should-haves, and he didn't see any reason to stop the lessons now.

His hand lingered, moving slowly up her calf to the delicate, sensitive skin behind her knee. Sand-washed silk, warm and sheer. He could feel her pulse pattering against his fingertips like a bird's.

He looked up and met her gaze, his resolutions quickly dissolving before the undisguised desire he saw. But it had to be her choice. "Next hand?"

She didn't speak for a moment before nodding and scooting back up to a sitting position. "Deal." This time it was her voice that rasped.

He dealt and in spite of his best efforts still managed to secure a pair of jacks. Happily, she came up with a flush. It didn't seem to elate her. She tossed the cards down. "I win."

Better to just get this over with. He'd take

off his jeans and embarrass the hell out of her. She'd feel like a fool, and that would be that. Except he'd be taking another cold shower and sleeping in that dinky chair again.

He stood up and unzipped his jeans the rest of the way. Then he peeled the well-worn denim off his hips, dancing on one foot as he got the pant leg off and then kicking the damn thing off the other. It flew off and hit the wall. He straightened, forcing himself to meet her gaze.

Only her gaze wasn't there for the meeting.

Boxers. Toni had known he'd had an erection. His jeans weren't tight, but they weren't loose enough to hide his state of arousal. But the old faded blue boxers he wore fit like skin around his heavy rugby player's thighs and across his groin, leaving nothing to the imagination.

Plainly the last half-hour hadn't been any easier on Dev's rising libido than it had been on hers. Unconsciously she drew the edges of her shirt closer. She looked up and met his gaze. He didn't smile. His face was tight with expectation and question. His gaze slowly fell to the front of his boxers and moved back up to her eyes.

"I want you. No surprise there. But it's damn hard standing here with you looking at me like that and not knowing what you're thinking or feeling or anything, so be a sport, eh, Minnesota?" The cajoling words didn't quite match the rough tone. "Tell me."

He didn't move, just stood there, big and heavily muscled, looking better than Mel, Liam, and any other male this country had to offer. Tanned, rippling, sexually primed, ready but waiting . . . for her to make a decision.

No more questions plagued her. She'd all the answer she needed in his willingness to wait. She stood up and moved directly in front of him. She was just a few inches shorter than him, her lips level with his throat. Perfect.

He still hadn't moved or said a word, but his breathing spoke volumes. His chest rose and fell like a bellows. His gaze followed her smallest move.

She reached under her T-shirt, unsnapped her bra's front opening, and then unhooked the straps. It fell to her waist, caught for a minute, and dropped to the floor. She saw Dev's eyes darkening, and a little tic jumped at the corner of his mouth.

Shyly she lifted her arms and settled them around his shoulders. He was hot, and she inhaled his scent, male and clean and intensely, richly Devlin. She touched her lips lightly to his throat and felt the tingle of response ripple through him.

"Isn't that enough of an answer?" she murmured, her lips never leaving his skin.

"No." He sounded like he was having a hard time talking, the word strained and clipped. "Tell me. Tell me you want this. You want me. Now."

Easy. She unlinked her hands, slipping them down over the hard muscle of his shoulders. Her fingers skated a languid trail down his chest to his ribs, to the taut rippling washboard of his belly, lower to the elastic waistband. She hooked a finger beneath it. He jerked back as if he'd been pricked with fire.

"I want you. Now. Here. Like this."

Whatever charge he'd given to himself to remain still dissolved. He grabbed her shoulders, pulling her close, turning his head and slanting his mouth down over hers. He kissed her hungrily, his tongue sinking deep within to mate with hers. Answering hunger rose within her like a tidal wave, swirling through her body, taking her out at the knees so that she had to cling to him, wickedly aware of the hard length of him. She pushed herself more fully against him.

He released her mouth with a growl. His gaze was intent, predatory, and certain. Slowly he released her arms and grasped the hem of her T-shirt. Gently, he rolled the material up, stripping it from over her head.

Almost casually he stroked the nether curve of her breast, his thumb brushing back and forth across her nipple. She shivered with longing.

"Please," she whispered.

His head dipped, and a jolt of sensation tore through her as his mouth fastened hungrily on her nipple, drawing the peak deep into his mouth. One strong, tanned arm looped around her waist and the other dropped, encircling her knees. He lifted her in his arms, his head dark against her pale skin.

Kneeling on the bed, he lowered her to it and turned, so that she lay on top of him. His hand flowed like liquid heat down her thigh to the back of her knee and to the front, tracing a slow path up her inner thigh, to the lace edge of her panties.

He did not wait for permission this time.

With a short, rough tug he pulled them off, peeling them down her legs to her ankles. Furiously she kicked free of them, wanting more, needing to feel all of his weight, heavy and powerful.

Eagerly she wedged her hand between them, pushing down until . . . There. Hard and long and surging into her hand. He hissed lightly as his hips jerked against her touch.

"Careful," he ground out in the lee between her neck and shoulder. His body was warm now, damp and taut.

"Careful?" she repeated breathlessly. "Too late."

She burrowed her fingers deeper under his waistband—

—and was tossed on her back. She stared, stunned by the sudden reversal of their positions, stunned even more by him, rising above her, arms bulging with muscle, chest heaving, a pirate's smile on his unbelievably handsome face, a dark promise in his gaze.

"Too easy. We'd be done too fast."

Before she could respond, he'd grasped each thigh, pulling her knees up over his shoulders and cupping her buttocks, lifting her.

He smiled and blew softly on the blond curls. Her whole body trembled. Her blue eyes were wide, a little frightened, and a great deal interested. Deliberately he covered her with his mouth. Her hands clenched into fists on the bedclothes, dragging the material toward her. Her back bowed.

"Please. Make love to me," she gasped.

"I am." He wanted her to need this, to remember this. To feel every touch, to tremble with desire as she'd made him tremble.

Slowly he lowered her, replacing his mouth with his hand. She was tight, and she arched against the touch. Her heels dug into the mattress as she gave herself to him, to the arousal he so expertly evoked, to the pleasure and the spiraling, coiling spring of need. And then the coil broke.

She climaxed, throwing her head back as pleasure ricocheted through her, flooding her. She trembled, drowning in physical gratification and floating back up through it. Her legs fell slack on the mattress; her hands un-clenched their handfuls of linen. Her body relaxed, sated.

When she opened her eyes, he was watching her. And the look in his eyes, the intensity of his gaze, started it all over again, the slow, inexorable building. She wanted him. That fast. That easily.

"Make love *with* me."

"Yes." He shoved the boxers off and quickly unpeeled a condom from its foil case, donning it and then coming back to her, using his knee to part her thighs. She felt him sinking into her, stretching her, filling her. The feeling was amazing. She wanted him to press deeper, to absorb the breadth and thickness of him.

He watched her. Her eyes were shut; her skin was flushed and damp. He pulled slowly back and her hips followed. He almost lost it then. He came back into her, a little roughly, a little desperately, bracketing her face and holding her head still to kiss her.

"I wanted to make you come again," he panted, "but I can't. You're . . ."

Whatever he'd been about to say was lost as he thrust deep inside her. She gasped and lifted her hips to accept him more fully, more deeply. He didn't need any further urging. The momentum grew, the pace quickened. She rode the rising pleasure, aroused by his scent, his feel, the sight of him bronzed with blood and desire, muscles hard and straining, a fine sheen of dampness glistening on his skin.

Her second climax struck suddenly, stunning in its force. She clutched him. At the same time, Dev surged downward, his arms wrapping tightly around her. His jaw clenched as, with a thick sound of pleasure, he climaxed.

His big body shuddered with his release, his heartbeat pounded against her.

She opened her eyes. His own were closed a few inches away. He was gorgeous. Supremely male.

And she loved him.

The realization hit her with the force of a lightning strike—and brought her just about as much joy.

She couldn't love him. She'd just met him. She'd come to Scotland and been primed for a fling and, by heavens, she'd had one. It was ridiculous to make anything more of it than that.

Hardheaded pragmatic Minnesotans did not run off on summer vacations and fall in love on the basis of one unforgettable night. If they did, they most certainly kept it to themselves. He'd think she was juvenile, self-delusional, susceptible, and *pathetic*. The sort of woman who has to gild animal instinct in romantic terms. She wasn't. She wasn't like that at all.

"Toni," Dev said, stroking her hair from her face. And suddenly she knew she couldn't stand it if he were to say something trite and clichéd and heartbreaking like, "I'll call you when you're back in the States." Not because she wouldn't believe him; but because she *would*. And when he didn't call, it would break her heart.

So when he started to speak again, she did the only thing she could think of to stop him . . . she kissed him. And so started the avalanche of desire flowing all over again.

7

They should have been edging around each other like stray cats caught in the same alley. She didn't want to speak about last night, and she wouldn't talk about tomorrow, leaving Dev at a loss as to how to act, what to say, how far to push her to make promises he wanted desperately to hear. But every time he tried to tell her how he felt, she shut him down completely.

It hurt. He had no idea what she was thinking, what it had meant to her. It had meant the world to him. He'd held her in his arms, and everything had come together. But if she didn't feel that way, if nothing remotely like it had happened for her . . . Yet she was still here, and she obviously felt something for him. He just couldn't risk pushing her away.

Ultimately, he could only accede to her unspoken entreaty and let the day happen. Whether or not either were willing to admit it, finding McGill had turned into an excuse to be together.

It didn't matter that Toni's future was at stake. Today, for this one perfect day, there was no future. It didn't matter that the fate of Dev's beloved Blackie still needed to be determined. There was only this day and their unspoken agreement to live it to the fullest, to hoard every moment of it.

Subsequently, their search for the missing manager was perfunctory. They strolled hand in hand among the crowds, talking, laughing, and nodding thoughtfully, meeting each other's eyes when some obscure reference was understood and appreciated, hoarding every second and storing it away.

In the end they didn't find McGill; he ran into them. They were walking along the edges of the RV park, well away from the crowds, engaged in a heated debate over which was more disgusting, lutefisk or haggis, when a small old man charged out between two campers. His face was bright red and glistening with sweat. He was in such a hurry he didn't see them in time to veer off but instead plowed into Dev, bounced off his far bigger frame, and landed on his bum.

"Watch out, ye big oaf! As if I don't have enough trouble without some great hulkin'—" He looked up. His little eyes grew as round as marbles. His gaze darted from Dev to Toni, and his mouth pleated into a sickly smile.

"Dev! Why, lad, what're you doin' here?" he asked.

"You old reprobate, try that innocent crap on me, will

you? Ms. Olson has a contract for the sale of Blackie that bears your signature. What do you have to say to that?"

"She bought the dog under false pretenses!" McGill declared hotly, glaring at Toni.

She crossed her arms over his chest. "I did not," she said. "I contacted you and told you exactly who I was and what I would pay for the dog, and you"—she pointed down at the squirming manager—" *jumped* at the offer."

"McGill?" Dev prodded.

McGill gave up any pretense at innocence, looking appealingly at Dev. "I did it for you, Dev. You said as how you wanted the kennel turned into a proper business, but you treated all the dogs like they were yer pets—"

"They *are* my pets. *Especially* Blackie."

"I know. But this spring I was going through the bills—"

"That must have been a first," Dev mutttered. McGill ignored him.

"I was going through the bills and I saw the papers, the *foreclosure* papers," he said dramatically, shooting a condemning glare at Toni.

Foreclosure? Toni thought on a wave of guilt. They didn't take private residences in foreclosures in the States. Did they still do things like that over here? Would Dev lose his castle if he didn't have enough money to pay—

"So what?" Dev exclaimed. "I filed for an extension. It hasn't been the first time it's happened in my family, and it won't be the last. We're extremely well-versed in bankruptcy laws, we Montgomerys. How do you think we've managed to stay afloat so long?"

"Afloat, aye," said McGill. "But I knew you were different, Dev. You wouldn't be content to eke by. You wanted to rebuild yer family's past glory—"

"I *wanted* a house with running hot and cold!" Dev declared in exasperation. "I couldn't give a bloody damn about my family's past glory."

McGill gave the requisite gasp at this bit of sacrilege, but his indignation was short-lived. Dev grimaced and reached down. "Here. Give me your hand. You haven't a clue the harm you've done." Most especially to his heart. "Ms. Olson can't afford to be tramping about after you. She's got a plane she has to catch, and"—he glanced down at his wristwatch. His mouth flattened into a taut, angry line—"about fourteen hours to do it in."

"Ach!" McGill groaned as he put his hand in Dev's and allowed himself to be pulled to his feet.

"'Ach,' indeed." Dev said grimly. "Now, where's Blackie? Ms. Olson will have to take a bus to Glasgow if she's to make the night train to London, so she has precious little time."

McGill put his hand to his heart, shaking his head.

"No more of your acting, McGill," Dev cautioned him.

McGill sniffed and took a rattling breath. Toni watched suspiciously. "Ah, Dev. Ye'd not take him *now,* would ye? He only has two more tests to run, and he'll win another championship. I was just going to have a word with Taggart about the call-back."

"He's not mine to run, McGill. And not yours, either."

McGill's skin tone looked off to Toni. A puce color underscored the ruddy wind-burned cheeks.

"I know," he said. "I see that now. But surely Miss Olson would want her dog to have another win to his name."

His breathing was shallow, and his beseeching eyes looked rheumy. "Wouldn't ye, lassie?"

She wavered. Yes, she would like Blackie to have another title to add to his credentials. But even more, she wanted to spend whatever time she had left with Dev. She couldn't think of anything better than watching a sanctioned sheepherding trial with the man she loved.

"Will it take long?" she asked and won a warm look of gratitude from Dev.

"No!" McGill assured her. "An hour or so at the most, and I'll drive you to Glasgow meself."

"No," said Dev, suddenly somber. "I will."

She felt a shiver in response to the promise in his gaze. "All right. But I have to leave in no more than ninety minutes. If I miss that flight, I don't know how I'll get home."

"I promise, Miss Olson. You'll not regret it. Wait'll you see Blackie run. He's a competitor, in't he, Dev? Loves the crowd, he does, and Dev always did know how to work that to his advantage."

"Dev?"

The old man had shooed them forward and was trotting after them, panting harshly as he went. "Aye. Dev. Didn't he tell you? He ran Blackie in every competition he won."

Startled, Toni stared at Dev. His expression hadn't altered, he showed no regret or remorse, but there was a hint of bittersweet in his voice when he said, "He's a good dog." And that was all.

McGill led the way to a tent where a plump and hirsute young man in an Edinburgh sweatshirt and flannels was checking off names on a clipboard. He looked up at their approach. "I thought you were going to miss your place, McGill. Hey, Dev."

"Taggart," Dev greeted him.

McGill drew to a halt and doubled over, resting his hands on his thighs, panting. "I . . . I can't handle the dog, Taggart. I come to tell ye."

"What?" All three of them turned to McGill, their faces reflecting their confusion and concern.

"It's me heart. I took a nitrate, but I . . . I don't dare put more of a strain on it. The pressure of the trial would be too much fer me, I fear. But Dev is here now; he'll run Blackie."

"*What?*" Dev asked. "I can't."

"Of course you can." Even in his present extremity, McGill's face managed a fierce expression of disgust. "You only done it about a hundred times before!"

"But I'm not even entered."

"It don't matter who runs the dog, as long as he's entered, and Blackie is, in't he Taggart?"

A look of amusement dawning on his pleasant face, Taggart nodded. "Apparently. I could have sworn the application we received said Nolly's Blue, but McGill has set that matter right."

The old pirate, Dev thought, regarding his manager with affection and exasperation.

"Do it, Dev. Please," Toni said.

Dev turned. Toni's face was aglow with something akin to the Mel-worship he'd seen on her face when he'd first met her . . . when? Only four days ago? She touched his arm, looking up into his eyes, and right then and there he knew he would have gone and fought the battle of Culloden all over again just to keep her looking at him like that. Preferably forever.

"It would be . . . I would always be able to . . ." She couldn't seem to find the words, but her grip on his wrist tightened. "I'd love to watch you win this trial."

He didn't stand a chance. And caught between his conveniently dying manager and the look of expectation in Toni's blue eyes, he didn't even try.

"All right," he said. "Let's get Blackie."

*T*he second test was a double lift—two groups of sheep in the same field. The dog would be sent for one group, bring the flock halfway back to the handler, and then leave them to go collect the second group of sheep, which he would herd back to join the first and then drive the entire flock to the handler.

For the first time Toni saw Blackie. For the second time in as many days she fell in love. Her dog was fabulous.

The other dogs performed well, making the competition fierce, but as soon as Blackie began working, it was clear he outstripped the rest of the field. Blackie and Dev worked as a team. The dog watched Dev with complete faith, took directions without hesitation, always working in tandem with Dev, never second-guessing him yet independent enough to catch any misstep a sheep made and bring it summarily back to conformity.

It was a breathtaking demonstration of what man and dog working together could accomplish. Twice the gallery burst into spontaneous applause, but not once did Blackie show a bit of distraction. His blue gaze was fixed on Dev, awaiting the next command, the next challenge, the next opportunity to show what hundreds of years of breeding could achieve. He was magnificent. *They* were magnificent.

There could be no mistaking the pleasure Dev took in handling Blackie. But even more than confidence, his expression clearly revealed his affection and pride in the Border collie.

A man like that, goofy over his dog.

Toni's heart melted, dissolved, puddled up, and drained away. There was no way she could take this dog away from him. He'd not once tried to get out of the deal his manager had made—well, okay, once at the very beginning. But as soon as he'd understood her position, he'd never pressed her or tried to get her to give up her claim. He'd been honorable to the end.

How could she not be in love with him?

"He's wonderful," she whispered, and McGill, seated in a folding chair beside her, nodded proudly.

"I told ye, lassie. Ye could live three lifetimes and never see his like agin."

"That's what I'm afraid of," she said quietly, her eyes fixed on Dev. She looked down at the old Scot. His color was better, but he was still in discomfort.

"Tell me, Mr. McGill," she said, "do you believe in love at first sight?"

He nodded at once. "Aye. I do."

"Really?" she asked. "You surprise me. I'd have taken you for a pragmatist like myself."

He chuckled, his gaze still tracking the action on the field. "There's nothing practical in being thick-headed, lass. If ye see sumthin' you know in your heart is the best of its kind ye'll ever find, only a fool would walk away from it."

Her heartbreak kicked into a faster gear. "But what if . . . what if this 'best thing' doesn't feel the same way?" she asked, unable to keep the quaver from her voice, stupidly hanging on his answer.

McGill tore his gaze away from the test field. "He might never be yores the way he's Dev's, I'll no say he will. But treat him fair and challenge his talents, and he'll be content."

Dear God, he thought she was talking about Blackie! She felt the heat race up her cheek and turned away, so that he could not read her embarrassment. At least she could give one thing to Dev that would assure he'd remember her.

She pulled the contract out of her pocket and ripped it in two. McGill whistled softly, his eyes round. "Ye'll let Blackie stay with Dev?"

"He belongs to Dev, anyone can see that."

McGill shook his head, staring at her in bemusement. "Yer a marvelous lass," he said wonderingly, "for an American."

She couldn't help a broken chuckle. "We try. Just don't sell the man's dog out from under his nose again. Your next American might not be such a . . . a *bampot*."

"Not I!" McGill swore solemnly as Toni turned. "Where are tha going, lass? Ye best have a care, or ye'll miss the final test, and Blackie's slated to be first dog out."

She smiled wryly. "I wish I could stay. But there's a bus leaving for the ferry in fifteen minutes, and I need to be on it to catch the bus to Glasgow."

McGill cocked his head.

"Don't worry," she said. "I won't make you drive me.

You stay and watch Blackie win. Just do me a favor, will you, McGill. Tell Dev—" she stopped, ambushed by sudden tears. She closed her eyes, willing them away, biting hard on her lip. She took a deep, steadying breath and opened them. "Tell Dev . . . I said good-bye."

Dev was waiting to be called near the pen at the top of the hill. Far away, at the opposite end of the field, a new flock of sheep milled uncertainly at the gate. Blackie had already spotted them. He crouched at Dev's feet, his wiry body vibrating with tension, licking his lips nervously as he waited.

One more test and, barring some unseen disaster, Blackie would win his last sanctioned trial in Great Britain. He hoped Toni would run Blackie in an occasional trial in the States. The dog loved it, and Toni would, too. He didn't have a doubt about it. He didn't have a doubt about her, come to that.

He looked around for her, the desire to preen—just a dram—for her irresistible. Instead of Toni, he saw McGill. The old man's face was creased with concentration, and his step was hesitant. If he had some bit of advice, some mistake he'd seen the other handlers make in reading the terrain, Dev hoped he had the good sense to clue him in on it. Quickly. The sheep were almost in, and they'd be calling him to enter the field.

"I have to go in soon, McGill," Dev called, "so if you have some wisdom to impart, make it quick."

The old man looked up at him. "She's going."

He knew at once who McGill meant. The world dropped out from under him; his heart beat in a crazed, thickened rhythm. He'd known this was taking too long, but somewhere in the back of his mind he'd hoped she'd become so involved in the trial she'd forget about the time, miss her train, and be forced to stay with him. But it hadn't worked out that way.

"Now, then, don't look so peculiar, Dev," McGill said. "Aye, I know you liked her, and it's too bad she lives across the sodding ocean, but here's a bit of somethin' that'll make you happy." The manager leaned closer. "She tore up the contract."

Dev stared at him mutely.

"Do you not hear me, Dev?" McGill insisted. "She's left you Blackie. Isna that wonderful?"

"Grand."

"Well," the manager said peevishly, "ye have a nice way of showin' yer elation."

It was too much. Dev stood stiffly, as if he feared releasing the tension in his body. "How am I to be elated, McGill? I'd give a hundred Blackies if she'd stay." His eyes were stricken, his voice hollow.

McGill drew back. "So that's the way of it?" he asked quietly.

"Aye. I love her."

"Then why don't you tell her, ye great grand fool?" the old man erupted, taking off his cloth hat and swatting Dev across the chest.

"She'd think I was daft!" Dev defended himself. "I only met her three days ago. If I went and declared my undying love she'd probably have me up on stalking charges, and I wouldn't blame her."

"Not if she felt the same way," McGill returned loudly.

Dev stilled. "What?"

"Mr. Devlin Montgomery to the line." A voice called over the loudspeaker system. Automatically McGill lifted the rope and shoved Dev under. Dev, still absorbing what McGill had said, allowed himself to be pushed, and Blackie slunk in behind him in a low, swift rush.

"How do you know?" Dev demanded.

"The last thing she asked me before she tore up the contract was if I believed in love at first sight."

"She did?" Dev straightened, swinging about, his eyes scouring the gallery. "Where is she? When did she go?"

McGill threw up his hands in distress. "About ten minutes ago. She was heading for the buses. . . . There she is!" With a cry of triumph he pointed down past the far end of the field. Over two hundred yards away, Dev could see a tall, leggy blonde heading for a thick flange of exhaust-spewing buses.

There was no way he was going to be able to get to her before she made it to them. And once she disappeared into that mess, he'd lose her for good. She was too far away to call, and . . .

He looked down. Blackie, crouched by his feet, swung his head up, staring intently into his eyes with almost preternatural intelligence.

It was crazy. It would never work.

It was his only chance.

𝒩olly's Black did not win the Great Hebrides Sanctioned Trial. He didn't even finish. But the crowd gathered there that day would never forget his farewell performance. One minute the spirited little dog was sitting atop the knoll while the northeast gate beneath opened and twenty stupid sheep bustled in, and the next he was peeling off at a dead run toward the north*west* corner of the field. He didn't look back once, never doubted his handler or his directions.

When he came to the end of the field, he cleared the fence with a grace that left the spectators gasping and rising to their feet. The black-and-white Border collie shot along the dirt path, heading for the auto park. Only when he came abreast of a tall blonde woman wearing a "Kiss My Thistle" T-shirt and heard the long rising blast of the cutting whistle did he stop and show confusion.

He herded sheep, not leggy Americans. The directions came again, this time the down whistle, curt and decisive. It was enough for Nolly's Black. He cut in front of the woman and crouched, eyeing her with all the power at his command. The woman shuffled to a halt, regarding the dog uncertainly. The audience stood in the stands, binoculars raised, as Dev Montgomery broke from the line and ran down the knoll heading for the bottom of the pasture.

The girl took a step, Dev whistled, and Blackie came in on a crouch, flat and intimidating. The girl hesitated; the dog moved cautiously forward. The girl made a gesture that even at a distance the crowd could read as part embarrassment and part annoyance and started to move around the dog. A long falling whistle sent Blackie scuttling to cut off her escape. By now Dev had vaulted the fence and was racing along the path. The girl turned and saw him, stood irresolutely for a minute, and then, with a defiant lift of her chin, marched to meet him. Blackie stayed put.

Whatever Dev Montgomery said to her, no one in that crowd was ever to know for sure. Donnie McGill, who later claimed to be instrumental in the odd, sensational courtship of the Laird of Oronsay and his lady, asserted that Dev asked her one question: "Do you believe in love at first sight?"

Whatever his question, Toni's answer was clear. She flung her arms around his neck.

The crowd went wild.

CONNIE BROCKWAY

Award-winning author Connie Brockway's books appear regularly on best-seller lists, including *USA Today* and the extended *New York Times* list. An avid traveler, animal lover, and history buff, Connie considers writing historical—and now contemporary—fiction the best of all possible careers.

Her next book is *The Bridal Season*, a romantic romp set in Victorian England. It will be available in November of 2001.

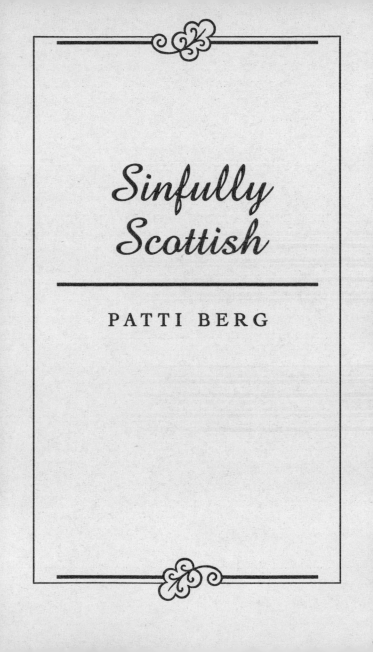

Sinfully
Scottish

PATTI BERG

Acknowledgment

Tons of appreciation to Maggie Crawford. Without her, I wouldn't have gotten to take such a delightful trip to Scotland, a land I have fallen in love with and hope I can someday visit for real. And many, many thanks to Michele Bidelspach for the eleventh-hour editing of this sinful little romance —and for loving it so much!

ust. Seduction. Sin. At last, everything Emily Sinclair had been searching for was only a few footsteps away, just behind the thick stone walls of an ancient Scottish fortress.

The last one off the tour bus, she ambled across the emerald green lawn and up the cobbled garden path. While others talked about the riotous purple and yellow flowers that surrounded them, it was only the Gothic castle that caught Emily's eyes. It loomed over her, its dark turrets and spires a menacing yet majestic display of grandeur, unlike anything she'd ever seen.

Amazed by the unexpected opulence, she drew in an awe-inspired breath and with wide, wonder-filled eyes walked through the first of several archways that led to the formidable stronghold. She'd never dreamed Dunbar Castle would be so . . . so unfairytale-like. Nor had she ever imagined it would be so . . . perfect.

"Our beloved castle, unlike others in Scotland," the tour guide said, "is not rich in glorious tales of Bonnie Prince Charlie feasting in our great hall or Mary, Queen of Scots slumbering in one or more of our bedrooms. Nay, Dunbar Castle canna boast about its lineage of heroes or braw warriors because, if truth be told, honor and virtue have not run rampant within our crenellated walls."

A definite understatement, Emily thought, especially if the incredibly wicked tales she'd heard in the village pub this afternoon could be believed.

"While other castle tours give visitors a glimpse into history with talk of war and political intrigue and possibly offer a few brief tales about a headless ghost or hauntings by a Green, Grey, or maybe a Pink Lady, we prefer to give our guests a fascinating taste of our castle's infamous past."

Infamy. Insatiability. Indulgence. That's exactly what Emily wanted to hear about, but the docent's voice came across as barely a whisper at the back of the gift shop, where the tour of the castle's interior began. Getting stuck behind forty-three other castle visitors would never do, Emily decided, and squeezed through the crowd for a better vantage point.

Not for the first time she wished she was five-foot-ten rather than five-foot-two—a height she achieved only by stretching on her tiptoes when being measured. She pushed past elbows and backpacks and emerged at the front of the group just as Gillian, their guide and the woman who'd driven them here from the quaint Highland village of Dunbar, led them through an impressive stone hallway lined with ancient tapestries and shining armor.

"Please follow me and remember, no food, no drink, and no cameras, flash or otherwise." The black-haired, blue-eyed beauty in a green-and-blue tartan jumper winked. "Black Andrew, our first laird—who, some say, still watches *everything* that goes on in and around the castle—would not approve."

No one mentioned tape recorders not being allowed, but just to be safe Emily kept hers hidden in the pocket of her blazer, and made sure her right side stayed fixed on Gillian so she could catch every intriguing word the young woman uttered in her soft, rolling burr.

"Andrew Dunbar was born in the thirteenth century. He was a very wealthy merchant who bought—and often-times took—whatever he wanted."

"You called him Black Andrew," one of the tourists said. "Why?"

"For his temperament, of course. And for the color of the blood that ran through his veins." Gillian grinned, obviously enjoying her tale as she led them up the circular stone staircase to the top of the keep. "It's said that Black Andrew lured puir wee lassies from the village to his . . . bed, and he had many, many beds within the castle walls. Then, when he tired of the lassies, he'd bring them here." She turned her palm upward and gestured at the scenery around them. "Bonnie, isn't it?"

It was magnificent. Emily shaded her eyes from the sun peeking through the early evening clouds and surveyed the ruins of the nearby abbey and its graveyard, the serene pastures where woolly, long-horned Highland cattle grazed, the cultivated pastures they'd been told were planted with barley, and the rolling green lawn that stretched from the castle to the placid, dark blue loch. It was hard to believe that anything wicked had ever happened in these pastoral hills, but she was very glad it had.

"If Black Andrew was tired of the women," one of the female tourists said, "why did he bring them up here?"

Gillian strolled toward the stone parapet and looked down, down, down at the ground below, as did every tourist, even Emily. "To kiss them heartily." She smiled mischievously. "To whisper sweet nothings in their ears. Then he'd lift them in his big, strong arms, and . . . fling them over the side."

A few women gasped. One slapped her hand to her chest in astonishment. The man standing next to Emily smirked as he shook his head, obviously not buying any of this. Emily didn't know if it was true or not, but it made for great storytelling, and that's exactly what she was looking for.

"I've heard tales," Gillian said, "that even though the women's bodies were shattered in the fall, each died with a smile on her face."

Black Andrew must have been quite a man, Emily thought. An attentive lover who believed in pleasing a woman, almost till her last breath. Andrew was a dying breed; at least that's what her somewhat limited experience with lovers led her to believe. For good reason, business—albeit a sexy business—was her only concern anymore.

"Tell me," a timid tourist asked, raising her hand slightly, "do the women Black Andrew killed haunt the castle?"

"Nay. He made their last days on earth such pleasurable ones that they had no reason to hate their killer or to come back and haunt the halls. Black Andrew is our only ghost, doomed to walk the earth until a Dunbar laird marries and lives happily ever after. He's been dead for eight centuries now and, sadly, still haunts the halls and the abbey."

With that bit of information dished out in a bubbly tone, as if the mostly American group visited haunted castles every day, Gillian headed back down the stairwell, a flock of attentive sightseers following behind.

"I heard Black Andrew had a bedroom hidden behind a secret passage," Emily said, catching up with Gillian. "I heard the room's magnificent, that the ceilings and furniture are gilt, and that the bed is draped in velvet, satin, and fur."

"I've heard those tales, too, but if the room exists, I haven't seen it."

Too bad, Emily thought. A secret room, especially one with a lascivious past, where unspeakable bliss took place, would provide the perfect backdrop for one or more pages of her next *Sinfully Delicious* cookbook. Already she could see something decadent, like Seduction, a frothy concoction of white and dark chocolate mousse capped with a swirl of rich ganache. The luscious dessert would float in a kaleidoscope of raspberry and dark chocolate sauces and be presented atop an antique gold platter nestled amidst the rumpled pillows and satin sheets on Black Andrew's bed.

And the caption: *The allure of silken smoothness and sublime pleasure tangled in a mysterious web of . . . Seduction.* She'd follow that with a tantalizing tale of sinful delights, leaving out, of course, the sordid endings to

Black Andrew's many romps. This new cookbook would definitely be another best-seller.

However, she'd have to get access to the secret room before she could photograph anything, a difficult task, indeed, since this tour was the closest she'd been able to get to the castle or its owner in three months of trying. Colin Dunbar, the current laird, was elusive, not to mention rude. He'd ignored every one of her letters and all of her phone calls. What he didn't realize was that she could be just as determined as he was difficult.

This tour might last only an hour, and an audience with the laird was not on the itinerary, but she didn't plan to leave with the rest of her group. She planned to find the enigmatic heir of Dunbar Castle and photograph the interior of his home—something that had never been done before.

She might be short, but she was extremely tenacious—and in business she always got what she wanted.

At the moment, however, she settled for being a regular tourist, gawking at the magnificence of the furnishings and antiquity as they passed through the great hall and moved on to the chapel, where the wives of the lairds had prayed for their husbands' fidelity—"An impossible feat for a Dunbar male," Gillian said—and finally entered a massive, high-ceilinged room paneled in dark walnut with a floor of flagstone.

"It was in this very room—the game room—that Black Andrew played chess with the devil," Gillian told them. "It's a tradition that has continued through the ages, although successive lairds have often chosen different games."

Fascinating, Emily thought, as she studied the room,

wondering what dessert would be most appropriate here. Blissful Victory? Hmm, not a bad name; not a great one, either; but oh, what fun she could have creating an incredibly decadent yet playful dark chocolate confection to photograph atop the ornate billiard table. Naturally she'd drape something sinful over the table. A lacy corset. A silk stocking. Maybe a pair of men's white dress gloves, an ebony walking stick, and a long rope of luxurious pearls.

There were any number of terrific photo backdrops in this room, which was a mishmash of centuries and styles. A scattering of elegant Louis XVI furniture sat on a colorful oriental carpet in front of the long and narrow windows that looked out across the loch. In one of the corners was a table set for chess with baronial chairs on either side, and at least an eight-foot-long plush black leather sofa rested in front of a fireplace so big she could drive her rented car inside.

Emily couldn't help but wonder what games the current laird played in this room, on *that* sofa, and if he played with the devil, his wife, or with puir wee lassies from the village. Surely he was just as wicked as his ancestors, the men in the portraits Gillian was pointing to now.

"Which one's Colin Dunbar?" a tall, buxom blonde asked. She wore three-inch red spikes, as if she needed any extra height, a tight, low-cut white tank top, with a lacy red bra underneath, and even tighter jeans. She'd been silent throughout the tour, as if she found the legends and history of the castle boring, as if she'd come here for one reason only—to see the castle's owner. Of all the nerve!

"Our current laird is a private man," Gillian told her. "You'll not find his picture here."

"Too bad." The blonde sighed. "Is there any chance we'll get to see him?"

Emily's ears perked up.

"Unfortunately," Gillian said quite emphatically, "he likes his privacy."

Darn!

"Are there any portraits of Black Andrew?" the woman who'd clapped her hand to her chest earlier asked. "I'd love to know what it was about him that was so fascinating to women."

"Our first laird lived long before portrait painting was fashionable, I'm afraid. But it's said that Alexander Dunbar, the man whose painting hangs above the fireplace, could have been his ancestor's twin."

The blonde stepped between the portrait of Alexander and Emily, as if she were invisible. Most people were courteous and realized that Emily didn't have X-ray eyes that could see through their backs. The blonde, however, was anything but courteous. Emily stared at the woman's tanned shoulder blades for less than a second, then took two steps to the right and gazed up at the gilt-framed portrait that had caught everyone else's attention. Her jaw nearly dropped to her knees. The man was absolutely gorgeous! Sexy and gorgeous! Wickedly gorgeous!

"He was a swarthy fellow with hair as dark as the night," Gillian said about the man in tall boots and riding attire, sitting astride a magnificent black stallion. "And even in the painting it's hard to miss the intensity of his eyes."

Or the color, Emily thought. The same deep, fathomless blue as the loch outside. Mesmerizing. Hypnotic, as if one brief glance from the man could make you his forever, could make you do anything he asked, make you even do things he didn't ask, and enjoy every moment of it.

His half smile was magnetic; his lips were slightly parted and glistened in the beam of sunlight the painter had swept across his face, making Alexander look as if he'd just licked them, as if he'd just kissed a woman and wanted more. A lot more.

"Castle records tell us that Alexander had a special bed made for him by craftsmen in France," Gillian said.

"Special?" Emily asked, immensely curious. Immensely enthralled. "Why?"

"He was too tall for any of the beds in the castle, even the bed that Black Andrew reputedly . . . *used*. Alexander ordered a bed that would comfortably accommodate a man of his height—for you Americans, that was about six-foot-five. Dunbar lairds have been quite tall ever since, and I daresay they've all looked quite similar."

"How lovely." The bosomy blonde moved so close to the portrait it looked like she wanted to climb right into Alexander's arms. The woman was obviously on the make, and more than likely she planned to sneak away from the group to find Colin Dunbar herself.

Well, Emily had first dibs on the laird. Once her business with him was successfully completed, the blonde could have him. She wasn't interested in anything more. Sex, as Emily knew all too well, wasn't one-tenth as satisfying as hard work.

"And now, if you'll accompany me to the gift shop, you may sample our very own Dunbar whisky."

"What about the arched hallway?" Emily asked,

wanting to see the place that held nearly the same intrigue for her as Black Andrew's secret bedroom. "Won't we be seeing it?"

"I'm afraid the arched hallway isn't on this tour. If you'd care to come back to Scotland on Halloween, we give a special ghost tour. It's quite exclusive. A two-hour exploration of the castle dungeon and, of course, the arched hallway . . . the place where the wife of each laird is said to have been buried or, I should say, walled up alive." A grin touched Gillian's face. "Wives have always been expendable at Dunbar Castle—after they've delivered an heir, of course—and mistresses have always been plentiful."

Again she smiled, definitely enjoying her job. "Now, to the gift shop."

Emily wanted to hang back, then slip away from the group when no one was looking and hide in the game room, but she'd seen the minuscule security cameras and alarms. The current laird had taken every precaution to keep trespassers from violating his space, to keep his treasures from disappearing.

Obviously Colin Dunbar trusted no one. Tourists couldn't picnic on the grounds or browse on their own, the way she'd done at other castles in Scotland. Sightseers couldn't even drive their own vehicles to the castle. Instead they were herded into a cramped bus and driven nearly three miles over a rutted, winding road, through a towering gate set inside a tall and thickset stone fence, to the castle grounds. It would be a long walk back to the village once she accomplished the first part of her mission, but it would be worth it.

Colin Dunbar wanted to make his home impenetrable,

but Emily was determined to stick around and see more—
and more included seeing the laird himself.

$\mathcal{C}$olin stood in front of the bank of security monitors,
hands folded casually behind him as he watched the
leggy, long-haired blonde sneak through the game-room
door and enter the Regency Room. She ran a delicate
hand over the gilt harp and the harpsichord. The same
hand trailed over the French writing table and the elegant
Grecian-style sofa. She moved languidly, her hips and
breasts swaying provocatively beneath her skin-tight
clothes, which left little to his imagination. Too bad. He'd
tired of women who blatantly showed off every facet of
their personality, and this one might as well have GREED
tattooed across her chest.

Losing interest in her, but not the security of his pos-
sessions, his gaze darted momentarily toward the monitor that gave him a clear view of the tourists milling
about the gift shop. A gray-haired woman pocketed a
Dunbar Castle souvenir magnet, a trinket worth not
much more than a pound, and then she proceeded to the
register and paid nearly two hundred pounds for a bottle
of Dunbar whisky. As long as he lived, he'd never understand tourists.

Again he caught a glimpse of the blonde, lounging
now in one of his chairs. If she thought she'd get to meet
the laird of the castle if she hung around long enough, she
was mistaken.

Looking back at the scene in the gift shop, Colin
searched the group for the one woman who'd caught his
eye when the tour began. Ah, there she was, the short red-

head with the curvy body she tried to conceal beneath an altogether too masculine looking suit. She was trying to conceal herself now, too, halfway hiding behind a rack full of whisky jiggers and silver spoons imprinted with the words DUNBAR CASTLE.

The redhead knew about the cameras. He'd seen her scanning the gift shop and hallway when the tour group entered the castle an hour before, and it hadn't taken her long to spot the security equipment. Of course, it hadn't taken him long to figure out that she had something hidden, too, but what she had secreted away in her coat pocket was still a mystery.

The woman intrigued him. Intelligent. Wary. Clever. From her movements he could tell she was after something, but he didn't know what. He couldn't read the redhead as easily as he could the leggy blonde, and that made her all the more interesting.

He wondered how long it would be before she figured out that if she were just a few inches shorter, there would be a lot of places she could go where she wouldn't be seen by the cameras. He'd find her again, however, because the monitors not only protected the castle's interior but its grounds as well. The secrets and legends surrounding Dunbar Castle, not to mention his exclusive, highly sought-after whisky, had helped to make him a rich man, and no expense had been spared to guard his privacy and those things he wanted to remain a mystery.

The blonde in the monitor to his left wasn't much of a mystery. She'd finally spotted the camera and walked toward it now, her hips and breasts swaying even more provocatively than before. A smile touched her wide, sensual mouth as she looked directly into the camera and motioned him, or whoever she thought was watching, toward her with her little finger.

"You're pretty, sweetheart, but it'll be a cold day in hell before I join you."

He chuckled as his gaze drifted back to the gift shop and searched the crowd again for the petite redhead. Maybe he'd stroll down there and make an uncharacteristic visit. Of course, the last time he'd done that one of the tourists had fainted at the sight of him, sure that the ghost of Alexander Dunbar had materialized before her. Strong genes had made him the spitting image of his ancestor, just one more Dunbar curse he had to contend with.

Contending with tourists could sometimes be just as big a blight on his existence, especially when they disappeared. "Blast!" Colin jabbed at a few keys on the security equipment and zoomed the camera in for a closer look at the people milling about. The redhead was nowhere to be found.

He quickly scanned the hallway leading out of the gift shop. Empty. Even the rooms she could access off the hall showed no signs of life. And then out of the corner of his eye he caught a flash of red behind the hedgerow leading to the distillery. Smart. Definitely smart. She'd figured out how to get out of the gift shop without being seen, even knew that the cameras didn't cover the strip of ground behind the hedge—a problem he'd have to remedy before someone else tried to outsmart his security system.

But what the redhead had failed to realize was that even though she was crouching as she walked, her wild curly hair continually bobbed over the top of the hedge.

What did she want? he wondered. Was she a spy sent to find the recipe for Dunbar whisky? He laughed cynically. Others had tried and failed, and she'd be unsuccessful, too, no matter how much she fascinated him. The recipe was in his head and nowhere else, locked there for safekeeping. It was tradition for father to hand the recipe down to son and no one else; that tradition, however, would end with him.

"Excuse me, Colin."

He turned at the sound of Gillian entering the room. "What is it?

"Two of the tourists failed to get on the bus."

"I know. I've been watching them."

Gillian crossed the room and stared at the monitors. "I see the blonde, but where's the redhead?"

"On her way to the distillery."

"Good. I was worried she might have gone looking for the hidden bedroom, since she was asking about it during the tour. I'll go after her now and make sure she gets on the bus."

Colin found himself frowning. "What about the blonde?"

Now Gillian frowned. "What about her?"

"Aren't you going to take her to the bus?"

"And why would I do that? She's tall. She's a bonnie lass, exactly the kind of woman you usually date." Gillian folded her arms across her chest. "Dinna tell me you're not interested in her."

"That's exactly what I'm telling you."

"But—"

"How much did you wager that she'd stick around and that I'd invite her to stay?"

"A week's labor! If I lose, I have to clean the Devil's Cup, and you've seen what that pub looks like on a summer morn. I'll be sweeping and scrubbing half the day . . . for seven days in a row. You canna do this to me, Colin Dunbar."

"If you and the rest of the villagers would quit betting on my love life, you wouldn't end up in these predicaments."

"And if you didn't flit from one woman to another, we wouldn't bet."

Colin shrugged and turned away from Gillian's nagging to look at the distillery monitor, where he caught a quick glimpse of the redhead knocking on the door, then unsuccessfully trying the handle. *Don't waste your time,* he wanted to tell her. *It's locked good and tight, and no one gets inside but me.*

Gillian cleared her throat to catch his attention, and he tilted his head to look at her annoyed frown over his shoulder.

"Meg bet on the redhead," Gillian said. "I told her she wasn't your type, so please dinna tell me you're going to let her stay."

Colin grinned, then turned his eyes back to the monitor. "Do you know her name?"

"Aye." Gillian drew in a deep breath then let it out in a huff. "Emily Sinclair. Age twenty-eight. Single, American, and never been married."

"You found all that out during the tour?"

"She's staying at the Devil's Cup, and Meg—dear, sweet Meg, whose pub I'll have to clean for *two* weeks, not one, if you let the redhead stay—plied her with stories this afternoon. If you give Meg a call, I'm sure you can find out an endless number of facts."

"All gathered for my benefit. Right?"

"If you dinna get married, if you dinna produce an heir—"

"The village will fall apart. Yes, yes, I'm well aware of your worries."

"You might take it lightly, Colin Dunbar, but there are forty-three people living in the village of Dunbar who take your love life quite seriously."

"And there are an equal number of people on the tour bus, plus a blonde in the Regency Room, that you should be taking back to the village. As for the redhead . . . she intrigues me. I'll watch her a while longer, and I'll make sure she gets back to the village . . . sometime."

Gillian harrumphed, spun around on her sensible shoes, and stalked out of the security room.

Again he turned his gaze to the redhead, who was still trying to find a way inside the distillery, but his mind wandered back to Gillian's words.

Marriage. He shook his head at the miserable thought. In eight hundred years only one Dunbar laird— Alexander—had had a successful marriage, and that had surely been a fluke. It was certainly not a fact anyone living in the village of Dunbar wanted to discuss or even believe, because it would tamper with their blasted legend about every Dunbar laird doing away with his wife in one lascivious way or another.

If truth be told, too many wives had run away from their philandering husbands, too many had died giving birth to an heir, and too many, like his own mother, had married only for wealth, and once they'd produced the obligatory son, took the money they were offered to get out of their husbands' lives and moved on.

No, he would not marry, and sadly, he would not produce an heir. Never. It was time the cursed history of the Dunbars came to an end.

2

$\mathcal{E}$mily was stuck—literally—and in an ancient graveyard, of all places. Ghosts haunted cemeteries. So did murderers and grave robbers, and they always did it at midnight. Didn't they? The witching hour was the perfect time for the unspeakable to happen, and it was bound to happen to her if she didn't get her ankle out of some long-dead person's blasted crypt.

She grabbed at the bend in her knee and tugged, but it did no good at all because she was wedged in way too far and way too tight. Obviously the fates were not smiling down on her this evening. Oh, no, why would they smile when they could roll in the clouds laughing themselves silly? "Serves you right for trespassing!" they'd probably say, followed by a stream of snickers. And they'd be right.

If she could just get out of this mess, she'd promise to make up for her error in judgment.

Until then, she gave herself permission to be a neurotic wreck. She drummed her fingers on the raised tomb to her right, jerked her stuck leg fruitlessly, and wondered uneasily why the slab covering the ground-level crypt she was caught in had been shoved aside. So a ghost could escape? It sounded reasonable, given her current state of near panic.

She tried not to think about her foot dangling in that person's burial plot, or the fact that her shoe might be touching someone's remains.

How, she wondered, could everything have gone so wrong after she'd executed such a brilliant, undetected escape from the gift shop? She'd made it to the distillery where Colin Dunbar reputedly spent the biggest portion of his time, but no one answered her knock on the door. And then a gardener spotted her with her hand on the knob and obviously thought she was a burglar trying to break in. He'd yelled, and she'd run—which proved to be her first really big mistake—straight for some hedges. Of course, the hedges turned out to be a maze. An endless, six-foot-high maze, which was not a good thing for a five-foot-two-if-she-stretched woman to get lost in, especially at night and for at least three hours to boot.

She drummed her fingers a little harder on the granite crypt, thinking about her relief when she'd finally escaped. She'd taken a deep breath and headed for the castle. Unfortunately, she'd always had trouble figuring out north, south, east, and west and ended up at the abbey instead.

The next time she was determined to have a conversation with an elusive, whisky-making Scottish laird, she'd pack a flashlight. She might even pack something to eat; her stomach had long ago started to growl.

It made one of its ridiculous little rumbles now, the sound horribly loud in the stillness of the night. And then the quiet was further disrupted by the shriek of wind through the menacing gargoyles and ghastly medieval carvings that glared down at her from atop the abbey ruins.

A chill snaked its way up her spine, and her nervousness became absolute fright when the ancient stone walls began to wail, as if the spirits of long-dead monks were crying over the devastation the centuries had wreaked on their cloistered home.

This was definitely not the place to be at midnight, all alone, with the moon and stars hiding behind the clouds.

She took a deep breath and tried to stay calm, but a bright circle of light suddenly appeared out of nowhere and joined the eerie screeching and crying inside the abbey, making her entire body tense up into a million unbearably tight knots. What was she witnessing here in the dark—at midnight? A ghost dancing from crypt to crypt? A spirit wanting to hightail it out of this place almost as badly as she did?

She squeezed her eyes shut, hoping that would make it go away, but when she cracked her left lid open the light was still there, moving closer. Closer.

Popping both eyelids open again, she tried frantically to get her ankle out of its trap, but it wouldn't budge. She swallowed hard, and her heart began a drum roll inside her chest as the circle of light grew larger and larger, blinding her when it stopped and stared her straight in the eyes.

Slowly the apparition began to materialize, a face from the past emerging from the cloud of light. It was swarthy and shadowed, and its wicked sapphire eyes burned into her. Hair so black that it almost blended in with the nighttime sky whipped around its face in the wind.

It was immensely tall. Its shoulders were broad.

If she didn't have a lump of fear stuck in her throat, she might have laughed at herself, because she found the apparition . . . stunning. She'd seen the face before, marveled at it in fact, when she'd gazed at a certain castle painting, one of a magnificent Highland laird on a massive black steed.

"Alexander." She whispered the name in awe, frightened but enthralled because he was far more gorgeous than in his portrait.

"Colin." It spoke, its voice a deep baritone, its Scottish burr soft, mesmerizing.

She frowned at the name the ghost had uttered. *"Colin?"*

"Aye. Colin, *not* Alexander, although it's his tomb you've been drumming your fingers on."

"Colin!" She swallowed hard when she recognized the name, but still a lump hung in her throat. "The current one or a long-dead ancestor?"

"Flesh and blood, although there are some who believe I'm made of stone."

Dizziness hit her—so did shock, but only an ounce of relief, and she clutched Alexander's tomb to keep from crumpling to the ground when her knees turned to quivering jelly. "I thought you were a ghost."

"I assure you I'm not."

His Sean Connery–voice all but echoed through the graveyard and abbey, a welcome and comforting respite from the eerie howling. At last he turned his flashlight so it was no longer half-blinding her, and she could see that the man was definitely 100 percent flesh and blood, not to mention solid-packed muscle, all wrapped up in an off-white Arran wool sweater and well-fitting jeans.

Slowly a smile touched her face as she realized she'd finally come face to face with the elusive man she'd set out to meet. The circumstances weren't the best, however. He'd caught her trespassing on his property at midnight, she'd almost fainted dead away at the sight of him, and her foot was stuck in one of his ancestor's graves. Not exactly a professional meeting, but she aimed to rectify that immediately.

She held out her hand in greeting. "It's nice to meet you, Mr. Dunbar. I'm Emily Sinclair."

He stepped closer, towering over her like one of the ominous dark spires on his castle, and took her hand. As intimidating as he looked, his grip was warm and almost gentle, and he didn't let go. In fact, it felt as if he planned to hold on to it indefinitely.

This was good, she told herself, trying to think about her agenda instead of the heat rippling through her. If he was in no hurry to let her go, she'd probably find time to discuss business. Of course, the fact that he wasn't letting go of her hand had some bad aspects, too, because that rippling heat flowing through her body felt really, really good, and everyone in their right mind knew that a smart businesswoman never mixed work with pleasure.

"Well, Emily Sinclair," he said, rolling the R in her name and halfway mesmerizing her, "did you enjoy your tour of the castle?"

She frowned at his question. "You knew I was on the tour?"

"I know everything that goes on here."

How could he possibly know? Unless . . . Her frown tightened. "Were you watching me in the security cameras?"

"I was."

His intense, dark-eyed gaze trailed over her body. Again he was watching her, as he had through his blasted cameras, only this time he was watching far too personally, which made her very uncomfortable.

When his stare fixed on the slab that held her captive, he let go of her hand and crouched at her side, wrapping his long, powerful fingers around her ankle. "Does this hurt?"

"No." Amazingly, it felt good, now that he was touching it. "I'm sure it's not sprained. Just stuck."

"Here, hold this." He handed her the flashlight. "I'll have you out in a moment."

Take your time. That was an odd thought to creep into her mind when only minutes before she would have sold her soul to the devil to get out of this place. But it was nice to have a moment or two to enjoy the heavenly sensation of his hands on her ankle, and from this vantage point she could leisurely enjoy the sight of his muscular arms and shoulders, their strength visible even through the wool of his sweater.

The aftershave he wore wafted around her, as did the now gentle breeze that tossed his thick and wavy ebony locks of hair. Why was it, she wondered, that men looked so rugged and handsome with their hair all mussed, while women usually ended up one big mess? She could only imagine what her springy bright red curls looked like at this moment. More than likely they stood on end, corkscrews flying everywhere.

Fortunately he wasn't gazing at her hair, only her leg, her ankle, and the heavy granite slab that held her prisoner.

"What did you think of my home?" he asked, pushing her pant leg up far higher than he probably needed to as he analyzed the tight spot she was in.

"It's . . . intriguing."

"What intrigued you the most?" His gaze flickered toward her for an instant, then focused back on his work. "The ghost stories? Tales of Black Andrew's escapades?"

She laughed, partially from the ticklish feel of his fingers sweeping over her ankle, partially from nervousness, partially because she was tongue-tied. Finally she got hold of her senses and tried to answer like a competent businesswoman instead of a giggling teen. "I thoroughly enjoyed the tales of Black Andrew. Of course, I didn't know any one family had such a dark past."

"You'd find the Dunbar family even darker if you heard all the stories."

"Are there a lot more?"

"Hundreds."

Oh, what she would give to hear every last one of them and print them in the pages of her cookbook! The sensationalism would send her book flying to the top of the charts.

After several attempts to maneuver her ankle so it would slide out easily, he gave up and tried to push the slab, and she tore her mind from best-sellers to flexing muscles.

"Did you enjoy the maze as much as Gillian's stories?" he asked, hitting her with a quick grin before concentrating on the stone again.

"You didn't really see me inside the maze, did you?"

"Aye."

This bit of news was really too much, and she felt her muscles tightening in outrage. "You let me roam around that blasted maze for hours on end and didn't bother to come out and help me?"

"I had work to do, and you were trespassing on private property."

"That's beside the point. I could have died in there."

"But you didn't. Besides, I kept an eye on you."

"And for that I should be grateful?"

"You should be grateful that I'm here now. If I weren't, you'd have to spend the night with your foot stuck in Robbie Dunbar's crypt."

"You haven't rescued me yet."

He frowned, and she could easily see him gritting his teeth as he shoved the slab one more time and finally budged it a fraction of an inch.

Freedom at last. She pulled her ankle out of the grave, and she would have bent down to rub some circulation into it, but Colin Dunbar, voyeur, whisky maker, and muscleman, lifted her from the ground and sat her down atop the raised tomb. Then, as if she wasn't already edgy enough, he lifted her leg in his hands and gently massaged her tender ankle.

Their eyes met, his intense sapphire ones staring down at her. He made her nervous. Made her tremble inside, but somehow she managed to smile. "Thank you."

"You're welcome."

He'd rescued her; now he was stroking, rubbing, and all but caressing her ankle. She assumed he'd stop at any moment, but he didn't. Instead he held her leg in the palm of one hand and her heel in the other and pressed his thumbs and fingers lightly into her muscles. She tried to hide her deep intake of keep-yourself-under-control breath and braced her hands behind her on the crypt.

"Tell me, Emily," he said in that Sean Connery voice of his, while his dark sapphires blazed a hole through her, "are you a spy?"

What an odd question. "Why would you ask that?"

"I watched you trying to break into my distillery."

"I did no such thing." She'd been accused of being a ruthless businesswoman, but never a thief. "I was trying to find you, and since I heard that you spend most of your time concocting new brews in the distillery, that seemed the perfect place to look."

"Witches concoct brews. I distill the best whisky in the world."

Oh, what an ego he had. "So I've heard."

A wry grin touched his face. "You're awfully petulant for a trespassing spy."

"All right, I admit to trespassing, but only because I wanted to meet you, not because I'm out to steal any secret recipes."

His brow rose, questioning her words. A moment later he stretched a hand toward her, fumbled with her navy blue linen jacket—of all the nerve!—reached into her pocket and pulled out her tape recorder. "What's this for?"

She'd been caught. "Nothing cloak-and-dagger, I assure you. I didn't want to miss a word of what Gillian said on the tour. I didn't take any pictures because we were told not to, and I didn't have anything to eat or drink. But I don't remember anything being said about tape recordings being forbidden." She turned her intense eyes on him now. "Please don't tell me you're going to confiscate it."

He shook his head slowly. "I'm already overfamiliar with the stories."

As if that subject was over and done with and he'd tired of rubbing her ankle, he lowered her foot to the side of the crypt, applied the heel of his hiking boot to the slab of granite, and inch-by-laborious-inch shoved the cover of Robbie's tomb back in place.

"So," he said, dusting his hands off on the thighs of his jeans, "what did you want to see me about?"

Finally they were getting down to business. "I have a proposition for you."

His grin was wicked. "It's been a long time since I've been propositioned by such a beautiful woman."

She should have known that typical male response was coming, but she couldn't keep from asking, "How long?"

He studied his watch. "Forty-six hours, give or take a few minutes."

Unfortunately his answer was probably the truth. Why it annoyed her was anyone's guess, but she forgot her irritation when his powerful hands wrapped around her waist and he lifted her down from the crypt. He watched her as she tested her weight on her ankle, then tucked her hand around his arm, and hit her with a smile. "Why don't we go inside and talk about propositions over a drink."

It wasn't an offer, it was a statement of intent, one she

couldn't refuse, considering that one drink might lead to a tour of the castle and Colin Dunbar's acceptance of her proposition. That was what she'd come here for. Wasn't it?

"What do you do when you're not spying?" he asked as they hiked up the hill from the graveyard to the castle.

"I write cookbooks." How unglamorous that sounded on the surface.

"You're a chef?"

"That's what I trained for," she told him as they strolled through the moonlit gardens and bailey. "Before that, when I was in my early teens, I barricaded myself in my bedroom and wrote lurid love stories."

"Sounds . . . intriguing."

"They were awful. Nothing but romantic drivel."

"I thought all women were romantics."

"A disastrous relationship cured me forever." It was ridiculous to tell him that, especially when he had no need to know. "When I was nineteen I got interested in photography and cooking."

They made their way through the great hall, past the drawing room and the library, the click of their heels and the sound of her voice echoing through the cavernous chamber. "A few years back I decided to combine all my interests—lurid love stories, photography, and cooking—into a cookbook. Three best-sellers later—and now I'm embarking on my fourth. That's what I want to talk with you about."

"I'm a lousy cook, so I'm afraid I can't be of much help."

"It's a business deal I want to talk about."

He removed the fat gold cord that had barricaded the

game room when the tour had gone through earlier, and led her inside. "I don't usually talk business after working hours."

"This won't take all that long."

He angled his head toward her—a long way down, considering his height and her lack of it. "Later, maybe. First we'll have some whisky."

A ploy to get her drunk? she wondered as he crossed the room in a few long strides, opened a cabinet, and took out a sparkling crystal decanter and cut-glass tumblers. As much as she enjoyed watching him, she turned her fascination toward the room. It was massive and masculine and a little intimidating, just like its owner, but she'd managed to get inside and she'd managed to get an audience with the laird himself, and she was darn well going to enjoy the experience.

She caressed the fine, highly polished woodwork scattered about the room, marveled at the exquisite oriental carpets, and was again drawn to the big black leather sofa in front of the fireplace, a fixture in the room that she assumed was used as much for sport as all the gaming tables.

"Is it true that one of your ancestors played chess with the devil?" she asked, her gaze fixed on the chessboard and its pewter playing pieces.

"The story has gotten skewed over the years," Colin said, walking toward her with two crystal tumblers half full of dark amber whisky. "Andrew *was* the devil, and many women sold their souls to play with him."

"I can't imagine anyone wanting something so badly that they'd sell their soul." Unless, of course, they were stuck in a haunted cemetery.

"It's not all that uncommon. I've had people ask to know the recipe for my whisky, and considering the prices they've offered, they might as well be selling their souls."

"It's in that much demand?"

"Enough for people to send spies here, people who've had as much success breaking into my distillery as you. The more secretive the recipe, the more value is placed on it." He took a swallow of whisky. "This isn't the high end of what I produce, but it's still one of the finest single malts you'll find anywhere. It's expensive, it has made me a fortune, and there are big corporations anxious to know what I put into it that gives it its distinctive flavor."

Curious now, she sipped slowly. She'd never had whisky straight before, and she understood why. Flames licked her insides as the liquor slipped over her tongue and down her throat.

"What do you think?"

"That it's hot." She took a deep breath. "That it lives up to its nickname: the Devil's Own."

"You know about my whisky then?"

"I'd heard stories, and naturally I did my homework to learn more about your company and your secretive ways. But it was the lady who owns the place where I'm staying who provided the extra details."

"Meg sells a lot of Dunbar whisky. She's proud that she's the only one in the world allowed to sell one certain mixture, and she likes to brag."

Emily frowned, uncomfortable with the fact that he'd watched her on the cameras, and now he seemed to know who she'd been talking to and where she'd found accommodations. Most people would have assumed she was staying in Inverness, not in a tiny hamlet with only one bed-and-breakfast-slash-pub.

"How do you know I'm staying in the village?"

"Gillian told me when she came to say you weren't on the tour bus."

"Is there anything you don't know about me?"

"Dunbar's a small village." He casually leaned a shoulder against the stone hearth. "The people who live there take great interest in anyone passing through. Tourists are always a prime topic of conversation. Stick around long enough, and they'll want to run your life."

"I only plan to stick around long enough to do business with you." It was about time she made her intentions clear. Of course, looking at the intriguing man over the top of her glass as she sipped his whisky, she had the dreadful feeling that if she stayed too long in his company, her intentions might stretch to wanting him as well as photos of the rooms in his castle.

Crazy! She had to remember that she was here for business, and for no other reason.

Suddenly he became the businessman, too, no longer leaning casually against the hearth but setting down his whisky and clasping his hands behind him as he stood straight, tall, and almost invincible. "Now that we've talked about whisky, the village, and the fact that you're not a spy, why don't you tell me your proposition?"

She didn't see the need to mince words. "I'd like to photograph the inside of your castle."

"No."

Obviously he didn't want to mince words either.

"You could at least hear me out before you say no."

"All right." He looked down at her from his lofty height and smiled. "I'll hear you out, and then I'll tell you no."

The man had ceased to be intriguing. Now he was merely a pain.

"While you make the finest whisky in the world," she said, throwing out a halfhearted compliment that might hopefully gain some points, "I create some of the finest, most sinfully decadent desserts in the world."

"Have you been given awards for your desserts?"

"No."

"Then how do you know they're the best?"

"Because I've received thousands upon thousands of letters from people telling me they've never tasted anything so rich, so luscious, so—"

"All right. I believe you." He grinned, and she wanted to smack him for being so smug. "So, what do your desserts and the interior of my castle have in common?"

"Your castle abounds with legends, with mystery, deceit, passion—"

"Lust." His gaze swept over her body, up, down, sideways. "Do your desserts cause people to feel these things? Mystery? Deceit? Passion?"

"I haven't taken any surveys." She took a swallow of whisky to quench her thirst and drown her annoyance and immediately began to cough.

Colin shook his head and plucked the glass from her hand. "I think you need something not quite so strong."

"What I need—" She coughed again. "What I need is the opportunity to present my proposal without interruption."

Colin handed her another glass of whisky, this one

lighter in color. "This is from my private reserve. No one drinks it unless I pour it."

She took a tiny sip, and it tingled in her throat rather than burned. It warmed her all the way down to her toes. Suddenly she realized Colin's sapphire eyes were bearing down on her, and she went from warm to sizzling.

"Feeling better?"

"Yes, thank you." It was a lie. She was burning up inside, and her heart fluttered. She took a deep breath in an attempt to calm herself, then looked up at his handsome, grinning face, and asked, "May I continue?"

"Be my guest."

The man was maddening. Gorgeous—but infuriating.

"What I'd like to do is photograph my desserts inside various rooms in your castle. When the cookbook is compiled, the photo of each dessert will be accompanied by a recipe and a story, a vivid retelling of one of your family's legends, leaving out the more sordid details, of course."

He frowned. "I believe someone already wrote to me with a similar proposal."

"That would probably have been me. I sent you several letters—none of which were answered."

"Did you call, as well?"

"Several times in the past month."

"I think my secretary might have mentioned your calls."

She wanted to scream, but she had to be a professional. "So why didn't you respond?"

"You're not the first one who's wanted to photograph the interior of my home. If I responded to the letters, I would have no time to distill my whisky. I'd have no time for other pleasurable pursuits, either."

"It's not my intention to waste your time. I thought by coming here I could expedite things. Now that we're together, now that you know what I'd like to do, maybe you could give me your answer."

"I already gave you my answer." He lifted his glass from the table and swirled the whisky around inside. Slowly his gaze fixed on her eyes, and he smiled smugly. "No."

Somehow she managed to keep calm and businesslike, although she was raging inside. "I'm more than willing to pay for the privilege. Just name your price."

He hit her with that sapphire stare again, crossed the room and took his time pouring himself another whisky, then stared out the window at the moonlight on the loch. "This means a lot to you, doesn't it?"

"I came all the way to Scotland to see you." She walked toward him, seeing his tall, handsome reflection and questioning look in the window. "I trespassed on private property. I sneaked out of a gift shop when I knew security cameras were aimed at me." She raised her glass close to her mouth. "I'm determined to get the pictures."

"All right, then." He turned and fixed her with a smile as she sipped her whisky. "Spend the night with me."

She choked on his words and began to cough all over again.

"Take another sip of whisky," he said calmly. "It'll make your cough go away."

A few more sips of whisky, and she'd pass out on the floor. Still, she did what he told her to do, and slowly the coughing eased. She took a deep breath and aimed a deadly glare at him.

"Are you trying to get me drunk, hoping I'll give you the price you want?"

He plucked the glass from her hand and set it down on a table. And then he did the last thing she expected. He curled his fingers under her chin and tilted her face up to meet his gaze. "I prefer my women sober and in complete control of their senses. It's not my intention to get you drunk, Emily, no matter how much I want you."

She tried to gulp down the lump in her throat, but it wouldn't budge. "You don't know me well enough to want me."

He smiled enigmatically. "I want you enough to risk getting to know you."

Oh, dear. "I came here to photograph your bed, not to sleep in it."

"Sleep has nothing to do with my proposition."

"You know what I mean."

"All too well. You want me to make compromises, but you aren't willing to do the same. In the end it all comes down to who wants what the most, doesn't it?"

"I want the pictures, but I'm not willing to sell my soul to the devil in order to get them."

"All right then." He took her arm and abruptly started walking toward the door. "I guess that puts an end to our bargaining."

She couldn't accept his price, but she wouldn't give up. "For now."

He laughed. "For good."

He made it sound so final, made it sound as if he had the upper hand, but she'd dealt with ruthless people before. She wouldn't argue now—but there would come a time when she'd get what she wanted.

He stopped under the archway just outside the castle walls, looked down at her, and smiled. "Good night, Emily."

Good night?

Good grief! She had no car, only two feet, and they were not about to walk three miles back to the village. In the dark. Even though she didn't believe in ghosts, just thinking that they *might* exist could still scare the beejeebers out of her. Oh, no, he'd have to take her.

"Do you think you might be able to drive me back to the village? As you might recall from your voyeuristic activities earlier, I got off a tour bus today, and I didn't get back on."

All he did was grin.

"I'd walk, but it's late, it's dark, and I have a habit of getting lost."

His grin widened. "Shall we attempt to strike up another bargain?"

She gritted her teeth. "What do you have in mind?"

He trailed his fingers across her cheek and lips. She wanted to slap them away, but the delicious tingle rippling through her body kept her from doing anything that might stop him. "One single kiss," he said. "That's all I want."

The ripple turned into great big waves, but she remained in control of her senses. "I don't conduct business that way."

"And I do very few things for free."

Budging on her principles irritated her as much as Colin's refusal to give her a ride out of the goodness of his heart. But it was either concede or walk back to the village alone. In the dark. And that made her shiver.

"Fine! One kiss, but nothing more, and only when you drop me off at the Devil's Cup."

"Agreed." He smiled all too easily. "But I'll decide just how long that one kiss will last."

$\mathcal{E}$verything in Dunbar revolved around legend, mystery, secrets, and the devil—the Devil's Cup pub, the Devil's Own Whisky, the golden pitchfork trademark that blazed on the side of Colin's black Land Rover, just as it blazed on the bottles of his whisky. Even though Emily knew it was all a myth, she was almost certain that something of the devil ran in Colin's veins.

She was a businesswoman who, until today, had had nothing on her mind but the pursuit of yet another best-seller, one that would top the last. Yet Colin was doing his best to bewitch her, to make her do his bidding. The same thing Black Andrew had reputedly done to all those puir wee lassies.

She almost laughed out loud as Colin drove along the narrow lane, and even though he couldn't have heard her, he looked at her out of the corner of his intense sapphire eye, as if he knew what was swimming through her mind. The devil could do that. Read minds, that is. And she was more than sure Colin Dunbar had more than just the ability to read her mind—she was almost positive that he could also make her body ignite.

She was being silly. Her head felt light from too much whisky, too little food, and a whole lot of nervous tension. One kiss. That's all it was. One kiss.

She'd never done business that way. Never wanted to. Till now, that is, and the anticipation was driving her mad.

He pulled to a stop in front of the Devil's Cup, stretched his arm across the seat, and tangled his fingers in her hair. "You're awfully tense. You've been that way ever since we got in the car. It's almost as if you thought I intended to do much more than kiss you."

"I'm hoping you're a man of your word."

The fingers of his free hand splayed over her belly and slid around her back, pulling her a little closer, a little closer. "I am. And true to my word, I'm going to exact my reward for driving you home. One kiss, the duration of which will be determined once we begin."

"You mean everything has to do with whether you enjoy yourself or not?"

"I'm going to enjoy myself, Emily. Have no fear about that."

How could she possibly fear that when she feared everything else—especially the beginning of the kiss?

Sapphire eyes bore down on her. Hot. Hot. Hotter!

His lips moved closer. Closer. Not close enough! And then they touched—his lips and hers. Gentle. So amazingly gentle. So wonderfully tender that he caught her completely off guard. Her lips parted of their own free will, and she gave him access to a part of her that she'd locked away so long ago.

The devil didn't hesitate to move past her lips. His tongue slipped inside and teased the roof of her mouth. He tasted hotter than his private reserve whisky, and she was sure he was far more intoxicating.

Her heart raced. Her stomach tumbled. She felt all achy and needy and quivery as every single one of her senses were caught up in his kiss, in the taste of whisky on his mouth, and the mesmerizing swirl of his tongue.

Somewhere outside the car a door slammed, and suddenly she was back in the real world again. It was two in the morning, and she was in a car kissing a man she hardly knew. It was too much, too soon, and she was not about to give in to Colin, even though giving in had been foremost on her mind a moment ago.

She'd come to Scotland to take sensual photographs of luscious desserts, not to get caught up in a sensual, short-term relationship with a lusty and luscious Highlander.

"I think we'd better stop." She shoved away, and he laughed, his fingers still in her hair, his hand still at her back.

"Have you forgotten that the duration of the kiss was up to me, that stopping was my prerogative, not yours?"

"That kiss was worth far more than the cost of a short drive home." She smiled, trying to regain control. "Let me take photographs inside the castle, and I'll let you kiss me again—but that's all."

He laughed, reached behind her, and opened the door. "Good night, Emily."

That's it? He didn't want to discuss anything more? Maybe she'd misjudged him.

Then again, maybe he'd misjudged her. Maybe he thought she'd protest his abrupt dismissal. Well, two could play this game as easily as one.

She smiled, just as he did, and stepped out of the car. "Good night, Colin." Shutting the door in her most businesslike manner, she turned, walked up the steps, and disappeared into the pub without looking back, hoping against hope that Colin wouldn't give up on this crazy game they were playing and that he'd make the next move.

3

The redhead was a tease. Her green-eyed smile, her freckled nose, and her soul-offering kiss had made him hard with want. And then she'd walked away when he thought for sure she'd stay, when he assumed she'd suggest they go back to the castle so she could see one of its many bedrooms. He would have made her want more after that. So much more.

But damn if she hadn't made him the one who wanted more. Made him want her in a way he'd never wanted another woman. If he got too close to this one, he'd be in danger of losing his heart, and he'd sworn he'd never give it to anyone.

Too many Dunbars had freely given their hearts, then had them stomped upon. It had happened to his father and his father before him, and Colin was not about to be trampled.

But as he lay in bed and stared at the ceiling, loneliness crept onto the mattress and kissed him good night. For the first time in his life, he regretted his inability to fall in love.

*E*mily bounded down the stairs feeling terribly perky for a woman who'd gone to bed at three A.M. and then lain awake the rest of the night and most of the morning concocting ideas for luscious new desserts, thinking of sensual ways to display them, and then plopping a conjured-up image of Colin Dunbar's deliciously nude body right down beside the rest of her sexy presentation.

Naturally, he was the most delectable feature, far more seductive and taste-tempting than any of her dark chocolate creations, and she wanted to taste him again. The hot, smoky whisky on his lips, his tongue, his breath, a taste that was intoxicating. Add a little sugar, a little butter and cream, not to mention the darkest, creamiest chocolate, and oh how sweet he'd be.

When she reached the bottom of the stairs, reality struck. She'd walked away from Colin Dunbar without looking back, and there was a very strong possibility that he hadn't cared.

Oddly enough, it wasn't the imminent loss of the greatest business opportunity in her life that suddenly made her miserable, it was the thought of losing what could have been—maybe, in her wildest dreams—a breathtaking and dizzying relationship.

Again she knew she was being ridiculous. Colin was

no different from any other man. His mind was on sex, and it didn't go any further than that. And because he was a Dunbar, with a whole history of misery, debauchery, and sin behind him, it was best that she focus on her original intent.

Get the photographs. After she got a bite to eat, she'd take a walk and think of nothing but work.

"Good morning, Meg." She slid onto a stool and smiled at the pudgy-faced lady standing behind the bar polishing glasses.

Meg harrumphed, shaking her head as if she were completely frustrated with the person who'd done nothing more than say good morning.

Emily took a quick glance around the semi-dark pub, and couldn't help but notice that every patron—the same ones who'd been here yesterday, at the exact same table, too—had fixed their eyes on her.

"Have I done something wrong?"

Meg harrumphed again, put the polished glass on the shelf behind her, then picked up another glass to dry. "I didn't expect ye to come walking doon those stairs till sometime tomorrow."

The odd, annoyed statement brought a frown to Emily's face. "You expected me to stay in my room for two days?"

Meg plopped her forearms—and consequently her ample breasts—atop the bar. The green of her eyes could barely be seen through her glower. "I expected ye to spend the night with Colin."

"Why would I do that?"

"Did ye not look at him?"

"Of course I did. He's . . . gorgeous." She whispered that last word so the attentive ears in the room couldn't hear her. "But I don't make a habit of spending the night with strangers." Emily rested her arms on the bar just as Meg was doing, and looked straight into the woman's eyes. "Is there some reason I should have stayed, something I know nothing about?"

"Aye," came a voice from behind. Emily spun around on her stool and looked at Billy MacGregor, Iain MacGregor, and Seamus MacGregor, triplets well into old age, who kept the Devil's Cup in business by drinking a minimum of three stouts every afternoon and every evening. They all stared at her now in deep silence.

"Someone seems to know what's going on. Mind telling me?"

"Meg wagered five pounds that ye'd not be back until tomorrow afternoon." Iain popped out of his chair and went behind the bar to pour another stout. "Show her how, Seamus."

Seamus, the quiet one, pulled a paper out of the pocket of his rumpled tweed coat and flattened the folded and wrinkled sheet on the table. Billy leaned over his brother and pointed to the chart. "It's all right here. Time. Date. Ye get to mark one square for every pound ye wager. The one who comes the closest wins the pot. Seamus won today."

It was a blasted football-type pool, and in their own way, they were betting on whether or not she'd score. Of all the—

"Meg had a different wager going with Gillian," Iain said, elbowing the older woman in her fleshy side, his grin wide. "Dinna know why she's all in a huff, since she won two week's worth of cleaning and scrubbing in that wager."

"Do you do this all the time?" Emily asked, appalled, yet slightly amused. She only wished she weren't the source of their entertainment.

"Aye," Meg said. "We bet on rugby, who's gonna catch the biggest fish in the loch on Saturday, and Colin's love life." She poured herself half a tumbler of Dunbar whisky and took a big swig. "It's all in fun, lass. Of course, no one likes to lose, especially me."

Emily didn't like to lose, either. "I'm going to be here for a few days, since I still have a mission to accomplish. Do you have any pools going that I can get in on?"

Seamus pulled a second sheet of lined white paper from his pocket and once again smoothed out the wrinkles after he placed it on the table.

"And what's this one?" Emily asked, pulling some pound notes out of her jeans pocket.

"Not too much thinking to do on this one," Billy said, lounging back in his chair with stout in hand. "It has to do with whether or not Colin will invite ye back."

Her eyes widened in shock. Of course she'd go back, but as her gaze drifted toward the paper, she saw that not many people felt the same way. A long string of names had been written under the nay column, and not a one had voted aye.

"Is there some reason every single one of you in here voted against my chances?"

"Aye," Billy said, drinking his stout without commenting further.

"I'm waiting," Emily said, glaring at the sly gentleman.

"Colin never invites a woman back a second time. They either stay, or they leave."

Well, that was a bit of news she didn't want to swallow.

Emily slapped her pound note on the table. "Put me under the aye column."

"Ye sure you wanna do that?"

She smiled, not the least bit sure she had any chance of winning, but she had to think positive. She wanted her photographs. She wanted to see Colin. "Aye."

Seamus pulled a pencil from his shirt pocket and scribbled her name on the paper. What do you know—she was betting on her own love life or lack thereof.

Climbing back on the bar stool, she ordered a ploughman's lunch, and just as Meg slid the heaping plate of ham, cheese, apple and a roll onto the bar, the door opened to let in a stream of light and a stranger, a short, thin man with a balding head that Emily hadn't seen before.

"Good morning, Meg." The stranger took the stool next to Emily and immediately slugged down a quarter of the stout Meg had poured for him before he sat.

"Good morn, Hugh. Yer in early today."

"Colin sent me, or I wouldn't have been in till dinner." He reached into his coat pocket and pulled out an expensive-looking cream-colored envelope with the distinctive Dunbar whisky pitchfork insignia embossed on the back flap. Slowly he cocked his head to his right. "Are you Emily Sinclair?"

"Yes."

"I'm Hugh MacTavish, secretary to Colin Dunbar. He asked me to give you this."

Meg leaned against the bar as Emily's trembling fingers reached for the envelope. For the longest time she stared at her name scripted on the front in bold black ink; then, taking a deep breath, she peeled open the envelope and took the embossed card from inside.

Behind her she heard the scraping of chairs and the clomping of shoes as Billy, Seamus, and Iain raced to look over her shoulder.

Reading privately was impossible, so she held the note up for all to see.

> Emily,
> I have another proposition. If you're interested, come for dinner at eight.
>
> Colin

Relief, not to mention sheer, maddening excitement, rushed through her, but it was a self-satisfied smile that touched Emily's face when she held her palm out to the characters in the pub.

"It appears I've won this morning's wager." Oh, the joy of victory. "So, what are we going to bet on now?"

*B*utterflies had taken up residence in Emily's stomach by the time eight o'clock rolled around, and they were furiously batting their wings as she stood in front of the great entrance to the castle. All day she'd wondered about Colin's proposition. All day she'd wondered if she was just another puir wee lassie being lured to the devil's lair.

The door opened slowly, and the stunning Highlander smiled down on her.

"Good evening."

Said the spider to the fly.

An off-white cashmere sweater hugged his chest and hard, flat stomach. A lock of ebony hair tumbled over his brow. Gorgeous! Just gorgeous. She quickly thanked the fates for putting him in a charcoal suit; she'd half expected him to be in a kilt, and then she would have spent the rest of the evening wondering what was under it rather than leading Colin toward a business deal.

Of course, the way his own gaze lingered over her attire gave her the distinct impression that he had no interest at all in talking business. She had, however, taken away his ability to study her anatomy too closely. Meg had told her to wear as little as possible—more than likely the woman and the gents in her pub had placed bets on how fast Colin could get her out of her clothes—but Emily hadn't dressed scantily. She'd dressed elegantly. Tastefully. In layers. She'd had to make a mad dash to Inverness to find something appropriate to wear out to dinner in a castle with a handsome laird, and in a petite shop she'd found a beautiful sapphire silk bolero, black silk tank top, and baggy black silk pants. She'd capped the outfit off with new silver jewelry and strappy, four-inch spiked sandals. She'd even found a manicurist to do her nails and splurged on a pedicure.

This was business, of course, but there was no rule that said she couldn't look her best. Considering the way Colin had looked at her, she felt she'd done a darn good job getting ready for their little tête-à-tête.

At last Colin tucked her hand around his arm, where she could feel big, strong muscles that made her all giddy inside, and led her through the great hall.

"So, Emily Sinclair, tell me what you did today."

What a great opening. "I spent a lot of time thinking

about your proposition." There was no need telling him about the massage she'd gotten to ease her nerves. "Could we discuss it before dinner?"

He stopped in front of a blazing fireplace, curled his index finger under her chin, and tilted her face to meet his intense but smiling eyes. "Could we pretend for an hour or so that you came here for reasons other than business?"

"Business is all I know."

He chuckled lightly. "It didn't feel that way when I kissed you last night."

It was time for a good explanation. She couldn't actually let him think that she'd enjoyed the kiss. "I'd had too much whisky."

He took a half step closer and tilted her face just a little higher. "Have you had any whisky today?"

Half hypnotized by his eyes and his Sean Connery voice, she shook her head.

"Good." A slight smile lifted the corners of his lips. "We'll try the kiss again."

Even if she'd wanted to, he didn't give her time to object. His mouth was on hers in an instant, and contrary to what she thought she'd do, she didn't fight. She simply enjoyed. Immensely.

Soft. Oh, so soft. She put a hand on his chest and felt his heart beating through his cashmere sweater. Felt her own heart quivering while the butterflies in her stomach began to kick up their wings. He felt good—wonderful— and it would be so easy to fall into his embrace, but she'd let that happen once before in her life. Let a man steal her heart, her dreams, her hopes, and then her ideas.

She would not fall so easily again.

With her hand still against his rapidly beating heart, she gave a gentle push and stepped back, giving herself room to breathe, to think straight.

"Did you ask me here to proposition me, or because you have a proposition to discuss?"

"Because you intrigue me. A lot of women have bored me lately. You don't."

"So I'm to be your evening's entertainment?"

"I thought we could entertain each other. I show you the arched hallway you expressed an interest in during the tour, and then we retire to the game room for a little fun."

The eight-foot leather sofa in front of the fireplace instantly sprang to mind. Was that the kind of fun he was thinking of? "What did you want to do? Play chess? Billiards? Gin rummy?" She had tried to sound professional, but she had the horrid feeling a touch of seductive temptress accented her words.

"Poker."

"One of my best games." Thankfully! "I have four brothers, and they never could figure out when I was bluffing."

"It'll be interesting to see how straight a face you can keep while we play."

"I'm very good at hiding emotions."

He smiled slyly. "Good. We'll have another battle of wills. That's one of the things I like so much about you."

At least she knew he liked her. Maybe he liked her enough to talk business.

"Now that we have the entertainment part of our evening planned, could we discuss your proposition?"

He tugged her hand through his arm again. "After dinner. As I said, pretend I'm not someone you want to do business with . . . at least for an hour or two."

It sounded like a fair enough plan. "All right."

Candles flickered in the great dining room, their glow bouncing off the crystal, china, and elegant silver. The fragrance of hundreds of roses engulfed her, and so did their blossoms, which sprang from nearly a dozen bouquets.

Ever the gentleman, Colin held her chair, then scooted it in once she sat down. At any moment now she expected a butler or two in elegant black livery to step out from behind the doors, but the only person who moved in the room was Colin as he walked to the far end of the table and took his place.

"Very intimate," she teased as she looked down the banquet table. "How many other people could you seat here?"

"Twenty on one side, twenty on the other. But tonight I made sure the table was smaller than usual, just for you."

"Thank you." A silver-domed plate sat before her, and she couldn't help but wonder what she'd find underneath. "Is this meant to be a surprise?"

"Only dinner," he said, a touch of mirth tilting his lips.

Hmm. She lifted the dome cautiously, wondering if the man were a tease and something would fly out to startle her. Doves, maybe. Or butterflies. Instead, something brown and terribly ugly sat on the plate before her. She frowned in confusion.

"You've never had haggis?"

"I can't say that I have." Or ever want to, she added to herself.

"It's spiced sheep innards and oatmeal. I'm sure you recognize the neeps and potatoes."

"Neeps?"

"Turnips." He laughed. "I thought you might enjoy a wee bit of Scotland."

"Then why didn't you wear a kilt?" The silly words flew right out of her mouth.

"I didn't want to alarm you with my hairy legs."

She raised an amused and very interested brow. "Are they that hairy?"

"That's something I'll let you wonder about."

Along with all the other images swimming around her head of Colin wearing a kilt.

"Go on." He lifted his knife and fork and posed them near the haggis. "Try it."

It wasn't bad, she decided after she popped the first infinitesimal morsel into her mouth. She wouldn't want a steady diet of spiced sheep innards and oatmeal, and the neeps weren't seasoned quite the way she would have prepared them, but all in all, she'd had far worse in other countries.

"Does your cook prepare haggis for you often?" she asked, slicing off another bite.

"Steak's more to my liking. Medium rare, with mushrooms and wine sauce. As for my cook, I'm without one at the moment." He chewed slowly, and she watched his mouth at work. A nice mouth. Sensual. Seductive. He'd taste quite good with wine, she imagined.

Her gaze flew back to the contents of her plate before her mind could pursue the image she'd conjured of his nude body drizzled with chocolate and raspberry sauce.

"Who made the haggis if you don't have a cook?"

"Meg made the haggis, and Billy—you may have met him at the Devil's Cup—brought it by shortly before you arrived."

"What happened to your cook?" she asked, making polite conversation.

"They don't stay long." He laughed devilishly. "There's something about the castle that frightens them away."

Her gaze flickered toward him, and she grinned. "You, perhaps?"

"I've been known to frighten a few people." His eyes seemed to smolder as he looked down the table at her. "Do I frighten you?"

She shook her head. "You intrigue me."

"Good. I'm a firm believer that all relationships should start with a little intrigue."

"I heard rumors in the pub that your relationships rarely last more than a day or two."

"Blatant lust withers quickly. Throw in a wee bit of mystery, and the desire is prolonged."

Prolonged desire sounded nice. Perhaps she could create a dessert with a lingering taste and dub it with that title. Maybe she'd feed it to Colin bit by bit.

A rush of heat blazed up her neck and into her cheeks at the thought. What on earth was going on in her mind? Was it this castle? The village? Colin? Surely they'd bewitched her; the last thing she ever did was picture herself in any of her sinful creations.

Somewhat embarrassed by her thoughts, she lifted her gaze to the far end of the table. Colin sat there, his fingers steepled in front of his face, and watched her.

"Is it too warm in here for you?" he asked.

"It's fine. Thank you."

He pushed himself up from the table, went to a side bar, and poured two tumblers full of whisky. How he could drink so much of the stuff and not get drunk amazed her, but he always seemed in control. Too much so.

"Come," he said, holding the glass out to her as she stood. "I'll show you the arched hallway now."

She took a sip of the whisky and felt the warmth drip through her until it reached her toes; then she took hold of his extended arm, and the warm drip was replaced by a flood of bubbling lava. The man was too hot, but she wasn't about to let go.

He led her through the armory, where bayonet blades and flintlock pistols hung on the walls beside decorative dirks, ancient claymores, and war-weary battle-axes. "My ancestors were merchants, not warriors," he told her. "Most of what you see here was collected by them from the battlegrounds long after the fighting ended. It's not an honorable tale, but it's true."

"Does it disturb you?"

"It's history."

But it seemed to bother him. It wasn't the first time she'd noticed him tense when he mentioned his family's past.

At last they stopped at one end of a long and wide, cold and stark hallway. "This is it. The hall of arches."

A slight shiver raced through her, and she could clearly see why the place was infamous, why tourists were only brought here on Halloween. A series of granite arches that must have been ten feet wide and fifteen feet high ran down each side, and shockingly, at least three-fourths of the arches appeared to have been sealed with a variety of different stones.

"The first part of the castle, where the great hall is, was built in the thirteenth century. This hallway, which connects the main castle with the coach house and stables, dates from the sixteenth." He took a sip of his whisky as they walked slowly down the hall. "Each archway bears a brass plaque to honor a Dunbar wife. They're all here—every wife after Alexander's."

"Is it true that they were buried—alive—behind the walls?"

Colin laughed, the sound echoing off the stone walls. "I could find out easily enough if I knocked down the archway walls, but the mystery is far more appealing than learning the truth."

He moved a little farther down the hall, taking another swallow of whisky as he stopped beside the last walled-in arch, its plaque engraved ELIZABETH DUNBAR—1978. "This one belongs to my mother."

Emily couldn't miss the flash of pain across his face "*Your* mother?"

"Aye." He laughed cynically. "She disappeared when I was two, taking with her far more wealth than she had when she married my father—at least that's the story I was told when I was old enough to understand. I've not seen or heard from her since. As far as I know, my father could have walled her up inside this arch."

"You don't believe that happened, do you?"

He shook his head. "I don't believe ninety percent of the tales that abound around here. For the most part they're stories that have grown out of proportion over hundreds of years of telling and retelling. I'm sure some of the murders are true, and probably most of the affairs. One thing I do know, Dunbars don't have a good record for happily-ever-after marriages."

"I'm sorry."

"Don't be. The stories breed curiosity, and curiosity has equaled money for our family." Somehow, without her even knowing it, his fingers had entwined with hers, and he squeezed them tightly now. "What about your family? Any scandal?"

"No divorces. No murders. Just a bunch of good old Californians who ate dinner together every night and went to church together on Sunday. The most scandalous tale I've heard told in years had to do with a panty raid my brother got caught in at college."

"I did something similar." He laughed, a faraway look in his eyes. "Except no one got caught, and the girls had to come to my room to collect their things."

"Did you exact a price from them before you gave back the panties?"

"A kiss. But just a small one."

They walked a little farther, and she sipped her whisky, thinking that he sounded like a man who'd like a regular life for a change, or maybe a combination of what he'd always had and what she'd always known. There may have been passion in his family, but apparently there'd been no love.

"This one," Colin said, stopping in front of an arch that hadn't been walled in, "is for my wife."

Her eyes widened. "You've got to be kidding!"

"No. If I don't fill this in, eventually, I'll break a long-standing tradition."

"You wouldn't break tradition, would you?"

"If the villagers have their way, no. If I have my own way, yes."

"Mind explaining that to me?"

"The villagers have a habit of sending women my way. They even wager on my love life."

"Oh, yes, I know all about that."

He chuckled. "I suppose I can't blame them. They feel their entire existence will crumble if I don't marry and produce an heir, someone I can hand the recipe for Dunbar whisky to."

"But what about your wife?"

"I'd definitely have to do away with her to keep the tradition alive. Meg, Billy, the whole lot of them, have presented me with a list of ways to get rid of her—all in jest, of course."

"And what do you tell them?"

He shrugged. "I've told them I don't plan to marry. The tradition ends with me."

"Is that what you really want?"

He angled his head toward her, sadness and a touch of mirth oddly mixed in his intense eyes.

"Murder's not my style, and I don't believe in divorce. I'm not going to marry someone, have a child, and let her walk away. The only option I see is not to get married in the first place."

"You don't believe it's possible to have a long and happy marriage?"

He shook his head. "No."

A look of annoyance crossed his face as he raised an empty glass of whisky to his mouth. "Come on," he said, gripping her fingers and tugging her back up the hallway toward the main part of the castle. "Talk of marriage and death bores me. I think we should go to the game room—"

"And discuss your proposition."

He laughed. "Aye."

At last. Business talk. Funny, though, as good as that sounded, she wished they could continue the privately escorted tour, and even more she wished she could continue their private talk, getting to know more about his life, what was in the past and what he seemed to see for himself in the future.

Later maybe. After business.

A fire blazed in the game room that had felt so cold the night before, and he led her straight to the windows, which looked over the loch. "Do you fish?"

"I have four brothers," she said, standing at his side. "I grew up fishing, hunting, camping, and even trying to play sports."

His gaze raked over the shortness of her body. She couldn't blame him when he laughed.

"No, I wasn't good at sports," she tossed out. "I wanted to play basketball, but oddly enough"—she laughed—"I was told I was too short, and that annoyed my competitive spirit. I couldn't beat my brothers at anything but poker. I started cooking because that was something they couldn't do. I wrote the first cookbook to compete with a man who . . . well, the reason I competed with him doesn't matter. Let's just say I'm very good at what I do, I've made best-seller lists worldwide, I've been on TV shows—and that makes me very happy."

"You're not much different from the people in the village. Always trying to beat your neighbor."

"I like to win."

"I thought so." He angled his head toward her and smiled. "Which leads me to my proposition."

"Does it have anything to do with the photographs I'm going to take?"

"Aye."

He led her toward a Victorian card table and pulled out a chair. She crossed her legs after she sat down, and smiled. "I'm listening."

He went across the room and brought back a decanter of whisky and a deck of cards, which he sat on the table between them. Then he took his chair.

"Here's the deal. We play poker until the stroke of midnight or until one of us has nothing left to wager."

"And what are we playing for?"

"You win . . . you can take all the photos you want inside the castle, but they're for use in your cookbook only. They will not go on the Internet. You cannot sell them to other publications."

That was good, for a start. "What about the secret room? Is that included?"

He shook his head. "No. That's my final word on that subject."

She gritted her teeth but didn't argue. "And what do you get if I lose?"

"If I win—and I will"—he grinned—"you move into the castle and cook for me for a month."

She couldn't help but laugh at that ridiculous suggestion. "That hardly sounds like a fair exchange. People pay a small fortune to have me as a private chef."

He shrugged. "Take it or leave it."

Time to bargain.

"One week. I'll buy the food."

"All right."

"Don't agree too quickly." She leaned back in her chair and folded her arms across her chest. "I want more than that."

His brow arched. "What is it you want?"

"I want permission to photograph the interiors in my spare time, I want you to tell me some of the stories that surround the various rooms, *and* I want to have the right to search for the secret room."

"In other words, you want to come out the winner even if you lose?"

She smiled. "That's right."

Colin frowned, obviously contemplating her words, and for a moment she thought he'd call off the whole thing. Instead, he leaned back in his chair and smiled slightly, apparently resigned to her demands. "All right, but the choice of poker games is mine."

His proposition was far better than anything she'd hoped for except for him leading her straight to the secret bedroom. Of course, this was one game she couldn't win. No, she'd have to lose, because in the end she'd come out ahead.

She reached across the table to shake his hand. "It's a deal."

He smiled wickedly. "Deal."

She poured whisky into his glass and hers, then leaned back and took a sip. "How much money are we each putting up? It should be equal so neither of us has the advantage."

He looked at her over the top of his whisky glass, his eyes dancing with something akin to laughter, and suddenly she knew she'd been conned.

"There's no money involved, Emily. My game of choice is strip poker."

4

*E*mily wasn't happy. Colin could see it in the way her shoulders tensed, her jaw tightened, and her knuckles turned almost white around her glass. His proposition had been simple; she was the one who threw in all the extra little details that had made losing sound so attractive to her.

Taking off her clothes, however, hadn't figured into her scheme.

The fact that she'd have to take off her clothes was attractive to no one but him. All night long he'd pictured her naked. Not only that, he'd pictured her naked and in his arms. There was nothing in Dunbar legend that said a man couldn't have a mistress and not a wife. Mistresses were happier, more content, and those relationships always lasted longer.

And there was a possibility that he might want Emily a good long time.

What she didn't know was that she'd never find the secret room, and he wasn't sure if he'd ever show it to her. He'd have to trust her first—he'd even have to love her—and he'd never trusted or loved a woman in his life.

He leaned across the table and pushed the deck of cards toward her. "Odds usually favor the dealer. I know how much winning means to you, so be my guest."

Her jaw was set, and she stole a glance at the porcelain clock that ticked atop the table beside her chair. "We stop at midnight. Right?"

"Or till you or I have nothing left to wager."

"Too bad you aren't wearing a kilt."

"Too bad you're wearing layers. I'd hoped you'd come tonight in a slinky evening gown. One ante—your dress—and I'd come out the winner no matter what."

She was loosening up a bit. Not as tense—yet. Her pretty green eyes sparkled as she dealt the cards, but she didn't look at him when she responded. "I was told your lady friends usually come to dinner scantily clad. I wasn't about to fall into the trap."

He found himself smiling. "That's quite all right. Slow strip teases are far more fascinating." And watching Emily strip would be the most enticing, exciting experience in his life.

He stood for a moment, took off his coat, and tossed it onto the center of the table. "That's the ante."

She slipped off her jacket, folded it carefully, and

placed it over his. She was stalling for time, and he knew it. That was quite all right. Stretching out the pleasure of her company was all he wanted right now.

Emily lifted her cards and watched Colin lift his, too. The game had begun, leaving her tense and even a little confused at why she was going through with this. Was getting photos inside Colin's castle all that important? Was it worth stripping for? How would she feel about all of this—about herself—when the game was over?

Suddenly the butterflies in her stomach had multiplied and were fluttering at a maddening pace. Her heart was doing the same. There was no need to worry about the consequences now; she was already in the game. She'd worry later.

Lifting her cards, she took a peak. A straight, ten high. Not bad for the first hand, but she kept her poker face, refusing to let her delight show.

"How many cards?" she asked.

He smiled slightly. Was his look one that said, I have a fabulous hand, or a smile that said, It's crap, but I'm planning to bluff? He closed the cards within his palm. "I don't need a one."

She tossed him the same enigmatic smile. "None for me, either."

Lifting his whisky glass, he took a sip, then stood, pulled off his belt, and tossed it atop the coats.

Slowly she did the same. "I'll see your belt and raise you—" What? She gritted her teeth, pulled off one of her strappy sandals, and plopped it on the belts. "I'll raise you one shoe."

Not the least bit daunted, he took off one shoe and

then another, and set them beside hers as the pile of clothing rose. "I'll see you another shoe."

She took off her second shoe, set it neatly on the table, then looked at her hand to decide if she wanted to go any further. Finally she said, "Call."

He laid his hand down on the table. "Full house."

Thank goodness! "Straight." She swept up everything but her initial ante and tossed his coat, shoes, and belt on the floor behind her. Slowly she put her shoes back on as well as her belt.

Emily couldn't miss his frown as he watched her dress. Colin Dunbar thought she wanted to win. Oh, no, not on her life. She planned to lose at the stroke of midnight, not before, and she planned still to be wearing clothes when it happened. She'd rarely lost at poker, but this time she had to, to find that secret room.

What Colin didn't know was that she planned to lose in her own way.

"Ante up," she said.

As much as she'd thought about Colin's naked body, she hadn't imagined anything quite like what she saw when he pulled his sweater over his head and tossed it onto the table.

Bronzed. Buff. Beautiful.

She took a quick sip of whisky and studied his muscles over the top of her glass. Lots of muscles and a dark mat of hair across his chest that V'ed into a slim line of hair right below his pecs. That slim line meandered under the waistband of his pants. It was a sinful thought, but she could easily imagine her hand meandering there as well.

The prospect of seeing Colin with nothing on fascinated her. So did seeing his secret room.

A tough decision lay before her: win, and she could see every inch of Colin's body; lose, and she could have a week in his castle, a week of taking photos, a week of searching for the secret room—and a week being with Colin.

And spending a week with Colin surely would lead to seeing every inch of his delicious physique.

A wicked smile touched her mouth. Losing was her only choice.

But . . . would Colin keep his promise if she lost?

She'd given a man everything once. He'd promised to love her forever, but everything he'd said had been a lie. He'd deceived her and in the end stole her recipes, her ideas, and ended up selling 2 million cookbooks before his second book fizzled and no publisher would option a third.

Would Colin end up hurting her, too?

"Getting cold feet?" Colin asked as she hesitantly dealt their next hands.

She shook her head, and decided on a whim that Colin would not deceive her. Something about him made her think that under the shameless behavior lay an honorable man. "I'm the one wearing shoes," she answered. "Remember."

"Things could easily change with just one deal of the cards." He grinned as he looked at his hand. "I'm going to win, Emily. Count on it."

Three hands later Colin was down to his trousers and nothing more. He casually leaned back in his chair, not the least uncomfortable that he was slowly losing all his clothes, that his body was exposed to her wandering eye. When Emily dealt another hand, he glared at his cards for the longest time, then stood, pulled off his pants, and tossed them on the table.

Emily's gaze drifted to his black silk boxers, which rested low on his hips. His legs were hairy, just as he'd said, but they didn't frighten her a bit. She wanted to reach over and run her fingers through the hair, wanted to know if it was soft or coarse. And then, goodness knows why, she wanted to know what his legs would feel like trapped between hers.

She dragged in a deep, calming breath and tried to concentrate on losing.

"Excuse me. Emily?"

Her eyes flickered across the table to catch the grin on his face. "Yes?"

"That was my raise. One pair of trousers."

"Oh."

She looked at her cards. A flush, something terribly hard to beat. What to do, what to do? The game could easily end here and now. She could take her photographs—of everything but the secret room—and be gone in a few days.

But she wanted more.

She wanted Colin.

So she folded.

He didn't question her move. He merely smiled, put his pants back on along with the watch he'd wagered during that hand, then tossed her bolero and shoes behind him.

Another hand was dealt. He drew three cards. She drew three as well.

He bet both socks. She tossed her ring on the table and called.

He had two eights. She had two sevens.

Again she dealt.

He bet both socks again.

She looked at him over the top of her cards. "I don't have any socks. I no longer have a watch. What would you say is an equal value?"

A wicked smile danced on his lips. "Your blouse or pants will do."

Either was worth far more than a pair of socks, but what was she to do when she had nothing else to bet?

Slowly she unbuttoned her blouse, watching the clock ticking closer and closer to midnight. If she drew this out, maybe she could lose with at least an ounce of dignity left.

Colin cleared his throat. "No fair stalling."

"Fine!"

She tugged the blouse from her body and watched Colin's gaze fix on her breasts. "I'd expected you to be the white cotton type, not sheer blue silk."

"That shows how little you know about me."

"I aim to know a lot more before we're through."

Afraid to go any further, to raise, she laid her cards faceup on the table. "Call."

His eyes darted from her breasts to her measly pair of jacks, then laid down his twos and sixs. "I'm afraid two pair win this round."

She put her hands on everything she'd wagered and shoved it across the table. "Why don't we just consider the game over? I lose."

His lips tilted at the corners as he shook his head. "It's not midnight, and you still have things left to bet."

He tossed his watch back on the table, then took a sip of whisky. "Ante up."

She slid her glass across the table, right in front of his

laughing eyes. "Could you fill this for me? Please."

"Gladly."

While he poured, she stood, unfastened the button on her pants, slowly peeled down the side zipper, and let her baggy trousers fall to the floor.

He pushed the whisky toward her. "Blue silk panties, too." His eyes flickered toward hers. "You have a lovely body, Emily. You shouldn't hide it behind suits."

She felt a blush rise to her cheeks—whether from his blazing stare or from the whisky she didn't know—but plopped back down in her chair and dealt the cards very, very slowly. It was five minutes until midnight.

At last she had a winning hand again. It wasn't enough to keep her from losing their match, just enough to keep her from losing her bra and her panties. It was her turn to bet first, so she merely laid down her cards. "Call."

He stared at her three jacks, then smiled and plunked down three queens and a pair of fours. "Full house."

He swept the pot onto the floor, all but his watch, then tossed a smug grin her way. "Ante up."

All she had left to ante was a sheer silk bra and matching panties. Oh, hell, what did it matter if she took everything off? What she was wearing didn't leave a whole lot to the imagination.

She sucked in a deep breath and let it out in a huff. Then her hands went behind her to unfasten her bra.

"Wait a minute."

"Is there a problem? Have you decided you don't want to see what's under here?"

"I'm very interested in seeing everything, Emily. I just think the moment calls for a more intimate atmosphere."

Emily looked at the clock as Colin walked across the

room. Three minutes until midnight. She was losing, and time was running out. If he wanted an intimate atmosphere, that was fine by her. The longer he took creating it, the longer she could keep her undies on.

Slowly the lights dimmed in the room, and then went off entirely. The only illumination came from the dying embers in the fireplace and the moonlight shining across the card table.

"There." He sat down again. "A more intimate atmosphere. A little more mystery and intrigue."

"You want to play in the dark now? You realize I could cheat."

"You won't. And you already know I'm going to win, but winning doesn't mean I want the mystery to end here and now. I can have the satisfaction of *knowing* you're wearing nothing. When I actually *see* you that way—which is going to happen sooner or later, because you want it as much as I do—I want to see you in full light, and I want you to be comfortable letting me see every beautiful inch of you."

"You're awfully sure of yourself, aren't you?"

"I try to be. You're sure of yourself, too. But underneath all that bravado you've got an innocence about you, too. The mixture is what I enjoy."

He was a smug devil—one who was surely out to take her soul.

Why couldn't this game just end!

The clock ticked. Two minutes to midnight. "Why don't we quit right now," Emily suggested, "since we already know I'm going to lose."

"I want you to lose fair and square." She could almost see his smile in the dark. "It's your turn to ante up."

She unfastened her bra and slowly pulled it from her body, hoping he wasn't deceiving her, hoping he didn't intend to flip on the lights.

The bra dropped from her fingers to the table. The only saving grace was that the firelight was behind her, making her body probably little more than a silhouette to him. Still, the thought of sitting in front of him, almost stark naked, made her anxious inside, wondering—fearing—what was going to happen next.

Slowly she dealt five cards. He took none. She took three, hoping she could at least draw a queen or ace to match what she'd kept in her hand. She didn't even come close.

He tugged his sweater off and tossed it on the table. "That's my bet. Are you going to see it?"

All she had left were her panties.

She folded.

He took a sip of whisky. "One more deal. One more ante."

"Fine!"

The butterflies had fluttered together into one big heavy ball that sat heavily at the pit of her stomach as she reached for her panties. Why couldn't this just be over and done with?

She took a deep breath, and Colin leaned across the table, reached for the porcelain clock, and pushed the minute hand to midnight. Mercifully it began to toll the witching hour.

Was he a gentleman? Or was he merely toying with her, trying to suck her into some other ploy? It didn't really matter what he was doing. She was annoyed with him for suggesting this game, for winning, and for being so smug. She was annoyed with herself for at least a million and one reasons, chief among them the fact that she'd agreed to this game in the first place.

To top it off, she hated what he might be thinking about her right now.

"Would you like some more whisky?" he asked.

"No, thank you."

"Would you like to slip into my sweater?"

The man was so completely maddening. Were his polite gestures meant to make her happy? He'd saved her from total humiliation, but she still felt as if she'd just sold herself to the devil.

No longer caring how little she wore, she stalked toward his chair, grabbed her clothes, and yanked them back on, knowing and not caring that she was a disheveled mess.

"I haven't congratulated you on losing," he said. "It was what you wanted, wasn't it?"

Annoyance burned inside her. "I lost fair and square. Please don't forget that that means I have complete access to your castle."

"It also means you'll cook for me."

"I haven't forgotten. I'll treat you to the best meals you've ever had."

He grinned in spite of her sudden fury. She'd wanted to lose, but now she just wanted to get out of his sin-filled castle and think about what she'd done.

"You won't poison me?" he asked as he turned the lights back on.

"That's how *Dunbars* get rid of people they tire of. Sinclairs do what they agree to."

"You agreed to live here for a week, too."

"Don't worry," she said, shoving her feet into her shoes. "I'll be back bright and early tomorrow morning."

She stalked out of the game room and headed down the hall.

"The front door's to the right, not to the left," came the laughing voice from behind her.

She stomped her foot, something she hadn't done since she was a little girl. She had to walk by Colin again to get out of the castle, and annoyingly, he latched onto her arm.

"Before you get lost, why don't you let me walk you to your car?"

"I'm perfectly capable of getting there on my own."

"But I'm a gentleman."

She stopped in the middle of the hallway and glared up at him. "Are you?"

"I can be."

"Prove it."

"All right, I won't touch you for an entire week. Fair enough?"

"Does this mean you'll stay out of my hair?"

"No, lass, it simply means I won't touch you. It doesn't, however, mean I won't watch you, that I won't try to get you to touch me. And let me tell you this, Emily, it definitely doesn't mean I won't want you."

5

*E*mily sat at one end of the exceedingly long dining room table and tried to concentrate on the
steak and eggs she'd prepared for breakfast, but it was
physically impossible to concentrate on anything with
Colin sitting at the far end of the table, watching her.

He seemed to have worked out a well-engineered
method for observation: cut steak, stab it, place in mouth,
lean casually back in chair, and stare while you chew.

They were having their first meal of Day Number 1. If
this went on through every meal—four of them each day
for seven days—it would be a very long week of servitude.

She lounged back in her own chair, finding it impossible to eat, and swirled orange juice in her glass. "Are you
going to eat or stare at me all day?"

Colin flashed a smug smile down the length of the table. "I have work to keep me occupied most of the day. During meals, however, I fully intend to enjoy myself, and that, lass, means looking at you."

He raised his glass of orange juice to his mouth and watched her over the top. "You're rather beautiful in the morning. No makeup, curly hair flying about, blouse buttoned crookedly."

Emily's gaze darted to the front of her shirt; sure enough, one side hung down farther than the other, and it gaped across her breasts. "I had a rough morning." Go ahead, Emily, tell him the truth. "To be perfectly honest, being here with you now and the thought of being with you for an entire week makes me terribly nervous."

"I can't think of a reason in the world for you to be nervous. I promised I wouldn't touch you for a week—a full seven days—and I always keep my promises."

"I hope that means you haven't changed your mind about me taking pictures of the interiors. You did say I could go anywhere I want in the castle."

"Feel free to go anywhere you want, except into the rooms I keep locked."

"And how many of those are there?"

"Two. My office and my bedroom."

Neither of which interested her. "There's only one bedroom I'd like to get into, and it's not yours."

"How could I have forgotten?" He leaned forward to cut another piece of steak. "You lost our little poker game just so you could have the privilege of finding the secret bedroom."

"Why does that annoy you so much? I made my intentions perfectly clear the first time we met. I came here to photograph the inside of your castle, something no one has ever done before, and now I'm going to have the privilege of doing exactly what I want."

"Does the end justify the means?"

"Don't go throwing that game of strip poker in my face. I had no idea you were going to impose something like that on me until after we'd made our deal. You could have chosen a regular game of poker, but no, you wanted to humiliate me—"

"I wanted to look at your body; that's why I chose the game I did. I wanted to see every inch of you because I like looking at you. That was my only motive. Humiliating you didn't enter the picture."

He shoved up from the table. "You're going to be here for a week, Emily. You can pretend to hate me for the next seven days if you want, but I assure you, this week would be a hell of a lot more enjoyable if you'd come down off your high horse and realize that you enjoy my company every bit as much as I enjoy yours."

With that said, he tossed his linen napkin onto his plate, favored her with a maddeningly seductive smile and walked from the dining room.

It wasn't until she sat all alone that she realized he was right. She did enjoy his company. He wrung every possible emotion out of her and made her feel really and truly alive.

And if truth be told, she enjoyed the way he watched her. In turn, she enjoyed watching him.

*C*olin hid in a dark corner of the stark, cold dungeon and watched Emily. By rights he should be in the distillery working, but he hadn't been able to concentrate on anything or anyone besides Emily since she'd arrived yesterday morning. She was the distraction he'd needed for years. A beautiful distraction, and it was going to be hell keeping his hands off of her.

She moved slowly, touching the rack, the manacles, the cold stone walls where dates and names had been etched hundreds of years before. She was dressed in walking shoes, jeans, and a bright green sweater, the same emerald color as her eyes. Her hips swayed. So did her breasts, and not for the first time he wondered how it would feel to cup them in the palms of his hands. Soft. Very soft, topped off by taut, pebbled nipples that he'd like to squeeze gently between his thumb and index finger, then suck into his mouth to savor, to tease.

But he couldn't touch her. That was the hell of it. He'd made a promise—a foolish one, but a promise nonetheless. He might not come from a family of honorable men, but he was trying damned hard to change the image of the Dunbar line before it died away with him.

Since honorable men didn't hide in the dark to watch beautiful women, he stepped from the alcove. "Looking for something?"

She spun around, and he could see a flash of surprised shock, perhaps fright, in her face. And then the look softened into a smile.

"You weren't watching me again, were you?"

"I could tell you no, but that wouldn't be the truth."

He walked across the dungeon and leaned casually against a wall. "Are you still looking for the secret bedroom?"

"I am, but I'm having no luck."

She could look forever, but she'd never find it. He was the only one who knew the truth about the secret bedroom, and he'd told himself he'd never tell a soul. Still, he didn't want to dash her hopes. Why shouldn't she enjoy the legends, myths, and beliefs surrounding the Dunbar family, just as the villagers did?

"Do you even know what you're looking for?"

She laughed. "No. I assume it's something grand and hidden behind a mysterious door that will fly open if I find the right thing to push."

"Could be."

"You're not going to give me a hint, are you?"

He shook his head slowly. "I don't think, however, that you'll find it down here."

"I didn't think so, but I thought I'd look while I was scouting out places to use as backdrops for my desserts."

"For some reason I don't picture luscious desserts finding their way down here any more than romantic trysts or secret bedrooms."

"You have to have a vivid imagination to put everything together, even in the best of places."

"Which one of your desserts would you put here?"

"Something new. I don't know. Maybe sweet chocolate crepes filled with fresh mixed berries, served on a cloud of thick whipped cream, drizzled with raspberry sauce, and garnished with entwined dark and white chocolate hearts."

"Just what every imprisoned man dreamed of having while he rotted in a thirteenth-century dungeon."

"Think pleasure, not pain."

He'd been thinking pleasure ever since he'd met her. He didn't even care what she wanted from him any longer. The secret room didn't matter. Photographing the interiors of his castle didn't matter. He liked her and would give her anything she wanted—except his heart and his soul. Dunbar men didn't have those to give.

"So, what are you going to call this latest dessert of yours?"

"I was thinking *Locked in Love's Embrace*."

Colin laughed, the sound echoing through the stark stone room. "People actually buy stuff like that?"

She hit him with a look of righteous indignation. "I don't laugh at your whisky."

"That's because it's straightforward. It's strong and potent. That's what a man needs down here."

"All right, loan me a bottle of your best, and I'll photograph it with my dessert."

"Only if I can watch."

A slight smile tilted her lips. "You have a thing about watching, don't you?"

"I have a thing about touching, too. Unfortunately, my hands are tied for the next six days."

"You don't have to keep them tied on my account."

Ah, she wanted him to touch her, to drive her wild. But he couldn't. Not now.

"I'm honor-bound. I promised not to touch, and I firmly intend to stick to it. Besides, if I could touch you, I might lose interest in everything else, and then I'd miss out on the talks we've been having. I've enjoyed learning about your business, your family life, and everything else about you far more than I ever imagined."

She looked overwhelmed by his statement. Surprised. Shocked. Hell, he was surprised and shocked, too.

And then she strolled toward him, her hips and breasts

swaying slightly. He was still leaning against the thick stone wall as she walked up good and close, stretched up on tiptoe, and planted a warm, soft, lingering kiss on his lips.

"Thank you."

"For what?" he asked, trying to keep control of his on-fire emotions as well as his hands, when she pulled away.

"For talking. I've enjoyed it, too."

Apparently Colin liked to talk. He'd done it nonstop for nearly seven days, and even though Emily had been interested in their discussions, there was so much more she wanted from him.

Darn it, she wanted Colin to touch her! A woman could only work and talk so long in the presence of a gorgeous hunk before she had every right to get frustrated. And she was frustrated now.

She'd never met a man who could make her want him merely by glancing up at her and smiling while he read the morning paper. Then there were those moments when he'd walk up from the distillery smelling like peat smoke, come into the kitchen and swipe a piece of cheese or fruit or one of her candies, toss her a wink, then disappear up to his room for a shower.

Seven days of being around him and not having him touch her had been torture. Seven days of his smiles, his friendly banter, his all-out sexiness and self-assuredness, had planted him firmly in her head and—lo and behold—in her heart.

Thoughts of him haunted her days as she worked in the kitchen, went into the village for groceries, and searched for the secret room. Dreams of him wakened her in the middle of the night, when she found herself rolling over and wishing he were lying by her side, keeping her company as he did when they shared their meals, when they talked and laughed, when he kept her caught up in his life.

She felt a closeness with Colin that she'd never known with any other man.

And she wanted him to touch her. She'd tired of his promise, tired of him smiling at her but never moving toward her. That was going to come to a screeching halt today—she had a plan. A good plan. A seductive plan.

If Colin Dunbar's resolve didn't crumble after she put this plan in motion, something was dreadfully wrong— with both of them.

At precisely eight P.M., Colin walked into the dining room, and Emily relinquished control of her heart and stomach to the butterflies that had taken up residence inside. They were flying fast, doing dips and rollovers that made her entire body quiver—not from nervousness, but from need. Every day she wanted him more.

As usual, he was stunning. While he wore bulky wool sweaters and jeans at breakfast, and a polo shirt with his jeans for lunch and tea, he'd come down to dinner every night in lightweight wool dress slacks—usually charcoal—and a cashmere sweater. Tonight his sweater was the palest cream, and it hung loosely over the hard, muscular angles of his body. If she hadn't already sold her soul to him, she might sell it again, just so she could have a chance to reach out and touch those muscles and angles and anything else she could reach.

She hadn't seen him since early morning, and as he

walked toward her, she realized just how much she'd missed him during the day. This morning, as part of her plan to seduce him, bewitch him, and otherwise drive him wild, she'd gone to Inverness and purchased a long, skimpy dress that was meant for one thing and one thing only: seduction.

Considering the fire dancing in Colin's eyes as he gazed at her now, her plan was going according to schedule. Considering the way he shoved his hands into his pants pockets, she knew she looked mighty tempting, and his hands-off stance might crumble at any moment.

"Did you get everything you needed in Inverness?" he asked, circling her slowly, getting a 360-degree view of her body and its skin-hugging black leather gown, with a slit that ran from hem to thigh.

"I did. Mushrooms. Shrimp. Asparagus. I also picked up this dress. I thought you might like it."

He withdrew one hand from his pocket and rubbed his fingers over his smooth, freshly shaved chin as he studied more of the skimpy dress. "Rest assured, Emily, I like it. Quite a lot."

She smiled softly, glad that he approved. That would make her plan of seduction a little easier.

"And what about the cold meals I left you? I know our bargain was for me to cook fine food, which to me means freshly prepared, but I hope you didn't mind pulling the plates out of the refrigerator."

"I didn't mind."

He stopped circling and stood in front of her now, hot, needy eyes staring down at her four-inch, strappy black leather sandals, not to mention her candy-apple-red toenails. Those big dark sapphires that sparkled in his eyes meandered slowly up her sleek and soft leather halter dress, hesitating for a moment at her knees, her hips, her waist, then taking a long, leisurely stroll over her breasts. At last he found her eyes.

She watched his powerful chest rise and fall beneath his sweater as he drew in a breath. "You look . . . beautiful."

"Thank you. I've decided business suits are too cumbersome when I'm working. Dresses like this give me more freedom to move."

He scanned the long, foodless length of the dining room table, then turned toward her and raised a questioning brow. "And what kind of work are you doing tonight? Obviously it has nothing to do with feeding the man who won your services for a week."

"I haven't forgotten your ravenous appetite. In fact, I've whipped up some delectable appetizers that will more than satisfy your hunger."

"And where, pray tell, is this food?"

"Upstairs. In a rather delightful room I discovered today. My camera's set up. The food's ready for you to enjoy. All that's missing is you and me." She smiled and held out her hand. "Come. I'll show you the way."

Just as she'd hoped, he reached toward her, then stopped when his fingers were only inches away. His grinning eyes looked down on her as he slowly pulled his hands back. Obviously he wasn't quite yet ready to go back on his word. "Why don't we walk side by side?"

"All right."

They walked silently through the great hall and up the circular stairs to the third floor, strolling down another hallway and up another set of steps until they reached a round tower room with cathedral-shaped stained-glass windows. They weren't just any windows, however. Each one depicted a man wooing a woman—from courtship to . . . well, to advanced stages of knowing and loving each other very, very thoroughly.

"I thought this tower would be the perfect backdrop for one of my desserts," Emily said. It was the perfect place for a lot of things, she thought, like falling in love—if she could just get Colin interested.

Instead he walked around the tower room, his hands folded behind his back as he inspected her tripod and camera, the lighting equipment, and the table laden with covered dishes. "What's under here?"

"Your dinner, and a few candies I whipped up yesterday. I've called them 'To Die For.'" He lifted the cover and took a peek at the chocolate confections. "They're truffles," she told him, "but not just any truffles. I've filled the inside with cream, dark chocolate, butter, and Dunbar whisky—from your private reserve, of course. They're delicious. Would you like to try one?"

"After dinner, maybe."

Maybe she'd feed them to him after dinner, then kiss the chocolate from his lips.

Goodness, her thoughts amazed her. Wasn't it less than ten days ago that she'd been not the least bit interested in men, only business? And look at her now. Work all but forgotten, she was out to seduce a tall, dark, and handsome Highlander. One who wasn't cooperating at all.

No, Colin was circling the room again, the truffles, his dinner, and his companion not capturing his attention quite the way she'd planned. Did she have to literally throw herself at him? Wasn't temptation enough? She was a businesswoman, for heaven's sake! She'd never seduced a man in her life.

This was going all wrong; he was much more interested in the dangerously sensual stained-glass windows than he was in her.

She sighed heavily, and he turned around and almost devoured her with his stare.

That was much, much better.

"I think you need one of my chocolates," she said, plucking one of her favorites from a plate. "Open," she said, and he smiled as she walked toward him. Slowly. Letting her hips sway just the slightest bit.

His lips parted as she held the truffle toward his mouth. He took only half, and she was forced to pop the rest between her lips and onto her tongue. They stared at each other as the richness melted in their mouths, as he tucked his hands into his pants pockets, as her heart raced.

If her seduction efforts weren't working on him, they were definitely working on herself.

"Do you like it?" she asked, licking the mixture of whisky and chocolate from her lips.

Intense eyes burned into hers. "I like it very much. All of it."

She circled around him, just as he'd circled her, looking at the contour of his body, the breadth of his shoulders, the slimness of his hips. The way he continually had to catch his breath.

"Do you like this room, too?"

He laughed. "I got quite an education coming here as a boy."

"I would have thought this place would be off limits to a child."

"Only if you got caught. I usually came in the middle of the night when people were asleep or . . . occupied. I could do all the looking I wanted."

She laughed at his declaration. "You didn't really learn about sex here, did you?"

"I learned that I wanted to know a lot more about it. In college I thought I'd learned everything there was to know, but I was wrong. And now I try to learn something new whenever I can." He casually leaned against one of the thick windows, a woman's naked, stained-glass breast peeking over his shoulder. "What about you?"

"All I know is what I learned from a chef who dumped me." It had stopped hurting years ago, and she could joke about it now. "He wasn't nearly as imaginative as the man who designed these windows."

"There's been no one since?"

She shook her head. "Only my work."

"Work never kept anyone warm at night."

"No, but I've bought some lovely down comforters, and I snuggle up with them while I write my stories."

"They provide warmth, but where's the inspiration?"

"That's what I get from my travels, from places like this castle of yours, and from people willing to tell me stories." She looked around her at the lustful illustrations. "There must be dozens of stories you could tell me about this room and the people who've used it, and I'm not thinking about daydreaming boys."

"I'm sure I could dredge something up and tell you later, maybe in front of a fire, with a glass of whisky."

Hmm, was he coming on to her now?

He walked to the far side of the tower and lounged in a gold brocade Louis XVI chair that was dwarfed by him, crossing his legs at the ankles. "Do you want a sinful story?" he asked. "Are you interested in murder and intrigue? Or do you want a combination?"

"A combination would be lovely," she said, handing him a tumbler of whisky. He wrapped his fingers around the glass, careful not to touch her, but still she could feel his heat, could feel the tension that crackled between them as they watched each other's every move.

"Are you hungry?" She used her most seductive voice when she asked.

All he did was nod, his eyes glancing from her face, down the curve of her throat, to her breasts, and then he looked up at her through his dark lashes and smiled. "Starved."

She sincerely hoped so!

She went to the table across the room and heaped a gold-bordered white china plate with a variety of cold finger foods like asparagus and cheese rolled inside thinly sliced ham and plump mushrooms stuffed with spicy marinated shrimp, giving him many tempting tastes and textures to dine on.

"I hope you'll like what I've prepared for you."

"I've enjoyed everything so far." His voice deepened. "Everything, Emily, particularly you."

"Enough to touch me?"

He shook his head slowly. "You know I can't do that. The honor of the Dunbar name is at stake."

She laughed. "I didn't think there was much honor to be found in your family's past."

"It's starting with me. New traditions, you know."

"Too bad. I rather like the lusty nature of your ancestors."

"And I rather like this new you."

"How much?"

A smile tilted his lips. "Have patience, Emily. When our week is over, I'll show you just how much."

"Can you wait that long?"

"I'm doing fine. How about you?"

She circled his chair, threading her fingers through his hair, sliding them gently over his cheek and lips, before she walked toward the table where their dinner awaited. "I'm doing fine, too." It was a bald-faced lie, of course. The fact that he wouldn't touch her made her want him that much more.

She selected one of the fattest shrimp-stuffed mushrooms from a china plate and walked toward his chair. "Try this."

He absentmindedly licked his lips before opening them slightly and biting into the succulent canapé. A small smile of delight danced in his eyes as he chewed.

When she pulled her hand away, she couldn't help but notice that a tiny speck of shrimp had caught between his lips. Unable to stop herself, she leaned forward and slowly licked it away with the tip of her tongue.

Shocked at what she'd done, by her sudden display of wanton hedonism, she backed away, feeling the heat rise in her cheeks.

"Don't stop, Emily. There's nothing in our rules that says you can't touch me."

"I've been in a one-sided relationship before. I'm not willing to go there again."

"When did this become one-sided?"

"When you decided not to touch me."

"Didn't anyone ever tell you not to touch something—your mother's best crystal, your father's autographed baseball?"

"Of course."

"And remember how it felt? The more forbidden it was, the more often you were told no, the more you wanted it."

"I remember."

"That's what I'm feeling right now. That's what I've felt since you moved in here. Every morning and every night I walk by your bedroom door, and I imagine you in bed. I wonder what you're wearing. If you're naked, in flannel, or in silk."

She drew in a deep breath. "You could always step inside and find out."

"I've rarely been curious about anything in my life. I've had almost everything handed to me. Money. Women. There's been little to dream about. To want or desire. Until you." His gaze searched her eyes. "Kiss me, Emily."

As if he'd hypnotized her, she walked toward the chair where he sat, slipped her hands around his neck and threaded her fingers into his hair, then leaned forward and touched her lips to his.

His chest rose as he drew in a breath. His legs parted, and she stepped between them, pressing her body close to his. He was hot. He was hard, and she could feel the tension straining in his muscles as he fought the desire to touch her.

Apparently the rules didn't apply to his mouth, because he nearly devoured her. His tongue swept around hers and danced, his teeth nipped her lips, his hot moist breath mingled with hers. She could barely breathe with a thousand and one tastes and sensations sizzling through her body, tormenting her, pleasing her. All with a kiss. An incredible kiss.

Warm. Sweet. Hot. Powerful.

Somehow she dragged herself away and drew in a ragged breath. "Touch me. Please."

"I can't. Not yet."

"I don't want to do this all alone."

"You're not alone. I'm here with you."

She knelt between his legs and lifted his sweater, pressing firm, moist kisses over his stomach, his chest. With her hands pressing against him, she looked up at his eyes and saw the desire, the passion, the need.

"Don't stop, Emily. Please. Don't stop."

She pulled his sweater up and over his head, tossing it aside as she kissed him again, his mouth joining hers in a dance that made her sigh.

Seconds ticked by. Minutes, as she luxuriated in his mesmerizing, soul-searing kiss. She wanted more, needed more, but even though he didn't touch her, she touched him, pressing her leather-covered breasts against his chest, so close his heartbeat became one with hers.

He sighed against her mouth and she knew he wanted just as much from her as she wanted from him, yet still he didn't reach out for her.

Tearing herself from the sensual feel and delectable taste of his mouth, she whispered kisses slowly down his corded throat, over his chest, which rose and fell heavily as if he labored for breath. Her tongue teased his hard, flat stomach, his belly-button, and traced the edge of his waistband. Slowly her trembling fingers touched his belt buckle, and she looked up at Colin and smiled.

Suddenly his hands were on her face, his palms cupping her cheeks and dragging her mouth toward his again. "God, Emily. Forgive me for touching you, but I can't hold back any longer."

"Forgive you?" She laughed with delight. "Touch me everywhere, Colin. Please."

In only a minute he had her out of the leather dress, and she had him out of every stitch of clothing. They stood in front of the stained-glass windows and looked into each other's eyes for just a moment, just long enough for her to see the longing in his eyes.

Slowly her gaze drifted lower, lower, and she saw what she wanted and desired, almost as much as she wanted and desired his love. He was blazing hot and ready. So very, very ready. Her gaze flicked back to his face, and she smiled. "I came to Scotland to find lust, seduction, and sin. I think I just found something a whole lot better."

"And it's all yours for the taking."

His fingers suddenly slipped under her bottom, and he lifted her till her legs straddled his waist. "Kiss me, Emily. Kiss me hard."

Even though he'd begged her to kiss him, his mouth was on hers first, capturing her, tasting her, his tongue dancing with her tongue, making her sizzle and burn with fulfilled desire.

Heat spread to her fingertips, to her toes, and blazed at the very center of her, heat that he'd ignited with his potent and powerful kisses. For a week she'd felt like she was starving, desperate for a taste of him, and now he was giving her so much more than she'd ever expected.

At last he laid her down on the oriental carpet, and his lips, his tongue, the moist heat of his breath, caressed the curve of her neck, the hollow of her throat, moving first to one breast then to the other, suckling and teasing, pleasantly torturing her nipples with nips of his teeth and the swirl of his tongue.

Her body had never tingled this way, had never been caught up in a torrent of such wicked and luscious emotions. She wanted to cry, she wanted to laugh, she wanted to pull him into her so she could know him fully and completely.

He rolled onto his back, and she straddled his hips, making herself comfortable, while Colin produced a condom from his pants pocket. With fast, fumbling fingers, they stretched it over him, then Colin's powerful arms all but lifted her up and set the hot, blazing center of her body on the hard, masterful length of him.

And then his hands went to her breasts, kneading them gently, drawing them to his mouth, as she lowered herself onto him. She moaned. Sighed. Gasped for breath as she took all of him inside her.

Then she rose slowly, smiling down on him as they moved together in synchronized time, as if they'd loved each other again and again throughout time and knew each other's needs, wants, desires.

His sapphire eyes blazed as he watched her, sending red-hot lava flowing through her breasts, through her heart and soul.

And just when she thought she couldn't go on any longer, he pulled her beneath him and thrust deep and hard. The first spasm hit, then the second and third. It was chaotic. It was bliss. It was potent and passionate, and she didn't want the impulsiveness of this act ever to end.

Colin smiled down at her, kissing her, and when every nerve in her body began to shout with joy, she watched his eyes slam shut. His body jerked and quivered, and a powerful smile broke across his face.

Slowly he wrapped her in his arms and pulled her against him, face to face, their legs entwined, still holding on to the love they'd just shared.

"I love you," she whispered.

His gaze flickered away from her for a moment, and a frown passed quickly across his face, then disappeared. She'd seen in his eyes and face everything that she'd feared. He didn't love her.

It wasn't supposed to happen this way. Not again. Definitely not with Colin. She tried to push away, but he held her in his arms.

"Love me, Emily."

"I do, but I want love in return. I told you before I don't want something one-sided."

"I don't know how to love," he said. "It has nothing to do with you. If I could love you, I would."

This time she did manage to pull away, the tears flowing from her eyes as she snatched up her clothes and stood in front of him, feeling naked and hurt.

He was beside her, trying to pull her into his arms, but she kept backing away, farther from him all the time.

"Stay, Emily. I want you here with me."

She laughed. "What, as some unloved mistress?"

"I'd care for you, Emily. I'd give you everything you ever needed or wanted."

"I want your love."

He laughed. "Dunbars don't love. They never have, and they never will."

"That's a myth, and you're a fool to believe it. A heartless fool who's made of stone."

"Then change me! Make me something else, because I don't want to lose you."

She didn't want to lose him either, but if she stayed, it would be too easy for him to accept things just the way they were. If she left . . . well, he'd have to decide what he really wanted.

Without thinking any further, she ran away, hoping he'd make the right decision about what he wanted.

Because she wanted him desperately.

6

"rink up, lass," Meg said, leaning her pudgy arms on top of the bar. "That whisky might not cure your ills, but it'll put a fire in your belly and take a wee bit of the pain out of yer heart."

Emily lifted the tumbler to her lips and took a sip of Dunbar whisky's next-to-the-best blend. "I've gotten attached to this stuff in the last week or so. Think you could send some to the States for me every so often?"

Meg shook her head. "Ye know good and well ye canna do that. That whisky's poured at the Devil's Cup and nowhere else. Ye'll just have to pay us a visit every now and then if ye want a taste."

"As good as coming back here sounds—Oh, who am I kidding? You and everyone else knows what happened between Colin and me, and you also know I won't be coming back."

"If ye ask me, yer giving up far too easy."

"The man's got a heart of stone, not to mention ice water for blood, and he's not interested in me. It's been two days since I ran off, and he's made no effort whatsoever. I'm getting on that plane this afternoon, and I won't be coming back."

"Want to bet on that?"

Emily turned at the familiar sound of Billy's voice.

It didn't surprise her that they were wagering on her troubles again. "I'm not going to bet on the inevitable."

"The entire village has wagered on this one." Iain popped up from the table to pour himself a stout, while Seamus smoothed out a piece of paper on their regular table. "Of course, everyone voted the same way, so there wilna be much to win."

"And how did everyone vote?" Emily craned her neck to get a look at the paper.

"That Colin wilna let you leave the Highlands. The man's stubborn as they come, but he's no fool."

"No, he's not." It was a voice from the near-distant past.

Emily choked on her whisky and coughed as the tall, swarthy Highlander pushed through the pub door.

"Give the lass some more whisky, Meg. It's on me."

Emily slapped her hand over the top of the tumbler and glared at Meg. "I've got a plane to catch"—cough! cough!—"and a long drive to get to the airport." Cough! "The last thing I need is more to drink before I get on the road."

Colin parked himself on the stool next to her and

wedged the glass from under her hand. "She's not going anywhere, Meg. A little more whisky will stop that cough of hers. At least, it always works for me."

Emily swiveled around on the bar stool and hit him with a frown. "I didn't cough till you walked into the pub. I never cough when I'm drinking—unless you're around."

"Then you'd better get used to coughing, because I'm not leaving your side."

"That's telling her, Colin," Billy hollered.

Meg glowered at Billy, Iain, and Seamus. "Mind yer own business!"

Emily leaned somewhat close to Colin, but not too close. He smelled too good. He looked even better. And he was the devil. "I don't know why you're here," she whispered, "but if you have something to say to me, could you do it in private?"

"Aye. And I've got the perfect private place to do it."

With that, Colin tossed her over his shoulder like a sack of barley and headed for the door.

"Put me down!"

"Not till we've talked."

"Should I pack the lass's belongings and bring them to the castle?" Meg hollered after them.

"You can pack them," Colin said, his arms trapping Emily's legs against his chest so she wouldn't kick him while she struggled. "But we're not going to want any visitors for a while. And Emily won't be needing any clothes, either."

"That's what you think!" Emily thrashed about, but it did no good. The Highlander wouldn't be stopped as he stalked out the door and into the sunlight, to the rousing cheers of the regulars at the Devil's Cup.

"Do you mind telling me what you're doing, Colin Dunbar?"

"I'm putting you in the car and I'm taking you home, and I'd appreciate it if you didn't make it any more difficult than you already have."

"My home's in California."

"Not any longer." He opened the car door and almost heaved her inside.

"I'm not going to live in that castle as your mistress. I already told you that." She tried to crawl out the passenger side of his Land Rover, but he latched on to her and pulled her into his lap, clapping a powerful arm around her middle.

She tried to wrench out of his arms, but he couldn't be wrenched. "It's dangerous to drive this way."

"It would be far more dangerous to drive with you trying to escape."

"I don't appreciate being kidnapped."

"And I didn't appreciate you running out on me."

"What was I supposed to do? I bare my soul and you . . . you—" Tears welled in the corners of her eyes.

Colin's warm and tender hand cupped her cheek. "I know perfectly well what I did. I hurt you, Emily. I drove you away, and I've been miserable ever since."

She shifted in his lap, turning until their eyes, their noses, and their mouths were mere inches apart. "You're not just saying that to get me back to the castle, are you?"

He shook his head slowly. "I'm saying it because . . ." He sighed softly. "Because I love you."

A searing heat flowed through her veins and into her heart. His confession thrilled her beyond anything she'd ever experienced in life, but it surprised her as well, and just to make sure she hadn't heard him incorrectly, she asked, "Do you really?"

His eyes sparkled as he caressed away the tears from her cheeks. "Aye."

Butterflies fluttered in her stomach once again. "Why didn't you tell me before?"

"Because I didn't know how I felt until you were gone, until I experienced the worst loneliness of my life." His lips whispered over hers. "I'll be breaking a long chain of Dunbar misery if I can make you love me as much as I love you."

Weaving her fingers behind his neck, she smiled into his beloved face. "Then the chain's already broken."

"It won't be broken until I take you to the secret bedroom," he said, kissing the tip of her nose, her eyelids, and then her mouth once again. "Until I make love to you in the mythical bed."

Emily tightened her arms around his neck and smiled. "Then start the car, Colin, and let's go break some chains."

 $\mathcal{C}$ olin pulled the Land Rover to a halt in the circular drive in front of the castle, and in just a few minutes, his fingers woven tightly around Emily's, he was tugging her through the great hall, his long legs moving much faster than her short ones.

Her anticipation-filled heart beat rapidly as she tried to keep up. But what excited her was something much more powerful than the prospect of seeing the secret room. It was the thought of being with Colin—of being loved by Colin and loving him back.

Suddenly he scooped her into his powerful arms and ran up the circular stairs, past the gallery and the bedroom where she'd slept the last week, past nearly a dozen other rooms, until they reached the double doors at the end of the hall.

Colin stopped, and she could feel the thrum of his rapidly beating heart against her breasts. "Here it is. The room you've been looking for."

He had to be mistaken. "But . . . isn't this your bedroom?"

"Aye. It's the one place in the castle that you never bothered to search."

"Because you told me your bedroom was off limits, remember?"

She couldn't miss the blazing intensity—or the desire in his eyes—as he held her close. "I promised not to touch you, Emily. If I'd found you here—stroking my bed, photographing desserts on it, doing everything in your power to tempt me—no oath would have held me back."

"Is that the secret of the room?" she asked, threading her fingers through his thick, wavy hair, loving the feel of his body close to hers. "That people can't keep from touching each other once they're inside?"

"I don't need a secret bedroom to make me want to touch you," Colin said. "If I did, I'd be sorely out of luck because there is no secret room in Dunbar Castle."

What? She pulled back just enough to hit him with a questioning frown. "Could you repeat what you just said?"

He kissed her ear and whispered, "There is no secret room."

Emily angled her head until their noses touched, and felt her eyes narrowing as she glared at him. "You mean to tell me I spent a week searching for a room that doesn't exist?"

"Aye."

"Why didn't you tell me?"

"I made that perfectly clear when we met. Because I wanted you, and you wouldn't have stayed here if there hadn't been a room to search for." His warm, tender lips trailed along her jaw, to the hollow beneath her ear, making her quiver inside. "I want you even more now, but if I didn't know better, I'd think you were still more interested in the secret room than you are in me."

"I'm *very* interested in you." She kissed him and a low, desire-filled sigh escaped her lips. "I'm anxious to strip you naked and make mad passionate love with you. I'll feed you chocolates and fine whisky, and maybe, just maybe"—she sighed again—"you'll tell me why so many people think there's a secret bedroom in Dunbar Castle."

"All in good time." He put the key in his bedroom door, shoved it open with his foot, and carried her across the massive, dark-paneled room to the huge, intricately carved four-poster bed.

He was tender, loving, and a master of seduction, and in no time at all she was lying in the very center of the plushy mattress, caught in a swirl of black satin covers, and Colin—her devil—stretched his long, strong body over hers.

"There is no secret bedroom," he said, wrapping one of her springy red curls about his finger, "only a story about a bed—this bed—that's been misinterpreted. Over the centuries it's been told and retold so many times by the villagers that they no longer know the truth."

"Do *you* know the truth?" she asked, working his shirt out from the waistband of his jeans, and smoothing her fingers over the heated skin of his back.

"Aye." He kissed her, and she thought for a moment he'd forget to tell her the story, but he spoke as his lips softly caressed her mouth, her cheeks, her chin. "Remember Gillian telling her tour group about my ancestor Alexander having a bed specially made for him in France?"

Emily nodded.

"The bed *was* made in France. And it *was* made extra large. But Alexander had it made as a wedding present for his wife. He loved her and she loved him—an unheard of occurrence among the Dunbars. This was the bed they first made love in and Alexander believed it had special powers, because he never slept with another woman after his wife. More important, he never wanted to."

"And this had to be kept a secret?"

"Just as Alexander created the secret recipe for Dunbar whisky and handed it down to his son, he also told his son that this bed would bring eternal love to any Dunbar laird and the woman he brought to it."

Colin laughed as he rolled over on the bed and carried Emily with him, holding her close, weaving his fingers through her springy hair and gazing into her eyes. "We

Dunbars have been a sorry lot. Gamblers. Womanizers. Men who believed in myths and legends. Some believed them so strongly that they kept this bed hidden away in an unused part of the castle for centuries."

She touched his face just as he touched hers. "You mean no one wanted to take the chance of falling in love?"

"No Dunbar wanted to risk being with just one woman for all eternity. No Dunbar, that is, until me."

She smiled at his declaration of love, but worried that he had too much faith in the legend. "It's just a myth, Colin. You don't believe it, do you?"

"I believe what I feel for you, that's all that matters. I'd never been in love until you walked into this castle. I never wanted to fall in love, never wanted to marry. But since that day I saw you on the security monitors, I've thought of no one else. Myths and legends are fine for marketing and making money, but when it comes to love—the only thing that matters is what two people feel for each other."

"What do you feel, Colin?"

"That I never want to let you go." He drew her face to his and kissed her gently. "Of course," he said, rolling over again in the massive bed and covering her body with his, "I believe in that myth enough to think we should make love in this bed—just a wee bit of insurance that you won't ever go away."

"I'm not going anywhere, Colin. I love you, more than I ever thought it was possible to love, and this is where I want to be—now and forever."

"Now and forever," Colin repeated, and Emily sighed

with happiness as her Highlander's mouth swept over hers.

She'd come to Scotland to find lust, seduction, and sin, but she'd found a most powerful and intoxicating love instead. He was delicious. He was Scottish. And oh, yes, at times he was a wee bit sinful.

PATTI BERG

Always a romantic, *USA Today* best-selling author Patti Berg spent her childhood dreaming about being whisked away by a knight in shining armor, a devil-may-care swashbuckler, a sheik on a shiny black stallion, or a broad-shouldered cowboy with a Stetson tilted low on his brow. Now she spends her days making up stories where her heroes do whatever she wants them to. It's almost as good as a dream coming true, she confesses.

Patti lives in northern California with her husband and real-life hero Bob and a very fat cat named Tootsie, who rules the house. She loves to hear from her readers. Please send email to patti@pattiberg.com or through her website at www.pattiberg.com.

Maddening Highlander

DEBRA DIER

Dedication

For my darling Sarah Louise,
Mommy's special inspiration.

1

"Aye, this is a photo of Ann Fitzpatrick. Do you mean to say you actually had an investigator poking about in Ann's life?" Rose Matheson looked indignant as she handed the photograph back to Iain. "You, a man who knows how dreadful it is to have people prowling about in his private affairs?"

"I didn't probe deeply into her personal life. I certainly did not violate her privacy." Iain Matheson sat on the edge of the large claw-footed desk in his library, facing his grandmother's displeasure. With her blue eyes wide behind the round lenses of her pink-rimmed glasses, she looked like a queen unhappy with one of her subjects. Over the years Iain had grown accustomed to this particular look of outrage in her eyes. He saw it each time his name appeared in one of the gossip magazines. Fortunately, he always managed to melt the icy scorn. "I simply needed to know if Ann Fitzpatrick was who and what she said she was."

Rose raised an eyebrow imperiously. "Apparently you no longer trust my judgment."

"It is not that at all."

"Since I invited her to stay, it certainly appears that way."

"I was a little suspicious of her story."

Rose huffed. "Because of the company you keep."

"Gram, a woman comes out of nowhere and claims she has just found the long-lost journal of Adair Matheson in the attic of a house in Chicago, of all places. She convinces my grandmother to invite her to Dunmarin for the summer to search for the Matheson jewels. It seemed a good idea to find out something about her." Iain winked at his grandmother. "For one thing, I needed to make certain she wasn't a reporter."

"A reporter. I hadn't considered she might be a reporter. After that incident at Christmas, I suppose I should have thought of the possibility." Rose sank into one of the leather armchairs near the desk. She smoothed her hand over the knee of her tweed slacks while she fixed a chilling gaze on Iain. "Of course, our family never needed to concern itself with reporters until a few years ago."

Iain grinned at his grandmother. "Father told me to enjoy myself while I was young. I am only doing what he advised."

"And a fine job you are doing of it too." Rose folded her hands on her lap. "Ann is a dear sweet lass, genuine in every regard. I am certain you found nothing at all to incriminate her in any way. She certainly is not at all like most of the females you tend to keep company with."

Iain flinched at the well-aimed barb. Too many times he had discovered that people were not what they appeared to be. Ann Fitzpatrick seemed to be an exception. Aside from her career as a professor of archaeology at Chamberlain College outside Chicago, her interests centered on her family. She lived with her grandmother. She had two sisters—Carol, who was three years older, and Ellyn, who was two years younger. Both sisters had married and started families. Ann spent her free time baby-sitting for her nieces and nephews or taking the children out on excursions. Except for her reputation for being a little absentminded at times, her colleagues had nothing but praise for the pretty professor. "Apparently she—"

"If you didn't keep company with such unreliable women, you might be quicker to believe a dependable one," Rose chided him. "If your great-grandfather thought it was all right to allow her great-grandfather to stay here, I am thinking it is all right to allow Ann to do the same."

"I don't mean to say it isn't, Gram. I just wanted to make certain Dr. Fitzpatrick is who and what she claims to be." He leaned forward and kissed Rose's cheek, inhaling the sweet scent of lavender. "And apparently she is. Your judgment was completely sound. I hope you can understand why I took the precaution of checking into her background."

A smile played about Rose's lips, and warmth entered her blue eyes. "Well, now, I suppose you were just being cautious. Although *cautious* is hardly a word I am accustomed to associating with you. I suppose I can understand why you might have been doubting the honesty of a woman you did not know."

"I am glad you understand." *A woman he did not know.* A woman he had never met. Iain glanced down at the folder lying open upon his desk. His investigator had included photos of Dr. Ann Fitzpatrick, photos that depicted a slender, rather serious-looking woman in her late twenties. He lifted a photo that showed her standing at the lectern in one of her classes. Although she was not beautiful in the classical sense, there was something about her that intrigued him. He could imagine being a young man in her class, watching her, wondering what it might take to make her smile.

Iain couldn't explain it, but each time he looked at her photo, he felt an odd sense of familiarity, as though he had known Ann all of his life. He had shifted three business meetings to come to Dunmarin earlier than he had planned, simply because he was anxious to meet the pretty professor from Chicago. "Where is the good professor this morning?"

"Ann has gone exploring. I think she intended to take a look at the caves."

"The caves." A chill crept through him. "She went exploring the caves. Alone?"

"I don't imagine she will do anything reckless. Ann appears to be a very sensible young woman. She knows how dangerous the caves can be. I'm sure she intends to just poke her head in and take a look around."

Iain glanced at the tall case clock standing against the

oak wainscoting in one corner of the room. It was nearly ten. The rising tide would have devoured half the beach by now.

"Is something wrong, dear?"

Iain hoped there wasn't. "I wonder if Dr. Fitzpatrick has remembered the tide."

"*D*on't panic," Ann Fitzpatrick whispered to herself, her voice swallowed by the roar of the sea. Morning sunlight glowed upon a fine veil of mist hovering at the mouth of the cave, less than ten feet away from where she stood. Safety lay in that mist. Yet it might as well be a hundred miles from her.

Her hands trembled as she gripped her leg. She tried twisting her foot, hoping to free herself from a stone crevice in the floor of the cave. Her foot wouldn't budge. Waves lapped at her knees, the icy water soaking through her jeans. Chills prickled across her skin, like frost painting a lacy pattern upon a windowpane. She had lingered in the caves longer than she had planned, distracted by a truly fascinating artifact she had found.

It didn't take a Ph.D. in archeology to understand the tide. From the watermarks on the stone walls, she knew the tide would rise in this part of the cave to at least six feet deep, a good five inches above her head. If she couldn't pull her foot free, she would drown. It was that simple. She now understood why an animal caught in a trap would chew off his foot to free himself.

Death by absentmindedness.

"Please, don't let that be my epitaph." Ann pressed

back against the wall of the cave, shivering, fighting the panic growing inside her. She tried to breathe, but the salt-tinged air hitched at the top of her lungs.

Would Rose notice that Ann had not returned to the castle from her hike? Would she think of the tide? Ann only wished she had remembered the tide. Perhaps Rose would send someone looking for her. Of course, by then it could be too late.

If she could loosen the laces of her hiking boot, then perhaps she could free her foot. She bent to work at the laces, her hands burning from the cold water. A wave crashed against the mouth of the cave, tossing foam into the air. The water roared, like a hungry beast wild with the scent of prey. The dark water plunged through the mist. It rushed into the cave, slapping the black stone walls. Before she could brace herself, the water slammed into her. Caught in the powerful grip of the wave, she threw out her hands, trying to save herself from the fall. Water flooded her mouth, her eyes, her nose, burning like salt in an open wound.

The rushing wave tossed her toward the belly of the cave as though she were a piece of driftwood. She struggled, fighting the water's pull, anchored to the floor of the cave by her trapped foot. The force of the rushing water pressed her down against the floor of the cave. She clawed her way through the water. She was not about to drown. Not here. Not now. She had not come to this remote island off the west coast of Scotland to end up as another tragic statistic.

A shadow crossed her periphery. Her right hand connected with something firm and warm. In the next instant, strong hands closed around her arms. Someone lifted her, pulling her through the churning water. When her head popped up from the water, she gulped at the air, inhaling salt and spray along with it. A spasm of coughing gripped her as her rescuer lifted her to her feet.

A man was holding her in his arms, shielding her from the pounding waves. She leaned heavily against his chest, her hands sinking into the thick soft wool of his sweater. He held her close against his big body, his arms cinched around her in a powerful embrace, his warmth radiating against her, while a paroxysm of coughing cleared her lungs of a small portion of the Atlantic.

When the spasm passed, she drew air into her burning lungs. A fragrance of citrus and spices swirled through her senses, easing the burn of salt from her nostrils. She turned her head against his chest, instinctively seeking more of his scent, his sweater warm and soft against her chilled skin, a sharp contrast to the hard plane of muscle beneath the white cabled knit. In spite of the fear gripping her, she acknowledged an odd tingling sensation rippling through her, an excitement that came from the mere presence of this stranger.

Startled by her own reaction, she tipped back her head and looked up at the face of her guardian angel. One look, and she knew if this man had ever been an angel, he had fallen from grace a long time ago. Hair as black and shiny as a mink fell in thick windblown waves around his face. Eyes darker than her deepest fear regarded her from beneath slanting black brows. Strong lines and angles shaped a face that could lead a woman straight to ruin—and had in fact done so on numerous occasions.

Although the photographs Ann had seen of him did not do him justice, she recognized the finely chiseled features of this man. Only now, standing close against him, did she truly understand the reason women kept tossing themselves into the inferno that was Iain Matheson.

She was a scientist. Her work dominated her time. Reason and logic ruled her life. She certainly was not the type of female who allowed a handsome face and splendid body to spoil her judgment. Yet here she stood, caught in a most peculiar web spinning around her, a force more compelling than the might of the ocean raging a few yards away from them.

In spite of the cold grip of the ocean, heat simmered through her in a tingling, swirling current that turned the air in her poor abused lungs to steam and melted her insides into hot chocolate. The roar of the ocean faded to a distant hum in her ears. The world seemed to contract and expand all in the same moment. She felt oddly suspended, as if time had caught its breath, making the rest of the world pause for this one startling moment.

It must be a trick of light or the result of nearly drowning that caused her to see what she saw in his eyes. For her own wayward mind imagined seeing the same confusion in his gorgeous eyes, as though he were experiencing the same reckless excitement at being so near to her.

A wave crested against the mouth of the cave, crashing into them with enough force to nearly tear her from his arms, ripping the sensual web to shreds. He held her close, defying the power of the ocean. When the wave subsided, he grabbed her arm.

"Come with me."

"Wait!" Ann shouted as he started hauling her toward the entrance.

Iain looked down at her. "In case you didn't notice, the tide is coming in, and we'll be fish bait unless we get out of here."

His deep voice reverberated through her. It was colored with a soft Scottish burr that made her want to hear her name whispered in that dark vibrant voice.

"Dr. Fitzpatrick," he said, his hand tensing on her arm. "Are you all right? Did you hit your head?"

Reality hit her squarely between the eyes. Her foot was stuck, the tide was rising, and she was staring at him like a demented schoolgirl. She collected her scattered wits and managed to make her voice work. "Yes."

"You did hit your head?"

"No. I mean yes, I am fine. Sort of." She shook her head, appalled at the way he could muddle her thoughts. "My left foot is caught."

Iain bent to examine the situation. She braced her hand upon the wall of the cave while he gripped her calf and explored the trap hidden beneath the water. In spite of her best efforts to ignore the startling sensations careening through her, she could not. Not while his hand rested upon her calf. He had such strong hands.

Ann shook her head. How in the world could she be thinking of his hands when she was a hairsbreadth away from drowning? Obviously she was in danger of completely losing her mind.

A wave crested as he stood. The water slammed into him, knocking him into her. He cinched his arms around her and turned, taking the brunt of the blow when the water tossed them against the wall of the cave. He pressed his shoulder against the wall, holding her close while he fought against the pull of the water. When the surge waned, he slipped his hand into the pocket of his black slacks and withdrew a pocketknife.

Ann stared, her breath trapped in her throat, while he unsheathed a rather sharp-looking blade. "What are you going to do with that?"

Iain lifted one black brow. "Amputation seems to be the only way to free you."

2

$\mathcal{A}$nn pressed back against the wall. "You cannot truly mean to . . . my foot!"

Iain grinned at her, a glint of mischief entering his dark eyes. "Relax, Professor. I think I can manage to cut off your shoe without taking any flesh."

He was teasing her. At a time like this, when she was scared to death, he had the audacity to tease her. She glared at him, the stern expression wasted, since he had already bent to his task. Ann pressed her shoulder against the wall and held her breath while he wielded the blade against the laces of her shoe and worked his fingers inside, until the leather gave way beneath his touch. He gripped her ankle and eased her foot from the trapped shoe, leaving her sock behind as well.

When she was free, he stood and slipped his arm around her shoulders. "Time to get out of here."

Before she could say a word, he bent and hooked his other arm beneath her knees. A startled gasp escaped her lips when he lifted her. She clutched his sweater in an effort to steady herself. He grinned at her, his dark eyes alight with humor as he settled her high against his chest. This was a man accustomed to sweeping women off their feet. A man for whom laughter came as easily as his conquests. It was important to keep that in mind.

"No need to look so tense, Professor, I'm not about to drop you," he said, that dark rich voice spilling through her.

Her tension had little to do with the fear of falling, even if the fall would be a long way. The man stood at least six-foot-three. Still, the powerful arms cinched around her provided ample security, at least from plunging into the water. As far as her wayward emotions were concerned, that was another story. Her heart thudded so hard, it threatened to bruise the wall of her chest.

She had lived nearly twenty-nine years, and this was the first time since she was a little girl that a man had swept her up into his arms. It was exciting. Far more exciting than she wanted to admit. Never in her life had she felt the immediate turmoil that this man evoked within her. Unfortunately that did not put her into a unique category.

Ann blinked against the misty sunlight as he carried her out of the cave. The thick muscles in his chest shifted as Iain trudged through the rising water, his body straining as he fought the pounding waves, the raw power of the man pitted against the raging might of the ocean. Still, she never doubted he would win. There was something about

Iain Matheson, an aura of power and conviction, a confidence that came from a lifetime of success. From what she had read about him, Iain devoured life.

A narrow strip of beach remained dry near the embankment. A hundred feet above them, Dunmarin Castle stood poised on the edge of the cliffs. She expected Iain to put her down once they reached dry land. Instead he continued to carry her toward the path that cut upward through the tall swaying grass, sand, and rocks that lined the face of the cliff.

"I can walk," she said, when it was clear he intended to carry her up the path. "My foot is fine."

Iain glanced toward the path. "You cannot be climbing with a bare foot. You would cut yourself or twist an ankle."

Ann acknowledged the wisdom in his words, even if she doubted the wisdom of remaining in such close proximity to this man. With each step he took, her side brushed against his chest, sending delicious sensations skittering across her skin. With each breath she pulled his scent deep into her lungs, where it smoldered like a mind-numbing drug. The lush masculine heat of his body radiated against her, seeping through her sodden clothes, warming her. If she was not careful, she would make a complete fool of herself over this man. Iain Matheson ate women like Ann for breakfast.

Once this initial excitement had past, she would be just fine, she assured herself. She was far too sensible, much too practical, to ever lose her head over a man like Iain Matheson. "I do not believe I thanked you for coming to my rescue," she said, pleased with the composed sound of her voice.

"I am only happy I was here to help, lass."

That soft Scottish burr brushed against her like warm velvet. She had a feeling the man could read a dissertation on the complexities of quantum theory, and she would sit enthralled by every word. "Rose said you were coming to Dunmarin on Thursday."

"I decided to come home a few days early. I was anxious to meet you."

She stared at him, her heart suspended near the top of her throat. "You were?"

"Aye. I am very interested to see the journal and hear about your plans for treasure hunting."

The journal. Her plans. Of course, that would be the reason he would want to meet her. It certainly did not involve anything of a personal nature. "Yes. It was an exciting find. All of these years the journal has been hidden in my grandmother's attic."

"I am glad Gram mentioned you might have taken a notion to explore the caves this morning." Iain smiled at her, and her temperature rose three degrees. "I only hope you don't plan to make a practice of running about like a perfect hen-wit. Next time you might not be so fortunate."

His words hit her like a cold glass of water. "A perfect hen-wit?"

"Aye. It's reckless exploring the caves alone." Iain paused when they reached the foot of the path. "Put your arm around my neck, to steady yourself a bit during the climb."

Ann was too stunned by his assessment of her intellect to move. "I assure you, I do not go running about like a hen-wit."

"No? And here I thought you were prowling about the

caves by yourself. Is there someone else back there we need to rescue?"

Ann bristled at the sarcasm in his dark voice. The breeze brushed her face, heavy with mist. "No, there is no one else. But that doesn't mean I am a hen-wit."

"I never said you were. I said running about the caves was a hen-witted thing to do. Far too reckless for your own good."

She did not appreciate being lectured on proper behavior from a man who had taken the meaning of *reckless* to new heights. "I was careful."

"Apparently not careful enough."

"I was anxious to see if I might . . . and I checked the tides . . . it was just . . ." She paused, appalled at the heat creeping upward along her neck. She was babbling like the idiot he thought she was. "My great-grandfather believed there was a major archaeological site hidden in these caves. I suppose I was overly anxious to see if I might get a glimpse of something. Perhaps I did make a small error in judgment."

"The caves are dangerous. Every year people wander in and don't come out."

"I know they are dangerous." Her great-grandfather Owen had been one of those people who had wandered into the caves one morning and had never been found. She didn't like to think about history repeating itself. Heat crept upward, burning her cheeks. She only hoped he thought it was the wind that brought the blush to her cheeks. It was embarrassing to be so quick to blush when one was almost thirty years old. "I didn't go very far into the caves."

"It is nothing short of reckless exploring on your own.

And as long as you are staying at Dunmarin, I will insist you not be doing it again."

"I am not a child. I do not appreciate being spoken to as though I were."

"Then perhaps you ought to stop behaving like a child. Now put your arm about my neck."

Ann had no intention of allowing this man to carry her back as though she were some poor helpless child. "You can put me down. I am quite capable of walking back to Dunmarin."

"You'll hurt your foot."

Somewhere in the back of her mind she realized she was being stubborn. Yet she would not allow this man to treat her as though she were a foolish little girl. She had fought enough prejudice in her given field. She certainly would not take it from an infamous playboy such as Iain Matheson. "I can manage."

He shrugged, then withdrew his arm from beneath her knees. Although he did nothing more than stand still and allow her to slide to the ground, the friction of her body against his was enough to vaporize the blood in her veins. By the time her feet touched the ground, her skin tingled with heat, which was almost as annoying as the pulse that had flared to life low in her belly. For the first time in her life she actually understood what it meant to have her knees turn to jelly.

Iain, on the other hand, looked completely unmoved. He stood smiling at her as though he found her amusing. Oh, she wanted to scream. She backed away from him, too quickly. Her instep came down hard on a rough-edged stone. The pain dragged a gasp from her lips. She stumbled and would have fallen if he hadn't grabbed her arm.

"I see you are also more than a little stubborn."

Ann rubbed her bruised foot and glared up at him. "I am not stubborn."

"No? Well, I am glad to hear that. Then you won't mind if I do this." He slipped his arm around her shoulders, hooked his other arm beneath her knees, and lifted her into his arms.

She gripped the shoulder of his sweater. "You needn't look so pleased with yourself."

He laughed, the deep rich sound almost musical. "Now, why wouldn't I be pleased to have a beautiful woman in my arms?"

Oh, he was good. In spite of the fact she knew perfectly well there was nothing behind the words but empty flattery, he still managed to send a ripple of pleasure through her. He had a way of looking at her that made her feel beautiful, even when she knew perfectly well she must look dreadful. She supposed that was simply one weapon in the arsenal any playboy needed to be successful in his given pursuit. No doubt seduction came as easily to him as breathing.

"Put your arm around my neck. It will steady you."

Even though she obeyed, she was determined to remain unmoved by the scoundrel. She stared at the ocean while he climbed the path. Still, she could not shut out the image of him in her periphery. In spite of her best effort, she caught herself turning her head to get a better look at him. His lips were full and smooth looking, lips that made women long to be kissed. She had never considered herself one of those foolishly romantic women. He was proving her wrong. She caught herself staring at the inviting hollow at the base of his neck, revealed by the round neck of his sweater, and an odd sensation coiled through her.

Strange, although she had not met him until today, she felt she knew him. She supposed it was simply from the stories she had read about him over the years. Yet being close to him like this felt so familiar, as if she had spent a lifetime being held by this man. Odd how the mind could play tricks on you.

He glanced at her and caught her staring at him. Staring in the same foolish lovesick manner in which she had always stared at Mike Campbell in high school. She was no longer the gawky girl in the back of the third-period English class, she reminded herself. She was far too old to indulge in foolish infatuations.

"I'm curious, Professor—how did Adair Matheson's journal end up in your grandmother's attic?"

"Apparently my great-grandfather bought it at a rare-book store in London," she said, relieved to have the conversation center on her work.

Iain's expression reflected his doubts. "If it is authentic, somehow it managed to slip out of the possession of my family. Which I find peculiar. I cannot imagine why a family journal would end up in a rare-book store."

"I can't say how it ended up in the store. But my great-grandfather was certain it was genuine. I had the journal examined. It dates from the period. And it appears as though the writing matches the writing on the photocopies of the letters your grandmother sent me, letters that are known to have been written by Adair."

"It's possible it is authentic. I suppose someone might have sold it without realizing the significance of it." Iain drew in a deep breath, his chest expanding against her side. "Still, I have to say, looking for the jewels is like chasing after a moonbeam. You have as much chance of actually grabbing hold of it. It certainly isn't worth taking risks with your life."

"I did not think I was taking any risks with my life when I went exploring this morning. I just wanted to have a look at the place where my great-grandfather Owen disappeared. And then I found this truly fascinating obelisk, sculpted black stone with symbols carved along two sides. It shall be very interesting to see what those symbols represent. If I hadn't found it, I most certainly would have remembered the tide, and you would not be so inconvenienced at the moment. 1 am afraid I lost track of the time. If not, I would have seen that crevice. But it was underwater, and I just stepped into it." She was babbling. She knew it. Yet there was little she could do about it. It was a nervous habit. Iain made her nervous and restless and defensive. "I never do anything that is reckless. I checked on the times of high tide before I left this morning. It was the obelisk that distracted me."

A pair of gulls swooped overhead on their way to the beach, their shrill cries rising above the sound of waves crashing against stone. "1 can see where the obelisk might have distracted you."

"You've seen it?"

"Aye. As far as I have been able to decipher them, the symbols on it deal with the passage of the moon and of time."

"You have deciphered the symbols?"

"I was raised on Dunmarin. From the time I was a lad, I have explored the castle and the land. There is little of the island I have not seen. I was naturally curious about the symbols I kept finding in various places. My father taught me. Before I went to university, I was already fairly good at reading the ancient ogham."

She stared at him, wondering if he might be teasing her again. "You can read ancient ogham?"

"Aye." He paused on the rocky path and fixed her in a steady look. "Now why is it that you are so astonished, Professor?"

The breeze ruffled his damp hair, tossing a thick ebony lock over his brow. Although his looks had been described as "Hollywood Handsome," he possessed a masculine appeal seldom found in leading men today. Two years ago he had been included in an issue of a magazine touting the most beautiful people in the world. He had been number nine out of fifty. Obviously the editors of that magazine had never stood with him on a misty Scottish beach, otherwise the entire issue would have been devoted to him. From everything she had read of the man, she was surprised his interests extended beyond the next woman he took to his bed. "It is . . . ah . . . I just . . . you don't really look like a man who would be interested in something such as ogham."

"Tell me, Professor, have you already slipped me into a nice neat little category?" Iain leaned toward her, his lips tipping into a crooked grin. "You wouldn't be one of those women who enjoy reading gossip magazines and newspapers, would you?"

Ann never did more than glance at the tabloids and popular magazines her grandma Evie devoured. Unless of course it had a story about Iain Matheson. She had to admit, she had been following his escapades ever since she was in college. It was convenient to say her fascination with Iain stemmed from the connection her great-grandfather had had with the Mathesons. Yet the truth was, she had been captivated by the handsome rakehell who was holding her close against his chest since she had first seen a photograph of him. "You are a bit infamous."

If she had not been so close, if she had not been so aware of him, she might have missed the flicker of annoyance in his expression. Yet he was so near, each exhalation of his breath brushed her lips. "Things are not always what they seem, Dr. Fitzpatrick."

Heat prickled her neck and crept upward into her cheeks. She refrained from citing some of the more scandalous episodes from his past. His past, his present, his future, had nothing at all to do with her. She had come here with one goal, and it had nothing at all to do with Iain Matheson. "With the journal, we have an excellent chance of finding the jewels."

Iain shifted her in his arms, adjusting her weight while he traversed a stony turn in the path. "Over the years a great many people have gone searching for the Matheson jewels. When I was twelve, I had a notion to find them myself. I spent a year searching every nook and cranny of the castle. I didn't find a trace of them."

"You didn't have the clues that Adair Matheson left in his journal. With them, I am confident we shall find the jewels."

"It will be interesting to see that journal."

The path led directly to a thick wooden gate in the stone wall that stretched along the perimeter of the castle. When they reached the top of the cliff, she said, "I think I might manage to walk from here, if you would like to put me down."

"There is no need to take the risk." Iain smiled at her, warm and genuine, a smile fashioned by God to tease any poor mortal female who wandered into his path. "You are as light as thistledown."

She resisted the urge to argue with him. Again. Her cheeks burned when she thought of how easily he had incited her temper. The man had the most infuriating way of ambushing her normally dependable emotions. She was not the type of woman who allowed emotions to rule her. Slow and steady, that was her motto. An archaeologist could not rush through a site without the risk of missing something important. She had always been well suited to her career. Until now, she hadn't even realized she possessed the capacity for a quick temper.

"Are you feeling all right, Professor? You're looking a little flushed."

She forced her lips into a smile. "The wind."

Thick black lashes lowered as he looked down, his gaze sweeping over her. Although he didn't touch her, her skin tingled as though he had brushed his hands over her breasts. "You're cold."

Strange, she *should* feel cold. Her clothes were soaked, the breeze was cool. And yet the cold didn't penetrate the odd warmth he conjured within her. As they approached the gate that opened into the sunken garden of Dunmarin, it opened. Rose marched onto the path, followed by three other ladies. They paused when they saw Ann and Iain.

"It looks as though you've been fishing, Iain." The lady to Rose's right lifted the glasses that hung from a gold chain around her neck. She peered at Ann through the lenses, her blue eyes filled with humor. "And you've caught yourself a mermaid."

"Aye, the fishing has never been better." Iain grinned at Ann, then looked at Rose. "Have you organized your bridge ladies to come hunt for us, Gram?"

"We were going to take a look about before we started our game. Just to be sure you were all right. Although I knew there was no real reason to worry. Ann is far too sensible to get into any real trouble." Rose patted Ann's hand. "Still, you look as though you have taken a soaking."

"Yes, I'm afraid I did." Ann glanced at Iain, expecting him to reveal the rest of the embarrassing story. Yet he merely grinned at her, apparently content to keep his own counsel.

Rose turned to her friends. "This is the young lady I have been telling you about. Ann Fitzpatrick, I would like you to meet three of my dearest friends. Deirdre Fraser," she said, gesturing toward the lady who had made the mermaid comment. "Beatrice Brodie, and Joanna Shaw."

Each lady expressed her pleasure at meeting Ann and she returned the favor. Short and thin, Joanna looked to be close to Rose's age, if not a little older. Beatrice looked to be in her late sixties. She also looked as though she enjoyed desserts more than exercise, a direct contrast to Deirdre, who looked as though she thrived on activity. Ann guessed Deirdre was the youngster of the group. She supposed the woman was in her late fifties or early sixties, although she could have been older and simply fought the battle against age better than the other ladies. Deirdre was also the only one of the group who had not allowed her hair to fade into gray, wearing her light chestnut locks in an elegant twist on top of her head. Deirdre was the type of woman who had been a notorious beauty in her youth and intended to maintain her looks until she died.

"You've lost your shoe." Beatrice winked at Ann. "Just like Cinderella when she left the ball."

"Now I would wager there is an interesting story behind that shoe," Joanna said.

"Well, I . . ." Ann hesitated, reluctant to betray the story behind her shoe, and her own negligence.

"Her foot became caught in a crevice. We had to leave the shoe behind," Iain said, quietly dispatching the curiosity Ann could see in four pairs of eyes.

"You better get out of those wet things before you catch your death," Rose said.

"Aye. Until later, ladies," Iain said, before leaving Rose and her friends on the path.

"You didn't tell them that I was a hen-wit," Ann said, when Iain carried her into the house.

"Your behavior was hen-witted, not you, Professor." He grinned at her. "And I saw no reason to add to the gossip."

After carrying her down miles of corridors, up two flights of stairs, and down another wide corridor, Iain set Ann on her feet in the hall outside her bedchamber. "Here you are. Safe and sound."

Ann curled her bare toes into one of the sapphire roses stitched into the thick wool of the carpet that ran along the center of the oak-lined floor. She felt like a child who has just been returned after managing to get herself lost in the woods. "Thank you, for everything."

"It was my pleasure." He looked at her, a whisper of a smile curving his lips. "I am looking forward to this treasure hunt, Dr. Fitzpatrick."

Ann stared at him. The last thing she wanted or needed was Iain Matheson poking about in her expedition. He had the most alarming way of turning her brain to mush. "I didn't realize you intended to stay for more than a day or two."

"I intend to stay for as long as it takes to solve this mystery. It has been plaguing my family for over two hundred years. It is only natural that I would want to be part of your quest."

"Yes. Of course." It was his home and his family treasure. She had no authority to ban him from searching for the lost Matheson jewels, even if she wanted to banish him from the island for as long as she was here. Since he was going to insinuate himself into her expedition, she would have to manage her reaction to the man.

Now that she realized how easily he could stimulate her sensibilities, she would be better prepared to handle these wayward emotions, she assured herself. She certainly had no intention of allowing a silly attraction to a scoundrel spoil the chance of a lifetime.

"When you change, would you mind meeting me in the library?" Iain smiled at Ann, one of those smiles designed to add a beat to a woman's heart. Her own heart was racing too hard to notice. "I am anxious to take a look at Adair Matheson's journal."

"Of course." Ann turned and walked into her room with as much dignity as she could muster, which wasn't much, considering the state of her clothes. Her wet jeans chafed with each step she took. Each step made her feel like a drunk on New Year's eve, since she wore an inch-high heel on one foot and nothing on the other. Still, she forced her shoulders back and her chin high.

She only wished she didn't feel his gaze. Without looking, she knew he was watching her. His gaze tingled along her spine, as though he were running his fingertips over her skin. As much as she resisted the pull, she could not keep from glancing over her shoulder. He was still standing in the hall, staring at her, a slight smile on his lips, a curious expression in his dark eyes. He looked at her as though she were some rare breed that he had never before encountered. She turned away from him and closed the door, appalled at the heat simmering in her cheeks. The attraction would pass, she assured herself.

She had an excellent chance of making what could be one of the most significant archaeological finds in history. And with it, she could give her great-grandfather the recognition he deserved. Nothing would keep her from solving the mystery that had led him to disaster.

3

*I*ain stood near one of the French doors in his library, watching the rain drift across the rose garden. The weather could change in a heartbeat on Dunmarin, which was nestled in the Atlantic just north of the Isle of Skye. It was one of the things he loved about this place—unpredictable, when so much in life was not. The fragrance of the sea and mist mingled with the scent of flowers from the garden, filling his every breath.

Beyond the cultivated expanse of the garden, with its neat beds of perennial flowers and rose bushes, stood the tall trees of a wood that one of his ancestors had planted. Mathesons had lived on this island for more than seven hundred years, and each generation had left a mark. Still, it was the very nature of the island that had always fascinated Iain.

In the distance, beyond the influence of man, the rugged slopes of Ben Alainn rose to embrace the sky, its peak dissolving into the mist as though it reached into another realm. Heather grew wild upon the rocky slopes, spreading like a lush purple quilt over the ground. Although he had houses in other parts of the world, this place was the one that always drew him back, where he always felt at home. His mother had told him it was because his soul had returned here time and time again.

His Highland blood allowed Iain to accept the possibility of past lives, just as he accepted the possibility there was more to the world than what could be seen and felt. He had been raised on tales of myth and magic, and all of his life he had believed there was more to the tales than simple imagination.

Although a sound did not betray her, Iain sensed the moment Ann entered the room. His skin tingled as though he stood naked in a summer storm. He turned and found her standing near the large claw-footed desk across the room. His gaze met hers. The attraction sizzled through him in a wave of heat that swept from the roots of his hair to the tips of his toes.

He stared at her, stunned by the sensations gripping him. It was the same as it had been that first time he had looked at her photograph, an odd familiarity, as if he had known her all of his life, as if she had always meant something special to him. It had been a very long time since he had felt an attraction this powerful. Now that he thought of it, he could not remember ever being hit with such force, as if a strong wind had snatched him up and set him down hard, leaving him dazed.

Although she was pretty—her cheekbones well defined, her nose slim, her face an appealing oval—when compared to the women he usually dated, there was nothing exceptional about her looks, except perhaps her eyes. They were beautiful, pale blue irises surrounded by a darker blue, the same color as the dark blue sweater she wore. Her hair was lighter than it appeared in photographs. Now that it had dried, he could see it was a light brown threaded with gold. The thick tresses fell in soft waves against her shoulders. Even as he tried to analyze the attraction she held for him, his instincts understood.

Indecision had never been one of his vices. He knew what he wanted when he saw it. He wanted Ann. In fact, he had wanted her from the very first moment he had looked at her photograph. He had a strange feeling he had wanted her even before he had known her name. He had dated some of the most beautiful women in the world, and not one had attracted him as this pretty schoolteacher from Chicago did.

Ann held a soft-sided briefcase against her chest, as though it were a shield. She was looking at him as though she were alone with a lion and she wasn't quite certain if he was hungry. What would she say if she knew just how hungry he was? What would she do if he crossed the distance between them and took her into his arms? Would her soft lips part for him if he kissed her? Would she slide her arms around his neck and hold him close against her?

The virulence of the desire pumping through his veins astonished him. It took every ounce of his will to maintain a thin veneer of civilized man, when all he wanted was to claim the female in his company.

Iain had no idea how long he stood staring at her, entranced by the spell spinning around them, finally broken when Ann looked away. She stood for a moment dragging air into her lungs, as though she had spent too long underwater. She felt it too, the same violent attraction. He knew enough about women to recognize desire when he saw it. It burned in her eyes when she looked at him. He could also see that the attraction she felt for him scared her half to death.

"I brought the journal. And a few things I thought you should see." She set the leather briefcase on the desk, her no-nonsense tone spoiled by the blush riding high in her cheeks.

Ann stepped back when he drew near, as if she were afraid she might get burned if she stood too close. He smiled at her. "Relax, Professor, I'm not going to bite. There is no reason to be frightened of me."

"Frightened?" She parted her lips as though she were going to say something. Yet it took another second for the words to flow. "I am certainly not frightened of you. There is no reason why I would be frightened of you."

"I am glad to hear that." He stepped around the desk, allowing a safe cushion between them. "We will be working together for perhaps the entire summer. In that time I hope we can become friends."

She glanced down at the floor. "Friends. Of course."

Friendship was just one thing he wanted from this woman. He opened the top drawer of the desk, pulled out a blue folder, and handed it to her. "Before we get started on the journal, I want you to see this."

"What is it?"

"A report. I think you should sit a moment and take a look at it."

She did as he suggested, her face revealing her curiosity as she sat in one of the leather wingback chairs near the desk. Iain sat on the edge of the desk in front of her while she opened the folder.

Ann glanced at the photos, then looked at him, her eyes wide with surprise. "What is the meaning of this?"

"I did some research about you, Dr. Fitzpatrick."

"Research?" She stared at him as though he had suddenly sprouted horns and cloven feet. "You had someone follow me?"

"I wanted to make certain you were who you said you were. If you look through the file, you will see there is nothing of a personal nature in it. It reveals no more than a job application might. Please take a look at it."

Although she looked doubtful, she glanced at the report, lifting each page as though it might leave stains upon her fingers. When she turned the last of the three pages, she looked up at him. Although he expected to see anger in her eyes, she surprised him by merely looking curious. "Why did you show this to me?"

"I have always held honesty in high regard. I wouldn't feel right if I didn't let you know that I had done some research about you, after you contacted my grandmother. On more than one occasion a reporter has tried to insinuate his or her way into my house. I wanted to make certain you were who you said you were."

"I can understand your concern." Ann drew her shoulders upward, as though she were cold. "Since we are being so honest, I should tell you that I did a little research into your family as well."

Iain cringed inwardly when he thought of all the articles that had been written about him over the past few years. "I hope you keep in mind, not everything that is printed is necessarily true."

Although Ann did not believe everything she read, particularly when it was written in a newspaper built on the gossip surrounding wealthy celebrities, when a man kept showing up in those newspapers with one famous woman after another, she certainly had to believe there was some amount of truth to the stories that followed him. It shouldn't matter to her. She could not possibly think of Iain Matheson in romantic terms, not unless she completely lost her mind.

She glanced down at the folder that outlined her nice, orderly, boring life. She and Iain Matheson resided in two completely different worlds. She taught archaeology. He ran a multibillion-dollar corporation. Her father was a retired aerospace engineer. His father was the earl of Dunmarin. She lived with her grandma Evie in a lovely 109-year-old Victorian house that Evie's grandfather had built. When he was not gallivanting around the globe, Iain lived in a huge 700-year-old castle on this remote Scottish island, an island his family owned. She had never in her life indulged in a casual affair. His liaisons were emblazoned across the pages of supermarket tabloids. Different worlds. Yet as much as she wanted to crush it with all of the logic at her disposal, she couldn't deny the attraction he held for her.

She set the folder on the desk and walked to the open French doors, needing to put some distance between herself and the maddening Highlander. The sound of rain pounding the stone terrace filled up the silence stretching between them. Although she kept her gaze fixed on a small statue of a sea lion just off the terrace, she could feel Iain's gaze upon her. Any thoughts of romance were insane. Yet here she was imagining what it might be like to feel his arms around her, his lips upon hers. "Your personal life is really of no concern to me. My only interest here is in finding the Celtic cross that was hidden along with the Matheson jewels. I need the cross to continue my great-grandfather Owen's work."

Ann heard him approach behind her. Her heart pounded so wildly, she was afraid he would hear it and recognize just how vulnerable she was when it came to this irrational attraction. Although he did not touch her, she sensed him standing close behind her, his warmth radiating against her, tempting her to turn toward him. She crossed her arms over her chest and sought some focus, some means to escape the need swelling within her. Yet she could not run and hide, no matter how frightening the sensations he evoked within her.

He rested his hands on her shoulders, his palms warming her through the soft navy blue cotton of her sweater. With gentle pressure he coaxed her to turn to face him. What she saw in those dark eyes startled her so completely, she forgot to breathe.

No man had ever looked at her the way he was looking at her now, as though she were not merely beautiful, but the most beautiful woman he had ever seen. Her life's experience had not prepared her for the potent masculinity of a man such as Iain Matheson. He was a man who had toppled the Hollywood marriage of America's sweetheart. A man who made a practice of dating women who made a living by convincing all the mere mortal females of the world that they too could look divine if they only used a certain brand of lipstick. She was just one of those mortal females.

He leaned toward her, so close the damp heat of his breath fell upon her lips, as he said, "My soul is not as black as they often paint it, Professor."

His Scottish burr stroked her, as dark as midnight, softer than the brush of a kitten's fur. He lifted a lock of her hair and slowly rubbed his thumb back and forth over the strands, a smile curving his lips, as though he savored the texture of her hair. The smoldering scent of citrus and spices drifted with the warmth of his skin, swirling through her every breath, coaxing her to move closer to him. Somewhere in the muddle he had made of her normally dependable brain, she realized she should step away from him. Yet his gentle hold upon her hair paled in comparison to the powerful grasp he held upon her senses.

She should not be standing here staring at him like a foolish, lovesick teenager. A magnetic current should not be swirling through her, making her feel more alive than she had ever felt in her life. Yet all the reasoning in the world could not keep the trembling from her limbs. Logic could not coax her heart into a nice sensible rhythm. Not while the heat of his body enveloped her. Not while the scent of him swirled around her. Not while he looked at her as though she were more important than anything else in the world.

As though drawn by invisible strings, she leaned toward him. He slid his long fingers into her hair, cradling the back of her head in his large hand. "There is something I have been wanting to do, Professor."

Ann had to swallow hard before she could use her voice. "What?"

"This." He lowered his head slowly, allowing her a moment of anticipation before he kissed her. His breath spilled across her cheek, warm and laced with a trace of cinnamon. He slid his lips over hers, claiming her completely.

4

nn was not a child. This was certainly not the
first time she had ever been kissed. Yet nothing
she had ever experienced compared to this kiss. It was as
if her entire life she had merely been an observer, existing
on the fringe of sensation without ever truly experiencing
passion or desire.

Longing swelled within her, rising from wells hidden
deep inside, in a place she never knew existed until she
felt the touch of this man. Although it defied logic, for
some reason she did not begin to understand, she responded to him as though she had been wandering lost all
of her life and had only now found her way home. As startling as it was, her own response did not astonish her as
much as his response to her.

He flexed his hands against her, squeezing her arm and her waist, as though he wanted to tear away every scrap of material that kept his skin from touching hers. Heaven help her, she wanted that too. She wanted to strip away his clothes. She wanted to feel the slide of his skin upon hers. The sheer power of her need for him ripped through her. Yet somewhere, in the part of her brain still functioning, screamed a very small, yet very loud voice. They were very nearly strangers. And she was on the verge of . . . She pulled back, terrified by the power this man held over her.

He looked down at her, his gorgeous eyes filled with questions, the answers to which she did not want to begin to contemplate. She pulled out of his arms and stepped back, straight into a small pedestal table near the door. She turned in time to see a tall brass figurine of a sea lion rising on a wave totter and plunge over the edge of the table. She snatched for the figurine. So did Iain. They collided, her brow ramming his chin.

The sea lion fell with a thump against burgundy and ivory roses stitched into the thick wool carpet. She looked up and found Iain rubbing his jaw, looking at her as though she were a puzzle he was trying to piece together. Not for the first time in her life, she wished she could wiggle her nose and disappear. Yet life did not follow the same rules as old television comedies.

"Are you all right?" he asked, his voice huskier than usual.

No. She was not all right. She had a feeling she would be far from fine for as long as she was within an ocean of Iain Matheson. "I came here merely to find the jewels and the cross. Not to be seduced by a man who apparently feels compelled to bed every female who comes within reach."

A glimmer of surprise touched his features before a lazy smile curved his lips. "Is that what I was doing, Professor? Seducing you?"

She was not so naive as to believe there was no intent to bed behind that kiss. "What would you call it?"

"A kiss." Iain brushed his fingertip over the curve of her jaw. She almost gasped at the pleasurable sensations. "A very nice kiss."

The man was dangerous. "You might find it amusing, toying with women, but I do not find it amusing to be toyed with."

"Toying with women." He released his breath in a slow sigh between his teeth. He retrieved the sea lion figurine and set it back on the table. "You have a fine opinion of me, I see. Do you truly imagine I spend all of my time seducing poor unsuspecting women into my bed?"

"I doubt you need to do much seducing. Women are only too anxious to fall into bed with men like you."

He held her gaze, while the sound of rain pounding the stone terrace filled up the silence between them. "What kind of man do you think I am?" he asked, his voice low and soft, a direct contrast to the hard glitter in his eyes.

"The kind of man who has always had things his way. The kind who was caught taking a moonlight swim with a supermodel in the Trevi Fountain in Rome last year. Naked and drunk."

He pursed his lips. "You enjoy the tabloids."

"My grandma Evie devours them. And you keep popping up in them."

"And what do you suppose I enjoy more than anything in a woman?"

"I suppose men such as you prefer either legs or bosoms."

"Actually, I have always liked a fine mind."

"Yes, I understand Jillian what's-her-name has graced all of those magazine covers because of her marvelous intellect."

"She graduated with honors in engineering from Stanford University. Not all beautiful women are stupid."

"I never meant to say a beautiful woman must be stupid. I suppose the fact she went skinny-dipping with you in the Trevi Fountain led me astray."

"If you want to know the truth of that, I was fully clothed and far from drunk. I went into the fountain because I was afraid she might drown. Jillian was not thinking clearly at the time."

"I suppose you didn't notice she was getting drunk when you were refilling her glass."

A muscle flashed in his cheek with the clenching of his jaw. "I had nothing at all to do with this particular vice. But I do not expect you to believe me, since you have already painted me so very black."

For some reason she couldn't understand, she did believe him. That was just one of the reasons he was so incredibly dangerous. "For a man who is innocent of all crimes, you certainly do get blamed for a great many of them. I suppose you are merely an innocent man who has been caught in compromising situations over and over and over again?"

"When I was at university, my father told me to enjoy my life." He smiled at her. "Have no regrets."

"And do you have any regrets?

"None that haunt me. At least not yet." He lowered his eyes, his gaze brushing her neck. A tingling warmth spread across her skin, as though he had touched her softly with his fingertips. "And you, Professor? Have you any regrets in your life?"

If she weren't careful, she would have one very huge regret. It took a certain measure of security to plunge into an affair with a man like Iain. A woman needed the confidence to know she could enjoy herself, then walk away with her heart still in one piece. She was not that type. If she became involved with this man, she would get hurt, deeply. She forced herself to maintain his direct gaze, even though she felt like running as far away from him as she could. "No. I cannot say that I have any major regrets. And I intend to keep it that way."

"It would seem we have at least something in common."

"Very little."

"Somehow I think we share more than you might want to believe." He lifted a lock of her hair. "I am going to enjoy getting to know you."

She pulled her hair free of his gentle grasp. "I think you are a consummate flirt, Iain Matheson. The kind of man who is not satisfied until every woman he meets falls beneath the blade of his charm."

He held her accusing gaze. "You have a clear picture of me, do you?"

Oh, she did not deserve that look of disappointment in his eyes. "Maggie O'Brien," she said, defending herself.

Twin lines formed between his thick black brows. "I see you have done some research, but then I doubt there is a supermarket in America that has not recently been filled with stories about how I have ruined the marriage of America's sweetheart."

"You destroyed her marriage, then refused to marry her. You made a fool out of her and her husband."

"I hate to spoil such a perfect picture of debauchery as you have painted, but the truth is, Maggie and I have been friends for about twelve years. One of her first movies was for the production company I started when I graduated from university."

"Beyond Forever."

"Aye. My uncle Nigel called it Iain's Folly. He was certain I would lose every penny that I had invested. Of course he couldn't understand why I would want to get involved with making films, of all things. Yet my parents understood." Iain smiled, a wistful look entering his eyes. "My father became my partner to show me how much he trusted my judgment."

A romantic comedy of a handsome Scottish ghost and a pretty American schoolteacher bound by destiny, *Beyond Forever* had received several Academy Awards as well as huge revenues at the box office. It had propelled Maggie O'Brien to stardom, and it made a major player of a small production company headed by the heir to the Matheson fortune. It reminded her of a movie that might have been made during the time of Cary Grant and Katherine Hepburn. Perhaps that was why she had enjoyed it so much. Old movies were still the best movies.

"It was a wonderful movie."

"Thank you." He smiled, warm and boyishly, a smile that revealed his satisfaction with life. "I wanted to make the type of movie I had always enjoyed, the old movies.

Something with the wit and warmth of *Bringing Up Baby* and the magic of *It Happened One Night.*"

He had just named her two favorite movies of all time. She stared at him, amazed to find anything in common with this man. "You like old movies?"

"Aye. No one makes a movie better than Howard Hawks or Frank Capra. And there are few stars who compare to the great stars of that era."

"Maggie O'Brien would have fit into that era well."

"Aye. She would have." He sat on the arm of a nearby sofa and stretched his long legs out before him. "Maggie and I are friends. We have never been lovers. She and her husband have been having trouble, it is true. But I have had nothing to do with it, except to be there when she needed to talk to someone. The photographs that appeared in all those tabloids were taken when Maggie and I went for a walk near her home in Malibu. Two friends on the beach, nothing more. Yet that would have been too innocent to garner any attention."

Innocent. It wasn't a word she associated with Iain Matheson. Still, there was a sincerity in his eyes that demanded rather than asked for her belief in him. "I cannot imagine what it is like to live under such scrutiny."

"Loss of privacy." Iain glanced toward the open French doors. "It makes you realize there is a price to pay for everything."

A price to pay for everything. What price would she pay if she indulged in this attraction to Iain Matheson? "I think we have somehow become a little diverted."

Iain looked at her, his expression revealing a flicker of curiosity. "Diverted? Is that what happened between us?"

Ann couldn't say for certain what had happened, except that she had lost a good portion of her common sense. "I think we should stay focused on the journal and the search for the jewels, rather than allow any . . . personal issues to divert us again."

"You want our relationship to be all business?"

"Yes. Business. All business. Entirely business."

He held her gaze, pure undiluted hunger smoldering in his dark eyes. "That is going to be difficult, considering how attracted I am to you."

She could not breathe. "Considering your reputation, I suspect you are attracted to most of the women you meet."

"My reputation is not who I am." He stood and moved toward her. "Perhaps you should get to know the man before you cast judgment upon him."

She stepped back when he drew near. "I suppose there isn't a trace of truth in any of the stories about you."

"It depends on the story."

He advanced. She retreated, backpedaling as he stalked her. "You don't actually date a new woman every week? Most of them gorgeous models or actresses?"

"Many of the women I meet are models or actresses." He shrugged, broad shoulders lifting the thick cabled knit of his sweater. "I haven't been fortunate enough to find the right woman. Yet."

She stepped back and bumped into the desk. "You are actually a nice, quiet man who is horribly misunderstood by the press."

"I am not a saint." Iain closed the distance between them, stepping so close his legs brushed hers. "But I am not quite the sinner they paint me to be either. I am just a man who finds himself in the company of a very desirable woman."

Desirable? Pleasure quivered through her. She quickly suppressed the need rising within her. She was certainly not desirable. She was dependable. Practical. Levelheaded. Efficient. Pragmatic. Any of her family could vouch for her character. She certainly was not the type of woman who would interest a man like Iain. At least not after the novelty wore off the situation.

Ann leaned back against the desk and held up her hand to hold him at bay. "I am not going to be the next notch on your bedpost."

"You have such a high opinion of me." Iain smiled, a glint of mischief entering his eyes. He braced his hands on the desk behind her, trapping her between his body and the solid mahogany. "I wonder how I shall manage to live up to it."

He lowered his head toward her. She felt a shifting within her, her will unraveling, her muscles tightening while she fought every treacherous instinct screaming inside her, instincts that begged for her to surrender. Instead she pressed her fingertips against his chin. "You don't happen to have a club hidden behind you, do you?"

He froze, as she hoped he might. "A club?"

"Since you seem intent to do your best impression of a caveman in heat, I was just wondering if you intended to hit me over the head with a club."

"I have never needed a club." He stepped back, allowing her room to escape. He smiled, his expression pure mischief. "Before now."

She edged away from him until she stood beside the chair behind his desk. "I realize you get a great deal of enjoyment in these little games you play with women, and I hate to spoil your sport, but I am not interested in participating."

$\mathcal{D}$ain sat on the edge of the desk, trying to ignore the discomfort of trousers that were suddenly too snug. Her kiss had told him all he needed to know. In spite of her words, she wanted him. She didn't want to want him, but she did. "I realize you think I am some kind of Lothario. But the truth is, I never play games of the heart. I have always been honest with every woman I have ever known. I was attracted to you from the moment I first looked at your photograph."

"My photograph does that to men all the time. I was actually asked not to put a photograph in the college yearbook, for fear of the damage it might cause to any unsuspecting male who might see it."

The sarcasm in her voice was spoiled by the soft blush that deepened the color of her eyes. The same rosy color stained the slim column of her neck. For all the world, he wanted to taste the heat of that blush upon his tongue. She stepped back and pressed her hand to the base of her neck, as if she knew what he was thinking. "I can imagine the havoc you wreak on the males in your classes. It's a wonder any of the poor devils can concentrate on their studies."

"Oh, yes. The poor things, what with the panting and salivating, it is a wonder we get any work accomplished at all. I simply cannot turn without bumping into one besotted male after another."

He nodded. "Lined up for miles, are they?"

She pressed her hand over her heart. "You cannot imagine the traffic hazard they cause, the way they overflow into the street. Unfortunately they serenade me at night, which drives my neighbors to distraction. I've tried tossing buckets of water on them, but it does no good. And I cannot step from my door without risking injury."

"Injury?"

"From nearly tripping over all of my admirers." She released an exaggerated sigh. "If they did not keep falling to their knees when they saw me, it would be much easier."

"And now here I am, just one in a long line of your poor besotted fools."

Ann rolled her eyes toward heaven. "I realize I may appear to be a little provincial, compared to the women you usually choose to be your next conquest, but I—"

"Conquest?"

"Yes. But I assure you, I am not foolish enough to leap at the chance to become a summer fling."

"A fling?"

"*Yes.*" She made a wide sweeping gesture with her hands. "So you might as well stop trying. I have no intention of being seduced by you today."

He grinned at her. "How about tomorrow?"

"Not any day. Not any night." Ann pulled a pair of wire-rimmed glasses from the pocket of her light gray slacks. She opened them and slipped them on, missing her left ear with her first try. Once she straightened the frame and hooked it around her ear, she grabbed her briefcase and pulled it open. "Now, if you are interested, I will show you Adair Matheson's journal."

He was interested, all right. He gestured toward the

large burgundy leather chair beside Ann. "Have a seat, Dr. Fitzpatrick. And show me the reason you think you can find the Matheson jewels."

Ann hesitated a moment before taking a seat on the edge of the chair. He noticed a fine trembling in her hands as she pulled a slim brown leather book from the briefcase. She then removed another book, this one covered in dark burgundy leather, photocopies of letters covered with a bold script, and a green velvet pouch. She opened the brown leather book and placed one of the photocopies beside it. "If you compare the journal to the letters that Adair wrote, it is obvious they were both written by the same hand."

Iain rested his hand on the desk and leaned forward to look at the journal and the letter she had laid beside it. When he drew near Ann, a delicate floral scent swirled through his senses, tempting him to press his lips against her soft hair. Since he knew where that would get him, he forced his attention back to the handwriting of Adair Matheson. "It could be his."

Ann glanced up at him, a determined look in her eyes. "It is his."

"After all of this time." Iain lifted the journal, a sense of wonder streaming through him. His life at Dunmarin had given him a strong appreciation of the past and of those who had come before him. He carefully turned the thick pages, glancing at the words written by one of his ancestors nearly two hundred years ago, accepting a possibility he had not considered since he was a lad. "You say he left clues to finding the jewels."

"I found four of them scattered throughout the book." She pulled a small black leather notebook from the briefcase and flipped through the pages until she found what she was looking for. She handed the notebook to Iain. "I listed them here."

Iain glanced down at the page, where four lines had been written in a precise script. "With the Sentinel of the Selkies you will take your first step. In the bosom of the Sentinel, find the lion who greets each day. In the jaws of the lion you will find the key. Seek the selkie's secret behind its stony face."

"The first thing we have to do is find the Sentinel of the Selkies." Ann pushed her glasses on top of her head, sweeping her hair back from her brow. "Do you have any idea where to start?"

"I think we should start with dinner, tonight. There is a pub in the village that has wonderful food, music, and dancing. Have you ever danced a Scottish reel?"

5

*A*nn stared at him, appalled at the swift flood of excitement rushing through her. She glanced down at the journal, hiding the expression in her eyes, afraid he might see too much. Yet she could feel the heat tingling her cheeks. Confound it, she really had to learn to control her blush. "I take my work seriously."

"I can see that you do. But I have to say in all honesty, even with the journal and these clues, finding the jewels will be next to impossible. Dunmarin has changed many times since Adair walked these grounds."

Her stomach clenched at that very real possibility. She had nine weeks before she had to be back home. Nine weeks to chase a dream that had haunted her all of her life. She was not about to give up without giving it her all.

She certainly would not allow a charming rogue to distract her. "I have to find the jewels."

He leaned back, allowing her a small degree of space. Yet she suspected it would take the span of an ocean to help ease this horrible turmoil he ignited within her. The man was definitely the most dangerous man she had ever met. "My grandmother told me you are hoping to find the missing half of a Celtic cross with the jewels."

"Yes." Ann removed half of an ancient cross from the green velvet bag. No matter how infuriating the man might be, she realized there was a better chance of finding the jewels with Iain's help. He knew the castle. If she could convince him to concentrate on business, they just might be able to solve a mystery. "It is the missing half of this cross. My great-grandfather Owen believed it was hidden along with the Matheson jewels. You can see there are symbols carved into the back of it. Owen believed that when the pieces of the cross were joined, the symbols would form a map that would lead to the lost city of Edaín. Have you heard of it?"

Iain studied her a moment, as though he were mildly amused by the question. "Edaín is a city in ancient myth believed to have been inhabited by the *sidhe,* or the Tuatha De Danann, the magical ruling class of the Celts. Through the years they have been called fairies, or sorcerers, or witches. Supposedly Edaín existed beneath Dunmarin."

She stared at him, wondering what other surprises the man held. "Apparently you do know a little about Celtic myths and legends."

"It is another thing we have in common, in case you didn't notice." He winked at her. "And you believe Edaín is more than a myth?"

"I think it is possible. This was Owen's last journal. I found it along with the journal of Adair Matheson and the cross in my grandmother's attic." She picked up the burgundy book, then glanced around the desk, searching for her glasses. She lifted the photocopies of the letters, then looked under the bag that had held the cross. "Where the devil are they?"

"What are you looking for?"

She glanced up at him. "My glasses."

"These glasses?" He leaned forward and slid the glasses from her head to her nose.

"Thank you." She pushed the wire rim against the bridge of her nose, embarrassed by how easily he could turn her brain to mush. She glanced through a few pages of the journal, checking her facts before she continued. "When he was a student at Oxford, my great-grandfather became fascinated by the work of Cameron Macleod, who was searching for Edaín in 1816. Owen believed Macleod found the city and etched the map to it on the back of this cross. He gave half of the cross to his cousin Adair Matheson to keep for him while he made a second journey to the city. Owen doesn't say how he ended up with the other half of the cross."

"Macleod never returned from the expedition to reclaim the cross. It is believed to have been hidden along with the Matheson jewels by Adair when he took a notion that he would be robbed. Apparently Adair was a wee bit of an eccentric. Unfortunately he died without ever telling anyone his hiding place."

"You know about Macleod?"

"It is part of the history of Dunmarin. And history has always been a passion of mine."

Ann stared at him, astonished by his knowledge. He leaned forward and tapped her chin. "Careful, professor, you'll catch a fly if you keep your mouth open."

She snapped her mouth closed, heat flooding her cheeks. "I was just surprised to hear that you enjoy history."

"Growing up in a place such as Dunmarin provided a wonderful chance to experience history."

She directed her attention back to the journal, trying to focus her thoughts. "Like Cameron Macleod, my great-grandfather also never returned from an expedition to find the lost city of Edaín."

"And now you are looking for the city."

"Yes." Ann tapped her fingertip against a page of the journal. "After all this time, we may actually find a way to prove that my great-grandfather Owen was very close to making a significant archaeological discovery."

"It is very important to you."

She glanced up at him, his features blurred by her reading lenses. "Edaín would be one of the most significant archaeological finds ever. Who knows what secrets would be revealed in that ancient city? Can you imagine what it would mean, finding a city that existed more than eight thousand years ago?"

"Aye, I can." He studied her a moment, as though she were glass and he could look straight through her. "Yet it isn't truly the discovery of Edaín that drives you, is it? It's your great-grandfather."

Ann glanced away from those perceptive eyes. "He never had a chance to prove his theories."

"Is that why you became an archaeologist? To finish what your great-grandfather had started?"

"I suppose it . . ." She hesitated, uneasy with sharing a part of her past. Yet she had a feeling he would probe until she had revealed everything about herself. "From the time I can remember, my grandma Evie would tell me stories about her father, Owen Grierson. He really had such fascinating theories and wonderful adventures. Unlike me, he actually practiced his profession in the field."

"And so you wanted to be like him?"

"It always seemed to me as though he had so many dreams that had never been fulfilled. I suppose I wanted to find the answers to the questions he left behind. I want people to know he was a brilliant man, not some fool who went chasing after a moonbeam and got himself killed."

Iain groaned. "I am sorry if it sounded as though I took your work lightly. I truly do not. I simply believe there isn't much chance in finding that cross."

"I have to try. In a way it feels as though all of my life I have been following a path that would lead me here." An odd feeling gripped her. Although she could not explain why, she knew with the same certainty that the sun would rise that she spoke the truth. She had been destined to follow a path that would lead her to Dunmarin.

"That is because we were destined to meet," he said, his voice soft and so very compelling.

Ann pushed her glasses to the top of her head to bring his face into focus. Since he could not truly believe such nonsense, she expected to see humor in his eyes. Yet the look in his eyes made her wish she had remained hidden behind the lenses. He was looking at her with such depth of feeling she completely forgot to breathe. He looked at her as though she were the only woman he had ever considered in terms of happily ever after. She tore her gaze from his, struggling to force her wits to function properly. **She** stared at her great-grandfather's journal, ashamed of how easily Iain had swayed her from her course. "The first step is to find the Sentinel of the Selkies. Do you have any idea where it might be?"

"Aye." Iain stood and offered her his hand. "Come with me, lass. Let's see if we can catch this moonbeam."

Ann stood without his assistance and faced him the way she might confront an annoying student. "I certainly would appreciate any assistance you may wish to give me. After all, if we find the jewels, your family will benefit."

"Aye, they will."

"I think we can work together, as long as it is clear our relationship is purely in the interest of science. I assure you I am completely prepared for any of your annoying attempts at seduction."

"Then you have nothing at all to worry about when you are in my company. You are immune to my dubious charm."

Oh, dear, she didn't like the look in his eyes. She had the uncomfortable feeling she had just dropped a gauntlet at his feet. "Completely immune, I assure you," she replied, raising her chin.

"So if I should decide to try to seduce you, I would fail miserably."

"It is pointless to try."

He leaned toward her, so close his breath brushed her lips when he said, "Are you certain you aren't a wee bit afraid of me and my terrible charm?"

"Not at all." She was terrified!

He ran his hand down her arm. "And if I were to take you into my arms and kiss you again, you would just stand there like a sack of flour?"

The heat of his palm penetrated her sweater, bathing her skin. "Completely unmoved," she said, her voice sounding breathy to her own ears.

Iain stepped back from her. "Then I can tell there is no sense in trying."

"None at all," she said, astonished by the disappointment rushing through her.

"At least not yet." He cupped her cheek in his large hand. "One of the things I have learned is that anything worth having is worth fighting for."

She stood captive to his gaze, stunned by the look in his eyes. Promises dwelled deep in those eyes, promises that couldn't possibly be true.

"Let's see what we can find, Professor. But first, let me show you the rest of the treasure that we are after."

Iain took her arm and ushered her toward the door. He led her through a maze of corridors and stairs until he reached a gallery in the south wing. He paused beneath a portrait of a woman sitting on a stone bench in a rose garden. The brass plate affixed to the ornately carved frame identified the woman as Lady Catherine, countess of Dunmarin.

Her dark hair was piled upon her head in the Grecian style favored during the early Regency period. The pale green of her high-waisted gown emphasized the darker stones in the necklace adorning her slender neck, three strands of emeralds and diamonds interconnected by a lacy pattern of gold. The smallest stones looked to be at least a karat, the largest four times that size. Catherine held her hands overlapped upon her thigh, as though careful to display the matching bracelet upon her white-gloved wrist and a ring that boasted a huge square-cut emerald surrounded by diamonds.

"Catherine was Adair's wife. I cannot imagine what she thought of him when she realized he had died without telling her how to find her jewels."

Ann moistened her suddenly dry lips. Until now she hadn't truly thought about the jewels as being anything but a companion to the cross. "Let's hope we can find them."

*S*heltered beneath a large golf umbrella Iain held, Ann walked beside him along a path that wound through the south gardens and the woods beyond. She soon regretted the fact they had taken only one umbrella. An unsettling warmth teased her skin each time his arm brushed hers. Although it was subtle, she could smell the tangy scent of his cologne, the scent tempting her to draw closer. After they had walked for nearly half an hour, she began to suspect he had something other than finding the Sentinel in mind. "You wouldn't just be leading me on a wild-goose hunt, would you?"

Iain lifted his brows, assuming a look of mock surprise. "How little faith you have in me, Professor."

"I suppose you think it's romantic, wandering about the countryside, huddled under this big umbrella as though no one else existed in the world."

"Romantic?" A smile slid slowly along his lips. "And here I thought you didn't believe in romance."

"I never said I didn't believe in romance. I simply

don't believe in indulging in romance with a man who has made it a sporting event."

"Careful, Professor, your flattery will have my poor head in a spin."

She suppressed the smile that threatened her stern look. "Do you really have an idea of where to look, or is this just a lark?"

"Be patient."

The woodland path led gradually upward. When they left the woods, they were on the brow of a hill overlooking the sea. A short distance away, perched near the edge of the cliffs, stood a small stone building that looked as though it had stood in this place for centuries.

Iain led her to the oak door and smiled at her. "This is where I thought we might start our search."

Ann's heart pounded with the possibilities hiding in this ancient building. "It looks like a tomb."

"It is a tomb." Rusty hinges groaned as Iain pulled open the door, releasing the scent of dust into the rain. "Be careful, there are steps just inside the door."

Ann hesitated at the threshold, a shiver rippling through her when she noticed the large cobweb that covered one corner of the doorway. "You want to explore a tomb?"

He grinned at her. "You aren't afraid of ghosts, are you?"

"No. But I'm not overly fond of crawly things."

"An archaeologist who is afraid of spiders?"

"Not afraid, exactly. Cautious." She walked past him, careful to avoid the cobweb, her head barely clearing the low doorway. Narrow windows just below the eaves cast a faint glow against the stone walls, illuminating a flight of stone steps leading down beneath the ground.

After leaving the umbrella near the door, Iain joined her at the top of the stairs, bending to accommodate his height. He pulled a flashlight from the pocket of his jacket and directed the beam down the narrow stone stairway. "I haven't been here in years."

"It looks as though no one has." Ann rubbed her arms, wondering what hid in the shadows. "What makes you think the Sentinel is here?"

"Because of the legend."

She stared at him. "The legend?"

"Aye." Iain took her arm and started down the stairs. "In 1435, the Matheson laird was succeeded by his only child, a daughter named Eleanor. Although many tried to coax her into marriage, no one succeeded until one day a stranger came to Dunmarin. No one knew from whence he came. No one knew his name, except that he called himself Dugald. Eleanor fell deeply in love. They married within days of meeting, and he assumed the name Matheson." When they reached the base of the stairs, Iain leaned toward her and lowered his voice as though he were divulging a secret. "It is said Dugald was not a mortal man, but a selkie who had left the sea to be with his one and only love."

Ann stared at him, trying to decide if he were teasing her. "And so one of your ancestors is actually a selkie?"

"If you are to believe in the legend." A smoldering scent of citrus and spices mingled with a scent that was his alone, the aroma enveloping her. "Do you know about the selkies?"

"Yes. They are enchanted beings, akin to fairies. They

live in the sea, wearing a second skin that makes them appear as seals, or sea lions, I'm not quite sure which one. When they choose, they can shed their skin and appear to be human."

"Upon each evening's low tide, a selkie male will hide his sealskin near the shore and go in search of a beautiful woman, with seduction on his mind. Handsome in face and form, charming in his manner—no maiden is safe," he said, his dark voice pouring over her. "One look in his eyes, and she will be his, body and soul."

Iain was the type of man who would consume a woman, body and soul. The type of man who would leave her grieving long after he had left her. "And after he has had his fill of the poor lass, he dons his sealskin and swims out to sea, leaving her heart broken."

"Not always." He smoothed his fingertips over her cheek, caressing her softly. A sigh quivered through her. "A selkie will wander the earth for an eternity, looking for his one true mate. According to the legend, Dugald had gazed upon Eleanor time and time again from the sea. He left all he held dear to be with her. It is said that in each firstborn male of his descendants the selkie blood still flows."

"And the firstborn male is always born with flippers?"

"The firstborn male is doomed to wander the earth ever searching for his true mate."

"Seducing every woman in his path until he finds her?"

"Incomplete until he finds her, as if he searches for the missing half of his soul."

"Soul mates." Such an alluring thought—yet she knew better than to believe he actually embraced such a concept. "I imagine that little piece of nonsense has served you well in the past."

"Nonsense?" The glow of the flashlight illuminated his look of surprise. "Do you truly have no belief in lovers who are destined to be with one another?"

"If you are asking me if I believe in the concept that our souls keep returning to earth, destined to find one true mate lifetime after lifetime, then I would say no. I believe it is possible to be happy with more than simply one person out of millions."

"Happy, perhaps. But not in the true sense of the word. Not with a joy that reaches deep into your very soul."

He looked into her eyes while he spoke, and for the life of her she could not see a trace of deception in those dark eyes. He was very good at this game. She intended to keep that in mind.

She directed her attention to the interior of the building, noting a pair of raised tombs at the far end of the structure. The light from Iain's flashlight illuminated numerous marble slabs on the walls. "In the bosom of the Sentinel, find the lion who greets each day. If this building is the Sentinel, we need to—" Her words ended in a shriek as something small darted across her foot. She grabbed Iain's arm and held him like a lifeline in a storm.

"It's all right," Iain said, covering her hand with his. "It's just a wee mouse."

Heat flooded her cheeks. "It startled me."

"I noticed." Iain grinned at her. "Would you like to wait outside while I look about?"

"No. I'm fine. Perfectly fine." She eased her hand out from beneath his warm grasp. "I just don't like to be taken unaware like that."

Iain tilted his head. "I'll keep that in mind, lass."

She lifted her chin and tried to appear as poised as possible. "I assure you, I am quite capable of handling all manner of irritating nuisances."

Iain grimaced. "That one hurt."

"I suspect you will survive." Her rejection would prove nothing more than a bump in the road for him. After she was gone, Iain wouldn't even remember her name. When she left Dunmarin, she intended to walk away in one piece. It would be wonderful if this tomb truly was the Sentinel. The quicker she could find those jewels and sever her connection with Iain Matheson, the better.

*N*ine hours later they were still no closer to finding the jewels. Ann stood next to Iain at the desk in the library and watched as he pointed out a large drum tower on a copy of plans made to improve Dunmarin in 1873. Since that major improvement, other changes had been made to the castle. Each change was outlined in one of the plans lying upon the desk. Hopefully the plans would give them an idea of where to find the Sentinel.

"You can see, that in the time of Adair, this tower and this wing did not exist." With the tip of his forefinger, he circled the depiction of the large drum tower that currently stood between two smaller towers in a great expanse that had become the face of the castle presented to the sea. "It was just the two smaller towers overlooking the sea. Nothing in between. I have to believe the Sentinel of the Selkies would overlook the sea."

"It would make sense." In the short time she had known him, it had become clear that Iain was a man who loved a challenge. When he put his mind to something, he attacked it with all the precision of a surgeon and the energy of a marathon runner. At the moment, she felt as though *she* had run a marathon. Aside from meals, she had been running all day. "Has there been much renovation done to the interiors of the towers since the time of Adair?"

"I know some renovation was made." Iain straightened and rolled back his shoulders. "The history of Dunmarin has been fairly well documented. We can take a look through the drawings that have been collected and see if we can find a clue."

Ann tried to stifle a yawn and failed. "Where do we begin?"

"We begin by getting a good night's rest. Tomorrow we can start with exploring the towers." He tucked a lock of hair behind her ear, his fingertip skimming her skin, sending shivers scattering along her nerve endings. "You look exhausted."

She stepped back from him, but that didn't ease the pounding of her heart. One touch, and her heart raced as though it had the Kentucky Derby to win. "I am a little tired."

"We shall get started again tomorrow."

"All right." She turned and headed for the door, her vote equally split as to whether or not it was a good thing that Iain intended to continue with the search. On one hand, he could prove to be a wonderful asset. On the other, he distracted her so much she couldn't think straight. Even as she debated, she realized she was being silly. The attraction would fade, she assured herself. When he realized she was not going to play, he would lose interest in this little game.

"Dr. Fitzpatrick, what do you wear to bed?"

His soft words wrapped around her like a velvet tether, halting her near the entrance to the room. She pivoted and found him standing near the desk, looking at her as though she were his favorite dessert. That look in his eyes did wicked things to her insides. "What did you say?"

"I want to know what you wear to bed. Since I am going to dream about you, I thought I might get your outfit fixed in my mind."

"My attire at bed is really none of your concern. And I would appreciate it if you—"

"A white cotton nightgown, long and full, the kind that hides everything and entices the imagination." He sat on the edge of the desk, his long legs stretched out before him, his gaze warm upon her. "The kind that would billow in the breeze, pressing against your body, should we walk along the beach."

Heat prickled her neck, then etched a scalding path upward into her cheeks, the blush pale compared to the heat blossoming in her lower abdomen. He had managed to describe perfectly the nightgown she intended to wear tonight. "Walk along the beach? I certainly would not wear a nightgown for a walk along the beach."

"In my dream you would." Iain smiled, a slow curve of sensual lips that coaxed memory to rise and flutter through her. Although she wanted to forget those few moments he had held her in his arms, the memories remained, etched upon her mind in bright colors. "Sleep well, Professor."

Ann turned without a word, knowing how easily her voice would betray her. The trembling in her limbs would not allow her voice to remain steady. Although she wanted to run, she forced herself to walk to her room. The man was the most infuriating creature she had ever met.

I am going to dream about you.

How many times had he used that line? She supposed it had served him well in the past. He would soon learn she was made of stronger stuff. She would not give the man another thought.

Come to me.

The words rippled through her mind. Yet there was nothing tangible to be heard, except the rush of the ocean lapping at the beach and the whisper of the wind against her cheeks. Still, Ann obeyed that soft command, following an instinct she could not begin to understand. The breeze caught the full skirt of her nightgown, billowing the white cotton behind her, as she stood at the edge of the water.

Mist brushed the top of the rolling waves, like a filmy veil. A sea lion dove from the rocks just offshore, his sleek body plunging through the mist. She watched as he arced in and out of the rolling waves. Yet it was not the animal who rose from the waves near shore, but a man. Moonlight poured over him, while the water spilled away from his powerful form.

Come to me.

The words rippled through her. Her heart hammered against her ribs while she stood mesmerized by the sight of him, his features revealed by moonlight. She should leave. It wasn't safe. He wasn't safe. Yet she could not look away from him. Mist swirled around him, as though anxious to touch him as he moved toward her.

Iain paused before her, tall and powerful, bathed only in moonlight and mist. "I've waited a lifetime for you."

His voice spilled through her, easing the fear coiling beneath the attraction that drew her to this man. When he reached for her, she went to him, her will bending to the need welling within her. At the first touch of his lips upon hers, she was lost. This is what she had wanted all of her life, this man, this moment of absolute freedom.

He peeled away her nightgown, drinking the moonlight from her skin as he exposed her breasts, her belly, her legs. She slid her hands over him, needing to claim him, as he touched and caressed and claimed her for his own. When he laid her down upon the soft white cotton of her nightgown, she welcomed him into her arms. The mist swirled around them, blending one into the other, two halves now whole again.

Ann awoke with a start, her body trembling, her heart pounding, as if she had just . . .

"No," she whispered, shifting upon the mattress, trying to ease the tingling sensation in her loins. She had not just made love to Iain on the beach. She was alone in her bed. The pale light of dawn drifted through the windowpanes, illuminating the bedclothes tangled around her legs. She straightened the covers, then lay back against her pillow. She stared at the dark canopy above her head while her pulse calmed and her breathing eased. She pressed her fingertips to her lips. They felt softly swollen, as if they had just been kissed passionately.

Apparently Iain Matheson's little comment had planted a suggestion in her mind. Strange, she had never had such a vivid dream before. She shook her head. The man was dangerous. Still, she was not about to succumb to his nefarious charm. If Iain Matheson thought she would be an easy conquest, he had a great deal to learn.

6

*E*ight days later, Ann stood at the large oak work-table that dominated the center of the family kitchen of Dunmarin, trying to concentrate on the task of cutting shortbread into leaf shapes. Unfortunately, even with the cutter she was using, her cookies resembled blobs rather than the elegant shapes Rose had made earlier. Iain kept ambushing her concentration. Yesterday he had left for London on business. She had expected to enjoy his absence. The man had bedeviled her for the past week, teasing her at every turn, provoking her in ways no one had ever done before. Yet instead of the very sensible feeling of relief that she should be feeling, she couldn't shake a horrible sense of loss. As much as she wanted to deny it, she missed the rogue. If the sense of loss was this bad after only knowing him a few days, what would it be like when it came time to leave at the end of the summer?

"The trick to making shortbread look perfect is to cut the dough into shapes on chilled baking pans, and then to let them chill again a bit before you put the pan in the oven." Rose pulled a baking sheet from the oven and placed it on the large oak table. "Mama would be proud."

"They look wonderful." Rose had insisted Ann join her this morning in the kitchen. Ann knew it was the help lift her spirits. They still had not made any progress in finding the Matheson jewels.

Rose inspected the pan of shortbread Ann had cut. "That's a good job, lass. Now we'll just put this pan back in to cool for a bit. And put the next one into the oven. The first pan should be cool enough now. Have a taste."

Ann lifted a cookie from the cooling rack beside the freshly baked pan of cookies and took a bite of the delicate shortbread. A rich buttery flavor spilled across her tongue and coaxed a humming sound from her throat. "Delicious."

Rose smiled proudly. "I have five sisters, and my mother made certain we each knew our way around a kitchen. Each time I make her special shortbread, it takes me back to those days when all of the girls and Mama would be crowded into her kitchen. Baking always has a way of making me feel good inside."

"Yes. It does." Ann took a deep breath, savoring the aroma of baking shortbread. "My mom was an accountant before she gave up her career to raise my sisters and me. From the time we were little, she would let us all help in making cookies. Once a week she would gather us in the kitchen for a new recipe. We still get together at Christmas and make cookies together."

"Family. Now there is the true joy in this world." Rose placed a mound of dough on a chilled cookie sheet. "I suppose you get a great deal of enjoyment from your work."

"Yes. I cannot think of anything I would want more than to find the lost city of Edaín."

Rose studied her a long moment. "Perhaps in time you might find something far more rewarding than an archaeological treasure."

What could be more rewarding than finding one of the greatest archaeological treasures of all time? Yet deep inside, in a place she seldom peeked, dwelt another longing. Each time Ann looked at her nieces and nephews, she felt a need she had always been frightened to explore. It was not extraordinary. It was simple in comparison to the dream of discovering Edaín. Yet within its simplicity lay a strength she could not ignore. The simple desire to love and be loved, to have children of her own. It certainly could not be compared to her work. Yet since she had come to this place, that one simple dream had haunted her more and more.

"How is it a beautiful lass such as you has not found herself a husband?" Rose asked, as if she could read Ann's mind.

"I suppose I have just never found the right man." With a spatula, Ann lifted cookies from the hot baking pan and placed them on the cooling rack while she spoke. "I'm not really very good at dating."

"Young people of today seem to take longer and longer to find their mate," Rose said, rolling the dough. "But you're thinking one day you might like to have a family?"

"I suppose, but I don't know if it will be possible."

"And why wouldn't it be possible?"

"I have always thought there is only one reason to marry, and that is if you meet a man you cannot live without, a man who cannot live without you." Ann glanced up at the copper pots hanging on a rack above the table. "I know it sounds overly idealistic, but my parents have that kind of relationship. They love each other, and it shows in everything they do. They respect each other. They are kind to each other. They are happiest when they are together. I don't want to settle for anything less than that. But I'm not sure I will ever find it."

Rose considered this a moment. "Perhaps it will find you."

"Perhaps. Speaking of finding things, I am beginning to wonder if we are going to find the jewels," Ann said, trying to change the subject to something less threatening.

"It's only been a little more than a week, lass." Rose patted Ann's shoulder. "When Iain returns from London, he'll find the Sentinel. He's a clever lad, always has been."

Iain had said he had several meetings he needed to attend. Ann wondered if he was meeting a redhead, a blonde, or a brunette. It shouldn't matter. The fact that it did matter irritated her to the point of pure frustration. "Does he actually spend a great deal of his time at his office?"

"A fair amount of time." Rose studied her a moment, her eyes narrowed behind the lenses of her glasses. "You shouldn't allow the rumors you might have heard about him to make you think he isn't serious about his work. He is."

"He just doesn't seem to be very . . ." Ann hesitated, searching for the right words. "It is just that I would never have guessed he would take his responsibilities seriously."

Rose nodded. "Oh, there were those who doubted the wisdom of turning everything over to him, including my son Nigel. But I never lost faith in Iain. Did you know the lad graduated with highest honors from Cambridge? Degrees in history and business he has. And he graduated from law school, while he was running his film business. Even if you feel the same as Shakespeare about lawyers, it still takes a fine mind to achieve what he did."

"Yes. It does." Iain might be a playboy, but apparently he wasn't the frivolous type. A scholar with a brilliant mind. It didn't surprise Ann as much as it should.

"Ah, fresh shortbread," Beatrice Brodie said as she entered the kitchen. "Obviously you knew I was going to visit this morning."

"Good morning, Beatrice," Rose said, obviously pleased to see her friend. "Sit. Have some shortbread. I'll make tea."

Beatrice took a seat at the table beside Ann and helped herself to a cookie. After complimenting Rose on the shortbread, Beatrice turned her attention to Ann. "You know, my dear, I have been thinking about your search for the jewels, and I have come up with a tremendous idea. I cannot imagine why no one has thought of it before."

Ann's breath stilled in her lungs. "You know something about the location of the jewels."

"Not exactly," Beatrice said. "But I know how you can find them."

"How?" Ann asked.

Beatrice smiled, her brown eyes as bright and shiny as polished pennies behind the round lenses of her glasses. "Ask the mad earl himself."

Ann stared at her. "The mad earl?"

"Aye." Beatrice lowered her voice. "He wanders the south wing. Many people have seen him. I caught a glimpse of him myself one evening during a party."

"After having a few glasses of punch," Rose said, lifting her eyebrows.

"It wasn't the punch," Beatrice said. "I shall never forget that night. He might have stepped down from his portrait, he was that clear."

"Punch has a way of clarifying some things," Rose said.

"I had a glass, no more," Beatrice said. "And I swear, it was the mad earl I saw."

Ann stared at Beatrice while she tried to make sense of her words. "Who exactly are you talking about?"

"The ghost," Beatrice said. "The ghost of Adair Matheson."

"Ghost?" Ann stared at Beatrice, thinking she must be teasing her. Yet Beatrice looked perfectly serious. "The ghost of Adair Matheson still wanders Dunmarin?"

"Aye. Rose can tell you."

"I have never seen him myself, but it is true that he has been seen by others." Rose pushed against the bridge of her glasses. "Of course it is usually after someone has had a wee bit of punch. It's made with Dunmarin scotch, you know."

"Now, Rose, I had only a drop of punch that night." Beatrice nibbled her shortbread. "And you know yourself several of the servants have seen him, as well as your brother Maxwell. And he wasn't drinking punch at the time."

"No." Rose walked to the stove to tend to the whistling kettle. "Maxwell was drinking his scotch neat the night he saw the earl."

"Well, I cannot say what state of mind Maxwell was in that night, but—"

"The state that sees ghosts," Rose said.

"Perhaps *he* was a bit tipsy, but I was not." Beatrice stared at the window above the sink for a long moment. "Still, I'm wondering how we could coax a ghost to tell us where he hid the jewels?"

"You could try offering him a glass of punch," Rose said, while she poured water into a teapot.

"It wasn't the punch." Beatrice brushed the crumbs from the front of her pink silk blouse. "My sister's husband has a cousin who dabbles a bit in witchcraft. I'm thinking she might help with contacting the mad earl. I'll see what I can do. Perhaps she can come up with a spell to help us."

Ann could see that Beatrice was completely serious. "I wouldn't want to put you to any trouble."

"No trouble at all," Beatrice said. "My pleasure."

There was a simple logic in her thinking—ask the man who hid the jewels where they were hidden. Pity it couldn't be that easy to find them, Ann thought. Yet she knew it would take work.

Later that night, Ann found a clue that might lead to the treasure.

Humid air lush with the mingled scents of jasmine and orange blossoms brushed her face as Ann walked into the huge conservatory of Dunmarin. Moonlight poured through the glass and steel that shaped the walls and the high domed ceiling enclosing a tropical garden. It was after midnight, but Ann couldn't wait until morning to see if what she suspected was true.

The splashing of water against stone echoed through the room from the waterfall at one end of the swimming pool, muffling the sound of her footsteps. She had traveled only a short distance along the flagstone path when a voice brushed against her back, freezing her where she stood. She pivoted and found Iain standing in the pool.

Lights glowed beneath the surface of the water, the pale light glistening on Iain's skin. Droplets of water glittered upon the hair that spread like an eagle's wings across his broad chest. His thick hair was swept back from his brow, betraying the sculpted perfection of his face. He was smiling at her, his dark eyes alight with mischief and more. In that moment she could almost believe he was a creature of myth, a magical being who had left the sea to seduce any unsuspecting female who strayed into his path. "What are you doing here?"

Iain lifted his brows at the sharp tone of her voice. "I live here, remember?"

"You're supposed to be in London."

"I came back a little early."

"And decided to take a swim?"

"When I can't sleep, I often come here. I like to swim. It's very relaxing."

Although the pool was the size of an Olympic pool, the resemblance to anything conventional ended there. It curved through ferns and plants along one glass wall. At one end flagstone steps dipped down into the water. The other end of the pool rose into a hill of sculpted black stone. Water bubbled from the top of the fern-swathed hill, tumbling over rocks until it plunged in a narrow stream into the pool.

"Did you come here to take a swim?" he asked.

"At midnight? Alone?"

"And here I was hoping you would surprise me. I thought you might have come here to enjoy yourself." He tilted his head, a challenge entering his eyes. "Look at you, the buttons on your shirt fastened all the way up to your chin, even though the heat in there is begging for you to loosen your collar a bit."

She rubbed her hands over the sleeves of her shirt, the white cotton damp from the humidity. "Is it warm in here? I hadn't noticed."

Iain pursed his lips. "Have you ever done anything that wasn't nice and safe and secure, Professor?"

Ann bristled at the censure in his tone. "I often have dinner at my sister Carol's house."

He stared at her, a glimmer of curiosity entering his expression. "And that is dangerous?"

"You have obviously never tasted my sister's meat loaf."

He laughed softly. "If you didn't come here for a swim, what brings you here at this hour?"

"I was studying the plans of the various improvements that have been made to Dunmarin. That's when I noticed that the conservatory was a garden in Adair's time."

"You were studying the plans at this time of night?" Iain released his breath in a slow sigh. "Do you ever think of anything besides work, Professor?"

Ann stiffened at the disapproval in his voice. "I am not here on holiday. I am here to work."

"Aye. And there is no room for a little pleasure in your schedule."

"I find pleasure in my work." She crossed her arms over her chest, resenting the way he made her feel so defensive. "According to the plans, this area was a garden in Adair's time. When the conservatory was built in 1932, the large fountain that once stood in the center of Adair's garden was left as it was. The fountain has a sculpture of a sea lion."

"Aye, I'm aware of it. We can look at it tomorrow."

"I was hoping to examine it tonight."

Iain folded his arms on the smooth flagstone edging the pool. "Have you ever gone skinny-dipping, professor?"

She molded her lips into what she hoped would be a sarcastic smile. "In a fountain?"

Iain grinned at her. "Anywhere?"

"Only in my bathtub."

"It is a very pleasant experience. But if you are a little too timid to try it, we keep bathing suits in the dressing rooms. I'm sure you could find one that fits you."

Ann's back stiffened. "I am not timid."

"I'm glad to hear it." He winked at her. "The water is fine."

Oh, the man was a master at this game. "I'll pass on the midnight swim."

Iain fixed his gaze on her. "Afraid of me?"

"No. I'm not afraid of you, I simply have more sense than to paddle about with a shark."

He placed his hand over his chest, grimacing as though she had wounded him. "My dear Professor Fitzpatrick, perhaps you should get to know the man before you cast judgment."

She knew him as well as it was safe to know him. "If you will excuse me, I have a Sentinel to find."

"It would seem you are determined to destroy a perfectly fine opportunity to have a wee bit of fun. I might as well help you, since you'll be prowling about with or without me." He walked toward the stairs at the end of the pool. The lights from the pool limned his body, confirming the fact he was as bare as Adam before the fall.

Images flooded her mind, memories forged on a moonlit beach in the realm of her dreams. The sudden surge of her heart set her blood pounding. She clenched her teeth, annoyed at the power this man held over her. She had heard of people having recurring dreams, but until recently she had never experienced them. Each night when sleep claimed her, Iain was there, waiting for her. Each night the dream was the same. A sea lion swimming in the surf, a man rising from the water, this man, only this man. Each morning she awakened in a tangle of bedclothes, hugging her pillow, restless and anxious and filled with a horrible longing.

Iain paused at the base of the stairs and smiled at her. "You might want to turn around, Professor. I'm not wearing a stitch."

He expected her to turn and blush like a fluttery old spinster. That was precisely what she would have done, she acknowledged, if he hadn't piqued her anger. Instead she returned his sarcastic smile, determined to turn the tables on the rogue. "Strange, I never would have suspected that you had a shred of modesty."

He lifted his brows. "I don't believe I have ever been accused of being modest before."

She walked to a nearby chair, where a thick white cotton robe and a large towel had been tossed over the wrought-iron back. She lifted the heavy white towel and held it out for him. "If you stay in the water too long, you get all shriveled. But then, perhaps you've already been in there too long. Is that why you are hiding?"

"Hiding?" Iain considered her a moment, as though he were assessing her. Finally a smile slid along his lips, shaping a grin wicked enough to please the devil himself.

Somewhere in the back of her mind she knew the folly of teasing a lion in his lair. Yet she had come this far; she had no intention of backing away now. Without looking away from her, he climbed the steps of the pool. As the water slipped away from him, moonlight embraced him, revealing every powerful line and curve of his body. Nothing about him looked shriveled.

Come to me.

The words rippled through her, tugging on her vitals like an invisible tether. She was staring straight at him. He hadn't spoken, at least not aloud. Yet the look in his eyes spoke those words as clearly as the voice whispering in her mind. The heat of the room pressed against her, a pale glimmer of the heat flaring to life inside of her. When he drew near, she clenched the towel, fighting the insidious need to touch him.

He slid his fingertips over her cheek. "You're blushing."

She glared up at him. "You aren't."

He slid his hand down her arm, the heat of his palm simmering through her sleeve. "How long are you going to deny this attraction that simmers between us?"

7

Heaven help her, she wanted him. Right here. Right now. She fought the urge to run, and an even greater need pounding through her. "I have no intention of getting involved with you."

He leaned toward her and whispered, "Perhaps you already are."

The truth in his words pricked her. She had hoped the attraction this man held for her would just run its course, the way a nasty cold might. Yet this affliction called Iain grew more virulent every day. "I suppose your pride won't allow you to believe a woman could actually resist your masculine charm."

"And I suppose it is your fear that keeps you from taking a chance with me."

"I prefer to think it is some measure of common sense." She opened the towel for him to don, hoping he wouldn't notice the way her hands trembled.

He took the towel and rubbed it over his arms and torso while he said, "I'm not the big bad wolf, Ann."

"Tell me, when was the last time you had an affair that lasted more than a month?"

Frowning, he tossed the towel to the chair and lifted his robe. "And when was the last time you had a relationship that lasted more than a month?"

The question caught her off guard. She started to reply, then realized the answer was far too embarrassing. "It isn't the same."

"Isn't it?" He donned his robe and cinched the sash around his slim waist. "Perhaps it is exactly the same. Only I keep looking, and you keep hiding."

"I'm not hiding from anything."

"I don't believe you, lass." He leaned toward her until his nose nearly brushed hers. "If you want me to leave you alone, you're going to have to do better at convincing me you don't want anything to do with me."

She stared at him, emotion crowding her chest. It was insane to even imagine making love with this man. Yet here she was with images flooding her mind. She stepped back, straight into a palm. Lacy fronds plopped over her head. She jumped as though someone had just come up behind her and poked her in the ribs.

When she pushed her way out of the palm fronds, she found Iain grinning at her. As much as she wished he might ignore her behavior, Iain missed nothing. He was far too experienced with women to miss her reaction to him. His was the smile of a man who knew precisely how easily he could send her composure straight to perdition. "The only thing I want from you is your help in finding the Sentinel."

He held her gaze. She held her breath, silently praying he would not press her. If he did, she wasn't certain she could resist him. Finally he released his breath on a long sigh.

"Come with me, Professor. Let's see if your Sentinel is hiding in here."

*T*he next morning Iain paused on the threshold of the library, his gaze fixed on the woman sitting at his desk. Since last night had turned out to be another wasted effort, he knew he would find Ann here, searching the plans and documents of Dunmarin for an elusive clue. Sunlight spilled through the windows behind her, shaping a golden halo behind her head. He could almost believe she was an angel sent to torment him for all of his past transgressions. Ann Fitzpatrick was the most infuriating female he had ever met. She haunted him, day and night.

The dream had come again to him last night, as it had every night since he had met Ann. Each night when sleep claimed him, Ann was there, waiting for him in the realm of dreams. Each night the dream was the same. He was swimming in the surf when he noticed her, a siren standing on the beach, luring him into her arms. Beneath the moon they made love, upon the soft white cotton of her nightgown laid upon the sand. Each morning he awakened wanting her more than he had the day before. Strange, his dreams had never felt so real before. Yet dreams could not satisfy this hunger clawing at his vitals, a hunger that grew each time he saw her.

Ann lifted her shoulders, like a doe who has caught the scent of a hunter. She looked up and met his gaze. Sensation ripped through him like current zinging across a wire. The swift surge of excitement caught him off guard, stunning him, as though someone had just landed a clenched fist to his jaw. With each passing day the attraction grew more powerful, until the ache of wanting her pounded through him day and night. "Searching the plans again?"

"Yes." She cleared her throat. "I keep thinking we are missing something."

"I'm sure we are." And it had little to do with a two-hundred-year-old mystery. He crossed the distance between them and sat on the edge of the desk. "Do you play golf, Professor?"

Her eyes grew wide behind the lenses of her glasses. "Golf?"

"Aye. It's a game played with a little white ball and a bag full of clubs."

She slipped off her glasses and looked at him with mock surprise. "I'm astonished."

"By what?"

"The fact you have any interest at all in an outdoor sport. I thought you reserved all of your energy for games of a far more private sort."

He laughed. "I'm Scottish. We lose our citizenship if we don't learn to play golf. And we learn at an early age never to waste beautiful days like this by remaining trapped inside. So tell me, do you play golf?"

She folded her hands on the desk, a smile curving her lips. "Are you asking me if I would like to play a round?"

"Lord almighty, I'm not that much of a cliché." He rested his hand over his heart. "If I promise to be on my best behavior, will you come and spend the day with me? I can show you how to play if you like. And you can show me how indifferent you are to my charm."

"I went to college on a golf scholarship."

"Then I think you would enjoy the course here on Dunmarin. It's beautiful, laid out right along the ocean."

She frowned. "I didn't bring any clubs."

"How can you come to Scotland, the birthplace of golf, without any clubs?" He shook his head, giving her a stern look. "Fortunately, we have a few extra sets here. I'm sure we can find a set you would like. As for shoes, we'll get a pair in the clubhouse."

"I really shouldn't." She glanced down at the plans. "I need to see if I can find something in these plans."

"You need to take a break from all of this. You'll be fresher and sharper if you take some time to relax. We'll play golf, then have an early dinner in the village. Afterward you can choose a movie from the film library. My great-grandfather had a theater built at Dunmarin in 1939. Have you ever seen any of the old classics in a theater? On a full screen?"

"No. I haven't." She drew her teeth over her bottom lip. "Do you have a copy of *Bringing Up Baby*?"

"Aye, lass. I do."

Have you ever done anything that wasn't nice and safe and secure, Professor? Iain's words kept haunting her. Perhaps she did live a very conventional life. Perhaps someone like Iain would think she was boring. Well, perhaps she just might prove to him that she could have fun just as well as he could. She left the castle in the morning determined to put aside all of her fears and doubts and enjoy herself. At least for the day.

The golf course was spectacular. On several holes she caught herself staring at the cliffs and the sea beyond, mesmerized by the sheer beauty of the island. Still, she managed to win the round—at least, her score was two strokes lower than his after she factored in the strokes Iain had insisted he give her as a handicap. Instead of being upset at losing to her, he had merely made her promise she would give him a chance to win another day.

After golf, Iain drove to a restaurant and pub on the outskirts of the village. According to Iain, the Golden Lion had been in Deirdre Fraser's family for generations, but under Deirdre's management the restaurant portion of the business had grown in importance and quality. The building—a large wood-and-stone structure that ambled along the edge of the cliffs—had been built in 1882, after a fire had destroyed the original inn that had stood on the same spot since 1712.

A warm aroma of freshly baked bread filled her senses as they entered the restaurant. Artificial candles burned in crystal and brass wall sconces on the oak-paneled walls, while real candles flickered upon each white-linen-draped table. The hostess showed them to a table overlooking the sea. Soon after they ordered, Deirdre stopped by their table. Dressed in an elegant black pantsuit, her hair in soft waves around her face, she looked as though she had stepped from the pages of a fashion magazine.

Deirdre smiled at Ann, then patted Iain on the shoulder. "I see you've brought your pretty mermaid, Iain."

"It's important to keep one's mermaid well fed, otherwise she will be wanting to return to the sea."

Deirdre winked at him. "A wise man knows how to hold on to a treasure when he finds it."

A treasure? Ann couldn't help but smile. "I suspect Iain finds treasures on a daily basis."

"You're the first lady Iain has ever brought to my fine establishment. You must be very special, Dr. Fitzpatrick. But then I can see you are." Deirdre rested her hand on Iain's shoulder. "If I were thirty years younger and he looked at me the way he looks at you, I would know precisely what to do about it. Ah, to be young again."

With that, Deirdre left them to visit other patrons. The woman no doubt had been teasing Iain since he was a lad. There was absolutely nothing behind her intriguing comments. Still, Ann couldn't completely erase them from her thoughts.

"Tell me, what would you be doing if you hadn't decided to complete your great-grandfather's dream?" Iain asked, after their entrées had been served.

"I suppose I would teach. But not at the college level." Ann cut a small piece of her duck and dabbed it into the thick raspberry sauce on her plate. "There are times when I think I would truly enjoy teaching young children something as basic and illuminating as the simple joy of reading. I suppose that sounds terribly pedestrian to a man in your position."

"Not at all. To know you have had a small hand in shaping a young mind must be truly rewarding."

Iain looked perfectly earnest, as though he truly understood her feelings. During dinner he managed to keep the conversation focused on her, as though he were genuinely interested in everything about her. Although she should have been surprised to find they shared a similar taste in music and movies, she wasn't. He had a way of making her feel as though she were important to him. He made her life seem somehow more than ordinary.

They had just finished dinner when the band in the pub began to play for the evening. Across the low wooden wall that separated the restaurant from the pub, Ann watched as couples crowded onto the dance floor, forming sets and dancing to a lively Scottish tune.

"Would you like to dance?" Iain asked.

"Yes, but I don't know the steps." Ann glanced to the dance floor. "It's too crowded. I could hurt someone."

"There's a room Deirdre uses for wedding receptions and other special occasions. I'll show you the steps, and when you're comfortable we can join the others." Iain stood and offered her his hand. "Will you join me?"

Ann hesitated just a moment before she slipped her hand into his. A shock of contact sang along her nerves, snagging her breath. Startled, she glanced up into his eyes, then wished she hadn't. She saw her own turmoil in his eyes, the same need that smoldered deep within her burning in their depths. Another time she would have been frightened of that look; tonight she chose to enjoy it and the excitement he always conjured within her.

He led her into a large room adjoining the dining room, flicked on the lights, then closed the door. Round tables were grouped around a wooden dance floor. The music from the pub rattled through the thick walls in a low din. "I expect they will be playing mainly reels and a few jigs."

"You are fairly familiar with the repertoire?"

Iain grinned at her. "There aren't many places to go for an evening of entertainment here on Dunmarin."

Yet he had never brought a woman here before tonight. Somehow Ann found that hard to believe. "Are there many dances you can dance without a partner?"

"Are you thinking about getting rid of me?"

"No. I was just wondering. If you have never brought a woman here before, then how did you enjoy the dancing?"

He leaned toward her, his eyes alight with humor. She had a funny feeling he could see right through her. "We are a friendly lot here on Dunmarin. Lots of people come here to dance, and the ladies don't mind if I am one of the men dancing with them."

"Oh." She glanced down at the wooden planks beneath her feet. "You think you can teach me to dance without fear of me making a wrong step and knocking down an entire line of dancers?"

"Aye. First I'll show you some of the basic steps." He took her hand, then placed his left hand at the small of her back, the heat of his palm soaking through her blouse. "Now this is what is called a traveling step."

Ann managed to hit his ankle and step on his foot with her first try. "Sorry."

Iain rubbed his ankle. "It's all right, lass. Just take your time."

Although she assaulted his toes more than a few times, he never grew cross or impatient. Instead he seemed to take delight with each small bit of progress she made. In a short while he declared her fit for action. "Come on, lass."

The man had the most uncanny way of making her

feel as though she was the belle of the ball. He soon found several of his friends to make up a set for the reel. No one seemed to mind when she bumbled the steps. Instead, they all gave her encouragement as well as instruction. Soon she was shuffling when she should, skipping when required, and traveling almost as well as the woman standing in line beside her. Her accomplishment pleased her even more when she noticed the look of approval in Iain's eyes.

Although the room was filled with pretty women, each time she looked at Iain, Ann found him looking at her, as though she were the only woman there. For the first time in a long time laughter poured from her, the kind that came when you allowed the pure joy of the moment to reach deep inside you.

*A*nn liked to tuck memories away in her mind, like roses pressed between the pages of a book. In all of her life she could not remember a more perfect day than this one. Golf had been wonderful. Dinner and dancing had been delightful. Now she sat in the large theater in Dunmarin watching one of her favorite movies. It felt as though she had stepped back in time, sitting here on this plush blue velvet seat, watching the antics of Katherine Hepburn and Cary Grant play across the large screen. Iain's great-grandfather had obviously felt the same passion for movies that Iain did. The auditorium was larger than most of the theaters found in multiplex cinemas in the States, with a screen large enough to accommodate an original screening of *Gone with the Wind*.

When the movie finished and they were walking out

of the theater, she thought of how very much she would like this day never to end. Yet midnight inevitably awaited Cinderella.

"Have you ever tasted Dunmarin whisky?"

Ann looked up at the man walking beside her, a warm tingling sensation simmering through her when her gaze met his. She could spend hours doing nothing but looking at this man. "I have never tasted scotch. Of any brand. I don't drink much."

"Ah, you really have to give it a try." Iain slipped her arm through his. "Come on, lass, it's time for you to see what you've been missing."

Ann was far too aware of what she was missing. Common sense demanded she refuse his offer. Yet she could not find the will to resist that smile of his. What harm could there be in tasting a little scotch?

8

$\mathcal{A}$nn sucked in her breath, stunned by the heat spreading like liquid fire down her throat and into her chest. A soft rumble of laughter brought her teary gaze to the man standing near the white marble hearth.

Iain winked at her. "I should have warned you it's a wee bit strong."

Ann coughed, trying to clear a passageway in her throat. "It really warms your throat."

He glanced down into his glass, and she had the distinct impression he was trying to suppress his laughter. "Perhaps it's a wee bit too strong for you. Would you like a glass of sherry or wine instead?"

Too strong for her? Ann's back stiffened against the thick cushions of the sofa. "No. I'm fine."

Iain lifted his brows. "Are you sure?"

"It's all a matter of getting accustomed to it. I can handle it." Ann lifted her glass and sipped the warm whisky. The potent aroma flooded her nostrils while the amber liquid streamed over her tongue. This time her senses were prepared for the lush heat that flooded her throat and chest. Either that, or she had gone numb from the first swallow. "It's actually very good."

"Be careful with it, lass." Iain rested his arm along the mantel. "It will sneak up on you if you don't take care, especially if you aren't used to strong spirits."

"I think I can manage, thank you." She leaned back against the sofa and sipped her whisky. Scotch wasn't bad at all, she decided, a nice comforting warmth spreading through her. "Have you really never taken another woman to the restaurant?"

He looked at her, his expression open and sincere. "You may find this difficult to believe, but I have never invited a woman to stay with me here at Dunmarin. This is a private place for me."

Ann resisted the lure of his words. After all, she hadn't really been invited here by him. She raised her glass, gesturing toward the sea lions carved into the cornice, intending to comment about them. It was then she noticed her glass was empty. She tipped the glass toward Iain. "A little more, please."

Iain took her glass. "Are you certain?"

A delicious sense of ease permeated every muscle in her body. She really could not remember the last time she had felt this relaxed. "I'm quite certain."

Iain took her glass and carried it to a cabinet across the room. While he refilled her glass, she glanced around the room, admiring the delicate lyre-backed chairs and Sheraton sofas, all upholstered in the same blue silk brocade. If she didn't know better, she could imagine she had been swept back almost two hundred years, straight to this drawing room and into the company of a charming Regency rogue. As the thought formed, her imagination sketched a scene from that period, of Iain sitting beside her on this sofa. Strange, the images were so real she couldn't help but laugh.

"What's so amusing?" he asked, handing her the glass.

"Nothing." She smiled up at him, wondering what he would say if she told him how very much she wanted to grab his hand and pull him down, straight on top of her. Wouldn't that surprise the rogue?

"You have a lovely smile." He sat beside her at an angle, his arm resting along the curved back of the sofa behind her. "I would like to see it more often."

She couldn't help but smile. Everything seemed so warm and lovely at the moment. She looked at him, etching each detail of his features in the book of her memories. "It seems to me that your family has run amok with sea lion images, or I should say selkies. They are everywhere in this castle."

"It's because of the legend."

"The legend of Eleanor and Dugald." Ann sipped her whisky, recalling all the beguiling nonsense he had related about the legend. *A selkie will wander the earth for an eternity, looking for his one true mate.* Strange, tonight it didn't seem like nonsense at all. "It's a very lovely fairy tale."

"What makes you think it is a fairy tale?"

"Can you honestly say that you believe in selkies?"

"I think it is possible."

Perhaps he did believe in selkies. For some reason she wanted to believe he did. She sipped her whisky, all the tension in her muscles melting, like wax beneath a flame. "You actually believe that you are destined to find one woman in all the world who can make you complete?"

He brushed his fingertip over her brow, slowly, as if he were an artist applying the last stroke to a painting. "I don't believe it happens with everyone. I think many times people settle for what they think is love. Sometimes they fall victim to circumstance, and never find that one person who is the missing half of their soul. Yet I believe when you come face to face with your one true mate, you will know. You will feel it deep inside. It will ring through you with the same sweet purity as a bell on Sunday morning."

Ann closed her eyes, enjoying his soft touch. "It is a lovely thought. But I suspect more times than not, love at first sight is actually lust at first sight."

"Are you really such a cynic, my bonnie Ann?"

"I am not a cynic. Not really. Simply practical." Yet she wasn't feeling practical at the moment. She looked up at him and wondered what it might be like to awaken to see his smile. Longing and need shifted inside of her, slipping from the nice tidy box where she kept them hidden, teasing her with glimpses of another path in life. Strange, she had never truly realized how lonely she felt until she had met this man. "There is nothing wrong with being practical, you know."

"Nothing at all." He drew his fingertip along the curve of her jaw. "As long as you remember to enjoy life. There is far too little of it to waste. When it is all said and done, we should have as few regrets as possible."

He was so close, all she need do was lift her head,

just a little, and she could kiss him. Strange she couldn't quite lift her head. Instead she stroked his cheek, enjoying the intriguing rasp of his awakening beard beneath her fingertips. "I wonder if all these selkie images are the reason I keep having the same dream, over and over again."

Iain stared at her, the smile slipping from his lips. "You have been having the same dream over and over again?"

"Yes. I'm on the beach, and a sea lion is playing in the surf. Only he isn't a sea lion at all, he is a man." Ann rested her fingertips on his chin. "You."

Iain released his breath slowly, the exhalation warming her fingers with a damp heat. "You have been having the same dream every night?"

"Yes. And I must say you are a very naughty man in my dreams." She laughed as a keen sensation of pleasure rose with the memories in her mind. "It's like Deborah Kerr and Burt Lancaster in *From Here to Eternity*. Only my imagination has filled in all the blanks."

He studied her as though he were fitting together the last piece of a particularly challenging puzzle. "You've been dreaming of us on a beach. How remarkable."

"Is it?"

"Aye." He brushed his lips against her right temple. "I've been having the same dream. I wonder what it means?"

It meant he was trying to seduce her. And the funny thing was, she wanted him to. She drained her glass, then slipped her arms around his neck, the glass dangling from her fingers. "Do you suppose we could go swimming in that lovely pool of yours?"

"Ah, lass." He rested his brow against hers. "You have the tolerance of a kitten when it comes to liquor."

She felt like a kitten stretched out in the warm rays of the sun. She nuzzled his cheek. "I want to go skinny-dipping with you."

He slipped the glass from her fingers and set it on the commode beside the sofa. "You don't know how tempting that is."

"Tempting." She snuggled her head against his shoulder, feeling deliciously drowsy. "You are so tempting."

He cradled her against his chest, holding her close with one powerful arm cinched around her shoulders. "And you are driving me wild."

"I'm glad." His heart beat comfortingly against her cheek. He slipped his arm beneath her knees and lifted her into his arms as he came to his feet. She looked up at him. "What are you doing?"

"There is really only one thing to do, my adorable temptress." He kissed the tip of her nose. "Take you to bed."

"To bed." The softly spoken words did something deliciously wicked to her insides. She rested her head against his shoulder while he carried her out of the room. Somewhere in the back of her mind, she realized there would be consequences to face for what she was about to do. Yet she could not utter a single protest. This is what she had wanted since the first moment she had met him. Perhaps even before then.

He carried her for what seemed like miles and miles of corridors until he finally entered her bedchamber. The bedclothes had been turned down, revealing white linen sheets that seemed to glow softly in the moonlight spilling through the windows. He lowered her to the bed, then stood looking at her, as though she were the most intriguing woman he had ever met. Just for tonight, she would allow herself to believe in the desire burning in those eyes. Just for tonight, she would indulge in this fantasy, accept all of his lovely tales of soul mates and destiny. Just for tonight, she would believe she was the one woman who could tame this beguiling man.

She stared up at him, watching in stunned disbelief as he slipped her shoes from her feet and drew the covers up over her. "You're leaving?"

"Aye, lass. I'll not have the first time I make love to you spoiled by too much whisky."

She giggled; she couldn't prevent the laughter from bubbling up inside of her. "I haven't had too much whisky."

"When I make love to you, it will be with no regrets for either of us." He stroked her hair. "Pleasant dreams, my bonnie Ann. I shall see you in my dreams."

He could see her now, if he would only stay. Yet she couldn't seem to grasp the words she needed to make him stay. Instead she lay with her head upon the pillow, watching him walk out of her room.

"I'll see you in my dreams," she whispered, singing the words softly. She closed her eyes and slipped into the sheltering arms of slumber.

𝒯he next morning, Iain leaned against the doorjamb of one of the gatehouses that stood near the cliffs, watching Ann explore the small room. She stepped in and out of a ray of sunlight slanting through one of the long, narrow windows, as though teasing the sunlight. Although there was a sea lion carved into a stone slab on the front of the building, they had not found a clue suggesting this was actually the Sentinel. Still, Ann was determined to examine every possibility, except of course when it came to Iain. Gone was the warm and playful lass from the night before. In her place stood an icy lady determined to keep him at a distance.

Last night the dream had come again, as it had every night since he had met Ann. This morning, as he lay in a tangle of bedclothes—heart pounding, skin tingling, hunger clawing at his vitals like the talons of a hawk—he finally understood something that had escaped him before he had heard Ann's sweet confession. The scene that kept unfolding in his mind each night had meaning in it—a meaning that defied logic; but logic had such an insignificant place in nature. The sea. The beach. The powerful need to possess Ann. The fact she was sharing his dream. It all made sense. If he was willing to accept the truth of a legend.

He lowered his gaze, sweeping the long length of her legs. Although she wore jeans, they were not the type that hugged her every curve. Her dark red sweater hung loosely from her shoulders, providing only a hint of the curves beneath. She never wore anything that exploited her natural loveliness. Yet it didn't matter what she wore. He could imagine the woman hiding beneath the layers. He felt as though he knew each sleek curve of her legs, every intimate inch of her slender form.

Ann turned and caught him staring. Even though she stood in the shadows beyond the sunlight, he could still see the rise of her blush. She glanced away from him, as though she were afraid of what might happen should she hold his gaze. "I think I should . . . I don't believe I have apologized for my behavior last night. And I should. I do." She cleared her throat. "I don't usually drink."

"You did nothing to offend me."

She glanced at him, then directed her gaze toward the stone floor. "You behaved as a gentleman. I appreciate the fact you didn't take advantage of the situation."

"It wouldn't have been fair."

"It is funny, the tricks the mind can play on a person when she is under the influence of whisky." Ann rubbed her hands together. "You say and do things you normally wouldn't."

"You were simply enjoying yourself. There is no need for all of this regret."

"I . . . it would probably . . . I would hope we can forget last night." Ann cleared her throat and continued before he had a chance to reply. "It would seem I have managed to hit another brick wall this morning. The Sentinel isn't here."

"Would it really be so terrible if you cannot find it?"

"It would mean I couldn't continue with Owen's work."

"Are you really chasing your own dream?"

"My own dream. What do you mean?"

Iain shrugged. "It seems to me that you have been chasing after Owen's dream since you were a child. I wonder if your desire to see his dreams come to fruition might have caused you to ignore your own."

"Of course it's my dream to find Edaín." Still, in spite of her words, she looked unsure of herself. She moistened her lips. "This is important to me."

"And it's dangerous. Except for Cameron Macleod,

no one who has ever gone looking for Edaín has ever returned. And Cameron vanished when he went back for proof of what he had found. Perhaps the *sidhe* don't want anyone to expose them."

"Perhaps the *sidhe* don't want anyone to expose them?" She rubbed her arms, as though she were chilled suddenly. "If Edaín exists, it hasn't been inhabited for a few thousand years."

He shrugged. "Time means nothing to the fairies."

She narrowed her eyes. "I suppose you want me to believe that you actually believe in fairies."

"And here you are, searching for a lost city of the fairies. I have read your great-grandfather's journal. According to Owen's notes, he believed these people existed. In fact, he believed it was possible that some remnant of the civilization of the Tuatha De Danann existed in his day. How do you reconcile your disbelief of the existence of these magical people with your quest to find their city?"

"There is often some kernel of truth in a legend. I suspect that is what my great-grandfather meant when he said these people existed. For some reason the people known as the *sidhe*, the Tuatha De Danann, the fairies, whatever you wish to call them, had technology that set them far ahead of most other people of their time. But there certainly is no such thing as magic."

"I was born and bred in the Highlands. Raised upon tales of magic and mystery." Iain glanced out the door, toward the castle that had stood for generations of his family. "Here we know there is more to life than what we can see and touch. Who is to say all the stories of fairies and magic are not true?"

"Magic has no basis in scientific fact."

He looked at her, meeting her steady gaze. "Life is far more than science and fact."

She held his gaze, as though she were trying to decide if he were being serious. "You actually believe in fairies?"

He drew in his breath, filling up his lungs with the salty tang of the sea, while he craved the scent of her skin. "I believe in the possibility of fairies. There are too many stories, too many myths, too many legends, to completely say they never existed."

"The next thing you will tell me is that you truly believe your ancestor was a selkie."

"I have reason to believe it is true." Until he had met her, he had never truly given the legend much thought. Now, he could not ignore it. "Do you ride?"

She stared at him. "A horse?"

"Unless you have something else in mind."

Ann pursed her lips. "I've ridden a few times. I am not an expert rider, but I'm not frightened of horses."

"I have a nice gentle mare I think you will find to your liking. Take a ride with me after lunch."

"I would like to keep focused on the matter at hand, not on the lark you have in mind."

"You have so little faith in me. After lunch, take a ride with me, and I will show you something extraordinary."

Ann looked at him warily. "Just what is it you want to show me?"

"Ah, now that would be taking a bit of the shine off the surprise. Come with me and I'll show you." Iain winked at her. "I promise, you'll not be disappointed."

9

Curiosity. Ann kept thinking of what they said about cats while she rode beside Iain along a bridle path that wended through the woods. She swayed in the saddle with the gentle gait of Fennella, the chestnut mare Iain had given her to ride. The tang of cedar chips rose from the path, tingling her senses. It would have been lovely, if she could just relax. Yet she felt as though something alive were trapped inside of her, something wild and restless and frightening. She suspected it had something to do with Iain's comments about following her own dreams. Unfortunately, the man riding beside her played far too large a role in those dreams.

When they left the woods and entered a broad field,

Iain halted his horse and turned to look at Ann. "Do you think you can manage a little gallop?"

"I think I might."

"Come on, then." Iain urged his large black gelding into a gallop.

Fennella didn't need any encouragement from Ann. She leapt into a gallop, following the gelding. Ann leaned forward in the saddle, trying to adjust to the rocking of the horse, while Iain looked as though he had been born in a saddle. Iain led the way across a wide meadow, scattering a flock of geese who had gathered around a large pond. A breeze heavy with the salty tang of the sea whipped the hem of Ann's sweater and tugged at her hair, dragging strands free of her ponytail. Fennella's mane streamed wildly in the wind, brushing against Ann's hands. A wonderful sense of freedom filled her as she felt the horse stretch out beneath her.

Iain rode toward the sea and brought his horse to a halt near a twisted oak tree just beneath a rise that led up to the edge of the cliffs. When Ann joined him, he grinned at her. "You're smiling. I like to see that."

Ann tried to suppress her smile and failed. She stroked Fennella's velvety neck. "She is a very gentle lady."

"Aye, she is." He dismounted, then lifted Ann from the saddle.

Iain held her just a moment longer than he needed—nothing overt, nothing threatening, but the simple touch of his hands on her waist was enough to set her legs trembling like gelatin in an earthquake.

After removing the horses' bits to allow them to graze, Iain took Ann's arm and helped her climb the steep rise that led to the edge of the cliffs. When they reached the cliff path, Iain glanced past Ann, directing his gaze toward the castle. The cool breeze had sketched color high upon his lean cheeks and tossed his hair into reckless waves. He looked like a handsome pirate straight out of an old movie, the kind who could steal a woman's heart as easily as he could wield a sword. Her own poor heart kicked into a sprint just being near him.

"At times like this, it is easy to imagine that we have stepped back in time." Iain kept his gaze on the castle as he spoke. "I like to think each of the Mathesons who have come before me once stood on this very spot and looked with pride at their home."

Ann looked back at the castle. Mist swirled in from the sea, embracing the gray stones of the huge structure. Sunlight sparkled on the mist, like a sprinkling of fairy dust. Although she had never placed any credence in the Celtic myths and legends she had studied, looking at the many turrets and spires and towers of Dunmarin, Ann could almost believe it existed in a different realm, a place of mystery and magic. Since she had never been plagued with a belief in magic, her thoughts startled her—but not as much as the sensations swirling through her.

It was odd, this feeling of familiarity. As though she had stood here like this before, many times. She probed the thoughts, seeking clarity. Yet it was like poking at images reflected on mist. Each time she tried to get a clear view, they shifted. In each image flickering in her mind, Iain was always there. The fashions altered, the style of his hair changed, marking the passage of time. Yet the man himself did not change. He touched her arm, and she jumped.

Twin furrows creased the skin between his thick black brows. "Is something wrong?"

"No." She was just having glimpses from lives that she had never lived. Memories she could not possibly have made. That was all. Just a bout of insanity. "Nothing is wrong."

Although he looked doubtful, he did not question her further. Instead he led the way down a path that dipped toward the rocky beach. The soft barks of sea lions lying on the rocks offshore mingled with the crash of waves and the occasional cry of a gull. About fifty feet before they reached the beach, he turned into a cave, the entrance partially hidden by an overhang of stone.

The thin beam of his flashlight reflected against the smooth black stone of the cave walls, illuminating their way. Occasionally crystals embedded in the stone caught the light and sent it back in a sparkling rainbow of color. Although the walls were dry, the scent of the sea lingered here, fresh and tangy.

Iain followed a twisting trail through the cave, taking turns at each junction, as though he were as familiar with this place as he was Dunmarin. After about ten minutes, they came to an arched opening that led outside. They stepped out of the cave onto a wide shelf carved from the sheer rock face of the cliffs.

It was the size of the library at Dunmarin, with three walls of rock, the fourth open to the sea. Mist swirled in from the sea, embracing the sculpted stones that stood in a ring in the center of the clearing. Each obelisk stood five feet from the ground. Twelve stones in all shaped a circle open to the sky.

"A fairy ring," she whispered.

"Aye. It is one of three I have found on the island. This is the only one still intact."

Ann knelt to examine the symbols carved into the side of one of the obelisks. When she touched the carved black stone, sensation darted along her nerve endings, as though she had touched a softly vibrating tuning fork. She snatched her hand away, then touched the stone once more. The same vibrating sensation rippled along her arm.

"Amazing, isn't it?" Iain knelt on one knee beside her. "It is almost as if the stones were tapped into some hidden source of power."

Ann rejected the doubts rustling inside of her. "There must be a scientific explanation for it."

"Perhaps." Iain tilted his head and regarded her a moment, a glint of mischief in his dark eyes. "And then perhaps it is magic."

Ann shook her head, trying also to shake the odd feeling gripping her. "There is no such thing as magic."

"Ah, lass. How can a woman with a name like Fitzpatrick not believe in the magic that is all around us?"

"Perhaps because I believe in science and logic."

"Come with me." He took her hand, helped her to her feet, then coaxed her into the center of the circle. "Close your eyes, lass."

She narrowed her eyes, hoping he wouldn't see the excitement surging through her. "What do you have in mind?"

"Nothing as black as you might imagine. Close your eyes for me."

Although he kept his voice low, she saw the determination in his eyes. He was a man on a mission. "If you think I shall suddenly believe in magic because—"

He pressed his fingertip against her lips. "Humor me, Professor. Just close your eyes."

Ann hesitated before she obeyed. She closed her eyes, feeling foolish and edgy. Still, she had no intention of allowing him to see how easily he could disrupt her thought functions. She sensed him moving around her, until he stood behind her, so close the heat of his body brushed against her. When he rested his hands on her shoulders, she looked back at him. "What are you dong?"

"Relax. I'm not doing anything but touching your shoulders. Now close your eyes."

Ann turned back to face the ocean. Sunlight skimmed the rolling waves, tossing light in all directions. Strange, it felt as though that same sunlight flickered inside her. She took a deep breath, then closed her eyes, curious about what he had in mind.

"My grandmother Rose is fond of saying that there is a wee bit of enchantment in each of us."

His dark voice washed over her, as though it were a tangible thing, like the thick warm fur of a Persian cat. "Superstition is more like it."

"I found this place when I was ten. And even then I knew there was magic here."

"Ten-year-olds often believe in magic," she said, her attempt at sarcasm spoiled by the breathless sound of her voice.

"I still do, lass." He brushed his lips against her hair. "I feel the magic when I am with you."

It was a line. It could not possibly be true. Men such as Iain Matheson did not fall head over heels in love with women such as Ann, except in fairy tales. Still, she could not find the will to pull away from him. He was so warm, so powerful. And deep inside her, she wanted to believe in the sweet treason of his words. She wanted to believe in the magic she felt flowing through her each time he was near.

"Do you feel it, Professor?" he whispered.

She did feel it, a vibration that rippled softly through her. "The only thing I feel is the cool breeze upon my face and the warmth of you behind me," she said, refusing to betray herself.

"My fine bonnie lass, open yourself up to the possibilities." Iain rubbed her shoulders, his hands strong and sure, melting away her tension, even when she tried to remain stiff. She felt herself easing in his hold, her muscles shifting, her body seeking more contact with the man who stood so close behind her.

A warm smoldering scent of citrus and spices swirled through her senses. The warmth of Iain radiated against her, seeping through her sweater, drenching her skin. Somehow every touch, every scent, every whisper, seemed sharper, clearer, than she had ever experienced in her life. It was as if this place, these stones, were somehow magnifying each sensation. Certain sensations should not be magnified, not safely. A sane voice shouted in her brain, *Run!* Yet she could not find the will to pull away from his light grasp.

"Imagine for a moment that time has no meaning." Iain slipped the elastic cloth-covered band from her hair. Slowly he combed his fingers through her hair, from her crown to her nape.

She should end this. Now. Yet the gentle touch of his hand upon her hair begged her to stay, just a little while. He eased his long fingers through the thick, waving mass of her hair, skimming over her neck, sending shivers rippling across her skin, like a breath of breeze whispering across a silent pond. She held her breath, waiting for the next caress of his hand, shamelessly hoping there would be more. He slipped his fingertips into her hair, gliding upon her scalp, her neck, skimming the hairline, back and forth, sensation whispering over her skin.

"Imagine that you once stood here," he said, his voice streaming over her like warm rain upon a parched garden, "in this place of enchantment, open to the power of the earth itself."

The breeze brushed a lock of her hair against her cheek, the ordinary strands sliding like silk upon her skin. The warmth of his body spread over her, warm as sunlight. He glided his hands down her arms, grazing the dark red cotton of her sweater. Her skin simmered with the need to feel his hands upon her, bare except for the whisper of the breeze and the brush of sunlight.

"My bonnie Ann, do you have any idea how much I want you?"

His words rippled over the pool of longing hidden deep within her. He gripped her hips and lifted her, until she could feel the hard bulge of his arousal pressing against her bottom. She could feel herself weakening, her will dissolving in the heat he conjured within her. The need for him curled into a tight fist that pounded deep in her woman's flesh with each quick beat of her heart. It took every last scrap of her will to keep from moving against that tempting ridge.

He was a notorious womanizer. She was crazy to stand with him this way. Yet even as the sane words formed in her mind, her body rejected them. For some reason she did not begin to understand, she felt as though she had known this man all of her life and beyond. For what seemed an eternity, she remained locked in his arms, trapped by her own wrenching need.

"I need you, Ann," he whispered, sliding his hand inside her sweater. He cupped her breast, then brushed aside the lace of her bra.

The first touch of his skin upon her bared breast sang through her, so familiar, so compelling, she could not keep her hips from moving against him, her jeans-clad bottom sliding against the hard ridge hidden beneath his jeans. He rolled her bare nipple between his fingertips, sending sensation shooting in all directions. She felt herself melting, a pulse fluttering at the apex of her thighs, need surging through her with each quick beat of her heart.

"Trust in this feeling that burns between us." He brushed his lips against the curve of her neck. "Trust me."

Trust me. His words acted like a sharp slap to her cheek. All the reasons she should not trust this man slammed into her. Her muscles jerked, as though she had suddenly come awake from a beguiling dream. She pulled free of his embrace, stumbled a few steps, then pivoted to face him. He was looking at her with the same aching need that gripped her like a vice.

As humiliating as it might be, the truth stared her in the eye: she would gladly surrender this quest for Edaín for the chance to live her life with this man. Only there was no future here, no matter how much she wanted to believe there was, no matter how tempting it was to embrace the need within her and deliver her own fragile dreams into his keeping. "I have no intention of indulging you in this little game."

He clenched his hands into fists at his sides, his expression betraying every nuance of his emotions. Anger and frustration, a desire so powerful it brushed against her at a distance, all of it and more simmered in his eyes. "I'm not playing some foolish game with you."

Ann backed away from him, afraid of the intensity of the emotion she sensed burning within him. Worse still, more terrifying than the emotion she imagined seeing in his eyes, were the emotions churning within her.

"We were destined to meet, Ann. Destined to love."

Soul mates. A love dictated by destiny itself. He was very good at casting illusions, so very good. Perhaps because she was so willing to believe in him. Yet she was far too practical to believe in all of this wonderful, seductive sorcery. It made absolutely no sense at all. "I did not come to Dunmarin to become embroiled in one of your romantic exploits."

"Ann, I . . ."

She backpedaled when he advance. It wasn't from fear of what he might force upon her; she knew instinctively Iain would never force a woman to do anything against her will. Unfortunately, he had the most infuriating way of bending her will to suit his own. "I will not stand here and allow you to manipulate me."

"Confound it, Ann, I . . ." He glanced beyond her, his expression changing, anger and frustration solidifying into a look of calm determination. He halted and lifted his hand. "Don't take another step."

The low command in his voice held no room for disobedience. Ann froze, trembling with the battle raging within her. She wanted to run into his arms nearly as much as she wanted to protect herself.

"Come to me," he said, lifting his hand toward her.

It took every scrap of will to step back, away from him. "I don't know what you are—"

Her foot slipped on the edge of the cliff. Her weight shifted. Her balance deserted her. She glanced back and glimpsed the waves pounding the rocks fifty feet below her. Her startled mind registered the horrifying fact that she was about to fall a heartbeat before a strong hand closed upon her arm. Iain hauled her back from the edge of the cliff and wrapped his powerful arms around her.

Ann leaned against him, absorbing the wonderful solid strength of him, affirming that life still flowed in her, while her heart slowly crept down from the back of her throat. The heat and vitality of the man washed through her, chasing away the icy fear of sudden death. She turned her cheek against his sweater, dragging the scent of him deep into her lungs. His heart pounded against her cheek, as quick and violent as her own racing pulse. A strange sense of familiarity swept over her. Each time he held her, she could not escape the feeling she had finally come home.

"Good lord, lass." He smoothed his hand over her hair. "You shaved ten years off my life."

His chest vibrated with the dark tones of his voice. A part of her wished she could stand this way forever. Yet reality would not be bought with wishes. She eased out of his embrace and backed away from him, careful this time to mind her step. He did not attempt to draw her back into his embrace. Instead he stood with his back to the ocean, his gaze fixed upon her, a look of calm expectancy in his eyes. "Are you going to deny you want me as much as I want you?"

"The problem is I want more than you do." She swallowed hard, forcing back the emotion crowding her throat. "I may not be as worldly as you, but I know enough to realize that if I get involved with you, I will not walk away in one piece."

He held her gaze, his eyes reflecting a terrible turmoil. "Who says it has to end?"

She laughed—she couldn't help it. The sound of her laughter surprised her with the bitterness it held. "You don't exactly inspire a great deal of confidence when it comes to happily ever after."

He grinned at her. "A man can change, for the right woman."

His words conjured incredibly beguiling, thoroughly foolish thoughts within her. Still, she was far too practical to believe in this fairy tale. "I prefer not to take the chance. I would like to return to Dunmarin now."

Iain stood tall and powerful amid the ancient stones, his gaze never leaving hers. Misty sunlight shimmered around him, as though the light emanated from him. Behind him dark gray-green waves crashed upon the rocks offshore, as if a mirror to the turmoil she saw in his eyes. In some primitive part of her brain she could believe he was a sorcerer of old, a conjurer of magic. After what seemed an eternity, he smiled. "If that is what you would like, Professor, that is what we shall do."

Ann didn't like the look in his eyes. It was the look a lion might give to an antelope who had just managed to jump out of reach for the time being. "You are giving up pretty easily."

Iain laughed, the dark sound melding with the low roar of the ocean. "When you get to know me better, you'll learn I never give up when I want something badly enough. And my sweet bonnie Ann, I want you more than I have ever wanted anything."

Breathe, she reminded herself. If masculinity were bottled and sold, it would be with his picture on each vial. Never in her life had she ever been confronted with a man like this. A man intent on seducing her. A man who could easily steal her heart—if he hadn't already managed to do just that.

She pivoted and bumped into one of the stone obelisks. Heat flooded her cheeks. She kept her gaze fixed on the arched entrance to the cave while she carefully made her way across the clearing, too embarrassed to meet his gaze. Somehow she had to find a way to resist the maddening Highlander. She could do it, she assured herself. The stakes were too high to lose.

10

"What are we missing, old man?" Iain looked at the portrait of Adair Matheson that hung in the second-floor gallery of the south wing. Tall and dark, Adair stood in a nonexistent garden that Iain supposed was meant to be atop Mount Olympus. Adair did have a wee bit of an eccentric streak. Dunmarin Castle spread out in the background, as though Adair were looking down upon it from his lofty realm.

Iain turned and marched to one of the sashed windows that overlooked the conservatory and the east wing. Perhaps he was becoming as eccentric as Adair. This afternoon, if Ann hadn't stopped him, he would have taken her right there in the fairy ring, like some great rutting beast. Was there any wonder she was frightened to death of him?

Waning sunlight glittered on the glass dome of the conservatory. He narrowed his eyes against the glare while he looked beyond the dome of the conservatory to the drum tower of the east wing. During his time Adair must have looked out of this window countless times. Only in his time, he could look straight to the ocean. Where was the Sentinel?

Iain stared for a long moment at the solid bulk of the drum tower, a thought teasing him, slipping out of the shadows of his mind, then ducking away from him each time he tried to grasp it. What was it? Something about the view of the ocean. He walked back to the portrait of Adair, this time concentrating on the painting of Dunmarin. The castle had stood then as it did now, except for the major improvements of the drum tower, and . . .

The towers.

Iain stared for a moment, clarifying the fact staring him straight in the eye. "That's it," he whispered. "That's what we have been missing."

He rushed from the gallery and nearly collided with his grandmother in the hall. "Sorry, Gram."

Rose glared up at him. "What has you running about as though you were a horse with the scent of fire in his nose?"

"Ann." Iain plowed his hand through his hair. "I need to find her."

"I see. It's not the scent of a fire that is in your nostrils." Rose studied him a moment, as though he were a book and she were slowly leafing through the pages. "You know Ann isn't one of your fancy women, my lad."

"Gram, there is no need to lecture me on the merits of Ann Fitzpatrick. I know she isn't like any other woman I have ever known."

"I see." Rose's white brows lifted above the rims of her glasses. "Well, now, isn't that interesting."

He touched her chin with his fingertip. "I would stay and indulge that wee curious look of yours, but there is something important I need to show Ann. Do you know where she is?"

"There is no need to indulge me. I have been able to see straight through you since you were a wee lad."

Iain grinned at her. "Where is she?"

Rose folded her hands at her plump waist. "I was just on my way to find you, to tell you to stop toying with the poor lass. She looks as though she hasn't slept well in a week. I would wager it is all on your head."

He hadn't been sleeping well himself. He intended to change that. "Where is she?"

"Anxious, aren't you." Rose tilted her head, a smug little grin curving her lips. "Perhaps you do have some of Dugald's blood after all. I was beginning to think it might have been wearing too thin to do you any good. Your father had already been married for eight years by the time he was your age. One look at your mother, that's all it had taken with him. And they are still just as happy today as they were thirty-five years ago. My Duncan was the same. We knew each other three days before he proposed. He was eleven years younger than you are now.

Iain gripped her arms. "Gram, I am growing older every second."

"When last I saw her, Ann was in the library, staring at the plans of Dunmarin. Now, you be easy with her. Impatience won't be serving you with this lass. If you aren't careful, you'll be scaring her all the way back to Chicago."

Iain kissed her cheek, sweet lavender swirling through his senses. "Thank you, sweetheart."

Iain found Ann where Rose said he might. She was sitting at the desk, staring down at a note, whispering softly to herself. When he entered, she glanced up and met his gaze. The same sweet heat simmered through him that came each time he saw her.

The lenses of her glasses magnified the wariness in her eyes as he drew near her. "Since you believe in fairies, can I assume you also believe in witches?"

"Witches?"

"Yes. It seems Beatrice's sister's husband has a cousin who is a witch. And she has written this spell for me." Ann handed him the sheet of paper. "It is supposed to convince Adair to tell us where he has hidden the jewels."

Iain glanced at the incantation, then at Ann. "Have you been sitting here, trying to cast this spell?"

"No." She glanced down at the plans scattered over the desktop. "I was simply seeing how it sounded."

"Isn't that odd. You see, Adair just told me what we have been missing."

She looked up at him, her eyes wide. "Adair?"

"Aye." Iain shuffled through the plans on the desk until he found the improvement that showed the addition of the drum tower and the east wing. He tapped the drum tower as he said, "This right here."

Ann glanced down at the plans, then back up at him. "I don't understand."

"We have been thinking the two towers at either end of the east wing existed in Adair's time. But they didn't. They must have been added in an improvement that wasn't documented."

She slipped the glasses from her slim nose and placed them on the desk. "And Adair told you this?"

"The portrait of Adair did. It shows Dunmarin as it stood in his day." Iain shuffled through the plans until he found a page that showed the entire layout of the castle as it stood today. He pointed to the tower that must have faced the ocean in 1816. "The only tower that faced the ocean was set back a good distance from the cliffs. My guess is, this is the Sentinel."

Ann's breath eased from her in a slow exhalation. "I hope you are right."

He grabbed her hand and tugged her from the chair. "Come on, lass. Let's see if we can solve a two-hundred-year-old mystery."

*A*nn hesitated on the threshold of the room. She glanced at the huge four-poster bed sitting at the far end, then at the man who had paused in the middle of the room to look back at her. What the devil was he doing now?

"Relax, Professor," Iain said, as if reading her thoughts. "This is my brother Sean's apartment when he is at Dunmarin. I brought you here only to look for the Sentinel, not to try to seduce you."

Ann tried to ignore the disappointment stabbing her, and failed. Since returning from the fairy ring, she had been plagued with doubts. For the first time in her life she had met a man who made her heart soar each time she saw him. Was it truly better to keep her distance? Would that save her from a fall? She had never been a gambler, and here she was contemplating a risk that could cost her everything.

Iain glanced around the large room, studying the oak-wainscoted walls as though he were completely unaware of the turmoil raging inside her. "No lions in here."

Unless one counted the tall, broad-shouldered lion who was currently headed for a door on the far side of the room. She realized she should concentrate on the puzzle Adair had left for them, yet putting together coherent thought when she was near Iain was next to impossible. As much as she wanted to deny it, the search for the treasure no longer held as much significance to her as it had. Iain had made her confront the truth of her existence. Most of her life she had been following someone else's dream—perhaps because it was too frightening to chase after her own.

Ann followed him out of the bedroom into an adjoining chamber. Iain touched a switch near the door, bringing life to the wall sconces. Artificial candles glowed behind cut crystal, casting a soft light upon the oak wainscoting, the Empire sofas and Queen Anne chairs, all covered in the same mint green silk brocade that shrouded the windows.

"Look, lass," Iain said, his voice filled with excitement.

Ann followed the direction of his gaze and found a lion peering down at her from the thick cornice. "In the bosom of the Sentinel, find the lion who greets each day."

"Aye, lass. And in the jaws of the lion you will find the key." Iain dragged a lyre-back armchair beneath one of the six lions peering down at them. "Let's see if we can find a lion willing to tell us something."

Three lions later, Ann stood a short distance from Iain, watching him explore another lion's head. She rubbed her damp palms against her jeans, hoping he might end the suspense with a positive sign this time.

Iain peered into the lion's jaw. After a moment, he slipped his fingers between the lion's fangs. "I wonder."

"You wonder what?" She curled her hands into tight fists at her sides. "Did you find a key?"

"I'm not sure. There seems to be a lever in here." Iain glanced down at her, his expression betraying his excitement. "Let's see if anything happens when I—"

A soft click sounded like gunfire in the quiet room. A panel of the oak wainscoting beneath the lion moved slightly, coming away from the adjoining panel. "Well, now, look at that."

Ann didn't need his encouragement. She closed the distance and gripped the panel. Hinges creaked as the panel swung open like a door, revealing a rough stone wall and a wooden staircase leading down into darkness. Iain's arm brushed hers as he looked into the alcove. "We need some light. I'll get a couple of torches."

It seemed an eternity, but soon Iain returned with two flashlights. Wood creaked as Iain stepped onto the first wooden step. He glanced back at her. "Perhaps you'd better let me take a look."

"Oh, no. I'm not about to stay here while you play Indiana Jones."

Iain drew in a breath. "Stay close behind me."

A damp musky scent swept around her as she followed Iain down the steep staircase. A sound echoed from beneath the stairs, growing louder with each step they took, a soft splashing sound, as though water were lapping upon stone. "Do you hear that?"

"Aye. I suspect the stairs lead into one of the caves beneath Dunmarin. It was probably the back door of the castle." He glanced back at her, his expression illuminated by her flashlight. "It's high tide—that's why we are hearing the water."

Ann shivered inside, remembering the cold rush of water against her legs and the colder threat of death. The stairs descended to a landing, then dipped at an angle before sinking deeper below the castle. Her breath caught when Iain's flashlight beam caught the figure of a sea lion in the light. It was carved into a stone slab about the size of an eleven-by-fourteen picture frame and affixed to the stone wall of the castle on the far side of the landing. "Seek the selkie's secret behind its stony face," she whispered.

"I'll see if this selkie is ready to divulge his secret." Wood groaned when Iain stepped onto the wooden platform.

Ann directed her light upon the wooden landing, her palm damp upon the steel tube of the flashlight. There were holes in places where the wood had rotted. "Be careful."

"Aye." Iain glanced over his shoulder and smiled at her. "Keep your torch focused on that selkie."

Ann did as he asked, her heart pounding at the base of her throat. She had waited a lifetime for this moment. Yet a chilly realization tempered the excitement singing through her. Recovery of the jewels would sever her connection with Iain. It was bound to happen, no matter what, she assured herself. She could not make time stop. She could not stretch summer into an eternity. Midnight was about to find Cinderella. And she hadn't even danced with the prince.

Iain examined the stone slab. "There's a gap here, between the stone and the wall. And I think—"

"What do you think?"

"Patience, lass." Iain rested his flashlight on the wooden platform and turned back to the stone slab. He lifted the selkie ornament away from the wall, revealing a cavity and a dark mound within. Ann tried to breathe, but the air only eased into the top of her lungs.

Iain set the stone on the platform, wood groaning beneath its weight. He reached into the cavity and pulled out a leather bag. The flashlight illuminated his smile when he turned to face her. "Now what do you suppose is in here, lass?"

"Aren't you going to look?"

"No, lass." He winked at her. "I thought we would take a look together."

She stood on the step, holding her breath while Iain walked toward her. Wood shrieked as the boards collapsed beneath him. She caught his startled look in the beam of the flashlight, before he fell out of the light. Ann reached out to save him, the flashlight tumbling from her hand. It smacked the step at her feet. Her fingers grazed his arm before Iain slipped away from her, plunging down into the darkness.

"Iain!" She snatched the flashlight from the floor and directed the beam toward the landing. The light grazed the ragged ends of the rotted boards and a gaping hole where Iain had fallen. She stepped onto the remnants of the platform, wood groaning, shifting beneath her weight.

"Ann, stay where you are!" Iain shouted, his voice echoing oddly against the stones.

He was alive. Thank God, he was alive. She knelt on the boards and peered through the ragged hole. The wide beam of her flashlight swept over the black wall of a cave before finding Iain. He was clinging to an outcropping in the stone wall near the ceiling of the cave, the leather bag clenched tightly in his hand. Water swirled around him, lapping at his chin. "Are you all right?"

In spite of the situation, he smiled up at her. "Cold. But nothing is broken. Still, I think I am going to need a wee bit of help getting out of here."

"Can you get to the other steps?"

"No, lass. I'm on the back side of them."

She lay on the platform, rested her flashlight on the edge of the hole, and reached her hand toward Iain. "Take my hand."

"It's too dangerous." He slipped along the wall before he braced himself once more against the strong current. "I could pull you in."

"The tide is rising, Iain. By the time I can get help, the water will be up to the ceiling, which means it will be over your head. And even a selkie needs to breathe." She reached for him. "Give me your hand."

"I'll tread water beneath the platform until help can get to me."

"The current is too strong. It will sweep you deeper into the cave."

"I'll manage."

"You'll manage to drown."

Iain fought the current, inching his way along the wall until he regained the ground he had lost. He lifted the leather bag toward her. "Take the treasure."

"To blazes with the treasure! Give me your hand."

A grin slowly slid along his lips. "You've worked too hard to let this chance disappear, lass. Take the bag."

She swore under her breath, then stretched to take the

bag from his outstretched hand. She tossed it behind her, the bundle landing with a thump on the step. "Give me your hand."

Iain glanced around as though looking for an alternative in the faint light shining from the flashlight above him. He shook his head, then looked up at her. "I'm too heavy for you, lass. I cannot take the chance of you falling in here with me."

"Iain Matheson, take my hand this minute, or I swear I'll jump in there, and we'll both drown." Even as she spoke the words, the truth of them sang through her with a sweet clarity. There was no sense in trying to deny a truth that kept staring her straight in the eye. She loved Iain Matheson, deeply, completely. She would rather die here and now with him than live knowing she had done nothing at all to save him.

He stared at her, his expression betraying the turmoil within him. "Ann, I—"

"I'll do it, Iain. Take my hand, or I will jump in there beside you. And I warn you, I will not be at all happy with you. So you'd just better take my hand now."

He released his breath in a quick sigh. "If you feel yourself falling, let go."

"Confound it, Iain," she said, trying to reach him. "We don't have much time."

He mumbled something about stubborn Americans, then reached toward her. She gripped his hand with both hands and pulled while he propelled himself through the water. She felt him surge upward, while she fought to keep from slipping headfirst into the hole. Cold droplets splashed her face as he threw his arm over the planks beside her. She tugged on his arm while he struggled to pull himself onto the platform. Wood groaned beneath them when his weight settled upon the remnants of the landing.

"Come on, lass," Iain said, grabbing her arm.

Together they stepped from the platform onto the bottom stair just as another plank gave way and tumbled into the water below. Iain clutched her to his chest, his arms steel bands around her, locking her against his big body. "Let's get out of here, before the stairs give way as well."

He bent and retrieved the leather bag before hurrying up the stairs, holding her arm as though he were afraid he might lose her should he slacken his grip. She followed him up the stairs, grateful for the strong grip on her arm steadying her wobbly legs, silently giving thanks for surviving near disaster.

The soft light cast by the wall sconces embraced them as they stumbled from the alcove into the drawing room. Iain pressed his back against a panel of the oak wainscoting and dragged her into his arms. His chest rose and fell against her cheek with each quick breath he took, his heart thudding in the same erratic race as hers. After a long while he said, "My sweet, brave Ann. You scared me half to death, lass. I thought for sure you were going to come sliding in after me."

She turned her face against his chest, feeling his warmth radiate through the wet cotton of his sweater. When she met his gaze, her breath stilled in her throat. The hunger in his eyes burned with an intensity she could feel, like the sun on a hot summer day. He wanted her. Here and now. She saw his need, recognized the questions simmering deep within his eyes.

From a secret pool of longing lingering within her, an answer rose to meet the questions in his eyes. He had once asked her if she had any regrets in life. At that time she had imagined the greatest regret might be to become involved with this man. Now she realized the greatest regret would be to walk away without ever knowing the reality of her dreams. Strands of sensation slipped around her, catching her in a delicate web of feeling that she could no longer deny.

Ann threw her arms around his neck and kissed him, allowing him to taste all the passion for him she had kept tightly clenched inside. Iain cinched his arms around her and held her as though he would still be holding her when the last star burned from the heavens. The hunger in him raged without disguise. He opened his mouth over hers, kissing her as though he took his every sustenance from her. In his arms she felt transformed. Gone was the nice, practical teacher from Chicago. In her place stood a temptress, wanton with the need for this man, only this man.

Together they pulled and tugged at the clothes that kept man from woman, until finally nothing barred the touch of skin against skin. When he drew her close against him, she sighed with pleasure at the soft brush of masculine hair against her sensitive skin. Never in her life had she felt this free, this alive, this frantic with the need to touch, to kiss, to possess. She slid her hands over his shoulders, down his chest, thick muscles quivering beneath her touch, as though he too were trapped in this vortex of need. She had never done anything like this before. Yet this man had altered her, had transformed the ordinary into the extraordinary, the timid female into a siren.

The look in his eyes burned away the qualms she had always felt about the quality of her slender curves. Iain provided no room for doubts. The look in his eyes told her precisely what he thought of her face and form. For some reason she could not begin to understand, he looked at her as though she were the most desirable woman he had ever gazed upon.

He slid his hands over the curves of her hips. "Do you have any idea how long I have been waiting for you?"

"Two weeks?" she whispered, her voice ragged with need.

He kissed the tip of her nose. "A lifetime."

As if to prove how much he wanted her, he flowed down her body, stroking her, kissing her, a hungry flame licking over her body, heating her, escalating the need within her until she feared she might come apart beneath his touch. Finally, when she thought she might die for wanting him, he lifted her into his arms and laid her down upon the cool, pale green silk of the nearest sofa. The first hard thrust of his body into hers nearly sent her over the edge.

She gripped his shoulders while she rose to meet his every downward thrust, pleasure expanding inside of her, welling upward until she could no longer contain it. Sensation ripped through her like light refracting through a diamond. Distantly she heard her name escape his lips while the pleasure gripped her, sending shudder after shudder rippling through her body. It was as if she had only been existing until this moment, until this man. In a distant part of her brain she acknowledged that they had used no precautions against pregnancy. Still, she was willing to take the consequences.

After a long while he lifted his head and smiled down at her. He smoothed a damp lock of hair from her cheek, then kissed her nose. "It's nice to know there are a few things in life that are truly worth waiting for."

"You have a way about you, Iain Matheson." She brushed her hand over the smooth skin of his shoulder. "A way of making me forget about all the things I once thought important."

"This is important." He shifted in her arms, pulling away from her. "And it's just the beginning."

She sucked in her breath when he lifted her into his arms, settling her high against his bare chest. "Just the beginning?"

"Aye, lass." He winked at her. "I'm not about to stop with just a wee bit of an appetizer."

"An appetizer?"

"Aye." He kissed the tip of her nose. "I think we should start in the shower."

Her imagination flooded her mind with naughty images. Her body tingled in response. She slipped her arms around his neck and snuggled against him while he carried her into the bedroom, thick muscles shifting against her breasts. It was so nice to learn that at times reality was better than dreams.

A long while later, Ann lay in bed, her head nestled on Iain's shoulder, feeling as sated as a starving beggar who has just polished off a twelve-course meal. The smoldering scent of his skin filled her every breath. The lush masculine heat of him warmed her. How glorious it would be to sleep like this every night and to awaken in his arms every morning. Unfortunately he had not mentioned a word about the future. She drew a serpentine pattern through the hair on his chest, while she considered the possibilities she might face with this man.

He brushed his hand up and down her arm. "There is something we really should do."

She lifted her head to meet his gaze. "Again?"

He laughed, the dark rumble rising from deep in his chest. "My goodness, Professor, I'm thinking you're a bit insatiable. I wonder if I can manage to keep you satisfied."

Ann liked the sound of that. It implied he intended to try. "I have a feeling you won't have any trouble."

Iain lifted her hand and kissed the inside of her wrist, sending tingles scattering along her nerves. "I was thinking of the treasure. I thought we might take a look at it."

"The treasure." Ann shook her head, amazed at how thoroughly he had chased every thought of work out of her head. "I completely forgot about it."

"You stay here." He threw the covers back and rolled out of bed. "I'll get it."

She watched him leave, admiring the view. When he returned, she lapped up the sight of him, like a kitten who had fallen into a pot of cream.

He paused by the bed, handed her the leather bag, and stood looking at her. Light from the wall sconces flowed over him, exploiting the sheer male beauty of his face, sliding lovingly over his broad shoulders, tangling in the hair that covered his chest, spilling over the sleek skin of his hip. Looking at him, she could believe he was indeed a creature not of mortal blood—a selkie who had come to her from the sea, a mythical lover, a man she could no longer resist, this was Iain.

"If you keep looking at me in that sultry way, I'll forget all about this two-hundred-year-old mystery."

She laughed and took the bag. She had never been accused of doing anything sultry until she met this man. It gave her a delicious feeling of power. She pulled open the drawstring and dumped the contents out of the wet leather pouch, spilling emeralds and diamonds across the sheet. A necklace, a bracelet, and a ring glittered in the light. The jewelry was more beautiful than the portrait had promised, the large stones shimmering with fire. They were obviously worth a fortune. Unfortunately there was nothing else in the bag. The cross was not with them. "It's not here."

Iain sat on the bed beside her, slipped his arm around her shoulders, and held her close. "I'm sorry, lass."

"It's all right, really." She leaned against him, oddly indifferent to the loss of this particular dream. What had seemed monumentally important before this moment now paled with what she had found on Dunmarin. "Still, I wonder what Adair did with the cross?"

"Perhaps he hid it somewhere else in the castle." He hugged her close. "We might be able to find it over the next fifty or sixty years if you care to look."

She looked up at him, afraid to read more into his words than what might be behind them. "*We* might be able to find it?"

"Aye. And there are amazing archaeological sites on Dunmarin. I could probably keep you busy for years just exploring the island. If you get bored with Dunmarin, we can always go off poking about elsewhere. Still, I suppose if you want to remain in Chicago, I will just have to buy a place there. But we could still come back to Dunmarin every summer."

Ann stared at him. "Are you asking me to . . . I mean,

you seem to have the future all planned, and I . . . are you?"

"You get a little crinkle between your brows when you are trying to figure something out." He smoothed his fingertip over her brow. "Do you mean to say you still don't know how much I love you?"

Her heart bumped into the wall of her chest. "You love me?"

"Aye, lass. And I expect a proper proposal of marriage from you."

Ann nearly choked. "A proposal of marriage from me?"

"My bonnie Ann, I cannot imagine you are the type of woman to take advantage of a poor lad." He kissed the tip of her nose. "I was thinking after you seduced me this way, you would be making an honest man of me."

"Me seduce you!"

"Aye. You were the one who kissed me first."

"I did not . . . well . . . maybe I did." She saw the glint of mischief in his eyes and realized he was teasing her. Again. "You've been trying to seduce me since the first day we met."

"It's my selkie blood. I recognized my mate when I saw you. You're mine. And I intend to keep it that way." Iain cinched his arms around her and dragged her down on top of him. "Any arguments, my bonnie Ann?"

She slipped her arms around his neck, snuggling against the long length of his powerful body. "None at all, my maddening Highlander."

Epilogue

"And one day you will meet your soul mate, lad. You'll know her the moment you see her."

Ann heard Iain's soft voice spill into the hall as she approached the nursery. She had just tucked their twin daughters into bed in the room next door. Sarah and Louise were four and determined to stretch their bedtime stories out for as long as they could coax Mommy into reading. Finally both little heads were nestled upon their pillows.

"Now she might be stubborn at first; your mama took a wee bit of persuading. But I finally convinced her I was the only man she could ever want. Remember, when you want something with all of your heart, go after it."

She paused in the doorway of the nursery, her heart

expanding with the sight that greeted her. Iain sat on a rocker near the crib, cradling their ten-month-old son in his arms. His dark head was bent over the infant, while he spoke his own version of a bedtime story to young Patrick.

"You see, it is Dugald's legacy to each firstborn male of the laird. A selkie he was, and selkies always know what they want when they see it." Iain glanced up and caught her watching him. He winked at her, a grin sliding across his lips, the pure love in his eyes reaching her across the distance. "Ah, lad, it's a joy it is, to find her, to woo her, to claim her for all your days. When you find her, hold on to her with all your might, and never let her go."

Ann crossed the distance between them and rested her hand on her husband's shoulder. She looked down into their son's sleeping face, seeing an image of Iain there. She bent and kissed Patrick's brow, the sweet powdery scent of him filling her nostrils.

"I think you have managed to put him to sleep," she whispered, squeezing Iain's thick shoulder.

"Aye." Iain stood with his bundle and carefully laid the child in the crib.

After turning off the light, he slipped his arm around Ann's shoulders and walked with her to their chamber. Moonlight flowed through the windowpanes, drawing them to the view of the beach and the ocean beyond. Although they spent several weeks each year in Chicago, Dunmarin was now her home. In a very real sense it felt as though she had always lived here. Iain liked to say it was because her soul had finally returned to the place where she belonged.

"Are your tired, lass?"

Ann looked up into his dark eyes, the breath growing still in her throat. She recognized the look in his eyes, felt the hunger in him. A warmth kindled deep inside her, desire stirring as only he had ever awakened it. She brushed her fingertips over the smooth line of his freshly shaven jaw and rose on her tiptoes to kiss his chin. A smoldering scent of citrus and spices and man swirled through her senses, doing wicked things to her insides. Need curled around her, tugging on her vitals, drawing her to this man as though an unseen tether wrapped one to the other. She looped her arms around his neck and leaned into the warm strength of his body. "I'm never that tired, my darling."

DEBRA DIER

A former manager in data processing, Debra Dier is the award-winning author of twelve novels. Although born and raised in Niagara Falls, New York, she currently resides near St. Louis, Missouri, with her husband and daughter and their Irish setter.

Castle
in the Skye

KATHLEEN GIVENS

This is dedicated

To Maggie,
who took another leap of faith,

To Peggy,
who walked away from advertising
into a whole new world,

And to Russ,
who will always be my hero.

1

"**N**o!" shouted Larry Marks, Creative Director of L & M Advertising. He threw his sandwich wrapper on the floor and glared at her. "It's terrible timing!"

Maddie Breen crossed her arms over her chest and bit her tongue. At the best of times her boss was a manipulator, a workaholic who demanded eighty-hour workweeks from his staff. To be fair, Larry worked the same hours at his advertising firm, where she was Art Director, but enough was enough. She hadn't had a vacation in three years.

"Larry, I gave the dates to Human Resources last month. I have plane tickets, and I'm leaving Saturday. You knew about this ages ago."

"I didn't think you'd really do it, Maddie. How can you leave us in a crisis?"

"It's not a crisis."

"Ever heard the word Super Bowl?"

"That's two words. It's July. Most of the work is done, and we've got two months to fine-tune when I get back. I'll only be gone for ten days."

"Ten days! The Gulf War was shorter."

Maddie shook her head. If only there were a trace of humor in this man. "We're not at war, Larry," she said evenly. "I've got everything covered."

"We've got the big pitch for the dot-com," he snarled.

"In October. I've already done the casting, and the artwork is ready."

"The radio stuff is two weeks late."

"That's not my project."

"We're a team, Maddie. I thought you knew that. If you leave, we'll all work even longer hours. It's a burden on the rest of us."

Maddie sighed. "Larry, I have to go."

"Why? To see some old geezer who was your grandfather's friend? Why do you have to be there? Go for the weekend and come back."

"I can't."

"Why can't someone else in your family go? Why you?"

"Because I'm the one who is friends with Magnus's granddaughter Sara. Because I promised."

"Well, unpromise."

"I don't unpromise."

Larry waved at the staff, who were all pretending not

to hear the conversation. "They'll pay while you play. We'll lose the account."

"We won't lose the account. I'll stay in touch; I'll call every day."

Larry's eyes narrowed as he watched her. Then he opened the drawer on his desk and handed her a cell phone. "Here. It's one of those satellite phones. Day or night, Maddie. You have to be available day or night."

"I will be."

"You'll never last two weeks. What the hell is there to do in Scotland? Where are you going? Skyeland or something?"

"The Isle of Skye. Off the western coast."

"I'm going on record that you are taking this time against my direct orders."

"You approved it."

"I don't remember approving it."

"That's a different problem. Look, Larry, I know you're not happy, but I've accrued six weeks of vacation, and I'm taking two of them. You approved it. In writing."

"We'll all be working twenty-four/seven until you get back. Think of us while you're playing with the boys in kilts," he said peevishly before stalking off.

*M*addie leaned against the railing of the ferry and looked across the water at the jagged mountains of the Isle of Skye. The dark peaks of the Cuillins dominated the skyline before climbing into the clouds, even more breathtaking than she'd remembered. Over the sea to Skye, she thought and smiled—she wasn't a Scottish prince fleeing for his life like in the song; she was an American on her way to a birthday party. She didn't need to take out Magnus's letter. Maddie knew his words by heart, had read them a hundred times since receiving it. It was a shameless maneuver, and she'd laughed when she'd read it.

"Madeline," he'd written. "Come to Skye. You have no choice. An old man who has loved you all your life humbly requests your presence at what may be his last celebration. Say yes. Please come and see me one more time."

And so she had agreed, just as he'd known she would. The invitation to his eightieth birthday party had triggered a flood of memories. She had not replied at once, wanting to go but knowing she couldn't even consider leaving her job just now. It was impossible, she'd told herself. But then Magnus himself had written, and she knew it was just as impossible not to go. How could she say no to him?

Her grandfather, Charles Breen, had been a paratrooper in World War II, dropped behind enemy lines in northern Italy. Separated from his unit, he'd found a wounded Magnus MacDonald hanging from a tree and had carried the Scotsman seven miles to safety. Later, when Charlie was wounded as well, the two men met in the hospital in England. And when victory in Europe was declared, Magnus brought Charlie to Skye to heal. Eventually Charlie went back to the States, but when he married, Magnus was his Best Man. And when Magnus married Anne the following year, Charlie returned the favor. Over the decades the two men had remained close friends, visiting as often as they could. When she was fifteen, Maddie spent a magical summer here with her grandparents and Magnus's granddaughter Sara. And when Charlie died, Magnus came to the States, bringing Sara with him, and a bagpiper who played "Amazing Grace" at the graveside while the skies darkened above them. How could she possibly say no?

Sara had offered to drive down to Glasgow and collect her, but Maddie insisted that she rent a car and save Sara the trip. It had been fifteen years, but she still remembered, sitting in the backseat with a sour face because she'd been forced to leave her one true love behind to spend the summer at Magnus and Anne's hotel, the Trotternish House. When she got home she'd hardly been able to remember the boy's name, but Skye's scenery and history had haunted her ever since.

This time she rented a convertible and let the summer wind blow her long dark hair out of its bindings and billow around her head until she arrived at Mallaig and boarded the ferry to Skye. She might have to stay in touch with the office, but she didn't have to look as if she was still there.

Maddie looked at her watch. Noon in Scotland; seven A.M. in New York. It was Sunday, but that wouldn't make any difference to Larry, who would be calling at any moment. He'd try to make her feel guilty for leaving, and he wouldn't have to try very hard. She probably should have stayed, should be working with the team, but it felt so good not to be there. As if on cue, the phone rang, and there he was, Larry Sunshine, curt and hassled.

"Maddie, did you e-mail the schedule to everyone?"

She sighed. Charming man. "Good morning, Larry. Nice to hear from you too. Yes, my flight was fine, thanks for asking."

"What? What about the schedules?"

"I did that two weeks ago. Look on your e-mail. You also have a hard copy in the file I gave you. It's all been done."

"What about the color blend on the brochures?'

"Corrected. Check the file."

She held the phone away from her ear and looked out over the water at the mountains as Larry continued to ask her unnecessary questions. It was no use. She no longer saw the Cuillins, but instead computer screens and the print campaign she'd approved in the taxi on the way to the airport. Larry hung up just as the ferry approached the dock and the people around her began to file down to the car deck. Maddie lingered, taking a moment to take one more picture, one more mental image of the blue water and the even bluer islands of Rum and Eigg on the horizon. She took a deep breath, smiled up at the gulls overhead, then followed the others below.

It took an hour to drive to the small harbor town of Portree, where she stood for a moment on the cliff overlooking the water, remembering being here with Sara. The two girls had become fast friends that long-ago summer, and the memory of their giggles and inept sailing in this bay brought a wistful smile. It feels like coming home, Maddie thought in surprise, looking at the pastel buildings that lined the shore of Portree Harbor. They hadn't changed at all, but she and Sara certainly had. It would be good to see Sara in person again, although they knew each other well after years of keeping in touch through letters and e-mail. Sara was a chatty correspondent, keeping Maddie up to date on her grandparents, her parents, her brother Derek, and her husband Keith. Maddie had written about her divorced parents, her married sisters and their children, her nonexistent love life. And her career. She sighed. She should be in New York. She called for her voice-mail messages as she drove up the coast.

She was still picking up messages and leaving her own for Monday morning as she passed the Old Man of Storr and started the last leg of her journey. The topography was dramatic here—the Sound of Raasay to her right, dark green hills dotted with gray rocks to her left, cliffs suddenly bordered by wide green pasturelands, but Maddie hardly noticed. She was explaining to her assistant Katie's voice mail how to solve the glitches with the brochure inserts when she took the turnoff to Trotternish House and slowed down on the narrow driveway. The trees grew close to the road here, but between them she could see a gravel track running parallel to the drive. The old road, she remembered, then slowed down even more as the pavement dipped down to a stone bridge that arched across the stream. Almost there. She told Katie three more things to look into, then hung up. Her mood lightened immediately. Katie could handle it, she assured herself with a grin. And if not, well, Larry would have to. It would serve him right. He hadn't given her a decent raise in three years.

The road rose sharply here, into a wide meadow where the Trotternish Games were held every summer, an emerald bowl with a view of the Quiraing behind and the sea below. Maddie slowed the car to a crawl as she remembered this meadow filled with color and activity. The Games were well attended, and this field would be teeming with hundreds of people watching the caber and hammer tosses, the putting of the stone, the dancing and piping competitions. Locals in traditional dress would mix with tourists in jeans, and this year she'd be among them. She'd paint the Games, Maddie thought, her pleasure growing.

One reason for this trip was to be here for Magnus's party, but another was to find the artist in herself, submerged under deadlines and advertising details for so long. She'd use acrylics to catch the vibrant colors, the tartans bright against the dark green landscape and the blue of the sky and sea beyond. If only the paints could hold the sounds as well—the laughter, the hush of the crowd as the competitions neared their end, the roar of applause when the winner was announced, the proud chatter of the parents when the children began their dancing. And over all the sound of bagpipes. She loved the Games, loved their drama and pageantry, and this time she'd capture them on canvas, or at least try.

She pulled to the side of the road and parked, then walked through the low bushes that separated the meadow from the sea cliffs. The old road was narrower here where it hugged the top of the cliffs overlooking the Minch, the sea strait that divided the Outer Hebrides from the mainland. Maddie took a deep breath as she watched the waves crash on the rocks below and pretended not to hear her cell phone ringing in the convertible, concentrating instead on naming the shades of blue in the sky and the water. Nothing changes here, she thought. This view had been the same fifteen years ago, and probably two hundred years before that. It might as well be the nineteenth century. Or perhaps not, she told herself—I wouldn't be wearing a black silk shell and slacks and ignoring my boss in New York. And I wouldn't have a warm shower waiting for me at Trotternish house. She turned from the panorama to head back to the car and that shower, then heard a pounding coming from the turn in the road that led to the hotel. Drums? But no, the very ground seemed to shake. She took a step forward, then gasped as a huge chestnut horse, mane and tail flying, thundered around the bend. Maddie stood frozen in the middle of the road as the horse charged at her. The rider was leaning over the horse's neck and urging it even faster, but as the chestnut lurched to the side, he looked up at her and straightened in the saddle, shouting something and waving his hand. They bore down on her, and Maddie prepared to die.

With a curse and a gust of warm wind the horse and rider pounded past her. She saw a blur of flying hooves, gleaming chestnut horse, and a bare, well-muscled male thigh at eye level before they flew around the next bend and out of sight. In the silence that followed, she began to breathe again and pressed her hand against her throat to still her pounding heart. My God, that was close, she thought; I'm out of here. She had started back to the car, her foot still in the air, when the horse came careening back around the curve, heading directly for her again. This time she screamed but was unable to move, watching in terror as man and beast raced toward her, then skidded to a stop ten feet away. The man threw a long leg over the horse, dropped to the ground, and stalked to stand before her. He was in his thirties, very tall, very blond. And very handsome, with sculptured cheekbones, a strong jaw, and brilliant blue eyes surrounded by thick lashes. He had broad shoulders and a trim waist under a white linen shirt. And he wore a kilt.

Maddie closed her eyes. I'm dreaming, she thought. I'll open my eyes, and I'll still be over the Atlantic. I knew I shouldn't have had that second glass of wine.

"Lassie, are ye a'right?"

The voice was real, she thought. She couldn't have invented that rich Scottish burr or the sound of him catching his breath. Or that body. She opened her eyes and looked at him. He was—impossibly—grinning at her!

"Am I all right? You scared me half to death!"

"Sorry. Perhaps ye shouldn't be standing in the middle of the road." He looked her up and down and fought a smile. "Ye look just fine, but let me look closer." He circled her, then nodded. "Aye, ye look fit enough. Not a scratch. A bit of dust here, though," he said, reaching out toward her leg.

Maddie stepped away, eyeing him suspiciously, brushing her slacks off. "I'm fine, thank you. What were you doing?"

He met her eyes with an amused glance. "Brushing dirt off yer leg."

"I mean racing down this road."

"Practicing."

"To kill people? I think you'll do quite well."

He laughed. "Glad to hear it. Might come in handy with the English around everywhere."

Maddie let her gaze fall from those amazing blue eyes past his shirt, open enough at the collar to let her see tanned skin and golden hair on his chest, and down to the kilt he wore with nonchalance, his legs bare below. His horse gave a snort, and they both looked over at the chestnut. The Scotsman patted him on the nose, then turned back to Maddie.

"I am sorry to have frightened ye, miss," he said, his voice sincere. "I didna expect to find someone standing in the middle of the road when we came 'round the bend. Ye near gave me a heart attack."

His contrite tone melted her resistance. "I'm sorry too. I didn't think anyone used the old road anymore. I was looking at the view."

"It's even better from the hotel. I assume ye're going to Trotternish House?" She nodded. "Are ye staying at the hotel?"

"Yes."

He smiled again, gesturing to the chestnut. "Do ye need a ride? I have a horse handy."

"No, thank you. I have a car."

She started to move away. He watched her for a moment, then called after her. "Are ye sure ye're not hurt? D'ye need me to drive ye?"

"I'm fine, thank you."

"Aye, that ye are," he said appraisingly. "And yer welcome."

Maddie gave him another glance before she walked through the bushes.

$\mathcal{T}$rotternish House Hotel stood on the northeastern shore, atop a small knoll overlooking Duntober Bay, protected from the worst of the weather by the Quiraing, the fantastically shaped lava formations that crossed the center of the Trotternish. It still looked like the rambling private home it had been before Magnus had converted it to a hotel twenty years ago, its three wings and four stories of gray stone dramatic against the surrounding greenery.

Anne's hydrangeas were six feet tall where they lined the circular driveway that climbed to the reception portico, the lawn lush and dark against the flowers that bordered it. The trees had grown considerably since her last visit, the white trim around the doors and windows had been recently repainted, and there were new benches under the beech trees in the side garden, but Maddie could see nothing else that had changed. Before she could even climb from the car, the side door of the inn banged open and Sara bounded out, her red hair streaming behind her like a banner. She gave a whoop and threw her arms around Maddie.

"Ye're here! Ye're here! I was about to send out a search team."

Maddie returned the embrace with a laugh. "The road has gotten smaller. And I'm driving on the wrong side of the road."

"Well, there's that," Sara said with a grin, grabbing a suitcase and leading the way to Maddie's room in the family wing.

Maddie couldn't help smiling as they climbed the carved staircase that swept up from the main foyer to the landing that separated the guest wing from the family wing. It felt so good to be back. Sara had redecorated the interior, preserving the comfortable elegance that was a Trotternish hallmark. The wings were named after their views—Garden, Mountain, or Ocean, symbols of each woven into the carpets and the upholstery in that wing. Maddie sighed with pleasure as she followed Sara down the long corridor of the Ocean Wing, with its blue-and-white color scheme. She remembered this so well, the walnut paneling waist high, topped by brilliant white plaster that showcased the hundreds of Scottish watercolors that Magnus and Anne had collected over the decades, seascapes in this wing. The windows were opened wide, and the sound of the sea rose above the conversation and laughter from the terrace below, where afternoon tea was being served. Sara opened the door to the room Maddie had had fifteen years ago, stepping back to let her enter first. The wallpaper and the bedding had been changed, but not the fine mahogany furniture. The room smelled, as it always had, like lilacs and lemon polish, and Maddie took a deep breath.

"I gave ye yer old room. Hope ye don't mind."

Maddie smiled. "I love this room, Thank you for remembering."

"Of course I remembered!" Sara went to the window and pushed the blue-and-white chintz curtains back. "But I warn ye, ye'll only be here long enough to throw yer exhausted self into bed. We'll have total chaos until the big day. My grandparents will see ye at dinner. They went to visit my great-aunt Eloise, the one who drives my grandfather mad. Hard to believe they're siblings." She plumped a pillow. "And speaking of siblings, Derek is in the kitchen trying to get something besides meat and fish and potatoes on the menu, and no doubt thoroughly upsetting my head chef. Can ye imagine the Trotternish changing its menu just because we're in a new century? Keith is down in Portree with a dead car. And my parents will be here next week, but enough about the MacDonalds. How are ye, Maddie?"

"Jet-lagged and grimy and tired—I had to work all night—but wonderful. It's so good to see you again." She gave her old friend another hug.

"And ye as well. Ye look splendid, not grimy at all, but very fit. Ye look exactly the same as the last time I saw ye."

"It's been five years."

"Is that possible?" Sara sighed. "Hard to believe. I suspect that means I'm five years older. Remember how we pretended to be in our twenties?"

"We were teenagers. We thought getting older was cool."

"We were idiots."

Maddie grinned. "We were, weren't we? But it was a wonderful summer."

"That it was. I don't think I've ever enjoyed one more. Well, now ye'll have another Scottish summer. Well, fortnight of a Scottish summer."

Maddie began to answer, but was interrupted by the ring of her cell phone. "Sorry, I have to get it."

"It'll be Larry Someone. Is that yer boss?"

"How did you know?" Maddie nodded and answered the phone, but the connection was gone.

"He called downstairs twice already. Maddie, really! Ye're on holiday. Can it not wait?"

Maddie shook her head. "You don't understand. I promised to be available."

"That's not much of a break."

"I shouldn't have left at all. It's terrible timing."

Sara put her hands on her hips. "When's the last time ye had a holiday?"

"I just need to get past the Super Bowl."

"But that's not until January! And then it'll be the next project. Ye've turned into a workaholic."

Maddie shook her head. "No, just someone with a very demanding job."

"Ye need a long, silly holiday, and that's just what ye'll get here." Sara gave Maddie a quick hug. "Have a nap and a shower and come down whenever ye wish. I'm off to get Keith, but I'll be back before too long. Help yerself to whatever ye need." She crossed the room and turned at the door. "Bless ye for coming, Maddie. It means the world to Granddad, and to me."

"And to me," Maddie said.

"Turn that damn phone off and rest! I'll see ye after a bit."

𝒯he shower felt good, and Maddie slept for an hour. It was late afternoon when she woke, or at least she thought so. Days were longer here, and Scottish summer nights very short; the gloaming lasted hours before the darkness came, and even then the night wasn't black, but rather a deep blue. At the longest the darkness lasted only a few hours, and then the sun rose again. Larry had left five messages on her cell phone, and Maddie called him at home, shaking her head as she hung up twenty minutes later. As usual, it all could have waited. The man was a walking cliché, poster boy for cardiac surgeon full employment.

Sara wasn't back when Maddie went downstairs, and after chatting with a few of the staff, she grabbed a windbreaker and set off. This was the perfect time to get started on her gift for Magnus. Even if she'd not needed to go there, she couldn't stay away. It had been her favorite place on the island and one of the scenes she'd not been able to erase from her mind. Duntober Castle.

2

Iain MacDonald looked at himself in the mirror and grinned. No wonder the American girl had been terrified when they'd appeared. The chestnut was eighteen hands, a huge brute who loved to run full bore. And he himself looked like a madman, hair too long and wild from the wind, shirt rumpled from leaning over Blaven's neck, legs muddy from crashing through the puddles on the old road. No wonder she'd been frightened; he'd had a hell of a scare himself when he'd looked up from coming around the bend and seen her in front of them. He turned from his reflection to pull his shirt over his head and toss it on the chest, where it was soon followed by the kilt. Thank God Blaven was as intelligent as he was swift; otherwise they would have run her over. And that, Iain thought, climbing into the shower, would have been a hell of a shame. She was damned beautiful; shaken, but definitely beautiful, tall, slender but curvy, just the way he thought a woman should look. Her brown hair had been tousled, giving her a look of abandon, and her eyes, fringed with long lashes, were splendid. Lovely eyes, he thought. Straight nose, delicate jawline that tapered behind her wavy hair, a definite beauty. Before she'd spoken he'd guessed she was an American; New York or L.A. where everyone seemed to wear black clothes every day of the year.

He'd have to apologize. And soon. Who knew how long she'd be staying at the hotel? It wouldn't be difficult to see her again. And if she was still angry, he could watch as her eyes flashed at him and her chest heaved. Iain grinned to himself. There was nowhere to go at the Trotternish but the pub or the lounge after dinner. He'd find her tonight, buy her a drink, and see just what color those eyes were.

𝒯his view is beyond beautiful, Maddie thought, pausing at the pile of stones that had once been a gatehouse. Below her Duntober Bay melded into open sea and flowed in shades of silver and blue to the mainland. The island of Rona was indigo in the channel, and the mainland mountains cobalt on the horizon. Whoever chose this site had chosen well. The castle was protected by the cliff that separated it from the water and by the Quiraing behind it. Duntober had passed into MacDonald hands in the early sixteenth century, and they had retained it ever since. It had been deserted in the eighteenth century, sometime after the Jacobite rising of 1715. There were several different stories for why the MacDonalds had left the castle, from a baby being dropped from a window to the ghostly visits of former owner Donald Gorm MacDonald. Maddie preferred the ghost story herself; it was easy to believe spirits roamed the ruins of Duntober.

Much of the castle was intact, although its walls were crumbling and many of the stones that had once formed the walls had been quarried for local houses. Magnus had told her that some of the stones used to build the Trotternish had been brought down from here. What was left was stark and lonely, but the ruin hinted at its former splendor and comfort. The wind freshened, and she turned to climb the short hill to the castle. The outer walls had once stretched from the gatehouse to enclose a courtyard and the castle itself, but there were gaps in it now. Stones were strewn along the pathway that had been clear on her last visit, and Maddie looked up at a sound from within the castle, half expecting to see rocks falling toward her. There was nothing to see, and she pulled her jacket tighter and told herself not to be so silly. No ghosts would disturb her visit.

As if to mock her last thought, the bushes and trees to her left rustled, the thick foliage blocking her view of whatever it was that shook the branches. She froze, feeling the hair on her neck rise. She took a step, then a second, off the path, pushing branches slowly out of her way and peering through the leaves. There was a movement; then the branch swayed again in the breeze, and she took a deep breath. Another sound, farther up the hill this time, assured her that whatever—or whomever—it was had moved away from her. Not enough sleep and too many ghost stories, she told herself. But something had been there.

At the top of the hill, the castle looked just as she had remembered it, the gray stone walls towering into the clouds. This graceful shell had once been a home, a refuge from the world, she thought as she moved to the center of the Great Hall. It would not be a shell for much longer. Magnus was going to restore Duntober, and Maddie was delighted. She and Sara had dreamed of doing just that and living here in luxury. They had spent hours here that summer fifteen years ago, planning their future together. Nothing of their dreams had come true except their continued friendship, although Sara's life was closer to their plan. She lived here now, having returned from London seven years ago and soon after married a Skye man. She and Keith had gradually taken over more of the responsibilities of the Trotternish and seemed content to stay right here.

Maddie, on the other hand, had had a disastrous marriage right out of college and a career that continued to consume her. Sure, it was exhausting, but the rewards were great. She made good money, and in another few years she'd really break through—if she could stand it. What had begun as an adventure had become tedious. She wasn't sure she had what it took to get to the next level, wasn't sure she wanted to try. You're just tired, she told herself, putting the office out of her mind.

There was obvious construction outside the castle, but inside the walls the restoration work must be in its very early stages. There was little change, although wheelbarrows lined the sides of the space, and piles of sand and bags of cement were stacked up next to them. The spiral staircase was dark, lit only by the arrow slits in its eastern side, but she remembered the way and climbed past the first and second floors, then stopped at the third level to stand in the doorway. She'd found what she'd wanted, the rooms that Sara and she had assigned to themselves. The one with the southernmost view would have been hers, the one next to it, facing the mainland, Sara's. She crossed the room to look out the window, stopping when she realized that the wooden floor was spongy under her feet, and turning back to the stone staircase with a sense of relief. Above her the stairs continued to the parapet, but they'd been wobbly fifteen years ago; she wouldn't risk it now. It was time to get to work anyway. Her gift to Magnus was to be two drawings of Duntober—what it looked like now, and what it would look like when restored—and she needed to begin her preliminary sketches if the drawings were to be ready in time. The ancient gazetteer she'd bought on the Internet had helped her to figure out perspectives and given some dimensions, but she wanted her gift to be more than a realistic rendering. She wanted it to show Magnus's pride and joy in his heritage, qualities he rarely spoke of but which were an integral part of his character. She found a spot to sit on the terrace, pulled her sketchpad out, and began to work.

An hour later Maddie leaned back, pleased with her work as she held the sketches up to the original and compared the two. Not bad, she thought as she put her things away. Maybe the old spark wasn't gone after all. It had been ages since she'd drawn for pleasure, since she'd done anything even remotely creative, and part of her had wondered if she still had it in her. She'd been naive when she first started working in advertising, thinking that she'd have a chance to create and still work in the real world. Instead, she'd found that since she was good at administering projects, that was what she did with most of her time. It meant she'd been promoted quickly, but she missed the thrill of picking up a pencil or paintbrush.

Maybe she'd do a whole series of Duntober drawings. She held her hand up against the glare and pictured tall ships in the harbor below. Duntober Bay had once been full of sailing ships that had traveled the world; what a sight they must have been, their sails sharply white against the water, tall blond men standing on the decks. Whoa, she thought, laughing at herself. Where did that come from? But she knew; she'd tried to erase the images from this afternoon's encounter, but they were too keenly etched in her memory. Gorgeous man. He'd looked so . . . male. She pulled the sketchpad out of her bag again. Could she capture him on paper? Almost, she decided after a few tries. She was sure she had the angle of his chin right, but those cheekbones couldn't really be that sharp. She needed to see him again. She'd have to ask Sara. Maddie smiled again and stretched. Maybe there was life outside New York after all. She'd heard rumors . . .

*W*hen Maddie got back to the hotel, Sara was on the side porch, talking with a man with brown hair and even features. Keith, she thought, recognizing him from the pictures Sara sent. He was even better looking in person. They made a striking couple.

"Here's Maddie," Sara said, and the man turned to greet her with a wide smile.

"Keith MacIver," he said, extending a hand to her.

"My husband," Sara said with a proud smile.

Maddie took his hand with a smile of her own. "Maddie Breen. I'm so pleased to meet you at last. I feel as though I've known you for years."

"And I ye. We're all pleased that ye've come, Sara most of all."

"I wouldn't have missed it."

Sara led the way inside, and Maddie followed. "Did ye sleep?"

"For a while. Then I showered and went to Duntober."

"I should have known ye'd do that straight away. Did ye find our rooms?"

Maddie nodded. "But of course. They look the same. The floor is squishy, though."

"Oh, grand. I'll tell Granddad tonight. Stupid place is falling down about our ears. The restoration is not a moment too soon."

Maddie laughed. "It lasted seven or eight hundred years. I'd say that's fairly good construction."

"Oh, well, there is that. Did ye see anyone up there? But no, it's Sunday, no one will be working. I sometimes forget I'm not in London. Hungry? I'm off to the kitchen to see how they're doing. Do ye want to come?"

"I can wait until dinner, but tea would be great."

"Come on, we'll get ye some at once."

Sara was as good as her word. Maddie met the kitchen staff and drank tea while Sara listened to the head chef's latest suggestions for the party menu, consoled him for Derek's intrusion into his kingdom, discussed last-minute details on tonight's dinner, and handled a minor dispute between two waiters. The Trotternish currently had fifty guests to feed and care for in addition to the staff and family now here, and more were arriving every day. Maddie quickly discovered that Sara's style and breezy cheerfulness disguised a deft managerial touch that made her a favorite with the staff. Before long Maddie was following Sara back to the family lounge for a drink with Keith. A tall man sat with Keith before the picture window, and Maddie recognized Sara's brother Derek at once. He hadn't changed much in the fifteen years except to fill out a bit. He gave Maddie a wide smile as he and Keith rose to greet them.

"Here's Maddie," Sara said. "Be charming to her while I check the dining room, lads."

"Welcome back to the Trotternish," Derek said, smiling again.

Maddie smiled in return. "It's lovely to be back. I had a wonderful time here."

"Ye won a lot of hearts in short order," Derek told her. "My grandparents adore ye, ye know. They often mention the marvelous Maddie."

"It's quite mutual. I've bored my friends for years with my Skye stories."

"Well, ye'll have more now. We've quite the party planned. Sara's outdone herself, and that's no mean feat. And then there'll be the Games and the big race."

"Ah," said Maddie. "That explains the man who was racing along the old road on my way in. I was nearly flattened."

Keith laughed. "Ye'll have to be careful, Maddie. Magnus has put a prize of five hundred pounds out, and half the island is mad for it. The kitchen lads were racing in the parking lot yesterday. Mad, the lot of them."

"Are you racing?" Maddie asked.

Derek shook his head. "We're not eligible. Granddad said no family; he's sure we'd win. Keith and I have our doubts, but this way we're not put to the test."

They all laughed, then turned to welcome Sara back. She smiled happily.

"All's well. No need for yer help tonight, Derek." She turned to Maddie. "My brother lives for the times we have him help in the pub."

"I'm considering leaving law to do it full-time," Derek said.

"As if ye would slow that career of yers," Sara said. "Ye're as bad as Maddie. Workaholics the two of ye."

"At least I take holidays," Derek said, grinning. "Maddie hasn't for years."

"I'm here now," Maddie defended herself. "And I'm determined to relax."

"She's promised us two weeks," Sara said, "which I'm holding her to. Imagine Maddie away from the office for two weeks. She's already gotten twelve phone calls, and it's Sunday."

"Oh, that's just Larry." Maddie laughed. "My lunatic boss," she told Derek.

"I was tempted to tell him ye'd never arrived," Keith said.

Maddie laughed again. "Another few phone calls like today, and you'll have my permission. He's a bit . . . hyper."

"Hyper! He's a heart attack in the offing. And soon. Oh, look, they're here!" Sara said as the door opened and her grandparents joined them, all smiles.

Magnus MacDonald held his arms open, and Maddie ran into them with a cry.

"Madeline," he said with moist eyes, "ye've done an old man proud, lassie. I knew ye couldn't resist me. Few women can."

Maddie laughed with him while Anne shook her head and reached to embrace Maddie, then Derek and Keith, who had risen as well. Magnus insisted that Maddie sit with them while Sara bustled around getting whisky and wine, and he studied Maddie while Anne asked her about her trip.

"The same dark hair, the same eyes," Magnus said. "Ye even have that way he always raised his head when he laughed. Ye look like Charlie's granddaughter."

"That's because she is," Anne said crisply. "Magnus, we said we'd be happy."

"My wife tells me that I'm no' supposed to remember anything," Magnus said with a wink at Maddie.

"No," Anne said. "Yer wife tells ye that ye're supposed to remember the happy times, not the sad ones. This, Magnus MacDonald, is a celebration." She turned to Maddie. "He still misses yer grandfather. Theirs was a wonderful friendship."

Magnus nodded. "He was my closest friend for fifty-two years. Aye, I miss him. He should be here, with a whisky in his hand. Is that not right, Maddie?"

Maddie felt her eyes fill. "He should. I miss him too."

"I know ye do," Magnus said, patting Maddie's hand and gesturing to Anne. "But for him I wouldn't be here, wouldn't have had this wonderful woman who has endured me with such grace for all these years. Wouldn't have had our children, or these grandchildren."

Anne leaned forward to kiss his cheek. "Ye're getting maudlin, love."

Magnus nodded and smiled more cheerfully. "I've earned it. And Bonnie Charlie always did love a good party. He should be here." He looked across the room. "Sara, tell me this is going to be a grand party."

"It's going to be a grand party, Granddad," Sara said with a grin. "It will be brilliant. Everyone on Skye will talk about it for decades."

"I love it when women tell me what I want to hear," Magnus said to Maddie. "Ye look the same, child. A wee bit pale, but we'll change that, aye?"

"She's not a child, Magnus," Anne chided. "She's a grown woman."

"She's a beautiful woman. We saw that when we went to Charlie's funeral."

Anne smiled and nodded. "We saw that when she was fifteen."

Maddie felt her color rise. "That's very kind of you," she said. "You two never change. You look wonderful, exactly the same as the last time I saw you."

And they did. Magnus did not look like a man about to turn eighty. His back was still straight, his posture as rigid as she'd remembered, his blue eyes still bright with mischief. Magnus MacDonald was a man who had lived life with enthusiasm and saw no reason to change that just because he was getting older. And Anne had the serenity of a woman who has been cherished for decades.

Dinner was wonderful, full of lively conversation and a lot of laughter, the sort of meal Maddie remembered from her last visit. Magnus and Anne had not changed, and Keith was a great addition, witty and affectionate with Sara, who beamed at him. It was obvious Sara's marriage was a great success, and Maddie felt a twinge of jealousy as Keith watched Sara with glowing eyes. Had a man ever looked at her like that? Sara, she decided, was very lucky. Magnus and Anne said their good-nights shortly after dinner, and Derek offered to show Maddie the pub while Sara and Keith checked the dining room.

The pub, in its own wing, jutted at an angle from the main structure to perch on the very edge of the cliff, its large flagged terrace overlooking Duntober Bay and the islands beyond. It was, Derek told Maddie, a very popular spot in the summer, both with hotel guests and locals, and tonight it would be jammed. As soon as they entered, she saw he was right. The bar was three deep, the servers hurrying to hand out drinks and food. She stood to one side while Derek braved the crowd, joking with many he knew among them. The pool tables in the back room were crowded with players and observers, and the terrace was beginning to fill up as well.

She saw him at once. He sat in the corner with three other men, his back against the wall. The table before them was littered with glasses and empty plates, the four men talking easily. He was smiling as he listened, then said something that had them loudly laughing while he drained his ale and rose to his feet in a single fluid motion. He wore a black knit shirt that outlined his shoulders against the light gray stone and jeans that showed off his lean legs. The light above his head made his hair, neatly combed now, look even more golden. Maddie caught her breath. No, she'd not remembered wrong, nor made too much of him. He was simply the most beautiful man she'd ever seen. He pulled bills out of his pocket and put them on the table amid protests from the others, saying something as he put the money down that made them laugh again. He grinned, waved as he left, then turned and saw Maddie. And smiled.

Maddie smiled in return and watched him walk toward her.

3

"*H*ere, Maddie," Derek said, handing her a glass of ale. "Pure Skye magic."

He sure is, she thought, turning to accept the glass with thanks.

Derek nodded and grinned as the blond man joined them. "Well, look who's here. I'm surprised to see ye away from the job."

The Scotsman grinned back. "It's Sunday, Derek. I am occasionally allowed time off for good behavior." He turned to Maddie with a softer smile. "Ye've no' told him about this afternoon, have ye?"

"Oh, God, it was ye who nearly ran her over!" Derek cried. "I should have known it, ye're that determined to win. Maddie, this is our favorite reprobate, Iain MacDonald. Same name, no relation, thank God, Iain, Maddie Breen."

"Can ye ever forgive me?" Iain asked her.

"For not being related to Derek? Easily," she said and watched him laugh.

"I think he meant nearly killing ye, Maddie," Derek said, looking from Iain to Maddie. "But I can see ye already know that. I'll just see if they're needing any help at the bar. Tread lightly, Iain. This is Granddad's favorite American."

Derek left with a grin, and Iain nodded at the terrace.

"Would ye like to go outside where it's quieter?"

Maddie nodded and followed him outside to a table next to the wall that overlooked the water. The light was diffused, and the moon was just rising. I'd love to capture that, she thought, then glanced at Iain as they sat down. Or capture him. Iain MacDonald. The name suited him. He looked tamer, more civilized, than he had earlier, but there was still that energy, that sense of power about him that was so arresting. His eyes were just as blue as she'd remembered, and yes, those cheekbones were as sharp as she'd drawn. He had a powerful face, a powerful body.

"'I was just coming to see if I could find ye," he said with a smile. "Didna know ye were *that* American."

"What American?"

"The one all the MacDonalds talk about with such affection. Magnus is very pleased that ye're here, I can tell ye that."

"You know Magnus too?"

He gave her an amused glance. "I went to school with

Derek, and I've known the family ever since. Derek and I spent a lot of time together in those days."

"And now?" She took a sip of her ale. Derek was right; it was wonderful.

"And now I'm here with them again."

"For the party?"

"Working. And where are ye from, Maddie Breen—New York or L.A.?"

"New York."

He laughed.

"How did you know that?" she asked.

"Black clothes. New York is the city of perpetual mourning."

Maddie looked down at her black short-sleeved sweater and slacks, then up to meet his eyes. He was laughing again, and she joined him.

"Might as well wear a sign, I guess," she said.

"It's in yer bearing as well. Ye look very . . . sophisticated."

She smiled, and he leaned back, crossing his arms over his chest as he watched her. "So, Maddie," he said, his eyes merry, "why are ye mad?"

She shook her head. "Do you know how many times I've been asked that?"

"And here I thought I was so clever. Well, lassie, what's the answer?"

"Maddie is short for Madeline."

"So ye have French blood?"

She laughed. "No, I'm all Celt. Irish and Scottish on both sides. My grandmother was a MacGannon. She and my mother loved the Madeline books, so I was named after the little girl in them."

"Ye're a MacGannon? From Kilgannon?"

"Originally. I'd love to find the castle while I'm here. I can't find it on the maps, and no one seems to know how to get there."

"I do. Ye have to go by sea. The old road's gone and has been for years. Did ye come across from Mallaig?"

Maddie nodded.

"Well, when ye return, look to the south. On the other side of the headland that juts out the farthest, the southernmost one ye can see, is Loch Gannon. It takes two turns and brings ye directly to the castle. It's a beauty, but ye need permission to visit it. It's unsafe."

Maddie leaned forward. "Who do I need to talk to?"

"I can ring a few people. One of them is sure to know how to do it."

"Oh, thank you so much! That would be wonderful! I'm very grateful!"

"A lovely emotion for a woman to have."

She laughed, then turned as Sara called her name from the doorway. Sara waved at them, then made her way through the tables.

"Sara has come to rescue ye," he said.

"Do I need rescuing?"

He let his gaze lift slowly from her waist to her eyes. "Ye tell me."

"I see ye've met our Maddie," Sara said to Iain with a smile. "That didna take ye long. She's been at the pub for ten minutes is all."

Iain grinned. "We met this afternoon. I was running Blaven and near trampled her. She dinna think it was a proper welcome to Scotland."

"I wonder why." Sara laughed and gave Maddie a measuring glance. "Ye didna mention that."

"She was still recovering, I'm sure," Iain said, then looked at Maddie. "I'll ring up about the castle on Monday."

"Iain's going to try to get permission for me to visit Kilgannon," Maddie said.

Sara nodded. "I'd forgotten ye wanted to do that. Listen, I came to steal ye away. And to tell ye that yer Larry called again. Twice in the last half-hour."

Iain arched an eyebrow.

"My boss," Maddie said quickly. "He's not my Larry, Sara."

"Well, ye're the only one who can abide him. He says he wants a quick word with ye and he canna reach ye on the mobile."

"That's because I left it in my room," Maddie said with a smile.

"That's a good lass! Ye're learning." Sara laughed and turned to Iain. "Maddie works too much. Ye wouldn't know about that sort of thing, would ye?"

Iain shook his head. "Not anymore, Sara. I've reformed."

"Good. We want this to be a memorable summer."

Iain stretched his arms wide and grinned. "I'll do my best to make it so. But dinna steal her, Sara. We're just getting to know each other."

"Ye'll see her again. She'll be here for a fortnight," Sara told him. "Iain MacDonald, ye are such a flirt. Off with ye, then. Make yerself useful in the pub."

"I will see ye again, Maddie Breen," Iain said and

made his way through the tables while both women watched him.

"Trust him to meet ye yer first day," Sara said. "Isn't he something?"

"Yes," Maddie said with a sigh, and Sara gave her a sharp glance.

"Ye didna mention meeting him earlier. What happened?" When Maddie explained, Sara nodded. "That stupid race! I'm just glad Keith and Derek aren't in it. Now, if ye're not too tired, I thought I'd show ye the ballroom and see if one of the dresses I have would fit ye."

"Dress? For what?"

"For the party. Ye didna think ye could wear a little black dress to it, did ye?"

Maddie laughed. "Actually . . ."

Sara laughed, then shook her head. "I knew it. Well, ye canna. We're all wearing traditional dress, and I don't think ye have anything that'll be right. Are ye too fashed to come with me? Want to wait until morning?"

Maddie glanced at the pub. She could see Iain and Derek laughing just inside the door. A pretty blond girl leaned against Iain, and he smiled down at her.

"No," Maddie said, standing up. "Let's go." She followed Sara without a backward glance.

The ballroom was huge, a simple rectangular space with high ceilings and French doors that opened onto another terrace. Maddie had not been in here during her last trip, but she remembered looking through the glass doors at the large paneled room. Cleaning supplies were in readiness next to the door, and chairs and round tables stood in a corner waiting to be unfolded. There was a stage along one side, already draped in white. Sara explained where the food and manned bars would be.

"And here's the dance floor," Sara said, spreading her arms wide over a portion of the hardwood floor. "Now, ye must picture all the chandeliers on and candles on the tables. Grandmother's doing the flowers herself—and we'll drape the room with MacDonald tartan. So, what's missing?"

"Nothing," Maddie said, turning to take it all in. "It looks like you've got everything well thought out. Will your grandfather be announced, or be here to greet people as they arrive?"

Sara explained the program as she switched lights off and led the way upstairs to the suite of rooms she shared with Keith. She pulled several dresses out of hanging bags and held them up to Maddie. Each was white, long, and very simply but beautifully made, with full skirts and dipping necklines.

"Granddad always likes us all to wear white. He likes the way the red MacDonald tartan looks against it," Sara said, smiling as she held a dress up to Maddie. "Ye'll look beautiful. It really suits ye."

Maddie looked at her reflection. Not her usual style, which was so tailored that it bordered on stark, but it would certainly do. She tried the dress on with Sara's help and laughed as she swished her way across the room.

"I can't remember the last time I wore a long dress," Maddie said. "I feel like Scarlett O'Hara." She twirled and watched the silk float back against her legs. "But what will you wear? Do you want to wear this one?"

"I'll be wearing one a size bigger than usual." She

paused, eyes filling with tears. "Maddie," she said, her voice full of wonder, "I'm having a baby!"

Maddie squealed and threw her arms around Sara. "Why didn't you tell me?"

"I wasn't supposed to tell anyone. It's meant to be part of our gift for Granddad. But I couldn't wait any longer to tell ye."

"Keith knows, right?"

"Of course! And Mother. But no one else. Father would tell Granddad immediately if he heard."

"So mum's the word," Maddie said and laughed with Sara.

A few moments later, as she eyed Maddie up and down, Sara said, "This was much too easy. We'll get this taken in, and ye're set. Ye look like a princess."

"I feel like one!"

Maddie embraced her friend again, then twirled, imagining dancing in this dress, in that ballroom. Perhaps with Iain? She felt her face flush and gave Sara a look.

Sara, however, was busy putting the other dresses away. "We'll have a fitting in the morning," she said and helped Maddie out of the dress. "Wonder who ye'll dance with?" Sara said with a laugh. "Haven't seen Iain move that fast in years."

"I thought you liked him."

"I do, very much. He's been a great friend to Derek, and Granddad thinks the world of him. Keith likes him very much, and so do I, but he's just Iain to us and I'm accustomed to him. But I'm always amused by women's reactions to him."

Maddie colored again, glad the dress was now over her head, hiding her face from Sara. "Well, not many men look like that. Did I look like an idiot?"

"No, not at all. Ye looked like ye were having a good time."

"I was. He's very nice."

"When he's not trampling people. "There", she said, arranging the dress on a hanger, then handing it to Maddie. "We'll have that done by tomorrow afternoon." She tilted her head. "Iain's not a bad man, Maddie, but he'll never marry again."

"He's divorced?"

"Years ago now. She was horrid. Unfaithful liar. He's better off without her. For years after that all he did was work, but now he's sold his firm and made a bundle of money. Derek handled all the paperwork for him. Lovely to have a lawyer for a friend. Now, what about shoes?"

*M*addie's dreams were a mixture of her late-night call to Larry, the airplane flight, and the drive to Skye. And a tall blond man in a kilt smiling down at her. The problem, she told herself in the morning, is that you haven't dated anyone in such a long time, so you overreact to the first really interesting man you meet. She might pretend not to be affected by him, but she'd fooled no one. Sara, certainly, saw too much. Today she'd be safe, however. She'd have the dress fitted, then she and Sara would go up to Duntober, taking lunch to Magnus, who was spending the day up there with the workmen. Last night at dinner he'd promised her a complete tour of the castle. She couldn't tell him she'd already been there, but she'd told Sara about the drawings she wanted to give him and that she'd need to visit Duntober a couple of times before the birthday party. Sara had laughed, saying she was sure Maddie would get cooperation from the man overseeing the restoration.

The fitting took only a few minutes, and then Maddie, Anne, and Sara took a ride down to Portree for floral supplies. They returned, laden with the things Anne needed for the party. Anne declined to join them for lunch at Duntober, saying she'd seen all the ruins in her life she ever wanted to and that she'd be much happier spending the day among her flowers.

Duntober Castle was alive with workmen. Maddie was surprised to see the crews of men manning big machines that were hauling rocks and dirt away. What a far cry from the lonely castle she'd visited the day before, she thought, looking at the men cheerfully calling to each other. The day had warmed considerably, and many had abandoned their shirts to work bare-chested in the sun. Several of the men called greetings to Sara as she and Maddie hauled the tote bags with their lunch up the stairs to the Great Hall, and Sara stopped to introduce Maddie. Most were local men, pleased at the chance to work on the project, but Magnus had hired a well-known restoration expert to oversee it all, Sara said, then gave Maddie a sidelong glance and laughed.

Magnus looked up with a smile from a set of plans spread across a folding table in the center of the Great Hall. "Ah, here ye are! I was just wondering when the two most beautiful girls on the island would be arriving."

"Just on Skye, Granddad? We must be slipping." Sara gave him a kiss. Maddie followed suit, and Magnus helped them set the tote bags next to another table set in the middle of the huge arched window that overlooked the bay.

"Perfect spot, isn't it?" He waved his arm at the hall behind him. "I can't wait to see this finished. We've been busy today marking up the spots that the engineers will need to survey. I had no idea I'd be hiring half of Scotland, but we need to do so many things to keep the restoration historically correct. I'll show ye what we're up to today," he said, leading the way back down the stairs. "We're making an area large enough to drive the delivery lorries right up here. I should have thought of it myself," he said over the din of the machines, "but this is my first restoration. By the time we're finished I'll know all these things."

Magnus led them around the corner of the foundation, where it was quieter, and pointed to several men who were measuring and marking the ground. One man, his naked back to them, was checking the blueprints he held. He pointed something out to a second man, then bent down and stretched out a measuring tape. Focused on his task, he didn't turn as they approached.

"Iain," Magnus shouted. "Let's have lunch."

"Aye, in a minute, Magnus," Iain said, then straightened and faced them, his obvious surprise at seeing Sara and Maddie quickly hidden.

Maddie caught her breath. She hadn't really considered what kind of work Iain was doing on Skye, but she'd not expected to see him here at Duntober, standing barechested before her, his jeans loose on his lean waist. His chest and abdomen were well-muscled and tanned from the sun, and she tried not to stare. Get a grip, she told herself. You've seen gorgeous men before.

"Maddie," Magnus said, "this is Sir Iain MacDonald. Iain, Maddie Breen."

Sir Iain, Maddie thought. This half-naked man was a knight?

"We've met," Iain said with a grin. "I'm sure Sara will tell ye all about it."

"Oh, I will, Iain," Sara said and laughed as he gave her a look.

"Didna know ye were coming here," he said to Maddie. "How are ye today?"

"Fine, thanks," Maddie said, feeling her cheeks flush. She looked away, then back as he explained to them what he was doing. She pretended to listen, but her mind was elsewhere. What would it feel like to touch him, she wondered? If she reached out now, she could find out. She could put her hands on each side of that trim waist, then glide them up his chest . . .

"We brought ye lunch," Sara said.

"Sounds good to me," Iain said and reached for his shirt.

4

Iain led them to the cellar he was using as an office and showed Maddie the architectural renderings they'd commissioned of the completed castle. Magnus chimed in with enthusiasm to point out details, and Maddie asked so many questions that Sara at last told them they would have to eat before the food spoiled. Over lunch they talked about the phases of the restoration work, and Iain explained the assessments that would have to be done before actual repair could begin.

"It'll be years before it's finished," he said.

"But it's a labor of love," Sara added.

"And we have the best man to do the job," Magnus said.

Iain laughed. "Said without a bit of prejudice."

"It's the simple truth," Magnus said and looked at Maddie. "Iain's become a celebrity with the restorations he's done. He has people willing to wait for years for him. He delayed several other projects to work here."

Iain shrugged. "How could I not? This one is special. A MacDonald castle being restored by MacDonalds. And I'm able to work with Magnus."

Magnus laughed. "It helps that I've known him for years."

"I'm glad to be doing it. It is a debt that I owe ye, Magnus," Iain said.

Magnus met his eyes. "There is no debt, lad."

"Aye," Iain said softly. "There is." He gave Maddie a glance. "I spent many summer holidays here on Skye when we were in school, and the least I can do is help Magnus with this." He pointed to the arched window before them. "This is a very special place. Most castles were built with no eye for their setting, but Duntober combines the best of the views with a canny eye for defense. Whoever designed it knew what he was doing. What other castle do ye know where a lookout window was made into a work of art?"

Sara nodded. "That's exactly what Maddie said. She's been studying Duntober since she was here last time."

"Maddie's the friend that Sara was going to restore Duntober with," Magnus said, with a glance at Iain. "Ye should really show her the castle, lad." He turned to Maddie with a smile. "Would ye like that, lassie?"

Maddie looked from Magnus's blue eyes to Iain's. "Very much."

"When?" Iain asked. "We'll need a couple of hours. Sara?"

Sara shook her head. "I canna help it if I do not find the bottle dungeon as exciting as some do. I'll pass on this one. But Maddie's free this afternoon."

Maddie laughed. "My social secretary," she said. "I'd love a tour."

"Good. I let the lads go about four. Can ye come then?"

When she nodded, Iain beamed at her.

"*W*ell," Sara said on their ride back to Trotternish House. "I haven't seen Granddad that animated in a while. And Iain loves that castle just as much. Whenever he was here, the two of them were always up there drawing layouts and making plans, but I never thought they'd actually do it."

"What is the debt Iain says he owes your grandfather?"

"Oh, that." Sara shrugged. "It's in his own head. Derek brought him home most summers because Iain had nowhere else to go. His parents are divorced and remarried, and Derek collected him and brought him here with all of us."

"That's what your grandfather did with mine after the war," Maddie said.

Sara nodded. "Derek's very like my grandfather. Everyone thinks he's just a quiet person, but we know him better. He gets quite wild with Iain and Keith."

Maddie laughed. "Which may be why they're friends."

"My parents always encouraged it too; Derek couldn't have had Iain here without their agreement. They adore Iain, but now Mother is trying to marry them both off. She's worried that Derek will never produce an heir and that Iain will be a target now that he has all this sudden wealth."

"Did he inherit money?"

Sara shook her head. "He designed software for architects and engineers that did something revolutionary. His firm went from five people to five thousand in ten years, then he sold it to a big American company and made millions. He signed a noncompete, so now he's restoring castles for fun. After he was knighted for his work on Brenmargon Castle, Grandfather asked him to take on Duntober."

"I thought at first today that he was one of the workmen."

Sara laughed. "If all the workmen looked like that, we'd have restoration groupies."

*L*arry had left two scathing messages for her, and Maddie's assistant had left two nervous ones. Larry was furious that he couldn't reach her and that she hadn't responded to his latest faxes. He gave her a deadline of six New York time, eleven Skye time, to answer the faxes and made vague threats about what he'd do if she didn't respond. It wasn't much of an ultimatum; it gave her ten hours. Maddie sighed as she settled on her bed and picked up the faxes. Larry was right to be angry—she had promised to be available and then hadn't been. But it felt so good to be away from the office. She plowed through the faxes, becoming annoyed by the unnecessary work. All of this could have been handled easily by Katie. And it took longer than it should have because she kept seeing Iain's face. She'd tried to be unaffected by him, but the more time she spent with him, the more he attracted her. There was a very simple reason. When was the last time she'd been kissed? Or anything else, for that matter? Enough, she told herself. Work.

At almost four Maddie stood at Duntober's gate. He's just showing me around, she chided herself. No big deal. She smoothed her hair and straightened her clothes. It had been hell deciding what to wear. She'd finished her work, then tried everything in her suitcase on. Oh, yeah, she wasn't nervous at all.

Iain wasn't in the courtyard or in the Great Hall, and she paused in the arched window that framed the islands offshore and the mainland beyond. Imagine seeing this view every day. She could hear men still working below and leaned out to see if Iain was among them. He was, standing in a group of men who were examining part of the foundation, their faces grim. Iain checked his watch and said something to the others, then shook his head. Maddie headed for the stairs. He looked up when she approached and gave her a tight smile, then turned back to watch the man who was apparently patching the foundation.

"Someone's undermining the wall," he said brusquely. "That'll do it, lads. Go on home. I'll see ye in the morning." He led Maddie away. "Sorry," he said in a lighter tone. "We've had a bit of vandalism, and it seems to be getting worse."

"Who would do that?"

He shrugged. "I'm not sure. But we'll find out." He turned his magnificent smile on her then. "Skye's a small place, and someone will talk."

"Who would want to stop the work?"

"The English, of course," he said with a laugh. "Or it could be the people who don't want any restoration done here at all. They say we're tampering with history. Or perhaps it's the MacLeods. We've heard some rumbling that the MacLeods are claiming this should be their castle."

"But they haven't held this land since the sixteenth century," Maddie said.

He gave her a surprised look. "How do ye know that?"

"I've studied Duntober's history. I've loved this castle since the first day I saw it. It's so amazing! Don't let them stop you from bringing it back."

He laughed. "We'll no' be stopped now. Come on, I'll show ye the rest of it." He led the way up to the Hall and raised a hand high. "We'll begin yer tour here, Miss Breen. The Great Hall was constructed some time in the eleventh to thirteenth centuries, built on the same site as the original wooden fort, or dun. This spot was probably used as a fort for centuries before the Norsemen came." He glanced at Maddie. "But ye probably know all this. Let's see if I can tell ye anything ye don't already know."

"First I want to show you something." He watched while she dug in her bag, then handed him a book. "This is part of my gift for Magnus, but I thought you'd like to see it."

He took the book with reverence. "It's a MacCurrie Gazetteer."

She nodded. "Eighteen hundred. It has a whole section on Duntober, with a floor plan."

"I've tried buying this for years! Where did ye find it?"

"I bought it on the Net. I buy everything I can find about Duntober."

"So do I," he said, looking up. "But I was outbid for the gazetteer."

"That must have been me."

"I'll be damned." He smiled widely. "Magnus will be very pleased."

"I want to do some sketches of the castle to go with it."

"He said ye were an artist."

She smiled. "Not really. I just want to give him something no one else can. Perhaps you'd let me come up here and draw when he isn't around?"

Iain gave her a slow smile that she felt all the way to her toes. "Ye're welcome here any time ye choose, Maddie."

*H*e showed her every corner, every floor, all the outbuildings and the fortifications. She surprised and pleased him by knowing more about Duntober and its history than anyone else but Magnus and himself. She made all the right comments, asked the questions he would have asked. He loved this castle, loved showing it off. Few people had the stamina and interest to tour the whole place, but Maddie seemed fascinated. She'd brought the gazetteer along and compared the actual layout to the book, and more than once he found himself leaning over her shoulder, inhaling her scent—a mixture of spices and flowers and something deeper, something that made him want to kiss her neck and see where that would lead them. He laughed at himself as he stepped back from her and continued the tour. When they'd finished, he led her back to the cellar, where he offered her a glass of wine. She agreed with a smile, and he opened the bottle, handing her a glass, then raising his high.

"A toast," he said. "To castles. To castles in the sky."

Maddie touched her glass to his. "To castles."

"Which reminds me." He smiled triumphantly. "Ye should be getting a fax at Trotternish with yer permission to visit Kilgannon. But only if ye're accompanied by someone with the correct credentials."

Her eyes flew wide, and she looked at him with delight. "Oh, Iain! How wonderful! But who has the right credentials?"

"Me, of course." He raised his glass again. "To Kilgannon."

They sipped the wine, and he looked deeply into her eyes for a moment before she colored and turned away.

*I*ain came to dinner at the Trotternish that night, and Maddie studied him. Something had happened at Duntober, and she wasn't sure what it was. She was more than just physically attracted to him. She liked his enthusiasm, his knowledge of and love for the castle, his positive outlook. This was a man who made things happen. Look at what he'd done about Kilgannon. During the meal he was silly with Keith and Derek, then Magnus engaged them in a serious discussion of the future of Scotland's independence, about which Iain was as ardent as Magnus. Anne met her eyes across the table and smiled, shaking her head and changing the subject, but Maddie hadn't minded. It was interesting to find out Iain MacDonald had more than just looks. But what looks! She watched the changing light play across his face, highlighting the hollows of his cheeks.

"*I*t wasna accidental, Magnus. And if we'd no' been going over every inch before the engineers come, we'd ha' missed it altogether. The bastard wanted to damage the foundation. He must ha' been digging out the mortar for a while."

Magnus's expression was grim. "Which would ha' led to the collapse of the corner of the tower. Eventually the walls themselves would ha' come down."

Iain paced the room, throwing his arms wide. "It was an evil thing to do, putting the sand inside in place of the mortar! I tell ye, Magnus, if I find the bastard I'll tear him limb from limb, consequences be damned! What kind of a man would do such a thing? And why? I canna find any sense in it except to stop us or to slow us down, and who would want to do that?

Magnus met his eyes. "Ye'll have to watch everything, lad. We were fortunate to find this now. There may be more we've not found."

"Exactly. But who?"

"Aye," Magnus said. "Start thinking."

*A*fter dinner, when they all went to the pub, Iain invited Maddie to come back to Duntober the following afternoon. Magnus, he said, usually left around three, and she'd still have lots of daylight in which to work. She agreed, very pleased, then sat with him on the moonlit terrace and talked. They talked about Scotland's future, their own childhoods, music, school, and work, smiling at each other when they discovered that they shared many of the same opinions. Iain really listened as she talked about her work. No one outside advertising had ever listened to Maddie talk about her job for more than a few minutes before they grew bored and changed the topic, but Iain asked questions and praised her for her success.

"So when ye go back, ye'll immerse yourself again," he said.

Maddie nodded. "I'll surface in February."

He toyed with his glass. "Is it enough?"

"Sometimes, sometimes not. After being gone, even for these few days, I've discovered there's a whole world out here."

"There is, Maddie. And it's beautiful. Ye should visit more often. What about yer art? Magnus says ye're very talented."

"Magnus is very kind. Someday I'd like to stop the madness and find out what I could do. It's just a dream, though. What about you?"

"I have Duntober. It'll keep me busy for years, and I'm quite content. It's my heritage. Ye know I'm a Mac-Donald? Well, my family comes from Duntober as well. I hate to admit it, but I probably am distantly related to Derek. I'll happily take Magnus and Sara, though. So ye can see why the castle is so important. It should be restored by someone who loves it."

"It will be," she said and smiled into his eyes.

*M*addie went to Duntober every afternoon to work on her drawings. Iain always greeted her with a smile, stopping his work often to watch her progress and compliment her. She took breaks as well, noting how easily he led the men and his obvious pleasure in the work. Her breaks became longer when she would look up and see him working shirtless, his smooth skin getting darker in the warm summer sun. Sometimes he would catch her watching him and grin and wave before he returned to his work. But sometimes he concentrated so fully on his task that she could really study him, memorizing the lines of his body, watching the muscles of his arms and back gliding under his skin, and she would have to tear her gaze away and try not to wonder what it would feel like to trace a finger along his ribs, to touch that paneled abdomen, to feel his flowing skin against hers. I'm simply studying the male form for my art, she told herself with a laugh, but she knew better. All the men might be working without shirts, but it was Iain she watched. She would shake her head then, trying to rid herself of the images before returning to Magnus's drawings. When she was finished for the day, he'd sit for a while with her, his long legs stretched out before him, his face animated as he talked about whatever came to mind. She decided that she loved watching this man.

She saw him at dinner every night as well, the meals often raucous and full of laughter. Afterward they'd go over to the pub, or sit in the lounge and talk. Sara would dart in and out, taking care of the dining room and lounge, drafting her brother and husband for tasks, but Maddie and Iain were left alone to talk. She'd learned much about him, told him a lot about her life—and learned some things about herself as well. She was lonely. She hadn't realized it in New York, had kept herself too busy to even think about it, but here, in the company of this dynamic man, it had hit her. If things were otherwise, if he lived in New York or she in Scotland, she'd definitely want to see him again. As it was, well . . . it was foolish to even consider. He'd given her no reason to believe he was anything more than mildly attracted to her. Still, there was something wonderful between them.

Sara and Derek's parents arrived on Thursday, and suddenly there was much too much to do in the time left before the party. Relatives and guests were arriving by the hour, and Sara was everywhere, seeing to details with her mother Mairi, who had turned out to be delightful. Maddie helped wherever she could and tried not to be disappointed when Derek said Iain would not be coming to dinner. He'd had some delays at the castle, Derek said. She finished her drawings late that night and helped Sara again on Friday. By evening she was tired, but the day, busy as it was, seemed incomplete without seeing Iain. Larry had eased up on his demands, and Maddie found herself not thinking about work for hours at a time; she thought about Iain instead. When Derek said Iain wouldn't be joining them again, she faced it. Obviously the attraction had been one-sided. All on her side.

And then it was Saturday, and the hotel bustled with well-controlled activity. By three everything was ready, and Sara gathered the family in the lounge for a light meal and a drink, then shooed them upstairs to rest and dress for the party.

Maddie dressed with care. The silk dress, full and fluid, floated around her ankles when she walked, and she felt transported to another time. She slowly brushed her hair into a chignon and watched her reflection as she put on her earrings. She didn't look like the Maddie she was used to, the advertising executive who dressed in black and carried files everywhere. She felt younger, lighter, she thought, as she put the final touches on the present for Magnus. She twirled in the center of the room, then went to find Sara.

𝒯he Trotternish's ballroom was aglow with chandeliers and candles, the high ceiling gleaming above the paneled walls. Flowers were everywhere, white roses and lilies and Anne's hydrangeas gathered into huge bouquets. The staff had outdone itself, and the tables were laden with dishes lavishly presented. The round tables, draped in white linen, were ready, their tops set with silver and crystal, and in the center of each a wreath of ivy filled with purple heather. The stage was filled with musicians, playing traditional Scottish melodies.

The party guests, all dressed in Highland formal wear, had been arriving in a steady stream, and the room was almost full. The women were in long dresses of every color, their skirts billowing as they moved. Each wore a tartan scarf proclaiming her clan allegiance, many held in place by jeweled brooches that sparkled in the candlelight. The men wore black formal jackets and lace collars above their kilts, dirks in their socks. Maddie stood at the side of the room by herself, marveling at the scene. She felt quite elegant herself. Sara's mother had provided a MacDonald scarf and the ruby brooch to hold it, and she fingered it now as she looked around.

Sara and Keith stood with Derek and Sara's parents at the door, greeting each guest. And then Maddie heard the pipers and knew what was next. The family stepped back as six pipers in full regalia marched through the doors. Behind them was a beaming Magnus, Anne on his arm. The guests roared their approval as Magnus and Anne circled the room, then stopped in the center. The musicians paused as Magnus raised his arms.

"Welcome!" he roared, then motioned to the musicians on the stage, who plunged into a reel. Magnus grabbed Anne, whirling her into the dance with him.

Maddie clapped time, but when her gaze drifted over to the French doors, her hands—and her heart—skipped a beat. Iain stood there, talking with Derek. He wore formal Highland dress, his hair golden over a black jacket that emphasized his shoulders and lean waist, silver buttons gleaming, his lace ruffle and cuffs brilliant white. His kilt was a MacDonald tartan, and long socks hugged the muscles of his calves above the traditional ghillie brogues. He looked at Maddie as she turned and flashed her a dazzling smile, then left Derek to come to her.

"Maddie Breen," he said, bowing before her. "Ye look beautiful tonight. I hope ye have saved me a dance."

5

"**I** was afraid you weren't coming," Maddie said, smiling up at him.

"I wouldn't miss this," he said with surprise.

They turned to watch Magnus and Anne finish their dance, then clapped with the others as Magnus, who had climbed onto the stage, held his hands up for quiet.

"I welcome ye all here," Magnus said and took a deep breath. "Whew! Anne is getting too old for this sort of thing!" He waited for the laughter, then smiled. "I thank ye all for coming tonight. Some of ye have come from far away to celebrate with us, and I canna tell ye how much it means to me. I have had a good life, a charmed life. Each time I thought disaster would strike, some kind angel watched over me. In Italy in 1944 it was Bonnie Charlie

Breen who carried me to safety. His granddaughter Maddie is here tonight, having come all the way from New York, and I'd like ye to give her a special welcome." He grinned across the room at Maddie, who blinked her tears away and smiled. "When I thought I would never find love, Anne came along and showed me, not for the last time, that I was wrong. When our son was ill, and we thought we'd lose him, he told me MacDonalds don't give up. Because he didna, I didna. He's given me years of proud fatherhood, a glorious daughter-in-law, and two magnificent grandchildren. And now, for my eightieth birthday, my granddaughter Sara tells me I'm about to become a great-grandfather."

Maddie looked at Sara, who met her eyes and smiled.

"And if that were not enough, I'm involved in two projects that will see me out. I have dreamed for most of my adult life about restoring Duntober Castle; Sir Iain MacDonald, there by the door with Maddie, is making my dream a reality. And Derek, the best damned barrister in Scotland and my favorite grandson, is helping me write my memoirs. No man has ever had a better family or friends, and I ask that ye celebrate both with me tonight. Slainte, and God bless ye all!"

As the applause died down and the music began again, Iain took Maddie's hand and gave her a crooked smile. "How can ye no' love the man? Let's do as he asks and celebrate, Maddie Breen."

"I'd love to, Iain MacDonald."

"Good. Than we shall."

"I've missed you," she said with a sidelong glance at him. "Where have you been? Working too many hours?"

His eyes flickered for a second, then he nodded. "I've

been at Duntober. I was hoping to see ye there. Where have ye been, bonnie Maddie?"

"I promised to help Sara on Thursday and Friday. I thought I'd mentioned that. I was hoping you'd come down to join us for dinner, or at least afterward."

He grinned and leaned over her. "Were yer evenings long then without me?"

She laughed up into his eyes. "Unbearable."

"Ah. As they should be." He paused, then his expression grew serious. "Well, the reason I was no' here is that someone drove through the wet concrete on Thursday night, so we had to cut out the whole thing and repour it. That took most of yesterday and today, the nights as well."

"Oh, Iain! I had no idea! Was there a lot of damage?"

He shook his head. "It was long hours and a lot of unnecessary money spent, but no' a real setback. Derek knew, he was there for most of it, but we didna want Magnus to hear before the party, so we didna tell anyone. We've fixed it now. I was hoping ye'd come up on yer own, though. I could ha' used yer inspiration, but I didna have time to stop to have dinner with all of ye. And I knew Magnus would see something was wrong just by looking at me. I'm no' much of an actor."

"I wish I'd known. I could at least have come and cheered you on."

"I would ha' liked that."

He brought her hand to his mouth and kissed her fingers one at a time while she watched, feeling her body react to his touch, a tingling warmth flooding through her. When her face flushed, he smiled. This man, she thought, knows exactly what he does to me.

"But now's no' the time for that," he said. "Now's the time for dancing. Ye look beautiful tonight, Maddie. The MacDonald tartan suits ye, and the dress is bonnie."

"Thank you, Sir Iain. You look quite wonderful yourself. Do you wear kilts a lot?"

He laughed. "Only for Magnus."

"And Blaven, apparently. You were wearing a kilt the first time I saw you."

"So I was. But that was just to get him accustomed to the kilt flying about."

She laughed. "Which it did."

He grinned. "So it did."

"Quite a welcome to Scotland."

He grinned. "I'm glad ye enjoyed it."

"Vastly. I felt very welcomed."

"I am a success at something, then," he said and laughed again. "Dance with me now, Maddie, if ye would. And promise me ye'll come and see me at Duntober. Did ye finish yer drawings?"

She nodded. "Yes, thank heavens. And I'd love to come back to Duntober."

"I'm thinking ye might like to do some more drawings."

She looked from his feet to his face, thinking of him working half naked in the sun. "Yes," she said, and he laughed again.

He took her hand and led her onto the dance floor to join the others. She didn't know the steps to the Scottish dances, but it didn't matter. Iain showed her how to follow him, told her what the next set of moves would be, and soon she felt more comfortable. Magnus was in the middle of the dancers, whirling Anne, who was smiling widely, and Derek danced with a young cousin while Sara and Keith stood off to one side with her parents. Maddie could see Sara's serene expression and Keith's proud one as they were congratulated on their news.

The hours flew by, a kaleidoscope of colors and music. She danced with Iain, with Magnus and Derek, with Sara's father, and then with Iain again. They ate a wonderful meal, sumptuous and delicious. Iain and Maddie were seated at the table with the MacDonalds for the nine courses, each a tour de force of presentation and flavor. The chef, trained at the best culinary schools, had prepared all the traditional dishes and many updated ones. Imagine wanting haggis for your birthday, Maddie thought and laughed.

Then they all danced again. The tempo suddenly changed, and all of the women and all but the youngest men left the dance floor. Maddie, who was standing next to Sara, asked her what was happening, and Sara beamed at her.

"Watch," she said.

Keith stood between Iain and Derek as the drums began. The rhythm went faster and faster, the fiddlers' fingers flying as the beat intensified. The men stomped their feet in time with the drums, raising their arms and whooping. The crowd loved it, clapping and cheering as the pace increased even more. Iain, Derek, and Keith joined hands and gave throaty cries as they pounded past Maddie, their kilts soaring high, revealing their thighs and occasionally more.

"I think ye've just discovered what a Scotsman wears under his kilt," Sara said, laughing. "This is Keith's celebration of fatherhood."

She was right, Maddie thought. The dance was a primitive demonstration of maleness, of potency and power, and the lesson was not lost on the audience. Nor on her. She felt her body respond as Iain flashed her a grin, meeting her eyes for just a second before he whirled to face the others. The dance ended at last, with a crash of drums and a quick skirl from the pipers. There was silence, then a roar from the guests before the music, much tamer now, started again. The dance floor filled as the men moved to the side. Keith wordlessly clasped Sara to him with a hearty kiss. Iain, his chest heaving as he caught his breath, looked at Maddie.

"I need a drink," Derek said, slapping Iain on the shoulder. "Come on." He started away, then turned. "Iain, Maddie, come on outside. It's too hot in here."

"That it is," Iain said. He reached for Maddie's hand and led her outside to the terrace.

$\mathcal{I}$ain drained the glass and put it on the table before him. He could feel the second whisky hit him. Or was it the third? Does no' matter now, lad, he told himself, watching Maddie laugh at something Derek said. Damn, the girl was perfect. He watched her mouth, watched her lips move, and wondered what they'd feel like on his skin. She slowly brushed her hair back from her cheek, and he wanted to do that for her, to feel her cheek under his fingers.

He wanted her. He thought of throwing her into the Rover and heading off for a weekend of lovemaking. A week maybe, he thought, grinning as he visualized her underneath him, her dark hair spread across a pillow, her breasts rising to meet him. He felt his body react and sat up straighter.

Derek poured him another glass of whisky, then said the bottle was empty and left to go get another while Iain studied Maddie. All right, lad, he thought, think about this now. Ye want her, but it's more than just physical. It'll be difficult to get this one out of yer head with some mindless sex. She's beautiful and she's desirable, both are true enough, but there's more and ye know it. Iain sighed. After just a few days he valued Maddie's opinion as well as her company. She seemed as thrilled as he was at returning Duntober from the grave, had held the renderings of the castle with a reverence that both pleased and unsettled him. No one else had the patience to listen to him explaining it all, no one else asked all the right questions. So is that what it is? Was he so hungry for someone to share the details of the project that the first person to show any interest in it had him falling all over himself? He didn't think so. Magnus had as much interest as she did, but Magnus did not attract him at all. Fine, that.

Maddie Breen attracted him on too many levels. He could talk to her. He'd talked to her more than anyone, told her more about himself than anyone else, probably said too much. But she'd talked just as easily with him. So what to do now? Sometimes she looked at him, like just now, as though she was ready to climb into his bed. Other times she held him away with a cool glance. Perhaps it was just a passing mood for them both, this attraction. Perhaps he'd not lifted enough weights lately.

Maddie smiled at him. Perhaps it's time to test the waters. He reached to touch her cheek.

"Maddie," he said.

"*M*addie," Iain said again, leaning forward, his fingers sliding through her hair to the nape of her neck. When she raised her face, he bent closer.

"Aren't they beautiful?" she asked.

"That they are," he said and lowered his head even more. "Beautiful lips."

Maddie leaned back against his hand to look up at the sky. "I meant the night. Look, Iain," she said pointing. "Look at all the stars. Aren't *they* beautiful?"

"I've seen stars, Maddie." He sat up straight, pulling his hand away from her head, then rubbed his chin as he watched her.

Whisky, she thought, and stood. "We don't get to see them in New York."

He rose to his feet with a slight frown. "I didna know ye were so fond of nature."

She smiled and moved to the other side of the table, putting the chair between them. "I don't get to see a sky full of stars very often."

"I don't get to see a girl like ye very often."

She laughed. "Iain!"

He spread his hands wide. "It's true, Maddie. Ye're what's beautiful."

"Thank you." She walked slowly over to the low wall that bordered the terrace. "My grandmother always says, 'Beauty is as beauty does.'"

Iain followed her, pausing at the table next to the wall. "And what does beauty do, Maddie?"

"Beauty behaves herself, Iain."

He took a step forward. "Perhaps beauty should get out more often. Remember, I told ye ye'd like the world." He took another step forward.

Maddie watched him move toward her while her heart began a staccato beat. How could he be so handsome? His expression was intent, his eyes watching her mouth. She walked to the next table.

"Ye might like it, Maddie."

She looked at him over her shoulder.

"The world," he said.

"Ah," she said, laughing. "Yes, the world." She looked at his mouth, then turned to look out over the sea. What would it feel like to kiss him? The crash of the waves was loud now, or was that rushing sound in her own head? He moved next to her, his finger tracing a line down her neck to her shoulder. She turned to face him.

"Maddie," he said. "Ye're so beautiful. There's never been anyone like ye."

"It's just the whisky, Iain," she said, trying to move past him.

He moved in front of her and leaned forward. She took a step backward and hit the wall.

"It's no' the whisky, Maddie. It's ye. I wasna drinking when I first met ye, and ye had the same effect on me then."

"Did I?"

He nodded.

"And you on me, Iain," she said and raised her face to

his. The first brush of his lips was so gentle she wasn't sure it had happened, but when he returned there was no mistaking his intent. He claimed her mouth with a ferocity that dazed her. He tasted like whisky, and for just a second she froze, then recovered, meeting his intensity with her own. His lips were soft, his body hard as he stood and pulled her up against him. She could feel his arousal when he pressed his hips against her, feel his hand on her back pressing her even closer, fell his knee squeeze between her legs. His lips claimed hers, then his tongue probed until she opened to him, the pressure increasing as he explored her mouth. One of his hands was tangled in her hair while the other slowly roamed from her cheek to caress her neck, then her collarbone, and then stopped, cupping her shoulder as he drew away.

"Good God, Maddie," he whispered. "Ye're even sweeter than I thought, and I've been thinking about kissing ye all night. I don't want to stop."

She gave a throaty laugh. Iain had kissed her, and she wanted more.

"Then don't stop."

"I should." He traced a finger from her temple, across her cheekbone to her lips. "I should send ye back to Sara as fast as ye can go."

"Why? You act as though I were dangerous."

"Ye are." He leaned to kiss her softly, then pulled back again.

"How am I dangerous, Iain?"

"I don't do this with Sara's friends."

"I never liked her," Maddie said breathlessly.

He laughed. "And ye're leaving in a fortnight."

"Which makes me less dangerous, not more."

He shook his head. "Ye are mistaken, Miss Breen. Ye are the most dangerous woman I've met in years."

"Then flirt with danger, Sir Iain. You're very good at flirting."

"I shouldn't do this," he said and lowered his head again to her mouth. This time there was no gentleness in his first touch, nor in her response. And this time his hand did not pause as he caressed her shoulders, but moved lower to cup her breast. She moaned when he touched her and moved closer, intensifying the kiss. At last he lifted his head and leaned back to look into her eyes.

"Damn! Damn and damn and damn!"

They turned to see Derek standing at the edge of the terrace, looking down at the glass he'd just dropped on the stones. Whisky streamed between the broken shards of glass, and he looked from it to them with a wide smile.

"I broke it," he said. "I'll go get another. But Sara's right behind me, so ye'd best stop that."

Iain laughed quietly and pulled Maddie to him for the briefest of kisses before he released her and stepped back. "To be continued," he whispered as Sara came into sight.

Sara looked from Maddie to Iain, then back to Maddie, putting her hands on her hips. "I should ha' guessed this. Come on, the two of ye. It's time to open the gifts, and I knew ye'd want to be there." She shook her head. "Maddie, ye'll be needing a comb."

*M*agnus cried when he opened Maddie's gift, wiping the tears away without embarrassment and calling her to him for an embrace. Anne kissed her cheek and cried unabashedly, holding the drawings up for everyone to see.

They did the same when Magnus opened Iain's gift, a model he'd had made of Duntober out of Scottish crystal, and Sara applauded them both.

"Great minds think alike," Iain said with a grin as he came back to stand with Maddie and watch Magnus open the rest of his gifts.

Many of the guests had gone, and when the music began again, there were fewer dancers. Maddie didn't mind. She danced with Iain, then Derek, then Iain again. He grinned when he held her tight against him, then frowned when he had to let her go. And when the music stopped he always came to claim her hand.

$\mathscr{B}$y three in the morning most guests had either retired to their rooms or had gone home, and Maddie sat on the terrace with Sara, Keith, and Iain. Derek had gone to the pub for a while and returned with the same pretty blond girl who had leaned up against Iain the night she'd been introduced to him at the pub. Derek led her into the ballroom to dance with him, and when she protested that she wasn't dressed properly, he undid the plaid from his shoulder and declared her a MacDonald. Iain watched them with narrowed eyes, and Maddie's heart constricted. Was there something between the two of them? If not, why was he so displeased with Derek's dancing with the pretty blonde? And if so, then why had he kissed her?

"Do you know her?" she asked, and Iain nodded.

"Everyone knows Joanie," Sara said, rolling her eyes. "She's quite . . . available. I don't know where's she's staying, but it has to be nearby. She's always up at Duntober talking to the men, and she's in the pub every night. She likes Iain and Derek a lot. Maybe," she said, with a significant look at Maddie, "she's a restoration groupie."

Iain snorted but made no comment, and Keith laughed, offering to get everyone another drink. Iain nodded absently as he looked through the French doors to where Derek danced with Joanie, his frown increasing into a scowl. Sara yawned and stood up, saying she was going to bed.

"Me too," Maddie said, rising. Iain looked at her in surprise but said nothing as she said good night, then followed Sara. Before they went inside, Maddie turned to see Iain still watching Derek and the blonde.

Maddie hung the ballgown up carefully and a little sadly. On the terrace below her room, Iain was at the table with Keith. Derek and Joanie had joined them and she could hear their laughter. Fool, she said to herself as she closed the curtain. It never could have worked, and that's fine with him. It was the whisky that made him kiss you, nothing more. She sighed and curled up in the chair next to the window to read the faxes that had come in Saturday morning. She'd been too busy to bother with them earlier, assuming that both of them were from Larry. The first one was—a long laundry list of details about the shoot in October, most of them things that had been thoroughly discussed before she'd left. Nothing worth even replying to, she thought, and unfolded the second fax. It bore the letterhead of the Scottish Historical Board and gave her permission to visit Kilgannon Castle, provided that she sign the enclosed waiver and be in the company of a member of their Board of Directors. Iain's name was of course on the list of the directors, and she gave a dejected sigh. He had done just as he'd promised, and she felt a wave of warmth toward him, then sorrow. He was a good man, but he was a man she could never have. The problem was that just now he was the only man she wanted.

Yes, he'd kissed her, she thought, touching her lips and remembering. But that was the whisky and the after-effects of that wild dance. It meant nothing more. He was gorgeous, true, and a very nice man. But he meant nothing to her, nor she to him. Sad, but for the best. What if they had really liked each other? He was geographically undesirable. He'd never leave Duntober, and she had a career she'd worked too hard for to desert. So the sensible thing was to wash her face and go to bed. Why then was she staring at the ceiling and thinking about kissing him? Maddie picked up her book and tried to read, then gave up and unpinned her hair, brushing it as she walked around the room. She'd miss him. She'd remember him the rest of her life.

"Maddie!" It was Iain's voice outside. She stared at the curtains. "Maddie, I know ye're still awake. Maddie!" She crossed the room and stood before the window. "Madeline Breen, I need to talk to ye!"

Maddie opened the curtains and leaned out. Iain stood alone on the terrace below, waving at her.

"Maddie! Come on down and see the sunrise with me."

She tried to whisper. "Iain! What are you doing?"

"Come on, Maddie. Put yer bonnie dress back on and come down."

Maddie heard Sara's window open. "Iain MacDon-ald!" Sara rebuked in a loud whisper. "For God's sake, go to bed. Ye've had too much to drink."

"I'm not drunk, Sara," Iain said, and Maddie had to admit he didn't sound it. "Ye go to bed; ye have to sleep for two now. This is between Maddie and me. Maddie, are ye coming down, or do I have to come up there and see ye?"

"Maddie, go down there before he wakes the whole hotel," Sara said urgently.

Her heart racing, Maddie called, "I'll be there in a minute, Iain," and closed the curtains.

It was more than a minute before she made it to the terrace. She left the ballgown on the hanger so it wouldn't get mussed, and threw some slacks and a silk T-shirt on, leaving her hair loose and blessing herself for not taking her makeup off. This is ridiculous, she thought, but smiled. He *must* be drunk. She'd talk with him for a minute and convince him to go to bed.

He waited for her at the table they'd been at before, his back to her, his legs stretched out before him. The ballroom was silent now, a few of the staff moving about, blowing out candles and closing the doors. There was no sign of anyone else, and she paused before she joined him. This was madness, she thought, then laughed. A little midsummer madness never hurt anyone.

"Iain," she whispered, and he turned, then rose to his feet to face her.

"Maddie," he said and held out his hand. "Why did ye go?"

"I . . . you . . ." She took his hand and came to stand before him. His eyes were dark in the dim light. "You seemed very preoccupied with Derek's dancing with Joanie," she said at last.

He laughed deep in his throat, then reached to pull her

against him. "I thought that was it. Damn, I love a jealous woman." He smiled down at her. "Maddie, how can ye think I'd care what that girl does? She's Derek's problem, and he can take care of himself. Lass, ye have no competition."

He kissed her, a soft kiss laden with promises, and she pressed herself against him, raising her mouth to him again.

"Maddie, I have a bottle of champagne in my room. Why don't we take it and watch the sunrise at Duntober?"

She shook her head. "I can't do that."

He touched his lips to her forehead. "Maddie, look at me."

She did, meeting his eyes with a tremor of fear. This man knew his power over her. He smiled now, slowly, as he ran a fingertip along her jaw.

"Ye'll ne'er see the like, Maddie. The sun comes up and lights each small bit of land and then sea, and the water changes from purple to silver. Ye should see it. For yer art."

She smiled. "For my art."

"It's research, lass." He kissed her hair. "Come with me and see the sunrise in a Scottish castle overlooking the sea." He kissed her cheek. "Who knows when or if ye'll ever be back here? Ye need to see this. Come with me, sweet Maddie."

"Yes," she said.

6

$\mathcal{I}$ain lived in one of the cottages at the back of the Trotternish, in a studio suite with a tiny kitchenette, decorated simply in florals and traditional furniture. Maddie looked around while Iain closed the door behind her and crossed to the small refrigerator, pulling out the bottle of champagne. She could see Sara's touch in the details, the patterns and colors that were so perfectly matched. But he didn't linger. He grabbed a blanket that was folded at the end of his bed, tucked it under his arm, and reached for her hand.

They walked to Duntober silently at first, then talking as they left the hotel grounds. By the time they reached the lower gate, Iain was swinging her hand and laughing out loud. Midsummer madness, Maddie thought, and looked at him again. If one was going to do something mad, this was the man to do it with. At the castle he unlocked the cellar and brought out two glasses, which he held up to her.

"No' crystal, but they'll do. Now, come on." He reached for her hand again and went up the stone stairs to the Great Hall. He led her to the arched window and gave her a smile. "In a few minutes it'll be spectacular. We have to be ready for it."

She fought a smile. "You'll have to tell me what to do."

He laughed. "Oh, I will. Here," he said, handing her the blanket. She helped him spread it out on the floor before the window, then stood on it, watching as he opened the champagne.

"Voila!" he said as he eased the cork out and grinned at her.

"You've done that before," she said.

"Opened champagne? Never with the likes of ye, Maddie," he said and laughed at her expression. He poured them each a glass, them held out one to her. "There's a toll, lass."

She laughed and lifted a hand for the glass, but he grinned at her, keeping it just out of her reach.

"What's the toll, Iain?"

"A kiss."

She tilted her head and looked him up and down. "One kiss?"

He laughed. "Can I get more? It's fine champagne."

She took a step toward him. "I might be able to arrange that."

"Payment first."

Maddie rose on her tiptoes and kissed his cheek. "Payment rendered."

He shook his head and leaned over her. "This is fine champagne, Maddie, I can no' accept anything less than the finest kiss." He handed her the glass. "Here. Take a taste."

Maddie took the glass and sipped as she watched him over the rim. He took a swallow of champagne and put his glass on the floor, then drew her into his arms.

"Now, lass, take another kind of taste."

She laughed and lifted her mouth to his. He kissed her gently at first, then with more intensity, pulling back to take her glass from her hand and put it next to his. He drew her closer against him.

"I expect full payment, lassie."

"Haven't you had it?"

"Oh no, Maddie. Those were just the samples. Let me show ye what I mean." He claimed her this time, wrapping his hand in her hair to hold her mouth to his as he parted her lips and explored her mouth with his tongue, then moaned as she responded. He pressed against her, holding her waist against his so she could feel his readiness for her, and leaning his hips into hers. When she stretched to wrap her arms around his neck, he moaned again and bent to kiss her cheeks and her neck before returning to her lips. He drew her down to the blanket and stretched out beside her, his hands roaming lower now, to cup her breasts and caress her hip. She was bolder too, running her fingers between the buttons of his shirt and finding the skin there, then reaching down to touch a naked thigh. He moved against her and lifted his head.

"Are ye wondering what a Scotsman wears under his kilt?"

She laughed softly and nodded, and Iain took her hand, placing it on the side of his knee, then, still holding it under his, ran her fingers slowly up his thigh to his hip. There was nothing but skin under her touch, and she shivered. If she moved her hand just a little to the side . . . He groaned as she did, and bent to her mouth again. The kiss was shorter this time, and he pulled away to stare at her.

"Damn, Maddie," he said at last. "Ye are dangerous, that's for sure. If we don't stop now, I won't. Are ye all right?"

Maddie caught her breath and smiled. Part of her knew they should stop, but part of her wanted him. Here. Now. "Yes. That was . . . amazing."

He grinned and sat up, straightening his shirt.

"Damn," he said as he reached for their glasses, handing hers to her with a shake of his head. He stood up and looked down at her, his breath still ragged. "How can I have known ye for such a short time? I feel as though ye'd always been part of me."

"I know," Maddie said, rising to face him. "I feel the same."

He sipped his champagne and studied her. She turned, suddenly shy, to look out over the water. It was as marvelous as Iain had promised, the sunlight just beginning to touch the top of Duntober's tower while the sea below was still wine colored. He came to stand behind her and pulled her against his chest, looking over her shoulder as the light claimed the castle inch by inch. And he did the same with her neck, kissing tiny portions, then moving higher, until at last she turned to meet his lips with hers again. Their glasses tipped and the champagne spilled on the cool stones at their feet, but neither noticed as they concentrated. Maddie's mind was swimming, her body crying for more while her mind refused to think at all. Just this one moment, she thought, I will enjoy this moment and look no further.

Iain lifted his mouth from hers and sighed as he wrapped his arms around her. "I will miss ye when ye return to New York, Maddie."

She nodded into his chest. "And I you, Iain. I never thought I'd meet anyone like you."

"Will ye no' come back again?"

She leaned back to smile at him, recognizing the words from the song "Bonnie Charlie."

"Better loved ye canna be, Maddie Breen. Will ye no' come back again? Or better yet, will ye no' leave?"

"I have to."

He nodded. "Aye. I knew ye'd say that. But promise me ye'll come back, lassie." He gestured at the Hall behind them, the ceiling details now visible as the light came through the window and lit the room. "Part of this castle will always belong to ye, Maddie. I don't think I can ever stand here again and no' think of this moment, with ye in my arms." He bent to kiss her with the gentlest of touches. "Do ye suppose we knew each other in a former life?"

Maddie smiled and reached to touch his cheek. "It would explain how I feel I know you so well. I'll miss you, Iain. Come see me in New York."

He nodded. "Haven't been there in years. Aye, I could do that. And ye'll have to come back to Duntober. Maybe we lived here."

They were silent then, and Maddie leaned her head against his shoulder. "Better loved ye canna be," she thought. If only that were true. Midsummer madness would fade with the first frost. But what memories she'd take home. She listened to his heartbeat and tightened her arms around his waist. I will enjoy this moment, this sunrise.

"Look," he said softly. "The light has hit the first of the water."

She turned to follow his gaze and smiled. He'd been right about the colors, too. The foam at the crest of the waves was a luminous white, the water below a slate blue that shimmered into silver as the light found it. Maddie sighed, feeling close to tears.

"I knew ye'd want to see this," Iain said, his lips at her ear.

She turned to him. "Yes," she said and pulled his mouth to hers for a short kiss. "Thank you. I'll never forget this."

He laughed against her lips. "I'd best take ye home, lassie, or I will no' answer for my actions." He kissed her again. "Or . . . Maddie, will ye come back to with me to my room with me and . . ." He pressed against her hips. "Maddie, will ye?"

She smiled up into his eyes and nodded. "Yes."

*H*is phone was ringing as he opened the door, and Iain threw the blanket on the bed and swore. "Who the hell is calling me at this hour?" He picked up the phone, then turned pale as he listened. "What? When? Which hospital? All right, I'm on my way. Ye have my mobile number, right? I'm coming." He hung up and looked at her with a stricken expression. "I have to go, Maddie. It's my father. He's had a heart attack. He's in hospital in Inverness. I have to leave at once." He kicked off his shoes, pulled his shirt out of his kilt, and unfastened the brooch that held the plaid, tossing it on a chair.

"What can I do?"

"Can ye make me some tea while I shower? I canna go like this."

Maddie made tea, then helped him throw some clothes into a suitcase. He paid little attention to what she packed, and she piled jeans and slacks and a dark suit, just in case, adding shirts and a sweater. He tossed in toiletries and zipped the bag closed, then looked at her.

"I'm sorry, Maddie. I have to go."

"Of course. But Iain, you haven't slept at all. Will you be all right?"

"I'll be fine. Ye'll tell Magnus and the others for me? I'll call and tell them when I'll be back."

She nodded. "I hope your father is all right."

He didn't answer, just leaned and kissed her deeply, then picked up the bag. At the door he paused. "If I don't see ye again, Maddie, I . . . I wish ye well, lass. And I'll always regret not . . . I'll miss ye, Maddie Breen."

"And I you. Drive carefully, Iain."

He gave her a ghost of a smile. "I will. Take care of our castle for me, aye?"

When he closed the door behind him, Maddie sank into a chair, watching the dust motes that swam in the diffused light coming through the sheer lace panels. She put a hand to her throat and tried not to cry.

*I*ain shielded his eyes against the sun's glare. He'd stolen an hour to drive over to Culloden, to walk the battlefield that never failed to move him. He stood before the monument stones that marked where the clans had fallen, then moved through the flocks of summer tourists and headed back to Inverness. His father would live. He'd been in intensive care for three days, unaware that his wife and three children were there. Iain had comforted his stepsisters, telling them that their father was strong and would pull through. Thank God he'd been right. And then, late Tuesday night, his father had rallied and been pronounced on the mend. He'd been his usual charming self when he'd seen Iain, asking his wife what the hell she'd done by calling his son and telling Iain he wouldn't inherit anything yet. Iain watched his stepmother try to placate his father, then turned on his heel and left. He would go back now and face them again, then go back to the hotel and sleep. And then go home in the morning to Skye, to Duntober. And Maddie.

He couldn't get her out of his mind. He'd tried, on the long drive here, to convince himself that what he felt was lust and some mild fondness for a charming stranger, but he'd not been very persuasive. And in those hours at the hospital, waiting to find out if his father would live, he'd had a lot of time to think about his own life. What did he want? Not to be alone forever. Not to be in the kind of marriage he'd already had. Nor one like that his father and stepmother shared. He wanted more. Could he love anyone again? He'd failed once already.

It still hurt. Iain looked through the windscreen at the A9, but he saw the note, so carelessly left on the foyer table. "Darling," she'd written, "Iain the Work-horse won't be home for hours. I've gone to get champagne. Be in bed and be ready when I come home." And he still saw her face when, enraged, he'd confronted her. He'd expected tears and denial, not her cold look and shrugged shoulders. "What did you expect?" she'd asked. "That I would wait while you built an empire? Marriages need attention too, Iain, not just businesses. I was bored."

Bored, he thought. He hadn't been. He'd been working as hard as he could to build the business so that he could give her everything she wanted, so that someday their children would be raised in comfort as both of them had. He knew how to work; he'd proved that much to himself. And he now had something worth his energy in Duntober. But work, even Duntober, wasn't enough anymore. He knew how to have a light dalliance, no strings attached. He'd had several in the years since his divorce; he'd not wanted anything more. He knew women he was fond of; and one or two who, with little persuasion, he suspected, would be happy to make their relationship much more. But each time he'd stopped short.

And now? He took the exit that would lead him to the hospital. Now he wanted what Magnus had—a loving family, a wife who adored him, children. Maybe grandchildren someday. He wanted to be eighty years old and tell the world how charmed his life had been and watch his wife smile at him as he said it.

He wanted Maddie. He didn't know the details of how he'd make that happen, but they didn't matter. Iain felt a burden lift off his shoulders. Now he knew where he was going.

*M*addie pushed her hair back from her face and sighed. Wednesday afternoon. She'd be leaving in four days. Her flight was Sunday night at six, but she'd have to drive to Glasgow beforehand, so three days left on Skye. The Trotternish Games would begin on Friday night with a ceilidh, a musical evening, at the hotel, then continue the next two days with the other competitions, culminating this year in the horse race. She wouldn't be here. She'd be somewhere on the road when Iain rode Blaven to victory or defeat. He'd called every day about Duntober, talking to Magnus and sometimes to Sara, telling them the latest news of his father's condition, each time asking them to give her a message. But he'd not once talked to her. And so she'd go home with bittersweet memories of a tall blond man with deep blue eyes, a contagious laugh, and a memorable body. The most remarkable man she'd ever known. She closed her eyes, remembering his laugh, the way he listened to her, the way he'd danced with Derek and Keith, the feel of his lips on hers. But it was obviously not to be.

She had her job, and it would help her get over this little madness called Iain MacDonald. She looked across the Great Hall of Duntober to where Sara and Keith pored over the blueprints with Magnus. The four of them had tried to replace Iain at Duntober, overseeing the work, but there were guests and relatives at the Trotternish who had come for Magnus's party and stayed for the Games, and they'd not been here as much as they'd hoped. Sara's parents had left, promising to be back for the weekend, but even without them, dinner had been an event with at least thirty people. After dinner each night Maddie had retreated to her room to work, or simply to think. Her calls to Larry had had a distant tone to them. He berated her for not being there, but there was no substance to his anger, and he hung up leaving Maddie with the distinct feeling that she was forgotten as soon as the receiver hit the cradle. It didn't bother her, and that bothered her. What did she have if she didn't have her job?

At least the wind had stopped. Two days and nights of high winds had left Duntober a mess, but there had been little real damage. She, Sara, and Keith had insisted on accompanying Magnus when he said he'd spend the day here and see what he could do to lead the men. The week had not been a complete loss. The driveway repairs had been completed, and two truckloads of lumber had arrived. The wooden steps had been finished yesterday, and it was now possible to climb from the newly created service entrance to the Great Hall and, on the other side of the castle, descend to the terrace that extended from the courtyard. Iain would be pleased, she thought, then sighed again as she flipped her sketchpad closed. She'd been like a madwoman, drawing without conscious plan, trying to capture him. She'd sketched him smiling at her on the terrace, lounging here in the Great Hall at the end of a long day, dancing at Magnus's party. She'd miss him so much.

It was impossible. She'd go home and forget these emotions; despite their current intensity, she knew they'd fade. She hoped they'd fade. It had been possible, standing in his arms, to let the glimmer of a future together cross her mind, but he'd never said anything about that, never had hinted at them being anything more than they were now. Which was? Not lovers, though she'd thought enough about that, when she'd faced her emotions in the hours between dusk and dawn. If he asked, she would, no regrets, no strings. And then what? She was going home in four days and might never see him again. It would be foolish. It would be heaven.

And if he returned and gave her that amazing smile, drawing her into his arms, what then? Even if they decided to give a relationship a try, how could they? She knew all the reasons they would fail. It was just not meant to be.

"Maddie," Sara called to her. "We have to get back to the hotel. Granddad, Keith, we've got people waiting for us."

"I'm coming," Maddie said and picked up her things as Keith left to put the blueprints in the cellar, using the old stone steps in the corner. Magnus waited for Sara and Maddie, then led the way down the new stairs, commenting as he descended that he was the first person to use them. Sara let Maddie go before her; she had just put a foot on the top step when Magnus gave a hoarse cry and tumbled down the last ten steps, landing in a heap on the stone terrace.

$\mathcal{D}$ain put the last of the flowers in the backseat of the Rover and smiled. Three dozen white roses. They looked beautiful. Roses because roses were for lovers, and that's what he hoped they'd be. And white because he thought red might scare her off. He'd called ahead to Portree, ordering the flowers to pick up on his way north, then stopped at a shop in Inverness where he bought Maddie a sleeveless pink sweater and another in a shade of green that reminded him of her eyes. No black. What did he have to lose? Either Maddie would be pleased and they could sort this out together, whatever it turned out to be, or she'd run back to New York and her career and he'd feel like a fool.

Surely they could find a way. How could a woman kiss him the way Maddie had and not care for him? He knew better. He'd been with women who had wanted something from him, his money, his title. Or a wedding ring. None of them had wanted him for himself, and none had fooled him. He'd enjoyed them for as long as it suited him, then moved on without regrets. But Maddie was different. Physically they'd be very compatible. She had responded with a passion that had surprised him, as though he'd breathed life into a banked fire. The flames had been instantly hot and quite intense. He smiled to himself. Damn Celtic blood. Next thing you knew he'd be writing sonnets to her beauty or composing songs to sing outside her window. Roses and sweaters were a good start.

At the Trotternish he stopped in the lobby to see if Maddie was around. It was almost time for dinner. The girl at the front desk looked at him with frightened eyes, and Iain tensed.

"What is it?" he asked, expecting to be told his father had taken a turn for the worse.

"It's Lord MacDonald," she said. "He fell down the stairs at Duntober this afternoon. They've taken him to Portree."

"Magnus? Where is he? How is he?"

The girl shook her head. "Haven't heard yet. Maddie

left her mobile number in case ye called," she said, handing him a slip of paper.

He went outside and stood next to the Rover while he punched in the numbers. Maddie answered on the second ring.

"Iain, you're back!" He heard the relief in her voice. "Magnus will be all right. He's only sprained his ankle. We're on our way back now."

"What happened?"

There was silence, and he thought he'd lost the signal; then Maddie's voice came back, quieter now. "We're not sure. The board was loose and he fell. The man who built the stairs said he checked everything four times, that the board couldn't have been loose. He says it was pried up after he nailed it down. He's furious, and he wants to talk to you. Magnus was the first one down the stairs. . . . Iain, he could have been very badly hurt. It could have been Sara. Or you."

"Where are ye?"

"At Staffin. We're almost there."

"Good. See ye in a few minutes."

He clicked the phone with a cold rage. The man who built those stairs was a good carpenter, a fine man. It was difficult to believe that he'd made a mistake like that. If he said the stairs had been checked, they'd been checked. It had been no accident. Whoever was making mayhem could have seriously hurt Magnus. Or Sara's unborn child. Or Maddie.

Who was it? It made no sense for the MacLeods to suddenly claim land they'd lost hundreds of years ago. A quick ring to Dunvegan would solve that mystery. And if some antirestoration group was really involved, why hadn't they picketed or made more noise in the press? No, this was a stealthy and nasty campaign, one aimed at stopping the work at Duntober. Why? Who would profit from that? Who had an old grudge? Who was it? Someone knew. And that skanky blond girl had something to do with it. He'd not really focused on her, although he'd been vaguely aware that she'd been around for weeks. But after Magnus's party, when Sara had made her remarks, he'd suddenly realized that the girl was always around, always asking how the work was going at the castle, always leaning her underfed body up against him or Derek. And when he'd seen Derek dancing with her, he'd watched her, had watched how calculated her attentions were. He wasn't worried about Derek—he could take care of himself—but he felt as though he'd just put a puzzle piece in the right place.

7

$\mathcal{I}$t was hours before Iain remembered the flowers. Magnus had arrived on crutches, Anne anxiously helping him through the door. And then there had been a flurry of activity, getting Magnus into the family lounge, where he sat, making jokes and trying to make light of it. But one look at Sara's and Maddie's faces, at Keith's fury and Derek's outrage, had let Iain know he wasn't the only one to suspect sabotage.

He and Derek had gone to Staffin, finding the man who had built the stairs and listening to his story, then assuring him that Magnus would be fine. The man, a carpenter who had worked for Magnus for twenty years, went with them to Duntober, showing Iain the pry marks on the wood where the step had been loosened. Iain told the man they believed him, then stood still as a thought occurred to him. He suddenly had an idea of who it might be. When they were alone, he told Derek, who agreed. They had called the police then to start the documentation process. In the morning the evidence might be gone.

$\mathcal{T}$wo hours later, back at the Trotternish, Magnus nodded slowly, looking from Iain to Derek to Keith. "Aye," he said. "It makes sense. Ugly sense, but it could be. Tomorrow I'll call Dunvegan, and that will eliminate that. If Iain's correct, we'll have more 'incidents.' Keith, Sara is no' to be at Duntober until we solve this. We're damn lucky it was me and no' her. If ye'd lost yer child . . ."

"I'd kill him," Keith said, and Derek and Iain nodded.

"I'll spend the nights there," Iain said, but Magnus shook his head.

"Spend tomorrow night there, lad. He'll no' do anything so soon after this. Go and get yer rest now, all of ye. This is a hell of a birthday gift. I need another whisky. Derek, find yer grandmother. I need a dose of Anne as well."

$\mathcal{M}$addie stretched her hands high above her head and tried to concentrate on Larry's latest fax. She'd have to call him, she thought, glancing at her watch, then looking up as Sara came to sit next to her in the hotel lounge. She had stayed downstairs hoping to see Iain alone, but it looked like a futile hope.

"I'm off to bed," Sara said with a wan smile. "I'm exhausted."

Maddie nodded and patted Sara's hand. "He's all right."

"I know. But . . . well." Sara straightened her back and sighed. "We all know it wasn't an accident, Maddie. Ye heard the man. He was outraged at the suggestion that he'd not attached the board."

"I know."

"And Granddad and Keith and Derek and Iain have been closeted for ages."

"I know."

"Did ye see Iain's face? He knows something."

Maddie nodded. She'd had the same thoughts. And others. This was not how she'd pictured she'd see him again, and she'd not had a moment to talk privately with him. He'd given her a warm greeting, but then had gone to Duntober, and when he came back he'd been in the lounge with the others. She sighed and patted Sara's hand again.

"Go to bed," she said, then leaned to embrace her friend. "All's well, Sara. We were lucky."

Sara nodded, yawned again, then turned as the men came out of the lounge. Keith, Iain, and Derek talked quietly together just outside the door, then Keith came to them and took Sara's hand.

"We're off to bed, love." He kissed her cheek and said good night to Maddie, leading a yawning Sara away.

Derek waved as he went through the front door. To the pub, no doubt, Maddie thought, then forgot about Derek as Iain walked toward her with an intent expression.

"Maddie," he said, coming to stand before her. "How are ye?"

"I'm all right," she said, trying to smile. Look at

him—was he not the most beautiful man who had ever lived? And in three days she'd leave and never see him again. "How is your father?"

"He'll live." He smiled wryly. "I've decided I was adopted," he said and paused. "I missed ye, Maddie."

She fought her sudden tears. It was going to be impossible to leave him. "Oh, Iain," she said and wiped her eyes. "I missed you so much." She took a shuddering breath. "I thought I wouldn't see you again before I left."

Iain held out his hand. "Will ye come with me, Maddie? We need to talk."

*H*e didn't speak on the short walk to his cottage, nor when he closed the door and turned to her, opening his arms. She went into them with hesitation, and when he wrapped his arms around her, pulling her closer, she raised her lips to meet his, surrendering all rational thinking. When it came to Iain MacDonald, her body had a mind of its own. He bent to kiss her with a hunger that surprised her, and she lost all conscious thought.

*H*e didn't want to stop, didn't want to lift his lips off hers, but he did long enough to whisper her name, then smile when she said his. He clasped her to him, reminding himself to slow down. He wanted to tear her clothes off, to fall on her like some savage beast. Instead he took a deep breath and held her at arm's length. Her eyes were dark, her lips swollen, and she smiled at him.

"Iain, what do you do to me?"

"What do ye want me to do to ye?"

"Kiss me again."

So he did, lingering over her lips, letting his tongue explore her mouth, and feeling his body react as she responded. He'd never wanted a woman more. He caressed her shoulder, then moved his hand to her breast. She moaned and leaned into his fingers, reaching for his shirt. He felt her undo the buttons and yanked the shirt loose from his jeans. Maddie slid her hands up his chest, lingering over the planes of his stomach and then reaching behind to pull him closer. He lifted his mouth from hers to kiss her throat, and when she arched her neck like a cat, he put his hands on her waist and slipped them under her top, lifting it gently over her head, bending to kiss her mouth again. He kissed the side of her neck, then her shoulders, then moved to the top of her breasts and unfastened her bra, peeling it slowly away, then leaning back to look at her.

"Maddie, ye're perfect," he whispered, cupping a hand over one breast and bending to take a pink nipple in his mouth. "Perfect." He looked up at her face as his thumb brought her other nipple to a peak. "Maddie, I want ye. Ye're all I can think about."

"I want you too." She reached for his jeans, fumbling over the fastenings. He took over, pulling them off with brisk movements, then pulled her to him again, pressing her breasts against his chest and running his hands down her back. She moaned at the feel of his skin on hers, and he leaned back with a smile.

"Maddie," he said, running a long finger down one side of her breast, then up the other. He kissed her shoulder. "Tell me what ye want."

"I'll show you," she said, putting her hands around his

back, then moving lower. She pushed his shorts down, then from him entirely, so that he stood naked before her, ready for her. She tilted her head.

"I want you. All of you," she said and let her fingers run along the length of him. "You're the most gorgeous man that has ever lived."

"No," he said. "Just the luckiest."

He undid her slacks, and she stepped out of the pools of material at her feet, then gasped as his hand slid down her stomach and inside her panties. His mouth devoured hers while his fingers found their goal at last, and he moaned as he felt her softness.

"Do ye want to stop?" he asked.

"No," she whispered, kissing his shoulder. "Do you?"

"No, but I want ye to be sure."

She leaned back and looked into his eyes. She could feel him hard against her stomach, feel the warmth of his arms around her.

"I'm sure I want you, Iain," she said. "Do you want me?"

"More than ye'll ever know."

"Then don't stop."

He pulled off her panties, his kisses making her forget she was standing naked before him. He led her to the bed, then stretched out beside her, using his lips and hands to excite her even more. She closed her eyes and concentrated on the feel of his skin under her hands, and hers under his. His mouth moved from her breast to her waist, then lower still, and she moaned as he touched her. He was a generous lover, making sure she was well pleasured before he let her guide him on top of her. He paused then, looking down at her with an intent expression.

"Maddie Breen," he said. "I love ye."

"Iain." She rose to meet him, gasping as he entered her, then holding him to her as he moved within her. She came in a daze of color and sensation.

*S*he woke wrapped in his arms, warm and satiated. Iain lay behind her, his breathing even, a long leg thrown across one of hers. He said he loved me, she thought, slipping out of his arms to sit up and look at him. He slept on his side, the blanket wrapped around his waist, his shoulders and chest bare. She sighed. Making love to him had been more wonderful than even she could have imagined. He was as magnificent in bed as he was outside it, a man any woman would want. And she did want him. She wanted to stay right here, to make love with him and pretend they were the only two people in the world. She wanted to have the freedom of reaching out and touching him whenever she wanted. She wanted to believe he loved her.

And if she did stay? Then what? What if it was only a short-lived infatuation and they had nothing in common? Would he ship her home to New York? She sighed again. At least she'd have memories.

"Maddie. Stay with me. Don't leave me."

He stretched a long arm to capture her waist, nuzzling her side, then threw the blanket aside and moved next to her. A naked Iain MacDonald was impossible to ignore, and she looked into his eyes, anywhere but that athletic body.

"Maddie, what's wrong?"

"I . . ." She couldn't say it, couldn't tell him how

much she wanted to believe his words, but how afraid she was that they were only words said in the heat of passion. "Nothing. Nothing's wrong."

"Are ye sorry we made love?" His eyes were worried.

"No." She smiled and touched his cheek. "It was amazing, Iain. Wonderful, spectacular. I'll never forget it."

"Nor will I." He kissed her gently, then grinned. "Don't move." He leapt from the bed and picked up the vase of white roses she had not even noticed on the table. So many roses, their blooms just opening. "I forgot to give ye these," he said, handing her one. "For ye, perfect Madeline." He bent to kiss her, then took another rose, putting this one next to her on the bed. "For yer right side." He did the same on her other side. "And yer left."

He kissed her again, then put the vase on the floor and tore the petals off a handful of flowers. He laughed at her exclamation, then tossed some of the petals onto the bed, bending her over them, and dribbling the rest of the petals on her stomach. "For yer perfect middle," he said and kissed her.

"Stay, Maddie. Don't leave me alone just yet." He rose to his knees and pulled her up with him, dropping rose petals between them as he pressed his body, ready for her, against hers. "Stay, Maddie."

Maddie laughed and kissed his shoulder, then looked up to meet his gaze, dark with desire. "Yes," she said, then forgot all about the flowers as his hands roamed over her breasts, her thighs, parting her legs as he claimed her mouth with a fervor that made her forget her fears and reach for him. They did not speak as they explored each other, then joined in a frenzy of moans and sighs. Maddie arched her back as she pulled him deeper inside her. He slipped his arm around her, then groaned as she climaxed. When she breathed his name and climaxed again, he lost control.

*M*orning came too soon, the light streaming through the lace panels. Maddie lay on her side, watching the roses he'd left in the vase catch the pink morning light, changing the white blossoms to rose. Three dozen white roses. Enough, he'd laughed, to make love with for a week. And he'd given her two sweaters. Not black, he'd said, and laughed again while she watched him, wondering what was happening to her. Behind her Iain stirred, then traced his fingers down her back. She turned to meet his eyes.

"I just wanted to make sure ye were real," he said.

She smiled and stretched. "Mmmm. I hope so. I wouldn't want to wake up and find out this was a dream."

"No." He sat up and grinned, then reached to caress her breast. "Aye, ye're real enough, lassie." He threw his legs over the side of the bed.

She leaned up against the headboard. "Look how beautiful the roses look in this light, Iain. I can't believe you bought me three dozen roses."

He laughed and handed her a petal from the chaos of the blankets. "And I helped ye press them too." He stood up and stretched while she watched him. He was the perfect man, she thought, letting her eyes drift over places her hands and mouth had visited.

"If ye look at me like that again, Maddie, I'll never get my work done."

She laughed and looked at the clock. "It's five A.M., Iain. What work do you have to do at this hour?"

"None just now," he said, pulling his jeans on. "But I'll have lots to do later. Tell me again what happened at Duntober."

She did, and he listened as he filled the electric kettle with water.

"It wasn't an accident, was it?" she asked.

"I don't think so."

"Who . . . ?"

"Ah, that's what today will tell us. Magnus will talk to the MacLeods. But it's no' them, and we all know it."

"Then?"

"Well," he said and came to sit on the side of the bed. "There is a man—Alan Loomis—who used to work for Magnus at the hotel. Magnus had to let him go after he found that Loomis was embezzling. Loomis swore he'd get revenge and did some ugly things, petty and nasty, letting people who worked at the hotel take the blame for them. When Magnus found out, he started telling people, and Loomis was all but run off the island. I'd forgotten all about that—it's been years now. But last night, when we were at Duntober, I remembered. It has to be him. He did the same loose-step thing at the Trotternish. No one else has any motive. And that blonde that ye were jealous of is part of it somehow."

"Why do you think that?"

The kettle began to whistle, and he crossed the room. "Well," he said, pouring water into the cups, "she's been around for weeks now, always asking questions and showing up at the castle."

"Maybe you're just irresistible."

He grinned. "Oh, I am, but this is different."

"What can you do?"

"We'll stop the information first. I think she's supposed to keep tabs on us and report what we're doing, and someone else is doing the damage. So, Derek's going to keep her . . . busy. And I'm going to stay up at Duntober tonight and tomorrow night. Everyone else will be here for the ceilidh Friday night and I'm sure they'll assume I will be too. I'll stay here long enough to be seen, then go and wait." He carried the tea over and handed her a cup.

"Iain, if you're right, if it's this Loomis creature, he might be dangerous!"

"He won't be." He sipped his tea, looking at her over the rim, then put the cup on the table next to the bed. "We have another two hours before the rest of the world will intrude, Maddie. Can ye think of any way to fill the time?"

She laughed. "We could watch the telly?"

He took her cup and placed it next to his, then leaned to brush his lips on hers. "I was thinking of something a bit more . . . vigorous."

*H*e was in the shower when she woke again, and she lay staring at the ceiling for a few moments, then glanced at the clock, rose, and dressed. It was, unfortunately, time to join the real world again. She was trying to smooth her hair with her fingers when he came out, and he stopped in the doorway, watching her run her hands through her hair. "Maddie, ye are very bonnie."

She laughed and blushed. "I'm sure I look dreadful."

"I'm sure ye don't." He came to stand before her, wrapping his arms loosely around her waist. "I meant what I said before, Maddie. I love ye."

Maddie's glowing mood faded, replaced by sadness.

"Iain," she said, her tone distant now. "That's very nice to say. It isn't necessary, but . . ."

"Necessary?" He felt his face flush with anger, and he let his arms fall from her. "Hell, no, Maddie, it isn't necessary at all. What do ye think it is to me, just a polite thing to say after sex?"

She shook her head. "I didn't mean it like that."

He stroked a finger along her jawline, then traced the outline of her lips. "Tell me ye feel nothing. Tell me ye don't feel yer body reacting."

"That's just physical, Iain."

"Of course it is. Part of it. . . . Oh, hell, Maddie—" He leaned forward and brushed his lips across hers, then pulled back. "Tell me why we shouldn't do this. Tell me, Maddie. Because I can't think of any reason why this is wrong."

"What if it doesn't work?"

"We'll make it work." He kissed her forehead, then her cheek.

"I . . . I think we're setting ourselves up for failure, Iain."

"I don't believe that."

"Nothing can come of it. You live on Skye, and I live in New York. I have my career, and you have Duntober. We're worlds apart. Nothing can come of it. It's too complicated."

"Why? Why is it complicated? Did ye enjoy making love?"

She sighed. "It was wonderful."

He met her eyes. "Aye, it was wonderful. But not good enough, is that it?"

"No, it's not that . . ."

Her eyes filled with tears, but he ignored them. "Let's be clear with each other, Maddie. What do think this is between us?"

"A strong attraction. A very strong attraction."

"Lust, then. Mutual, apparently. But now ye've satisfied yer curiosity, and ye're finished with me. Is that correct?"

"No!"

"I told ye I loved ye, Maddie!"

"In the middle of sex, Iain!"

"Then I'll tell ye again now, when we're not. I love ye, Maddie Breen."

She wiped her tears from her cheek, then shook her head. He felt his chest tighten. "Ye don't believe me?"

"You've only known me for days, Iain. Yes, there's something very strong between us. But it's not love. It's an infatuation. It'll pass."

He stepped back from her. "I've having an infatuation."

"It's a mutual infatuation." She met his eyes. "This was wonderful, Iain. Amazing. I'll never forget it. But it's not love. Love doesn't happen in days. One of us has to be realistic."

"Why?"

"Iain!"

"I'm serious. Why can't this work? I love ye."

"Don't say that! You can't love me. It's not possible to fall in love so soon."

"It is possible. Look, I don't understand it either. But I want to be with ye, Maddie. I don't understand it, I can't explain it, but there it is. I'm finding myself thinking about buying a house and getting a dog and coming home to ye each evening. I love ye, Maddie. Look at me and tell me ye feel nothing for me."

"I can't. I do care for you, Iain. A great deal. If things were otherwise, I would love to be in love with you. But this is impossible."

"Why?"

"Because I live in New York, and you live in Scotland."

"That's a choice on both parts. I could move to New York."

"You'd hate it. I'm not sure I even like it anymore."

"Then ye could stay here."

"I can't do that. I have a whole team of people depending . . ."

He stopped her with a raised hand. "God, Maddie, don't give me that. I've been there. It's not enough to fill a life. I ruined my marriage, I lost friends. And for what? There are other ways to live."

"I have responsibilities. I can't just walk away."

"Yes, ye can. It is possible. Ye're not saving lives in advertising. Life will go on whether the art is well done or not. Ye like to think ye're indispensable, but there are hundreds of people waiting to take yer spot."

"I worked hard to get where I am."

"I'm sure ye did. But will it keep ye warm in yer old age?"

"I'll deal with that if it happens." She spread her hands. "Look, Iain, you want me to walk away from everything, to leave New York and my family and my job. You want me to give up my life."

"No, I don't. If ye say the word, I'll move to New York."

She stared at him. "You would do that?"

"I would go anywhere to be with ye."

"But what would you do?"

He shrugged. "Dunno. Start a new firm?"

"What about Duntober? What about Magnus?"

"I haven't worked out the details."

"It would never work."

"We could make it work if we tried. Ye could stay here. Ye could do the art for the Duntober brochures. Or paint whatever ye wished for a change."

"You'd be bored with me soon, and then what?"

He flushed with anger and turned to stare through the window. Don't explode, he told himself. He looked back at her, his tone glacial now. "That's damn insulting, ye know. I'm not some sort of halfwit. If I say I love ye, I love ye. It's not a mood, Maddie. It's not an infatuation that will pass. I agree it's an astonishing timeline, but there it is. Life is about choices, and I get the message loud and clear. I chose ye, but ye don't choose me."

"That's not fair."

"It's very fair." He shrugged. "Maybe ye just wanted a summer romance, something to remember in the middle of a long winter. Hot sex and then, bam, off to New York. Well, I want more. All or nothing, Maddie. Love me like I love ye, or get the hell out of my life. Which ye already plan to do."

"Iain, it's only been ten days! We don't know each other! How can you think we can live together?"

"I'm talking marriage, Maddie."

"You are asking me to marry you?"

"Yes. What the hell did ye think?"

"Iain! How can you think I'd marry you so soon?"

He froze, then shook his head. "I don't know. I guess I thought what I felt for you was reciprocated. Hell, ye couldn't be more patronizing, could ye?" He held the door open for her and nodded with his head. "Go on, run away, back to yer safe job and yer empty life. I won't bother ye again."

"You're just hurt, Iain. When you have time to think about all this, you'll be glad we didn't—"

"Get out, Maddie."

"Iain . . ."

He drew himself up straight and glared at her. "Get out."

8

*M*addie ran all the way to her room and threw herself on the bed, crying into her pillow. The knock on her door made her sit up in panic, looking for tissues. She called out hesitantly, relieved when Sara's head poked around the door.

"May I come in?" Sara asked.

When Maddie nodded, Sara came to sit on the foot of the bed. "Are ye all right?"

"Yes. No."

"What happened?"

"Nothing."

"Nothing? But ye spent the night with him."

"Sara! Does everyone know?"

"Just me. And Keith and Derek. We all saw ye run out of his cottage this morning."

"Oh, God!" Maddie wailed, hiding her face in her hands.

Sara's eyes widened in sudden worry. "Did he hurt ye?"

"No!" Maddie wiped her eyes. "He's not like that . . ." She took a deep breath. "We didn't do anything I didn't want to. That part was wonderful."

"Then can't ye just talk and work it out?"

"No. Some things can't be fixed, Sara."

"Do you want me to talk to Iain?"

"No! He's not the problem. I am."

"What do ye mean?"

"He says he loves me, Sara!"

"Well, I'm no' surprised. We've all seen him the last week. So why are ye this unhappy?"

"He wants me to marry him."

Sara threw her arms around Maddie. "That's wonderful!"

"No, that's horrible!"

"Wait, I don't understand. Iain says he loves ye, and he wants to marry ye."

"Yes."

"I'm trying to see why ye're so upset, Maddie." Sara tilted her head. "Oh! Ye don't want to leave yer job. Ye don't want to move to Skye."

"Iain says he'll move to New York."

Sara's eyes widened. "He did? What did ye say?"

"I said no."

"Ye turned him down? Iain asked ye to marry him, and ye said no?"

"I've only known him a few days."

"He seems sure enough."

"It's a mirage, Sara, not reality."

Sara cupped her chin in her hand and studied Maddie. "Ye're afraid."

"No, I'm not."

Sara nodded vehemently. "Yes, ye are. Ye're afraid ye'll fail."

Maddie met her eyes. "What if it didn't work out?"

"Then ye'd be older and wiser. What if it did?"

"What if I left my job and then we failed?"

"Ye'd get another job."

"It's not that simple."

"It looks simple to me. If ye want to keep yer job, he'll go to New York. If ye don't, ye can come here. He says he loves ye. The only reason I can see to turn him down is if ye don't love him in return."

"People don't fall in love this fast."

"Some people obviously do. It's yer decision of course, Maddie, but if ye don't even try, it's an automatic failure. Do ye not love him at all?"

"Yes. No. Oh, I don't know. I know I care a lot for him. He's a wonderful man. He's a good man. He's gorgeous."

"Problems in bed?"

Maddie met her eyes. "None."

"Then? He's nice, but not nice enough? No magic?"

"Oh, there was magic! Wonderful magic. No, that's not it. He's amazing. I'll always remember him. Why does that sound so lame?"

"Because it is." Sara stood up. "I think ye're afraid, Maddie."

"It's all too much, too soon."

"Then stay longer and see what ye think in a week."

"I have to get back to work."

Sara shrugged again. "Then go home to yer job. I hope ye'll be very happy together."

*M*addie showered, then quietly went downstairs and outside. The hotel suddenly seemed claustrophobic. The path she chose led down to the water, then to the rocks at the north end of the bay, where she stopped and looked across at the blue islands and the cloud-spattered sky above. Iain in New York. She pictured him bundled against the cold at Christmas, walking with her on a spring day in Central Park, standing with her before the Temple of Dendur. Maybe they could make it work if he came to New York. Maybe she could have it all, her job and Iain. No. It would be selfish of her to ask him to leave Duntober, and a horrible thing to do to Magnus after he'd told everyone it was his dream. And if she came to Skye . . . ?

Why was it so hard to breathe? Iain's expression when he told her to leave would haunt her forever. She hadn't meant to hurt him. How could this have happened so quickly? He doesn't really love me, she told herself; it's just his pride that's wounded. Or was Sara right? Was Iain right? Was she afraid to try because they might fail? Any relationship might fail. If she was too timid to try with a man like Iain, what did that say about her? About the rest of her life?

But it was so sudden. She needed more time. She'd stay another week, and when they both calmed down, she'd talk to Iain again. If he was serious about moving to

New York . . . But no, that would never work. Even if she could reconcile her guilt feelings about Magnus, Iain wouldn't want to wait for her to get home at eight or nine every night. And he'd never understand why she had to work all weekend, every weekend. She took a deep breath. She didn't understand it either anymore. Why did she buy into the whole workaholic syndrome? Iain's right; this career is not enough. She pressed her eyes closed. Life without Iain. Life with Larry. Is that really what she wanted? She'd had no idea she could feel this way about anyone, nor that anyone could feel this way about her. If she walked away now, would she ever find a man his equal? What if this was her only chance for a real love, and she was so stupid that she let it slip through her fingers?

She needed another week. She pulled her cell phone out of her pocket and called the office, leaving Larry a voice mail saying she was going to take a third week. That should get a response, she thought, and went back up the hill.

She had to find Iain.

$\mathcal{D}$untober was crowded with men, but none of them Iain. The workmen were cheerful, but no one knew where he was.

"He's gone, miss," one said. "He was here for about an hour, then he left. I haven't seen him since." The man shrugged. "Is his Rover at the hotel?"

"I don't know; I didn't look."

He gave her a smile. "He'll be back. Why don't ye wait for him to find ye?"

$\mathcal{D}$ain's Range Rover was gone, and Sara gave her a blank look when Maddie asked her where he might be. "He could be anywhere. He's got a lot to do just now. It may be ye're worrying for nothing."

"No one knows where he is."

"Maddie, ye should just leave him alone."

"I need to talk to him."

"A little late for that, isn't it?"

"Sara!"

"Look, Maddie," Sara said with a sigh. "He'll be back. He knows where to find ye. It's not everyday a man's proposal is turned down. He may need to get off by himself."

$\mathcal{M}$addie had lunch with Magnus and Anne and their friends who had stayed for the week. Soon after that Magnus went to call the MacLeods, and Sara took Anne and her friends to Portree. Keith and Derek went to Duntober, and Maddie tagged along. She tried to sketch, but found herself staring off into the distance.

Her phone rang at three o'clock, and she took it out of her pocket and looked at it. The last thing she wanted to do just now was talk to Larry. She let it ring twice more, then answered. It wasn't Larry, but a breathless Katie instead.

"Larry says you can't take another week. You need to be here by Monday."

"Why?"

"The account execs have moved the deadline for the dot-com presentation up five weeks, and we're expanding the scope. We're adding TV and outdoor." Katie paused for dramatic effect. "Media bought time."

Media bought time, Maddie thought. That meant that the Media Department had bought television airtime, not at all what they'd discussed. The client had originally agreed to do only a radio and print campaign, and those were near completion, most of the details arranged. Now she'd have to plunge into development and casting for the TV spots, coordinate with the copy writers and account execs, start from scratch. All the deadlines she'd worked out so carefully would have to be revised, and possibly everything her team had worked on for months would be scrapped and something new thrown together in its place. It meant that this was not a good time to be gone from the office, but it wasn't the end of the world. It just meant more work to do in less time when she got back. She forced herself to be calm.

"When did this all happen?"

"Last night. Larry's furious that you're gone," Katie said in hushed tones. "He says you've let the whole team down by not being here. He says—" She paused, and Maddie knew she was wondering how to say what was next.

"Just tell me, Katie."

"He says if you're not here on Monday . . . he says you're fired."

"He doesn't mean that."

"He does, Maddie. He's faxing it to your hotel. What should I do?"

Maddie's laugh sounded brittle. "Don't worry, he's just bluffing."

"I don't think so. He's been talking to HR."

Maddie held her breath for a moment. "I haven't taken any vacation in three years." She forced her tone to be bright. "Don't worry, I'll call him and get this straightened out."

"I hope so. Maddie, just get back here, and it'll all blow over."

"Katie, let me think. I'll call you back."

"Call Larry. Think on your way to the airport."

Maddie sighed and dialed her boss's number. "Larry," she said. "It's Maddie. What happened?" She listened quietly while Larry shouted out the details. "But I don't understand. We went over this five hundred times with the client."

"It doesn't matter. Get your butt back here. Now."

"I'll see what I can do."

"You'll do as I say. Get back here."

She tried to repress her anger. This was a crisis, but it could be contained. It was time for rational thought, not bullying.

"Larry, you're the Creative Director of the firm. You own the agency, for Pete's sake. Tell the account execs to tell the client we have to keep the original deadline. We can't change both the scope and the deadline. It's not reasonable."

"Don't tell me who I am, Maddie. Just get on the next plane home."

"I'm staying another week."

There was silence, then Larry hung up. Maddie looked up from the phone to the water. Larry's latest power play was having the reverse effect. Instead of making her want to rush back to be by his side to fix this, she was resentful, seeing him and his machinations with clear eyes. So why was she thinking of leaving to be with him instead of here with Iain? Why didn't this bother her more? Maddie laughed. Damn, she was a slow learner.

$\mathcal{I}$t wasn't quite so funny when Sara handed her the fax. Katie had been right. Larry's letter was carefully worded, saying that if she weren't back in New York on Monday, she'd be fired. Her call to HR was even more chilling. Larry, Susan reported, kept two complaints about everyone on his team on file at all times.

"That way," Susan said, "he can let anyone go and let the lawyers sort it out later. I thought you'd gotten copies of the complaints."

"No. What are the complaints?"

"Missing deadlines. Like that's not normal around here when the scope changes. But, Maddie, understand. This is a power play. You're either here on Monday, or you're out."

"I'm taking a third week."

"You didn't request it. It hasn't been approved. You know the rules."

"I'm taking a third week."

"Ooh, then this is going to be ugly. Sorry, Maddie, you're on your own."

Maddie called Larry, but he and Katie were in a meeting and couldn't be disturbed. She drafted her response fax carefully, saying that she was still taking the third week. Let the chips fall. She called the airline and rescheduled her flight.

$\mathcal{D}$ain didn't come to dinner, and no one mentioned him. Magnus said the call to the MacLeods had been cordial, that they'd be coming to the Games, and that they were delighted he was restoring Duntober. After dinner, when everyone went into the lounge, Magnus asked her to sit with him, and when she did, he gave her a measuring look.

"What happened?"

"What do you mean?"

Magnus frowned. "Don't be evasive. Between yesterday and today, with ye and Iain. What happened?"

She told him the bare bones of it. At the end of her story he smiled.

"Did I ever tell ye I had to beg Anne to go out with me?"

She shook her head.

"And when I proposed on the first date, she slapped me." He laughed, and Anne looked up and smiled at him. "But I knew what I wanted, Maddie, and I knew there was a chance as long as she was still talking to me."

"But he's not talking to me. He's gone."

Magnus snorted. "I know Iain. He heals alone and then comes back to the world. He'll be back. I know where he'll be tonight, lassie, and tomorrow night."

"At Duntober? He said he'd be there, but will he?"

Magnus nodded. "If Iain says he'll do something, he does." He patted her hand. "He loves ye, Maddie. Ye must decide if ye want him, lassie, but I can tell ye, he's yers for the asking. Mind his pride, though."

Maddie thanked him and kissed his cheek, then

looked up as Sara came to stand over them with a worried expression.

"Larry's on the phone, Maddie," she said. "And he's quite angry."

*M*addie listened for a few minutes to Larry's diatribe, then cut in. "Look, Larry, let's stop the posturing. I'm going to take the third week. We'll still get everything done." She held the phone away from her ear while Larry ranted. Like in a bad movie, she thought. He's a cliché. "Larry, it's not going to work. I'm taking the week." She hung up and met Sara's eyes.

A half-hour later, Katie called to tell her that Larry was in the office roaring that he was going to fire her whether she came back or not.

"For what?" Maddie asked.

"Insubordination. Desertion. Betrayal. You name it."

Desertion, Maddie thought. All she'd done was take a few vacation days. Wasn't this all a bit out of whack? Betrayal, for God's sake. Get real.

"Everyone's mad at you for not being here. Larry says you don't have any work ethic, and if you're not here by Monday morning, your job is mine."

"It's an empty threat."

"I could do it, Maddie. I'd be good at it."

Maddie felt a chill. She worked with vultures.

"He said he owned the agency and could do whatever he wanted. Then he threw his phone through the window."

"Through the window? You're on the fourteenth floor!"

"I know. He just looked at all the broken glass, then told me to find out if he'd killed anyone outside."

"Good Lord!"

"Maddie, you should get back here as soon as you can."

Maddie called Susan in HR again, who said not to worry, that the legal team told Larry he would never make it stick. "Larry can't win this one, and when he cools down he'll see that."

Great, she thought as she hung up. My future is secure, but my boss hates me, and people are salivating over my job. That's a really good atmosphere to be creative in. Creative, she mocked herself. When was the last time you were creative in that job?

She went to find Sara, who was at the pub with Keith. She'd visit with them for a while, then go to Duntober around eleven and try to talk with Iain.

But she didn't need to go to Duntober. When she walked into the pub, Iain was at the bar. He turned, two glasses of ale in his hand, then looked past her, walking to a table in the back. He sat down and handed Joanie a glass. She gave him a dazzling smile and snuggled up next to him.

Maddie stood by the door for a moment, watching them. Iain looked up at her and she met his eyes across the room. He held his glass up in a salute, and she spun around and fled.

9

*M*addie watched the dawn from the porch at the Trotternish. Iain had not come back to the hotel, and she hadn't gone to Duntober. Maybe she should now, she thought. Maybe they could talk this through. Or maybe Joanie had spent the night with him. Well, she thought, if that had happened, she'd just go home and try to patch it up with Larry.

The lower gate was locked, but she climbed over the fence without difficulty. Anyone who wanted access to Duntober could get it easily enough, she thought. That would have to change if the vandalism continued. She paused on the terrace, then climbed the wooden stairs, repaired now, to the Great Hall. The castle still had the power to touch her, to spark her imagination. I don't want to leave, she thought as she came to stand in the arched window. I don't want to plunge back into the madness of advertising, to spend my life picking out the right person to eat a hamburger in a TV ad. It was entirely possible that her career had reached the end of it's life all by itself. Weird, but it didn't faze her. Iain was right. There was a whole world out here, and she wasn't exactly saving lives in advertising. Maybe it was time to start living. Maybe on Skye. Maybe she should start building a castle.

She felt a weight leave her and turned to look at the Hall again. I want to see this castle come alive again. I want to dance in this room with Iain. I want to stay and try to make this thing we have between us work. Whatever happens in New York can happen without me. I want to be here with Iain. She laughed out loud. It had taken long enough to see the light, but she sure saw it now.

*I*ain stood at the bottom of the stairs to the Great Hall and listened. He thought he'd heard a woman laugh. He must be hearing things. He'd not slept well, rolled into a sleeping bag in the Hall, and had risen, stiff from the night on the cold stone, to go down to the cellar and fix a cup of tea. I'm too old for this. I should be in a comfortable bed. With Maddie. No, he wouldn't even think about her. He ran a hand through his hair and went up the stairs slowly, careful not to spill his tea, then stopped when he saw Maddie standing in the arched window. His heart began a slow thumping.

"Maddie," he said.

She turned to face him with a faint smile. "Iain. I didn't know whether you'd be here."

"I said I would be." He sipped the tea and watched her. "I am."

"I couldn't sleep."

He brushed past her and sat in the archway. "I couldn't either. A bed is always nicer than stone." As soon as the words were out, he regretted them. They conjured up too many images. "Why are ye here, Maddie?"

"Did you spend the night with Joanie?"

"What?" He tried to hide his surprise. Her face was scarlet, and he felt like laughing. He'd bet that wasn't what she'd intended to say. "It's none of yer business." He sipped his tea and looked out at the water, watching the light change the gray sea to blue when it touched it.

"Iain?" He turned to face her. "Can't we even talk about it?"

"Me spending the night with Joanie?"

"No. Us. But did you?"

"No, Maddie, I did not."

"Were you trying to make me jealous?"

He smiled; he couldn't help it. He did like the idea of Maddie jealous. "No. I won't say I didna consider it. But I was only trying to get information from her. She does not attract me."

"Good. Now talk to me."

"I'm not feeling particularly civilized."

She took a step closer. "Talk to me, Iain."

He studied her for a moment. Even now, even with the signs of strain apparent in her face, she was beautiful. Why didn't she go home and leave him alone? "All right," he said. "What do ye want to hear?"

"What you're thinking."

He glanced through the window, then took a sip of his

tea. "I'm thinking I'm not too happy just now, Maddie. I fell in love with ye. I didna expect it, didna ask for it, and I don't know how to control it. The sex was brilliant, though."

She flushed, but lifted her chin. "Yes, it was, wasn't it? I changed my flight. I'm staying another week."

"Won't that upset Larry?"

"It did. I'll probably be fired on Monday if I'm not there. I thought it might please you."

"That ye'll be fired?"

"No, that I'm staying."

He watched her, his thoughts tumbling.

"I want to try, Iain. Let's give it another week—"

"A week."

"I thought—"

"Ye thought what, Maddie? That I'll be a different man in seven days? Or that we'd have sex for a week, and then ye'd decide if I'm worthy of more?"

"No, Iain, I love you. I want to stay, I want to see Duntober come alive."

He stood up and drained the tea cup. "Too little, too late, Maddie. Go on home."

He turned and stalked from the room. Her voice reached him as he started down the stairs. "Good try. I'd give it an eight."

He stared at her. "What?"

"You know, like the Olympics. Good form, lots of drama. An eight."

"Maddie, what are ye doing?"

"I quit my job."

"What?"

"Well, not yet. But I'm going to today." She turned

away and started for the stairs to the terrace. "You can't get rid of me that easily, Iain MacDonald."

He stared after her, kept staring even when she was gone. Damn, she made him crazy.

*M*addie chewed her lip. Maybe she'd played that all wrong. Maybe she should have let him stalk off with his wounded pride. He probably thought she'd gone over the edge. Well, she thought as she walked through the hotel lobby, he'd be right. She had. She felt like it was the last day of school with a long summer before her. When was the last time she'd done anything unprofessional and impractical? When was the last time she'd fallen in love? It wouldn't be easy to win him back. His pride was hurt and his heart wounded. But he loved her. And she loved him. She'd have to find a way to make it work.

Sara looked up from the front desk as Maddie went past. "What are ye doing up at this hour? It's not half past six yet."

Maddie grinned. "I changed my flight, Sara. I'm staying."

Sara shook her head. "Where have ye been? Did ye ... ?"

"Spend the night with Iain? No. But I saw him this morning."

"And?"

"And nothing. He's not too thrilled about the idea."

"Maddie!"

"I'm quitting my job today."

"Maddie!"

"And maybe I'll start a painting. And I need to get into Iain's room."

"I can't let you do that."

"Then talk to him. He's at Duntober. Call him and ask him if I can have my sweaters and my roses."

Sara watched her go up the stairs, but Maddie didn't mind. Being ridiculous was kind of fun. The euphoria even lasted through the phone call to Larry. She'd waited until seven A.M. in New York, then called his house. At first he'd refused to talk to her and his wife tried to cover it, but finally he came on the line.

"See you Monday, right?"

"No, Larry. That's why I'm calling."

"Dammit, Maddie, we've gone over this. I'll fire your ass if you're not there."

"So do it."

"What?"

"Fire me. I'm not coming back yet, Larry. What's the line you love? Do what you gotta do."

"What are you on?"

"Love Potion Number Nine. Skye Love Potion Number Nine. Bye, Larry."

*S*he called her mother next, then both of her sisters, and warned them that she might not be coming back, hanging up with the distinct impression that they all thought she'd lost it. She grinned to herself and went to find Sara, to thank her for having the roses and sweaters brought to her room.

The ceilidh started at eight, but Sara and Maddie had everything ready hours earlier, and Sara went to take a nap while Maddie had a talk with Magnus and Anne. She poured out her heart, told them all of her fears and what she'd done. When she finished, Magnus and Anne had exchanged a look, then Anne had leaned forward to pat Maddie's hand.

"He's a good man, Maddie, but a stubborn one. I wish ye luck."

Magnus thought for a few minutes, then nodded. "There are some people, Maddie, who need seven years to know someone. There are others who only need seven days. What have ye talked about?"

"Everything, Magnus—our divorces, our parents' divorces, our sisters, about politics and money and working and art and travel. And India, for heaven's sake! We talked about clothes and furniture and cars. We talked about you and Anne and how much we admire you both and how much we'd like to be your age and still be happily married."

"Have ye talked about marriage? About children?"

"No."

"Did ye know Iain's buying Duntober from me? He'll be living here."

"No, but that doesn't surprise me. He loves that castle."

"Aye. And I love that lad. Maddie, don't do this unless yer certain."

"I won't hurt him, Magnus."

"I don't want either of ye hurt, Maddie. What about yer job?"

Maddie sighed, then smiled. "I don't even know if I'll have one next week. But it doesn't matter. Being away from the office for this long made me remember that there are other ways to live. I forgot that there is a whole world out here. And I don't want to go back to that, no matter what. I'm going to start painting again. I'm going to paint the Games."

Magnus nodded. "Talk about marriage, lassie. And children."

*P*eople were arriving as Maddie hurried to get dressed. She could already hear hotel guests gathering on the terrace below, their excited chatter drifting through her thoughts. Pink or green? She had the hardest time deciding and finally wore the pink. It was summer, after all. No more black.

At eight Maddie was busy helping Magnus and Anne settle their guests at a table near the stage. At nine she danced with Derek, who promptly deserted her when Joanie arrived. At ten she stood alone at the side of the room and watched the dancing, her exhilarated mood long gone. Iain had been here for half an hour, talking on the other side of the room to Derek and Joanie. He'd looked at her once, without expression, then disappeared. Too little, too late, he'd said.

"Maddie."

She turned to see him behind her, wearing a midnight blue shirt over khakis. He looked wonderful, and she smiled tentatively.

"The sweater looks very nice," he said.

"Thank you. It was a gift."

He nodded. "Did ye really change yer flight?"

"Yes."

"What about yer job?"

"I don't know. We have time to get everything done when I get back. It'll be tight, but it can be done, and Larry knows that. On the other hand, he says he'll fire me if I'm not there on Monday. So I don't know."

"What are ye going to do if he lets ye go?"

"Well, I suspect my days at L & M are numbered no

matter what. I was hoping to be offered a better position elsewhere. Perhaps in Scotland."

"Ah. Well, Edinburgh has lots of firms."

"I was thinking about the brochures for Duntober."

"Ye'll have to talk with Magnus. Those won't take ye more than a week."

"How many children do you want, Iain?"

He stared at her for a moment. "What?"

"How many children do you want? Or do you not want children?"

"Aye, I do." He gave her a sudden grin. "Ten."

"No, no more than three."

He shook his head. "Maddie, yer mad."

"About you."

His expression sobered. "Don't do this. Don't play games."

"It's not a game, Iain." She looked up into his eyes and smiled. "It's not a game. I just needed to get used to the idea, Iain. Don't give up on me."

He nodded. "Works both ways, Maddie."

"I know. We have a week to decide."

He stroked her cheek with the back of his hand. "I have to check Blaven, then I have to get back to Duntober."

"Are you still in the race?"

"With Blaven? Of course. Derek ran him while I was gone. Or did ye mean in the race with ye? That's for ye to say." He leaned forward and brushed his lips on hers, then turned and left without a backward glance.

𝒯he Trotternish Games began early, and Maddie was there for the opening parade, next to Magnus, who rose to salute the MacDonald pipers and contestants. It was as colorful as she'd remembered, the competitors, and many of the spectators, in their clan tartans, the reds and blues of their plaids bright against the greens of the grass and the surrounding trees. And beyond the meadow, the sea shimmered in the summer light, blue and silver, the mountains of the mainland an even deeper blue in the distance. Like Iain's eyes, she thought. She took pictures, then sat by herself to try to sketch it, enjoying the pipes and laughter around her.

Maddie was in a hushed mood today, trying not to think about tomorrow. Or Monday. Katie had left a message on her cell last night, telling her Larry said to overnight the phone to New York. There had been a new note in Katie's voice, a quiet triumph that let Maddie know that Katie expected to have her job next week. So be it, she thought. If I've learned nothing else from this trip, it's that life is for living. There is room for work, but there also should be room for people. And for love.

She loved him. Last night, when he'd been so remote, she felt a wave of yearning wash over her. How foolish she'd been not to throw her arms around him when he told her he loved her. If she ever got the chance to hear it from him again, she'd not make the same mistake. He was as lonely as she was, but he was willing to walk away now, if she let him. What if they did fail? It could happen. They'd each failed before at marriage. How could they know if they'd do better this time? It might be, just as she'd feared, that the attraction was purely physical. They might wake up in a few months and wonder what they'd done. She looked over at Magnus and Anne, Sara and Keith beside them, watching the first of the dancing competitions. Or they might be lucky enough to grow old together, to have children and grandchildren. They might have a wonderful, happy marriage. And live in a castle on Skye. She grinned to herself. Rough job, but someone had to do it.

The caber competitions began with a flourish of pipes and drums, and Maddie wandered over to see the first throw, sketching frantically. The colors were impossible to duplicate on-site; she wouldn't even try until later, but she wanted to capture the shapes, the lines of the men's bodies as they strained to carry the huge pole, then heave it into the air. A shadow fell across the page, and she looked up into Iain's eyes.

"That's very good, Maddie," he said quietly, looking from her sketchpad to the contest. "May I?" he asked as he took the pad from her.

10

$\mathcal{H}$e flipped the pages, then caught his breath as he saw the drawings of himself. So many drawings. Of him. He studied each one, then returned the pad to the page she'd been working on and handed it to her.

"Yer very good, Maddie," he said. "Ye have a real talent."

"Thank you."

He met her eyes. "How are ye today?"

"I'm fine. And you?"

"Tired. We had a visitor last night."

"At Duntober?" He nodded. "What happened?"

"Derek and I heard the bastard drive through the gates and came down, but he must have seen us, or the light. He was gone when we got there. We had wet down the dirt around the gates, thinking we might get footprints, so he left all kinds of tracks. He drives a Rover, I think, or at least has tires like mine. They're the same kind of tires that ran through the concrete. If ye see a Rover with scratches and dents on the front, let me know. We have the police looking for it and checking to see if Loomis is back on the island. And Joanie did her best to keep Derek at Trotternish last night."

"Iain, he's getting bolder. This can't go on."

"Actually, I'm liking it. Keeps my mind off other things."

"And if he's dangerous?"

"He's a sneaking coward, Maddie. We'll get him. And soon, I think."

"Iain, please be careful."

He nodded, then turned as a roar came from the hammer toss audience.

"Do you ever compete?" she asked.

"In these Games?" He shook his head. "Never had time. I was always too busy working to even come to see them."

"And now?"

"Now," he said, watched the sunlight play on her hair as the breeze moved it, turning strands from deep brown to cinnamon, "now I have other things to do."

"Iain . . ." She touched his hand. "Can we go somewhere and talk?"

"I . . ." He pressed his lips together, then shrugged. "I think New York still has quite a hold on ye."

"I see." She stood up, holding her sketchpad against her chest, then reaching down for her bag. When she straightened and looked at him, he could see the anger in her eyes. "Perhaps it does."

He was silent as he watched her walk away.

*T*he Games were well attended and the hotel full of people. The pub and lounge were so busy Saturday night that people spilled out into the parking lot and the center lawn, sitting on the grass under the stars. Maddie didn't join in. She'd put a brave face on it through dinner, which Iain did not attend, but she was miserable and went to bed soon after. If he'd wanted to put her in her place, he'd certainly done it. All the silliness, all the lightness, had gone from her mood, replaced by a dread that by next week she'd have nothing. No job. No Iain. So be it, she thought. Maybe he wasn't worth all this. Maybe he was just a stubborn Scot who liked to have his way, on his terms, on his time. Maybe she was better off without him. So why did it hurt so much?

*S*unday's Games started later, and Maddie spent the morning drawing the field, empty now of competitors, but with all the booths and flags still in place. The wind was brisk today, and everyone was complaining about the lack of rain, worrying about a drought. She loved it. The breeze held the flags out for her to get each detail and brought the clouds billowing overhead, then pushed them out of the sunlight. Summer on Skye was breathtaking, she thought as she headed back to the Trotternish to eat.

She was back at two, with Sara and Keith, standing at the front of the crowd as the final competitions got under way. She loved to see the children dance, but when a little blond boy danced with wild abandon, his long legs pounding into the stage, she turned away, overcome, remembering Iain's dance at Magnus's party. That's what our son would look like, she thought, and felt a wave of loss that chilled her. She smiled as Sara said something, then followed them to the next contest.

At four she stood with Anne and watched Magnus thank everyone for attending the Games. The final event, he said, was about to begin, and would everyone please gather along the old road for the horse race. Maddie had tried to leave, not sure she could stand here and smile while Iain competed. If he lost, she'd feel terrible for him. And if he won, it would be a hollow victory for her. But she had no choice. Anne brought her to where the horses had lined up at the starting line, talking to each of the riders, wishing them luck. The men wore kilts and white shirts, their plaids attached with brooches. Some wore boots, some ghillie brogues, but there were no saddles, no stirrups. Iain sat straight on Blaven, his muscular thighs hugging the big horse's sides, his kilt already high on his legs. Don't look, she told herself, but she did anyway. Iain smiled at Anne and thanked her for her good wishes, then met Maddie's eyes.

"Good luck, Iain," Maddie said.

"Thank ye," he answered, then turned at a series of shouts from the spectators. "What the hell?" he asked, trying to calm Blaven, who started to dance.

Maddie and Anne turned to see what everyone was looking at, and when Maddie followed their gaze, her heart froze. From the top of the hill, where the castle was, tall plumes of dark smoke rose into the sky.

"Fire!" someone shouted.

"Dear God, it's Duntober!" Anne cried.

Maddie turned to Iain, but he was staring up at the fire.

"No!" he cried.

"Iain," she said, putting a hand on his leg.

"Get out of the way, Maddie," he said, looking down at her with a fierce expression. "Get back, love," he said and pulled Blaven back.

She took a step backward, trying to avoid the horse behind her. All the horses were moving restlessly now, and she realized she and Anne needed to get off the road. She took Anne's arm, then turned at a movement next to her.

Iain leaned over Blaven's neck and called to him, digging his heel into the big chestnut's side. The thoroughbred responded at once, breaking away from the other horses with a leap, and Maddie watched in horror as Iain and Blaven thundered down the road. Toward Duntober.

"No!" she screamed, but her voice was lost in the roar from the crowd.

*M*addie didn't remember moving, didn't remember starting to run, but she had to stop to catch her breath at the foot of the hill below the castle. She held on to the gate, shaking it in frustration when she realized it was locked. As if that had helped, she thought, looking up through the trees where the clouds of smoke had thickened. She could see the flames now, greedy tongues of fire licking at the roofs, then climbing in triumph to the sky.

"Iain!" She screamed his name as she clambered over the fence, then turned to see the men behind her tearing the gate from its hinges.

"Hurry!" she shouted at them, then continued up the hill.

This is where I heard him before, she thought, as she ran up the path through the trees, certain now that it had been Alan Loomis skulking away in the bushes that first day she'd come here.

"Iain!" Her call was lost in the crackle of the fire, and her throat constricted as the acrid smoke reached her. She raced around the foundation, then stood on the terrace, her hands clasped at her throat as she looked up to the Great Hall. The stairs so recently built, the same ones that Magnus had fallen down, were in flames, the Great Hall an inferno above it. The ceiling, that beautiful hammered wood ceiling, was burning. She couldn't get through here; she ran past the men who had gathered around her to the other side of the castle, past the cellar where men were handing blueprints and the renderings from one pair of hands to the next. Blaven stood nervously at the base of the stairs to the Hall, reins dangling from his bridle. He trotted away, then came back to look up the stairs again. Behind him was a white Range Rover with a dented front grill. She put a foot on the first step, then turned at a shout.

Derek put his hand on her arm and pointed at the Great Hall. "Ye'll not get through, Maddie!"

"Iain's in there! Let me go!"

"No!" He pulled her back to stand with him on the driveway, and pointed to the top of the keep. "He's up there! Look! With Loomis!"

She stopped struggling as the two figures came into sight. She couldn't tell who was who at first as they battled, their bodies entwined as one man pushed the other back against the stone battlements. The back of a blond head leaned over the parapet, Loomis's hand pushing his chin back. They both disappeared as Iain kicked Loomis off him. Maddie held her breath, then turned to see Keith come to stand next to her. He raised a pistol and aimed at the top of the castle, but no one was there. The smoke shifted away from the castle, a sudden change in the wind pulling the smoke out to sea, and Maddie saw a flash of white in the window of a third-floor room.

"There," she screamed. The two men passed before the opening, Iain's face drawn into a savage snarl as he reached for his opponent. Smoke billowed from the spiral stairs, the column acting as a chimney, and that drew her attention for a second before she looked back to see the window empty. She began to pray.

Long minutes passed and they waited, a tiny zone of quiet in the madness around them. Men tried to go up the stairs to the Hall, but backed down as the smoke and flames blocked them. Others threw ropes up into the windows where the men had been, the ends trailing down the outside of the structure like long strands of hair. Maddie pressed her hands to her mouth.

Then a long, agonized scream, a howl of terror that continued for several moments, then trailed off into silence, came from the tower, and everyone gasped. No! Dear God, no! Not Iain! Please, don't let that be Iain! Please, dear God, let him still be alive. Spare him and I'll do anything, anything. She blinked her tears back and looked at the empty window again. Was that a sleeve she saw? A patch of white against the gray stone? But no, it was nothing, and she covered her face.

"Maddie! Maddie!" Keith pointed to the side of the tower, where a man in a white shirt was slowly climbing down one of the ropes. "It's Iain!"

Iain moved awkwardly down the rope, his movements stiff. The wind changed direction, and the smoke, which had been blown away from him, now surged around the tower again, driving the rescuers back. She ran to stand below him with the men who waited to catch him. At fifteen feet above the ground he fell, and the men surged forward, catching him and laying him gently on the ground.

His eyes were closed, his breathing ragged, but he was alive. Soot streaked his face, his clothing was torn, and he had some nasty lacerations on his arms. She could see nothing more serious, but he might have internal damage from the smoke or the fall. She covered his face with kisses and murmured his name. He turned his head, then opened his eyes.

"Iain! Oh, thank God," she cried.

"Maddie." His voice was a croak, but he smiled through cracked lips. "Maddie." He put his hand on her arm. "Will ye marry me?"

"Oh, yes and yes and yes!"

The men around them exchanged looks and began to laugh.

"Damnedest proposal I ever heard," Derek said.

Alan Loomis's identity was confirmed, and the inquest absolved Iain of any blame. Joanie, who had given a terrified account of her relationship with Loomis, testified that he had been the vandal. The legal details were still being sorted out, but Maddie would leave that to Magnus. It was over.

The castle was gutted now, its walls blackened by the fire, the beautiful ceiling, all the wooden floors in the tower, gone to ashes. It had been the floor on the third story, rotten from the years of exposure to the elements, that had given away under Loomis. As the two men had struggled across the room, he fell through, dangling in air for a few fateful moments, then plunging through the burning lower floors to his death. Only a quick leap and the grace of God had saved Iain from the same fate.

Magnus hosted a dinner the night that Iain came home from the hospital. It had rained all day, which made the long drive back to the Trotternish tedious, but Maddie didn't mind. Iain was alive. He'd had some injuries to his back and to his lungs, and a bad burn on his leg, but he would recover in time. The sun had come out as they'd turned into the hotel's driveway, turning Anne's hydrangeas vibrant pink and blue against their green leaves, and she'd decided it was an omen that their life together would be as beautiful.

At dinner Maddie held Iain's hand and accepted Magnus's good wishes for their future together, then laughed as Derek's mother asked him when he would be marrying. Afterward she and Iain sat on the terrace with Sara and Keith and Derek, enjoying the clear air and the light breeze.

"Ye look mighty cheerful for a woman who lost her job," Iain said to Maddie, and she smiled.

"I didn't lose my job," she reminded him. "Larry

called three times and begged me to come back. But I won't. I'm going to marry a rich man and live in a castle in Scotland."

"Not for quite a while, princess."

She laughed. "It doesn't matter. I have captured my golden prince."

"Ugh," said Derek on her left, rolling his eyes, but Iain just grinned.

"Come on, Maddie," Iain said, pulling her to her feet. "We have to leave before we're thrown out."

*H*e held her hand as they walked back to his cottage, his hair catching the evening sunlight. Golden man, she thought. Alive, thank God, and with her.

"Maddie," he said as he opened the door and pulled her inside with him. "Maddie," he said again, and she went into his arms. He swung the door shut.

His kiss was not gentle as he pulled her against him. He deepened the kiss, and when she opened her mouth to him he groaned, tightening his arms. When at last he withdrew from her, sighed, then leaned back.

"Champagne," he said.

"Perfect."

She watched him open the bottle and pour her a glass. She lifted her mouth to meet his kiss, then raised her glass in a toast.

"To Duntober."

He touched his glass to hers. "To us, Maddie."

"To our castle in the Skye."

"To castles and dreams," he said and kissed her again.

"Do you love me, Iain?"

"Do I love ye? Beyond words, Maddie. Beyond reason. Until we're four hundred years old."

She laughed. "Longer. I want forever."

"Ye'll get whatever ye want, love. Just stay with me. Forever."

"Forever."

He kissed her again.

"You know we'll have a lot more work at Duntober now," she said, but he laughed and shook his head.

"We'll have less. Now we don't have to tear the floors out. And I'm thinking that when we're finished with Duntober, we'll buy Kilgannon and restore that. I still owe ye a trip there, ye remember. I don't know what we'll do after that. Move to New York and start an advertising agency and put Larry out of business. Anything ye want."

She put her hand on his cheek. "I'm sorry you never got to race Blaven."

He shrugged. "I did race him, right past ye, lassie. No, I don't mind. My competing days are over; I've already won the prize of my choice." He gave her a wide grin, his eyes twinkling. "Frankly, Maddie, I don't give a damn."

She laughed and reached to pull him close. His kiss tasted like champagne. A good start, she thought.

KATHLEEN GIVENS

There is a spot on the northeastern coast of the Trotternish Peninsula of the Isle of Skye that belongs to me. Not literally, but to my soul. It is there that "Castle in the Skye" is set, on that amazing island off the west coast of Scotland. Skye is home to legends, myths, and incredible history; astonishing topography; distinctive hotels and evocatively ruined castles. I have taken the liberty of adding Trotternish House and Duntober Castle to the list of Skye's attractions. Although neither of them actually exists, the scenery is very real—and breathtakingly unforgettable. The blues are bluer than is possible, the Outer Hebrides fade into the western horizon, and the mountains of the mainland draw your gaze to the east. It is the kind of place where even the artistically challenged want to pick up a sketchpad or paintbrush—and I swear there is the faintest hint of bagpipe music coming from the very air. (This without any whisky or the fine local ale.) What could be more wonderful than to have some artistic talent and visit Skye? Well, to be there with a man you love. And he should wear a kilt, right? Why not?

I became fascinated with Scottish history while researching my first two books, *Kilgannon* and *The Wild Rose of Kilgannon,* and will return to the west of Scotland again for my next two historicals, *The Legend* and *The Destiny,* to be published by Warner Books in 2002. I can't think of a better place for a wild romance than the Highlands and Islands, where the men are manly and the views are glorious!